ELECTRIFYING PRAISE
FOR HARRY HUNSICKER'S *STILL RIVER*

"Hunsicker does everything right—no-nonsense prose, a tough but sympathetic hero, and a case that pulls at the heartstrings. *Still River* proves that the modern private-eye model is alive and well. I can't wait for the next in this series."

—Rick Riordan,
Edgar and Shamus Award–winning author of
Southtown and *The Devil Went Down to Austin*

"*Still River* is a marvelously written debut with vivid characters, a terrific plot, and a richly portrayed Dallas, from its glories to its gutters. Private eye Lee 'Hank' Oswald is everything a reader wants in a hero: tough but good-hearted, fearless but flawed. Harry Hunsicker puts Dallas squarely on the modern mystery map with this outstanding novel."

—Jeff Abbott,
three-time Edgar nominee and author of *Panic*

"Take a wild ride down the dark, dusty, and often dangerous streets of Dallas with Lee Oswald, PI. *Still River* is a terrific debut."
—Chuck Hogan, author of *The Standoff*

"This is fast-paced action, with plenty of laughs along the way. Harry Hunsicker creates characters as big and bold as Dallas."
—Ben Rehder, author of *Bone Dry* and *Buck Fever*

"Lee Oswald is the kind of man you want on your side—hard as titanium but with a heart as big as Texas. Hunsicker really delivers the goods in this impressive debut."

—Steve Hamilton,
Edgar and Shamus Award–winning author of *Ice Run*

STILL RIVER

A Lee Henry Oswald Mystery

HARRY HUNSICKER

St. Martin's Paperbacks

STILL RIVER

Copyright © 2005 by Harry Hunsicker.
Excerpt from *The Next Time You Die* © 2006 by Harry Hunsicker.

Cover photo by Peter A. Calvin.

ISBN: 0-312-94090-4
EAN: 80312-94090-4

Printed in the United States of America

St. Martin's Press hardcover edition / May 2005
St. Martin's Paperbacks edition / July 2006

St. Martin's Paperbacks are published by St. Martin's Press, 175 Fifth Avenue, New York, NY 10010.

10 9 8 7 6 5 4 3 2 1

*For my lovely wife, Alison, and
my parents, Harry and Foree Hunsicker,
thanks for all your help and encouragement.*

Acknowledgments

The book would not have been possible without the help and advice I received from Erika Barr, Jan Blankenship, Amy Bourret, Victoria Calder, Will Clarke, Kevin Crank, Alan Duff, Jeff Epstein, Ginna Getto, Dan Hale, Susan Huber, Fanchon Knott, David Norman, Brooke Malouf, Barry Philips, Christine Phillips, and Randy Spence. A special note of appreciation goes to Suzanne Frank for her early encouragement as well as her guidance throughout the entire process. Very special thanks to Richard Abate and Sean Desmond for their wisdom, professionalism and unwavering support.

STILL RIVER

CHAPTER ONE

Vera Drinkwater had been a slut in high school, or so they said. According to Artie Galbreath, she'd traded a blowjob for tickets to REO Speedwagon in the back of his Goodtimes van, the kind with the shag carpet on the walls. Artie was the class dealer and liked to sample his own inventory, so you had to take that into account. I had no firsthand knowledge of her morals as I only knew her from the two or three classes we had senior year. As I recalled, she looked the part back then.

She didn't appear very slutty now, sitting in my office crying. She looked pathetic, sleazy, and frumpy at the same time in a too-tight running suit with mascara drizzling down her face. Her hair was stringy and fried blond one too many times.

"Hank, you've got to help me." She blew her nose into a crumpled paper napkin. "I don't know where else to turn."

"Vera, why don't you take a moment and get yourself together. Then start at the beginning." I pushed a box of tissues across the desk.

She grabbed a handful and blew her nose again. "It's my little brother. He's missing. He was supposed to come to my birthday party, two days ago, and he never showed up. It's not something he would do; it's not like him at all." She coughed and shifted her weight. Her chair squeaked on the worn hardwood floor. My office was the back bedroom of a converted 1920s Tudor house, on Reiger Street, in old East Dallas. For that era, it was a large room, with plaster walls, crown molding, and built-in bookcases. Everything about the place squeaked or groaned.

"What's your brother's name?"

She rubbed her nose with another wad of tissues. "Charlie. I mean Charles. Charles Wesson."

"I remember him." An image came to mind: little Charlie Wesson, all arms and legs, gawky with thick glasses and an overstuffed backpack, two grades below me. The stoners who hung out behind the gym used to pound the hell out of him until I intervened that one time. That stopped them for a while. The downside was that I couldn't get rid of Charlie, always tripping over himself to be in my general vicinity.

"He's my half brother; my mom remarried a couple of years after her and my dad split." Vera tugged at a lock of blonde hair, wrapping it around her thumb. "My stepfather's name was Ketch Wesson. He's Charlie's father."

She seemed to say the name of her mother's second husband with a vengeance, as if she wanted to expel the words before they lingered on her lips too long.

"I take it you didn't like Ketch too much."

She grimaced and made a hucking sound that ended with the clearing of her throat. "Ketch was an asshole. Ex-marine, big run-a-tight-ship kinda guy. Lots of chores. And rules. Still, he kept a roof over me and Mom's head when no one else would."

I remembered Ketch now. Ketch had been one of those *involved* parents, especially when it came to athletics. He'd been at all the practices and games for his son and stepdaughter, wearing those god-awful polyester shorts, and a sweatshirt with the sleeves torn off, yelling at the coaches and refs. He looked like an ex-marine, all muscles and sinew, covered by hard, leathery skin. Charlie took after Vera's mother. Bookish. Bet it was fun growing up with Drill Sergeant Ketch as a dad.

"When was the last time anybody saw your brother?"

"Monday afternoon. He was at work and then coming to my birthday party. He left at about four and no one's seen him since."

It was now Tuesday morning. He'd been missing for a little less than twenty-four hours. Too early for the police to be notified but not too soon for a big sister to become worried. "Where did Charlie work?"

"Callahan Real Estate Company." She pulled a piece of paper from her purse and slid it across the desk. "I wrote down the address and the name of Charlie's boss. Also, where Charlie lives. That's about it, I guess."

She'd come prepared, sure I'd say yes. After all, I was a private investigator, licensed by the good people at the state capitol who handled that sort of thing. Why wouldn't I take the case? Maybe because I tried to have a rule that I wouldn't do business with a friend, however remote. Maybe because I felt like there was something Vera wasn't telling me. I didn't take the paper. Instead, I leaned back in my chair, put my hands behind my head, and didn't say anything.

Vera watched me and then fumbled with her purse. "I understand that most investigators work on a retainer. How much would you like?" She pulled out a wad of cash.

I ignored it and said, "Is Charlie married?"

"No. Divorced now for two years."

"Children?"

"No."

"Girlfriend?"

"No, not really. He dated a couple of people, here and there. Nothing serious."

"Did he gamble?"

"No. He wouldn't even play the office football pool."

"Booze?"

"No." Louder and more forcefully than the rest.

"Drugs?"

"No." Much quieter. Too quiet.

Bingo. I leaned forward. "Charlie in some kind of recovery program, twelve-stepping it, maybe?"

Vera didn't say anything. Instead she dug a rumpled pack of Capris from her purse and lit one. I reached into the middle drawer of my desk and pulled out an ashtray. It was made out of the bottom of a fifty-millimeter mortar shell. I slung it on the desk and waited.

Vera smoked and then started to cry again. She put out the cigarette and honked into a tissue. Her nose was red now, mottled to the color of a moldy tomato. "He's been straight almost eighteen months. He'd worked so hard at being clean."

"Booze or drugs?" There was a stack of Styrofoam cups on my credenza and a half bottle of mineral water. The minerals in the water came from the rusty faucet in the bathroom, but I didn't mention that. I poured a cupful and put it in front of her.

She slurped it down and said, "Both. Mostly drugs, though."

"What's the longest he's been sober?"

She sniffled. "Before this, it'd only been a month or two at a stretch. It was for real this time, though, I know it. It was after his second stint at rehab." Her tone implied that rehab twice was an automatic guarantee of sobriety. She leaned into my desk and the edge caught the zipper of her running suit top, pulling it down a couple of inches. "A year and a half, Hank. He'd been clean and sober for a year and a half."

To avoid looking at the top of her breasts I shuffled some papers on my desk. "Vera, here's the deal. Statistically speaking, Charlie's fallen off the wagon. He's on a bender somewhere and will surface eventually. You ever given him money before?"

She nodded.

"Then he'll probably come to you again for a handout. Does he go to anybody else when he's in trouble? Your mother? His father, a college buddy? Anybody?"

She shook her head. "Mother died right after Easter, last year. Cancer. Ketch had a heart attack about ten years ago, dropped dead. After Charlie sobered up he didn't hang around his old friends. Other than a couple of cousins he never sees, the only family or friend he's got left is me."

I rubbed the bridge of my nose and was suddenly tired. Charlie Wesson. Zitface, one of the cheerleaders who actually acknowledged his presence had called him. I remembered more. There was something about the guy; the smallness and insecurity made him mouth off when he shouldn't. The stoners had come back, a few weeks after the first time. I hadn't been around and they'd gotten in some good shots before a teacher had intervened. I remember Charlie's dad showing up later. And slapping his son once across his already bleeding mouth because he hadn't fought like a man, like the marine he was gonna be soon as graduation passed.

Vera looked at me from across the desk, one eyebrow raised. The ancient air conditioner stuck in the half window across the room was the only sound, chugging away to keep the morning heat at bay.

I rubbed my eyes and said yes; I would make some calls and nose around a little bit.

Vera jumped out of her chair and clapped her hands. "Thank you, Hank." She came around the desk and hugged me, pulling my body into hers and holding us together a little longer than necessary. I smelled her, cigarettes and cheap perfume covering a layer of grease. She'd cooked bacon that morning. She let our bodies part, reluctantly, it seemed to me, and smiled. "Thank you so much, Hank." She kissed me on the cheek, turned and left.

The phone book listed Callahan Real Estate, same number and address as on the piece of paper Vera had given me. That proved absolutely nothing except they'd been in existence since the last publication of the directory. As I dumped Vera's cigarette butt into the trash I heard a crack of thunder and the first fat drops of an early summer thunderstorm splat outside. I thought about where a myopic ex-hype might run to, or why.

I thought about people from high school who might know something. None of the answers added up to anything good.

The rain fell harder. I knew this not from looking out the window but because I heard swearing in the hallway, where the roof leaked in a downpour. I shared the house on Reiger with two other people: a lawyer named Ferguson Merriweather and a real estate appraiser named Davis Marcy Howell. Both men were in their late forties and on the downside of what once had been promising careers. Liquor is a cruel mistress.

It was the crack of eleven o'clock and about the time Ferguson showed to work. I stuck my head into the hallway and there he was, all five foot five of him, dressed in a pair of gray dress pants, a threadbare button-down, and a stained red tie. He looked at me and said, "The roof's leaking again." He sounded like it was my fault. A drop of water dribbled down his face.

"Call the landlord." I handed him the bucket we used for these occasions and walked around the drip, heading toward Davis's office, at the front. Davis, the appraiser, had real estate connections that in moments of lucidity he was willing to share. I thought he might know something about the Callahan Company, Charlie Wesson's employer.

When you walked in through the front door, his office was to the right. To the left was a living room that served as a reception area. Our receptionist du jour, Amber something, was out for the morning, so I walked straight into Davis's office, rapping on the door as I opened it.

Davis sat at his desk with a cup of black coffee, a glass of water fizzing with Alka-Seltzer, and the *Daily Racing Form*. He glanced at me for half a second, then turned back to his reading. "What do you want?"

"Information." I pulled up one of his two extra chairs and sat down. "Ever heard of Callahan Real Estate Company?"

"No." He took a sip of coffee.

"How about a guy named Charlie Wesson?"

"Uh-uh."

"Have you stopped beating your wife?"

Davis looked up and smiled, a rare occurrence. "I'm currently not married. Perhaps you would be referring to an ex-wife?"

I chuckled. He was more awake than I thought. "So you've never heard of Callahan Company? They office up north, in Addison."

He downed the rest of his fizzy water in one gulp and stifled a burp. "What do they do? What kind of real estate?"

"Beats me." I shrugged my shoulders. "The kind where you could hire an ex-junkie."

Davis massaged a spot on his stomach and grimaced. He took a sip of coffee. "That doesn't narrow it down much. What's the address?"

I pulled the slip of paper out of my pocket and read it to him.

"Is this about that platinum blonde that was in here a few minutes ago?" He was looking out the front window, onto Reiger Street. I nodded, but he couldn't see me. He took another drink of coffee and leaned back in his chair. "I used to date a girl looked kinda like her. Dancer at Baby Dolls."

"Really." I sighed. Davis's imaginary love life was legend around our small office.

"She drove a maroon Corvette." He scratched his armpit and stared at the ceiling.

"A Vette, no kidding." I stood up. "Fill me in later."

Davis blinked and looked at me again. "What'd you say the name was?"

"Callahan."

He grabbed a soft-cover book from the floor and flipped it open. "Here we are. They do commercial leasing and brokerage. That help?"

"Maybe." I moved to the doorway.

"You're welcome." He dropped the book back onto the floor and looked out the rain-streaked window. "There's a Camaro out front. Been there for thirty minutes or so, motor running."

I stepped back into his office and looked out the window. The car was beige, early nineties vintage, a trickle of exhaust coming from the tailpipe as it idled across the street. The windows were steamed so I couldn't see inside.

Davis opened a bottle of Advil and dumped a couple into his mouth, swallowing them with coffee. "I just paid off my bookie so I don't think they're after me."

"Maybe somebody's just waiting for a friend." A siren sounded in the distance.

Davis nodded. "Yeah. Maybe."

CHAPTER TWO

grabbed my gun, a matte black Browning Hi-Power, slipped it into the holster behind my right hip, and covered the butt with the tail of the denim shirt I wore untucked over a pair of faded jeans. The rain had stopped as quickly as it started, a shaft of sunlight slicing through the humid air as I exited by the back door. The rainwater made the streets steam, and the air smelled of ozone and wet asphalt and the heat of the day that was yet to come.

My current transportation was a two-year-old Chevy Silverado, dark gray with tinted windows and four-wheel drive. The truck was perfect for my line of work since it looked like one of the fifty thousand or so other nondescript, late-model pickups in North Texas.

I turned the AC on high, pulled onto Reiger Street, and the Camaro followed. I made a left, went two blocks and turned right. The Camaro did the same. So much for the waiting-on-a-friend theory. At a traffic light on Munger Boulevard I adjusted one of my side mirrors and got a look at the driver. It was hard to tell much about him with two windows and a mirror between us. Thirtyish, kinky-curly hair. Maybe a mustache. Maybe not.

The light turned green. I floored the Chevy and kept both hands on the wheel to navigate between the line of cars parked on either side of the narrow roadway. The Camaro followed, bottoming out on a small hill at the end of the block.

In the second block there were even more parked automobiles. Almost halfway to the next cross street, I stood on the brakes and jammed the transmission into park. I heard the tires on the Camaro squeal as I jumped out of my truck and slipped between two cars. I used the parked automobiles as a shield and ran back the way I came, keeping low.

The Camaro had managed to stop a few feet before hitting my truck. I darted between two more cars and found myself facing the left front window. The driver's hands were visible on the steering wheel. He wore a tank top. The thin material and skimpy coverage of the shirt accentuated the man's biceps and deltoid muscles, rippling beneath the skin like stringy meat in an overstuffed sausage casing.

I rapped on the window with the muzzle of my gun. He jumped at the sound, and I saw he definitely had a thin mustache and hair so curly it appeared to be permed. He said something I couldn't hear because of the glass between us. I made a twirling motion with my gun, indicating for him to roll the window down.

He blinked a couple of times and looked from my face to the muzzle of the pistol before shifting the car into reverse and pressing on the accelerator. He probably could have avoided sideswiping three or four of the cars he hit, if he had looked in the rearview mirror instead of at me. After forty feet or so of mashed metal and broken glass, he back-turned into the cross street, put the car into drive, and sped away. I holstered my piece, ran to the truck, and drove off in the other direction as the first of the owners of the damaged vehicles emerged to see what all the racket was about.

A couple of turns later I was on Gaston Avenue, headed to my home on Sycamore Street, a few blocks north of the office. I'd bought the house three years ago. The place was solid, made from rough-cut stone and one of about three in the city that had a basement. The neighborhood was an interesting mix: working class, half Asian and half Hispanic, and a handful of expatriated white guys like me. The homes ran the gamut from wooden shacks held together with little more than a coat of peeling paint to a handful of new brick cottages, snug little places with bars on the windows and outside lights triggered by motion detectors. This part of town was as far from the Dallas of J. R. Ewing as you could get, though a lot of the Cowboys buy their drugs from a dealer two streets over. That's not really touristy, though.

I pulled into my gravel drive and got out. Mr. Martinez, my neighbor to the left, stood in his backyard, scattering corn for the chickens he raised. He waved and said hello in Spanish. I stopped and leaned over the top of the chain-link fence separating our yards. A retiree, Mr. Martinez liked to talk and I could count on ten or fifteen minutes of uninterrupted neighborhood gossip. He'd gotten through the Hidalgos on the corner and the trouble their son had at the border in Laredo last week, when we heard shouting from the house on the other side of mine. He shook his head. "*Muy loco.*"

I nodded and we looked in the direction of the shouting, waiting to see if anything else happened. No more commotion erupted so Mr. Martinez continued as if nothing had happened. My other neighbor was Edwin, an artist who sculpted in bronze and iron and became terribly agitated when his art went awry. Which was often.

After Mr. Martinez finished his rundown, we said good-bye. I walked into my house and got the mail. Nothing of importance except for some bills. The rest was junk mail. I put the whole lot of it on the table in the hall, next to the latest issue of *Model Railroader*. The magazine was for my next errand, and I ignored it.

Since it was lunchtime I went to the kitchen. The room was half finished, a mess of power tools, paint, and wooden debris. I'd redone most of the place myself, from refinishing the hardwoods to renovating the turn-of-the-century bathrooms. The kitchen I'd saved for last, and it was nearing completion. The nice people from the building supply company had delivered the new granite countertops last week, courtesy of a man named Phil. Phil built homes, nice ones in the good part of town. His daughter had fallen in with a couple of ex-ballplayers, third-string losers who had suited up for the Mavericks for a couple of seasons until no amount of strong-arming by the union could keep them on the team after a series of failed drug tests. They'd done some bad things to the girl, and he'd hired me to rectify the situation. They were punks and it hadn't taken much time or effort. I'd tried to tell Phil that, but he wouldn't listen. He insisted on paying my fee as well as a gift of the countertops. What can you do but smile and accept graciously? He'd call again because his daughter was that way.

I got some stuff from the refrigerator and made myself a sandwich: corned beef and Swiss on whole wheat with mustard. Half an onion, wrapped in foil, called my name, so I added two thin slices to the mix and ate over the sink. The last two bottles of Carta Blanca beer called my name also, but I pretended I didn't hear. I had work to do.

Glenda, the chocolate Labrador retriever I sometimes think of as a pet, padded into the kitchen and sat on her haunches, watching me eat. Glenda was mean and smelled bad. She reminded me of the girlfriend who gave her to me.

"Here you go." I flipped her the last quarter of the sandwich. She managed to eat it and growl at the same time. That reminded me of my ex-girlfriend too.

I checked the messages on my machine. Nothing but a pre-recorded solicitation for vinyl siding and a secretary I'd had a date with two weeks ago who wondered why I never called back. I erased both and rifled through the mail again. I popped open one of the Carta Blancas, went into the living room and thumbed through the model railroad magazine. My eyes saw things but my brain refused to read so I tried to concentrate on the pretty pictures of locomotives and cabooses. After a while I gave up and stared at a stain on the Oriental rug on the floor.

When the beer was empty, I looked at my watch and swore. It was time to go to the hospital. My breathing became labored, lungs fighting imaginary smoke. I shivered even though I wasn't cold as the walls of the living room seemed to shimmer and sway, like reflections in a pool. I swore again and slung my empty bottle into the fireplace, where it broke. I felt tears well up in my eyes but managed to fight them back, sheer will power keeping a weak corral around an onslaught of emotions.

Baylor Medical Center was on Gaston Avenue, not far from my house but closer to downtown and Deep Ellum, one of the more popular bar districts in town. Everything in my seedy little neighborhood is close together: home, work, hospital. A liquor store on every corner; everything a body could need. I wheeled into the parking lot and got out, the model railroad magazine cradled under my arm. The early afternoon sun made the asphalt seem like a sauna. I leaned against the truck and let the heat work the kinks out of me, trying to regulate my breathing. The Dallas skyline loomed ahead, a textured wall of stone and glass phalluses jutting from the black-land prairie.

A crew of window washers were cleaning their way down the Adam's Mark Hotel, their scrubbing actions barely visible from the distance. I smiled, remembering the stories my partner and mentor Ernie Ruibal used to tell me about his father working as a bouncer at the illegal casinos when it was called the Southland Hotel back in the 1930s. Benny Binion had been the undisputed king of the Dallas underworld at the time, running craps and blackjack and working girls out of the top floor, the Dallas establishment turning a blind eye to the activities since it was good for business and the upcoming 1936 Texas centennial celebration. When a zealous new sheriff and district attorney had finally closed him down for good, forcing Binion to run with his millions to Vegas, where he would soon become a legend, he had given Ernie's father one of the two pearl-handled .45 automatics he carried as a gift for a special job. To this day, Ernie never knew what the job had been.

A lump of emotion hit my throat. I shrugged it off and headed to the front door of the hospital.

Ernie Ruibal was on the fifth floor. He'd been there for the last five days, ever since the cancer had gotten so bad that the pain medication they gave him didn't work anymore. His wife had been so fearful that she'd called 911 and then me. I'd held one hand and she the other on the ride to the emergency room. I'd visited him every day since then, at the same time. When he was lucid, we talked about cases and people we'd known over the years: cops and crooks, hookers, grifters, gamblers, and other assorted lowlifes. When he'd gone to see Morpheus, I'd sit for an hour or two, flipping channels or reading a book. Sometimes his wife, Miranda, was there, or one of his sisters. Sometimes not. He and Miranda had two children, boys. One was dead, the other in prison.

Ernie also had a heart condition that precluded the transfer to a hospice the doctors wanted. "To die with dignity, you understand, don't you," they said. I didn't understand shit when I saw a fifty-six-year-old man, the closest thing I'd had to a real father, wasting away as his olive skin turned yellow and his hair fell out. Go to hell, Marcus Welby.

The door to Ernie's room was open and I walked in. Miranda stood up and kissed my cheek. "He's awake, not too bad today. Why don't you sit with him while I go get a cup of coffee."

I said okay and walked over to the one chair that would fit in the cramped room. The door shut on her way out. Ernie opened one eye and looked at me. "Is she gone?"

"Yeah."

"Thank Jesus. That woman's about to drive me to drink again." Ernie had quit the booze when he was in his thirties. He'd gone to AA meetings five times a week ever since. Until he got liver cancer. Ernie liked to point out how funny it was, in a sick kind of way, the irony of a recovering drunk getting liver cancer.

"What's she doing now?" I said.

He reached for the tumbler of water on his nightstand and took a drink. "I told her that I wanted to be buried in my blue suit. That's all I say, and she starts to cry." The outfit in question was baby blue and had a golden wagon wheel embroidered on the back. That was just one of its many western themes. When Ernie wore it, he looked like a Mexican Porter Waggoner.

"Here's your magazine." I decided to ignore the Miranda/burial suit situation.

"Thanks. What's up at the office? The roof leaking again with that rain?"

"Yeah. Ferguson's about to have a stroke."

"A stroke would do him good. That or a high colonic." Ernie flipped a couple of pages in the magazine and then closed it. "We got any new business?"

"It's not much but we do have a new client." I related the story of Vera Drinkwater and her missing little brother. Then I told him about the guy in the beige Camaro.

Ernie scratched his scalp. "And you didn't recognize him?"

I shook my head. "He's not in the business. He wouldn't have followed that close or panicked."

My partner nodded. "Maybe just some whack job."

I shrugged but didn't say anything.

"But you coulda handled him, right, Hank? You got the best moves of anybody I've ever seen." In his youth, Ernie had boxed some, Golden Gloves and then a few professional fights as a welterweight. He held up his hands in the way a boxer would, one forward, the other back, waiting to strike. The IV line in the back of one fist slid across the metal bed rail.

I didn't reply, suddenly overcome with a sadness I couldn't put into words.

"You remember that loan shark on Ledbetter Avenue, that time he—" He stopped abruptly and grimaced, eyes shut so hard his brow furrowed.

I waited without speaking, almost without breathing, painfully aware of my impotence when it came to this. A metal and glass contraption sat next to the bed, connected to the patient by a thin IV and a push button. Pain medication a touch away. He held the button in his hand, thumb poised to go. Another grimace and a groan and his thumb wavered. The spell passed and he opened his eyes. "Cancer sucks, Hank." His breath was ragged.

I nodded but didn't say anything.

"I need a favor, I hate to ask."

I took his free hand, the one without the IV. "Whatever you need, Ernie. What are partners for?" *Hate to ask? Since when?*

"My sister, Isabella, she's been up here but you haven't met her, have you?"

I shook my head.

"Her youngest girl is Nolan—"

"Nolan?"

"Yeah. Her father named her." Ernie drank some more water. The tumbler was empty so I filled it again. "Nolan just moved here from San Antonio. She used to be a cop down there, but she's not anymore. Got her license and does what we do, skip tracing, missing persons, industrial security, that sort of thing. Anyway, she's here now and there's a certain person who is going to be at a certain place tonight. She's supposed to serve papers on him."

"What's the favor?" Serving papers is to a private investigator what fixing a hangnail is to a heart surgeon.

Ernie knew this and avoided eye contact. "I promised my sister that I would look after her kid, including her first . . . uh . . . assignment here." Ernie sighed dramatically. "I told her someone would be there, tonight, when she serves this man's papers."

I tried *not* to sigh. "All right. I'll do it. Tell me where and when."

"If you can't be there, I could always call Delmar or Olson."

"I said I'd do it. Tell me the particulars." Delmar and Olson were two psychopathic gun dealers we used occasionally for heavy muscle work and backup. They referred to themselves as "arms merchants" and wouldn't be caught dead serving papers. They'd wad the papers up and shove 'em down the guy's throat, but they wouldn't serve them.

Ernie coughed and grabbed his stomach. "Enrico's, on McKinney Avenue. Tonight at eight o'clock."

"How am I supposed to recognize . . . Nolan?"

Ernie held the dope button, thumb resting on the switch. "Her name is Nolan O'Connor. Dad's Irish. Irish-Mexican-Catholic, how's that for a mix? You'll know her. Always wears her hair in a ponytail." Something started at his toes and worked its way upward, causing his body to ripple like a piece of garden hose snapped at one end. When it got to his midsection, he let out a yelp and pushed the button. A few seconds later tension, pain, and coherency started to drain out of his body. He managed a few more words. "D-d-don't worry. Blue eyes. And pretty." Then he was asleep. I put the magazine I'd brought on the bedside table, pulled the covers up, and slipped away.

The sky was the color of hot brass and the air had started to shimmer just above the concrete of the parking lot. I felt the heat worm its way through the soles of my shoes. The temperature on the bank sign across the street read 98 degrees.

Visiting Ernie was the same way every time: I struggled not to lose it before going in, then felt nothing when I left. I looked at my watch: two o'clock. I had six hours before babysitting Nolan O'Connor. It was time to head north and visit Callahan Real Estate and see what they could tell me about Charlie Wesson.

CHAPTER THREE

Dallas, the northern portion anyway, owed its appearance to several things. Chief among them was structural engineering and the ability to mold concrete into any design imaginable. Additional factors included a flat, stable terrain and creative mortgage lending. But that's another story.

I made my way up the Dallas North Tollway, the turnpike that split the northern sector of the city. It was before rush hour and the traffic moved well. Since a portion of the highway sat below ground level, you felt like you were in a concrete canyon, swimming in some river of internal combustion engines. Above the walls of the canyon came the jungle. Like the vegetation at a creek bank, the buildings closest to the tollway were bigger, sucking their nourishment from the torrent of cars that passed by every hour. Those farther from the stream of automobiles grew smaller, content to feed on the eddies and tributaries that are the side streets leading off the highway. Beyond those sprawled the dwellings, thousands and thousands of houses and apartments, homes for the workers who toiled in the tall buildings at the edge of the canyon. Nobody kept chickens in their yard up here.

I drove ten miles per hour over the speed limit, in the right-hand lane, and was the slowest-moving vehicle. At my exit, a Mercedes swung past me and cut across my lane to make the off-ramp, desperate to save those four or five seconds that would have otherwise been lost. I slid in after him and exited on Belt Line Road, crossing over the tollway and heading west. Traffic flowed heavier here, six lanes between a strip of offices and shopping centers, each disgorging a torrent of cars at one end while taking in an equal number at the other.

Callahan Real Estate Company officed on Lindbergh, a side street in an industrial park near Addison Airport. Addison sits on the far northwest side of Dallas, one of a handful of suburbs bordering the city there. Addison was the only area for miles around to serve liquor by the drink. Consequently it had more restaurants per square mile than any city in America. They were classy places, usually part of some corporate chain, with names like T. J. McFunFuns or Bobblers—A Place to Ogle Teenage Waitresses While You Wait for Your Buffalo Wings.

Lindbergh ran into the airport on the west side, one block north of Belt Line. I turned right on Midway Road, then a quick left, and idled down the street. Nothing remarkable, just a strip of dingy, one- and two-story offices and warehouses masquerading as offices. 3912 Lindbergh was a squat, cinder-block building. Gray paint peeled off the sides. A red awning, weathered to the color of three-day-old hamburger, proclaimed this the location of "Callahan Real Estate, Your Full Service Property Company." A thin strip of grass and a scrawny pear tree served as landscaping.

I parked in front, next to a late-model Cadillac and an elderly Pontiac Sunbird. A new Mercedes, complete with gold wheels and tinted windows, sat on the other side of the parking lot.

A bell sounded when I pushed open the door and walked in. The front room was a small reception area with cheap carpet and cheaper wood paneling. The place smelled of coffee, cigarettes, and copier toner. Sofa and chairs left over from the last Howard Johnson's redecoration clustered to the left; on the right was a receptionist desk.

A woman in her early twenties, a panorama of cleavage, eye shadow, lip gloss, and that big hair that they only do in Texas, looked up from her romance novel and blew a plume of smoke my way. "Yeah?"

"I'm here to see Mr. Callahan. About the office space, the one on Arapaho Road."

She took another hit on the smoke and squinted her eyes. She was marginally pretty, in a fourth-string Playboy Playmate kind of way, until she frowned. Then she was ugly. "What office space are you talking about?"

"The one on Arapaho."

"We don't have anything on Arapaho." She pulled a sheet of paper out of the top drawer and studied it. I didn't think she could squint any harder but she did. "Nope, nothing on Arapaho. We got, hmm, lessee . . . two thousand feet on Spring Valley."

I pulled a piece of paper out of my pocket and looked at it. "My mistake. You're right, it's two thousand and fifty feet on Spring Valley."

She smiled, apparently unused to being right about anything.

"I need to see Mr. Callahan about that space. I've got a tenant for it."

"Mr. Callahan?"

"Yes. I need to see Mr. Callahan." I tried not to sound or look exasperated. "About the space on Spring Valley."

She squinted again and I could see the wheels turning underneath all that hair spray. "Mr. Callahan is . . . in a meeting."

I sighed elaborately and put my hands on my hips. "Look, I've got a tenant who needs two thousand square feet, and he needs it yesterday. We've got an appointment in an hour at another building. It's a little farther away than he wants but the agent is willing to deal. Do I take my guy there or can I talk to Callahan?"

She looked scared and I almost felt sorry for her. Almost. "I . . . I'll buzz him." She picked up the phone and punched a button. "I'm sorry . . . I know . . . there's somebody here about some space . . . I know . . . he's got a tenant for the office on Spring Valley. . . . Yes. Yes, I will." She put down the phone and pointed to the door behind her desk. "If you'll go right through there, sir. First one on your left."

I said thanks and walked through the door. There was a narrow hallway and the first door on my left was open. I walked in. It was a larger and better furnished office than the one in the front. A middle-aged man sat behind an oak desk, white button-down shirt and tie undone, a stack of files in front of him. He stood when I entered and came around the desk, hand extended. "Howya doing? Tom Callahan. Nice to meet you. What can I do for you?"

I shook his hand and said, "How are you, Tom? My name is Hank Oswald. My client is Charlie Wesson, and he needs to lease some space from you."

He gave me a blank stare, then a frown, then a blank stare again. "What?"

"Miss January, out front, said you were in a meeting. I hope I'm not interrupting, but my client Charlie Wesson wants to lease some office space."

Confusion disappeared, replaced by hostility. "Who are you?"

I didn't reply, just stared at him. Silence was an old technique; don't say anything, let the mark get nervous and fill the quietness. Tom Callahan must have seen that episode of *Dragnet* too, either that or he'd been negotiating real estate deals for too long to let a method like that get to him. Five seconds stretched to thirty and then a full minute. Finally he spoke. "There is a man named Charlie Wesson who works here. He didn't show up today."

"Do you know where he is?"

"No."

"Who'd he work with?"

"That really is none of your business. I've got things to do. I think you should leave."

"I was hired by his family to find him. It is my business."

Tom Callahan walked back to his desk and sat down. He began to shuffle papers. "Get out."

I didn't move. "You're pretty nonchalant about this. Do you have employees disappear all the time?"

Callahan put down the file he was holding and looked at me. "Charlie Wesson was a druggie. I hired him to try and give him a chance at a normal life. But once a doper, always a doper. It's a fucking disease, like epilepsy or herpes. Once you get it, you never get rid of it. Charlie fell off the wagon. He may be dead for all I know. That's what you get when you deal with junkies." His tone was angry and bitter, more so than the situation warranted, I thought.

He seemed to read my mind. "My son went through rehab three times. Nothing worked. He died six months ago. Overdose. I thought maybe I could make a difference with Charlie."

I flipped a card on his desk and said, "If he turns back up, or you hear anything, I'd appreciate it if you'd let me know."

At the front, the receptionist was back at the romance novel and sparking up another smoke. She ignored me. I stood in front of her desk and said, "Did you know Charlie Wesson?"

She didn't put down the book this time. "I'm not supposed to talk to you about that. You should leave now."

I left another card on her desk with the same request that I'd given her boss. Her eyes were pleading this time. "Really, for your own good, just leave."

Something was funny here. I couldn't figure out how she had been told not to talk to me. There wasn't time from when I left Callahan's office and got to her for him to have called.

I walked out into the heat of the afternoon sun. A single-engine Cessna sputtered in the rubbery-tasting air, heading across the horizon toward Addison Airport. Two men stood in the parking lot, leaning against the Mercedes. As I walked down the steps, they came forward, blocking my way to the truck. They were big, obviously strong and well built even though they were wearing loose-fitting clothes. One was white with a goatee, the other black and clean-shaven. The white guy had one hand in the pocket of his oversize jeans. His partner kept both hands hanging loose by his sides. They were professionals, hired muscle.

The black one spoke first. "I hear you're asking questions about Charlie Wesson." He smiled as if enjoying the punch line of a joke. "That's not a real smart thing to do."

CHAPTER FOUR

I kept my eyes on the white guy with his hand in his pocket but talked to the black one. They weren't amateurs like the guy in the Camaro, they were the real thing. "Yeah, I'm asking around after Charlie. What's it to you?"

The black man smiled, displaying a set of perfect white teeth, movie star cuspids. He didn't say anything, just held out the index finger of his right hand and pointed it heavenward. His partner grinned and moved a few feet to the side. He had a gold filling in his front tooth.

"One time," the black man said.

I didn't respond, figuring he would explain himself when he wanted to. Goatee took his hand out of his pocket and stuck a cigarette in his mouth. No guns so far.

"You've got the look of a professional so I'll give you this as a courtesy. One time only." He waved his solitary finger at me. He spoke in clipped tones, without an accent. "Do not ask any more questions about Charlie Wesson. Do not make any more inquiries into his health or welfare. As far as you or any member of his family is concerned, he is fine." He lowered his finger and clasped his hands in front of himself, parade rest. "Are we understanding each other, Mr. Oswald?"

They knew my name so they must have been somewhere in Tom

Callahan's office, listening in on an intercom. Either that, or they'd placed a bug there and were outside eavesdropping. Neither of which was a particularly pleasing scenario. What had Charlie gotten himself into? I debated responses: be polite like he was, or surly. "Where is Charlie Wesson?" was the best I could come up with.

Goatee started to flex his fists and the black man made a tsking sound. "I thought you were smarter than that. Did I not just say you were only going to be given one warning? Now my associate is going to have to explain the ramifications to you." Goatee threw his cigarette down and started to come toward me. I could tell by the way he moved his feet and held his hands that he'd been in the military sometime in the last decade. Probably tried for some branch of the Special Forces and washed out. Maybe he'd stayed long enough to take the intro course in their particular brand of hand-to-hand fighting. Too bad for him I helped design the curriculum.

He came in low and fast, feinting with his left and throwing a short knuckle jab with his right. I slapped his punch away and went lower, grabbing his right with my left and pulling him over my shoulder. My right arm looped under his leg and he fell on his back, behind me and to my left. One foot shot out and connected with the side of his head at the same time as I pulled my pistol out of the holster behind my hip. The black man and I were pointing nine-millimeters at each other.

Standoff.

I kept my gun at the ready and moved slowly in an arc, around the two men, toward my truck. Goatee lay on the asphalt, not moving. A trickle of blood seeped from his temple. He was mildly concussed, I didn't put that much into it. His partner didn't say anything, just tracked me with his gun as I moved.

I was ten feet from my truck, walking backward now. "Is Charlie Wesson alive or dead?"

He didn't say anything. When my back was against the driver's door, he holstered his gun and kneeled by his partner but kept his eyes on me.

I got in the truck and drove off, pistol in my lap.

I left the parking lot on Lindbergh as fast as possible and drove west on Belt Line, the opposite way from the tollway and home. I cut across two lanes of traffic and headed down a residential street. The area was bland, row after row of identical floor-planned, subdivided houses, circa 1970. No one was home yet in this corner of suburbia, so a tail would be easy to spot. It never hurts to be too careful, especially when you just kicked a muscle-bound gorilla in the head.

I prided myself on keeping abreast of the latest personnel changes among the criminal element in North Texas. My line of work often depended on the knowledge, plus it was an excuse to hang out in a lot of sleazy bars. Neither of these thugs' faces registered with me. Ernie might have an idea but I didn't want to bother him. That left Delmar or Olson.

It was Tuesday afternoon. Olson had dinner with his mother every Tuesday. He usually went over early to her house in Fort Worth, and worked on the odd jobs that had accumulated during the week. She fixed chicken casserole and fussed over him about not settling down and finding a nice girl. Tuesdays put Olson in a bad mood. All six foot six and two hundred and eighty pounds of him.

I decided to call Delmar. He didn't have a mother and his father was doing twenty to life in Huntsville for trying to whack a municipal judge in Lufkin. He was always in a bad mood but couldn't do too much damage over the phone.

He answered his cellular on the first ring. "Yeah?"

"It's Hank. I need some info."

I could hear movement and talking in the background. "This really isn't a good time. I'm in the middle of something."

"The middle of something" could mean a lot of things with Delmar.

I waited a moment but didn't hear any gunfire or screaming. "Call me back when you've got a minute."

"Hang on." More talking in the background, Delmar and someone with a German accent. I could hear Delmar's voice: "Of course, Herr Muller. We shall talk in the morning. *Auf Wiedersehen.*" He came back on the line with me. "So tell me why the hell you are bothering me."

"Herr Muller?"

"Yes. Herr Muller. He's the German equivalent of the Duke of Earl or something. He's got a matched set of prewar Purdeys, originally made for the British royal family. We're in the middle of negotiating a price for them."

I noticed thunderclouds forming again. "What's a Purdey?"

"It's the Rolls-Royce of shotguns, you fucking Philistine. Why are you calling me?"

I chuckled to myself. Delmar specialized in exotic shotguns and custom rifles that usually cost more than a nice house in the suburbs. While I didn't know much about either, I knew enough to enjoy playing dumb from time to time. It was fun to get Delmar riled up, especially at a distance. Olson dealt in machine guns, semiautomatic rifles, and pistols. I knew a lot about those.

"I need some information. Two thugs. They were in a late-model Mercedes, gold stuff hanging everywhere and tinted windows. One black and one white. White guy has a goatee and a gold tooth. Both in their mid-thirties, six-foot plus, two-hundred-pounders. The white guy was military, no question. And they are definitely in the game, professionals. They tried to warn me off a case I'm investigating."

"What happened with the warning?"

"The white guy got himself a concussion. The black guy stayed out of it, except to pull a pistol."

Delmar didn't say anything for a moment. Then, "What kind of pistol?"

"I couldn't tell." I was out of the residential area with nobody tailing me. I pulled onto the LBJ Freeway, the inner loop of the city. Time to head home.

"Think they were with Omar?" The cellular crackled in my ear as he spoke. Omar ran the largest gambling operation in the area, in addition to occasionally dabbling in other things like prostitution and drugs. He kept himself and his people close to home, though, in Arlington, one of the midcities between Dallas and Fort Worth.

"I tried to make him work for this but couldn't. He's geographically undesirable. Plus this has to do with a real estate broker somehow."

We talked over various possibilities for a couple of minutes, assorted hoods and wiseguys, without finding a likely candidate. Delmar said he would make a couple of calls and get back to me. I drove to my neighborhood, anxious to be among the lowlifes and the relative safety of the narrow streets there, away from the chain restaurants and tract houses of the northern environs.

I'd signaled to turn onto my street when I realized that the pantry at Casa Oswald lay bare. I sped up and headed for the nearest grocery, on Gaston Avenue. It was late afternoon and people thronged the aisles, a chattering blur of browns, yellows, and other earth tones. Their voices filled the air; mostly Spanish, followed by Vietnamese, then a slew of unidentifiable Central Asian dialects. The place smelled like a grocery store should, fruity and warm, the temperature of the air only slightly less warm than outside.

I picked up a pair of bone-in chicken breasts, a bag of onions, some Asian greens for a salad, and a head of cauliflower. That seemed too healthy so I grabbed a twelve-pack of Coors.

Back at home I put the chicken breasts in a casserole dish, drizzled them with olive oil, added salt, pepper, and a handful of rosemary from the bush that grew wild between my house and Mr. Martinez's. There was a half bottle of decent Chardonnay in the refrigerator so I poured a couple of slugs in the bottom of the dish. A piece of foil over the top, and I popped dinner in the oven. The dog looked friendly, and I fed her.

The chicken would take about an hour, so I changed into an old sleeveless sweatshirt and a pair of shorts and headed for the basement. My regimen is simple and I keep to it at least four times a week, religiously, unless I'm hungover or have something better to do. Fifteen minutes of skipping rope to warm up, followed by a half hour of work with the free weights. I ended my workout with some stretching exercises and a little time on the punching bag hanging from the rafters. On alternate days I run through the neighborhood for an hour. That's the Hank Oswald Exercise Program. I ought to get my own video.

I emerged from my home gym sweating and feeling virtuous. I drank a liter of water to rehydrate, then popped open a Coors to sip while I fixed the rest of my dinner. The aroma of roasted chicken and herbs wafted through the kitchen. I turned on the local news while I chopped cauliflower and prepared a salad. Authorities found a twelve-year-old girl, weighing fifty pounds, locked inside a closet in a double-wide trailer in Forney, a rural suburb to the east of Dallas. She was filthy, lying in feces and a pile of empty dog food cans, evidently her primary means of nourishment. The authorities also discovered the badly decomposed body of a prepubescent male under the trailer. It was thought to be her brother. The parents were members of a strange religious sect that worshiped the moon. They had a combined IQ of 150.

I drank the rest of the beer and poured myself a glass of the Chardonnay.

A radical environmental group staged a sit-in protest at the site of the Trinity Vista, a new development between North and South Dallas. The group of environmentalists said the land, a floodplain but soon to be reclaimed by the U.S. Army Corps of Engineers, housed a rare species of lizard.

I mixed some dressing for the salad: mustard with extra-virgin olive oil and balsamic vinegar.

Police arrested a Dallas city councilman for drunken driving, his second time in as many months. A man with no legs sank a hole in one at a local golf course. The weather guy talked a long time about an un-seasonable low pressure trough in the Gulf of Mexico. Expected temperatures to be higher than normal for the early part of the summer, certainly in the triple digits.

I raised my glass in a toast to lizards, drunken city councilmen, and central air-conditioning. The chicken and cauliflower went on the next-to-last clean plate, the salad would do straight from the bowl. I pulled a bar stool up to the kitchen counter. Another glass of wine, a squeeze of lemon juice on the vegetables, and dinner was served, chez Hank. After eating, I cleaned the kitchen and then showered for my appointment with Nolan O'Connor, Ernie's niece. I dressed for the evening: a clean pair of khakis, black rubber-soled shoes, and a navy silk Tommy Bahama shirt, untucked to hide my pistol. I strapped the usual assortment of weapons and private investigator paraphernalia to my body and went forth to meet the evening.

CHAPTER FIVE

The woman stared at me when I said my name, a quick frown and raised eyebrow. Sometimes it's not easy being named Oswald, not in the city where Lee Harvey grabbed his infamy by the throat and choked it to death. I probably shouldn't have introduced myself using my first name, Lee, but something about her and the place we were in made me irritable and belligerent.

I tried again. "Just call me Hank." I held out my hand. Hank was short for Henry. Lee Henry Oswald. The third. Thanks a lot, Dad.

She shook it. "My name's Janice. Didn't you say your name was Lee Osw—"

A waitress interrupted her. "What can I get you to drink?"

Janice looked at me, then the waitress, then back at me. She finally ordered a Cosmopolitan and I got a Carta Blanca. She was pretty, slender with blond hair and green eyes that twinkled in the thin light. Thirty lay a couple of years down the road.

"So, Hank, what brings you out tonight?" She earned points for not asking what I did for work or where I lived as her first question.

We were in the bar at Enrico's, the newest, hippest, place-of-the-moment for the young and pretty crowd. Enrico's featured the latest trend in haute cuisine: Spanish-Asian fusion. A spring roll of shrimp paella for twenty-six ninety-five, washed down with a jasmine martini. The decor was raw brick, exposed wiring, and oddly spaced spotlights. You could see the whole place from where we sat. No sign of a woman with blue eyes and dusky skin, her hair in a ponytail.

"No particular reason," I said. "It's been a long day. Thought I'd slip in and have a quick drink." The waitress arrived with our order, and I paid her.

Janice took a sip of her Cosmopolitan. "Yeah, me too. Just a quick drink. So what do you do for a living?"

A direct girl, she was prequalifying me before she wasted any more time. I decided not to lie. "I'm a private investigator. What about you?"

"I'm a-a-an, um—" She had trouble getting the words out. "I'm in advertising. Are you really a private investigator?"

"Yep. Really and truly." She didn't say anything for a minute, just took a couple of sips of her drink. I figured she was trying to decide if I was telling the truth, and if I was, how much effort should she expend on a private eye.

She was about to say something when there was a commotion at the front door. An entourage had arrived. Four burly guys in bad suits surrounded two smaller ones with cell phones glued to their ears who flanked a man and a woman. The man appeared to be in his mid-forties, six feet tall and trim, slicked-back hair, three-button black suit over dark blue, spread collar shirt. No tie. He walked the walk of one who was Important with a capital *I*. His companion slinked beside him, moving with that particular stride of a professional runway model. She was maybe twenty-five, blond, and excruciatingly pretty in a black, clingy cocktail dress.

Wait staff and manager types scurried around them like so many sucker fish swarming about a shark. Before you could say leveraged buyout, they'd cleared three tables in the center of the room and the group sat down, the man and woman inside a protective circle of yes men and hired muscle.

There was something familiar about him that I couldn't quite bring to mind. I turned back to Janice but she'd left already. I saw her against the far wall, talking to a knot of other young women, dressed the same way. They had their eyes glued on the man and the woman in the middle of the bar. I scanned the rest of the place but didn't see anybody resembling Nolan O'Connor. It was still early, though, only seven forty-five.

The waitress tapped me on the shoulder and handed me a folded cocktail napkin. I opened it and read the message. *If you want to help and not just babysit, "accidentally" knock over your table when the man selling roses approaches the group in the middle. Nolan. P.S. I'm wearing a denim jacket and my hair is in a ponytail. The man in the dark suit is Lawrence Shagan.*

Real smooth, Mr. Private Eye. I mentally berated myself for not spotting her, even if she was trying not to be seen. I stuffed the note in my pocket but resisted the urge to scan the crowd again. Instead, I kept my eyes on the now familiar face of Lawrence Shagan, the CEO *Business Week* headlined the month before as the Man Who Made Us Forget Ken Lay and Enron. Indicted a half dozen times but never convicted, he was the subject of scores of lawsuits from disgruntled investors. Then there was the not-entirely-legal animal testing one of his pharmaceutical companies had engaged in, sending the PETA crowd into orbit. He spent most of his time offshore, cruising the Caribbean in his yacht, and dodging additional lawsuits. I recalled that his mother lived in Dallas. Somehow, Ernie's niece must have gotten the word that he would be in town today, and end up here this evening. Evidently another group had filed another lawsuit, and she'd been hired to serve the papers.

I took another sip of beer and looked around the room without moving my head. No denim jacket with a ponytail visible.

A man with a thick mustache, wearing a red hat and matching windbreaker, walked in the front door. He was carrying a basket of roses. The manager stopped him. They talked for a few seconds, the manager shaking his head. A couple walked between the rose man and the manager at the same time as the phone rang at the front counter. The couple stopped to talk to the manager while he tried to answer the phone. They were angry about something. The man with the roses slipped through. He approached several people but was rebuffed. Lawrence Shagan and his entourage watched him come toward their tables. The bodyguard closest stood up as he approached and held his hand out, stopping the man. They exchanged a few words until the man with the roses shrugged his shoulders and appeared to turn away.

A voice behind me said, "Do it now."

I kicked the table over, ashtray, beer bottle, and glass crashing to the floor. Everybody turned my way as the rose man shrieked, "*Save the animals.*" He slung the flower basket at Shagan and his companion, as roses and something liquid exploded everywhere. A shower of either blood or red food dye splattered over Shagan and his party as well as the surrounding tables.

Shagan's team jumped at the man.

Unfortunately the couple who'd been talking to the manager when the rose man slipped in decided to head back to the bar and walked right between the man and the bodyguards.

Extreme confusion ensued.

The action was a thing of beauty to watch from my point of view, more of a ballet than a serving of papers, each move evidently choreographed and planned beforehand. The bodyguards got tangled up with the couple, who were tangled up with other groups of people sitting nearby. More glassware broke as more tables fell over. The rose man disappeared; one instant he was there, the next he was gone. From behind me I caught a flash of denim glide through the mess, up to Lawrence Shagan.

My evening's appointment, it had to be.

She tapped Shagan on the back and said something. He turned and looked confused. She spoke again and he nodded. In a flash, she thrust a white envelope into his hand. She turned and ran to the back, toward the restrooms and the rear exit.

People stood, craning to see what the fuss was about. I could hear Shagan's girlfriend, swearing like a twenty-dollar hooker as she tried to mop up the blood off her dress. It was time to leave, so I headed to the rear.

The back opened onto the restaurant's parking lot. I eased out the door and stood against the wall. The lot was empty except for two people standing by the street, away from the lights on the building. In the dimness I recognized the denim jacket and ponytail. She saw me and waved. I walked up as she finished counting out a wad of cash.

"One eighty, two hundred. And here's a hundred each for Mary and Sid." She handed the money to the man standing next to her. I realized he was the rose man, minus his mustache, red jacket, and cap. He must have slipped out of his disguise in the confusion. "Thanks, Benny. I appreciate your help, especially on short notice."

"Anything for you, Nolan." He pocketed his money and looked at me. "Animals do have rights." He turned and walked into the night.

Across the street, someone started a car and turned on the headlights. The light shone on Nolan O'Connor. She was better-looking than anything related to Ernie Ruibal had a right to be. Early thirties, five eight and slim, she had high cheekbones and pale blue eyes set in an olive complexion. A hot wind blew across the parking lot, whipping a loose strand of hair across her face. The air smelled of the city: diesel exhaust and trash.

"You done checking me out?" She took off the jacket and slung it over a shoulder. She wore a pair of navy slacks and a sleeveless silk blouse, the faint silhouette of a handgun barely visible against one hip, underneath her top.

"Yeah, pretty much."

"Good. How about giving me a ride?"

"Sure. My truck's around the corner." We left the parking lot as the first police car rolled up, lights flashing. The two uniformed officers that got out paid us no mind. We walked down the side street, toward my car.

"So I bet you're wondering how I figured out who you were," she said.

We reached my ride. I hit the remote and the locks popped open. "You're the youngest child, probably the only girl."

She didn't say anything, just hopped in the passenger's seat.

I continued. "You come from a close-knit family and know your mother pretty well. You knew she worried when you were with the San Antonio PD, knew she worried even more when you went freelance. You also had an uncle in the business, here in Dallas. You knew he was sick but had a partner. It's not too much of a stretch to see you parking down the street, checking out our office. Which you did before I knew you existed."

She nodded her head slowly but didn't say anything.

I drove down the side streets, zigzagging away from McKinney. I had no particular destination in mind since she hadn't told me where to take her. They called the area Uptown, denoting its location just north of downtown. High-rise apartments and exclusive shops dominated the narrow blocks. We passed several galleries, each with a series of abstract sculptures in the front, illuminated from the ground up by different-colored lights. They were across the street from a nightclub with the doors open to the warm evening air. The effect of the multihued lights combined with the music and noise from the club was surreal. I made another random turn and the noise faded.

"What I don't know is how your mother, and then Ernie, came to know about your little rendezvous with Lawrence Shagan."

Nolan tugged at a strand of loose hair and stared out the window at the tourists spilling out the front door of the Hard Rock Cafe. "I told my mother. I wanted to see what Uncle Ernie could come up with." She looked at me. "That's a polite way of saying I wanted to see how good you were."

"Well, as you saw, I can kick over a bar table with the best of them."

She laughed and started to say something when my cell phone rang. It was Delmar. "Get over here. ASAP."

"Good evening to you too." We were on Turtle Creek Boulevard now, heading toward downtown. "What do you have for me?"

"I did a little research on that thing we talked about this afternoon. We need to visit. Immediately."

"I've got company right now. Give me the highlights."

"Not on the phone. If you're still with Ernie's niece, bring her. You might need help on this one."

"I probably don't want to know how you knew about her."

"Ernie called me this morning. I'm at the usual place. Get here. Now." He hung up.

I put the cell phone back in my jacket. "Have you ever been to the Purple Pagoda?"

Nolan shook her head. "Nope."

I made a U-turn and headed north. "You're in for a treat."

CHAPTER SIX

The Purple Pagoda sat behind a Mexican restaurant on Oak Lawn Avenue, not really a building, more of a zoning anomaly. In a different era it had been a house, a stucco, prairie-style dwelling; home to some upper-middle-class family at the beginning of the last century. Sometime in the past, someone had glassed in the front porch, added a bar and small kitchen, and knocked out a few interior walls, turning it into a restaurant of sorts. Vegetation ran amuck on the lot; ivy covered the house and a stand of hackberry trees hid what the ivy didn't. Purple neon that said "P.P." served as the only signage. For whatever reason, the city inspectors allowed it to exist. I always suspected they were afraid to venture inside to see what was really there.

At about nine o'clock I pulled off Oak Lawn, drove past the restaurant in front, and parked. It was a humid night with a threat of more thunderstorms in the air, and there weren't many patrons at the Purple Pagoda. I saw Delmar's Lexus, Olson's Ram Charger, and a handful of other cars parked by the front door.

"Tell me again who these guys are," Nolan said. She was standing in front of my truck, looking at the stores on either side. The one on the left was called the Man from Nantucket, the one on the right, the Southern Cross. A Confederate flag covered the door of the Cross, and a dozen or so Harleys sat parked in front. Two figures stood by the front door of the Man from Nantucket, locked in an embrace.

"We're going to see Delmar and Olson." I chirped the locks shut on the truck. "We use them occasionally when we need an extra hand. They're good for information too."

"Is that a gay bar?" She pointed at two men with their mouths locked together, in front of the Man from Nantucket.

I pushed open the entry without replying. Olson and I had served together in the Persian Gulf, a few years after he had been cut by the Cowboys for throwing a reporter through a plate glass window. He and Delmar were what modern society termed same-sex life partners. I called them friends, loyal to the last ounce of energy they possessed. They were lifetime members of the NRA, paid their taxes on time, voted a straight Republican ticket, and asked only to be left alone. Sometimes that was hard because of their chosen occupation, hence their desire to keep their sexual predilections under wraps. Which made it all the more confusing why they would hang out at a bar called the Purple Pagoda in the gay part of town.

The smoky darkness washed over me as I squinted to see where they were. The Pagoda was one big room, bar to the left, fireplace on the right wall. No illumination except for the string of white Christmas lights running along the trim, and the candles on the tables scattered around the room. Light purple paint and posters from 1940s musicals covered the walls. Frank Sinatra sang on the jukebox about the summer he turned seventeen. The place smelled like whiskey, cigarettes, and some really nasty incense.

A couple of people sat at the bar, nursing draft beers. Nolan was the only woman in the room. I spotted them in the back, sprawled at a table near a lacquer and marble grandfather clock. They both stood for Nolan when we approached, full of that old world charm. They made quite a sight. Olson was big, blond, and fair, with a long, thin face and blue eyes. He looked like a Norwegian professional wrestler instead of an all-pro linebacker who spent most of his career playing next to Ed "Too Tall" Jones. Delmar stood four inches shorter than Olson, about my height but stockier. He was swarthy, with a full face and bushy mustache. Olson wore his standard uniform: cowboy hat and boots, faded Wrangler jeans, a white pearl-button shirt, and a leather vest.

And mascara.

He swept his hat off and shook Nolan's hand. "It certainly is a pleasure to meet you, ma'am. We've heard so much about you." He ignored me.

Delmar wore his cool-guy city clothes, an Armani suit and black T-shirt. He held a cigar the size of a loaf of French bread in one hand. No mascara. "Ernie's a good friend of ours. Anything we can ever help you with, let us know."

I pulled out a chair and sat down. "Thanks, fellas. I'm doing just fine too."

Delmar frowned at me while Olson waved at the waiter. They signaled for another round. Bourbon and vodka respectively. Nolan got a beer. I ordered a single-malt scotch old enough to vote. The Purple Pagoda was their turf and they paid the bill. Those were the rules. We made small talk until the waiter brought the drinks and left.

Delmar sparked up his cigar. "You ever hear of Coleman Dupree?"

I took a taste of the water of life from the Scottish Highlands and shook my head.

"The guy you ran into today, the black one. Name is Jack Washington. Jack the Crack, they call him, and it ain't because he sells a lot of dope. It's because he likes to crack bones. He's Coleman Dupree's number-one enforcer, his go-to man."

"And Coleman Dupree would be?" Nolan asked.

"Dupree's the man in charge of ninety percent of the drugs in South Dallas, which means ninety percent of the drugs in all of Dallas. Which means—"

I finished the sentence for him. "Which means probably fifty percent of the drugs in North Texas. Which explains why he has an enforcer named Jack the Crack. How come I've never heard of this Dupree guy?"

"He's new in the last month or so." Delmar paused and relit his cigar. "Just took over a couple of operations and consolidated. The details are a little hazy."

"Hazy?" Nolan said.

"Uh-huh." I took another taste of whiskey. "Most of the hard stuff around here is controlled by eight or ten people, sort of like distributors. They have a network of retailers they sell through. One guy taking over another's operation is a big deal, it's not like buying the corner grocery store. Usually involves dead bodies. We'd have heard about it. If not on the news then on the street."

"That's right," Delmar said. "And there hasn't been a peep about any kind of takeover or war or anything. Except for one little thing." He pointed to Olson, who continued the story.

"About two weeks ago, a guy approached me. Wanted to buy some hardware. He was fourth-hand, friend of a friend. I said sure, but I need to know who I'm dealing with, you understand, I'm a reputable businessman and all. That's when he gets all jiggy and weird. Says for me to fucking mind my own fucking business, do I want to deal with him or not because he's got cash money and is ready to go."

I bit the inside of my cheek to keep from laughing. Maybe the Jaycees would honor Olson with their Reputable Businessman of the Year Award. Olson: the honest, illegal gun dealer. "What kind of hardware did he want?"

Olson drained his drink and scratched his chin. "Hmm, let's see. He wanted some nine-millimeters. A lot of them. Think it was twenty-five. And twenty-five submachine guns. Mac-10's, because I had them on hand."

"What? No bazookas?" I said. "What about land mines?"

Nolan choked back a laugh, staring at the last half inch of her beer instead.

Olson missed my humor. "No, just the nines and the subs. Well, come to think of it, he did inquire about some of those new shoulder-mounted antitank rockets, but I didn't have any. A couple of guys from South Texas had been by the week before and cleaned me out on the big-ticket stuff."

I reiterated my New Year's resolution for the umpteenth time: Do Not Ever Piss Off Delmar or Olson. "So how does this guy figure in with Coleman Dupree?"

"Delmar says you said the other guy with Jack the Crack was a white dude, ex-military, maybe Special Forces. Early thirties with a gold filling in one of his front teeth. Right?"

I nodded.

"That's what this guy looked like. The guy that wanted to buy all that hardware." Olson ran an index finger along the tiny scar on the side of his neck, a subconscious gesture, the wound courtesy of an Iraqi soldier's bayonet during a particularly nasty skirmish a couple of clicks on the wrong side of the Euphrates River. Fortunately I had been able to get my sidearm unholstered in time and all Olson had to show for the encounter was a scar.

I debated the wisdom of having another cocktail while I tried to puzzle out the information. Delmar solved one part of the equation when he signaled the waiter and ordered another round for everybody. I rattled the ice in my glass, watching the dim light reflect off the cubes. "What do we know about Coleman Dupree?"

"Born and raised in Dallas." Delmar toyed with his mustache as he talked. "About thirty. Very intelligent, and very mean. Runs the operation like a business, with a corporate structure. He's layered, never gets his hand dirty with the actual material. He's got what he calls 'vice presidents.' They're in charge of different divisions of the operation: marketing, sales, product development, you get the idea. Then they've got people below them who've got their own people, et cetera."

"Hell, that's what the police report said about the last ten dealers they busted," I said. "Everybody they nail is a Fortune 500 drug lord."

Nolan shook her head. "That's just publicity crap they put out so they can squeeze some more money for the budget."

"She's right." Delmar nodded once. "But according to my source, this guy really is like that."

"Is your source reliable?"

Olson swallowed his drink wrong and started coughing. "Jesus Christ, Hank . . ."

Delmar looked hurt. "That's a low blow. Do I question your ability with that kung fu shit you use?"

"So is your source reliable?" It was the same every time. And every time I wanted to know how reliable the source was. Bad intel's killed a lot of folks over the years.

Olson managed to quit spluttering vodka for a minute. "He's with the DEA. He's a friend of a friend. A very good friend of a friend. He has also been reliable in the past."

I nodded but didn't say anything.

Nolan made little circular motions with her glass on the tabletop. "Dupree feels disenfranchised."

"Disen . . . what?" Delmar said.

Olson frowned and raised one eyebrow. I took another sip of scotch.

"Dis-en-fran-chised." She said the word slowly, enunciating each syllable. "Guy's from the bad part of town. No economic opportunities for an ambitious young man."

"He's a drug dealer," I said. "Coke, heroin. Bad guy. Bad stuff."

"I didn't say he was a *good* guy." Nolan removed the rubber band from her ponytail. She brushed her fingers once through her hair before replacing it. "Helps to understand what you're up against."

Delmar changed the subject. "So how'd you get involved with this anyway?"

I thought about it for a few seconds and then told the whole story to the three of them.

"You realize that Charlie's dead, don't you?" Delmar said.

"As the proverbial doorknob," Olson added. He pulled a cigarillo out of a pocket and lit it, blowing a plume of smoke skyward.

"Yeah. It looks that way."

Nobody said anything for a while. We sat and drank and looked at the purple walls. The waiter came back around. Delmar paid the tab and then put out his cigar. "What's your next move?"

"Try his apartment tomorrow. See if there's any info there." I stood up.

Delmar stood also. "Watch your backside. Anybody named Jack the Crack doesn't suffer a defeat quietly. We'll keep our ears open, see if there's any word on anything."

"Remember, there's no *I* in *team*." Olson patted me on the back so hard I thought my shoulder would separate. "Call if you need backup." He loved to play the ex-jock sometimes, spouting off bumper sticker philosophy about winning and losing and the competitive spirit.

"Thank you, Tom Landry." I rubbed my throbbing shoulder and headed to the door. "You're right; there's no *I* in *team*. Only an *m* and an *e*."

"You're not talking trash on Coach Landry, are you, Hank?" Olson stopped and frowned.

"Me? Never." I could sense Nolan a step behind me, trying not to laugh.

We walked out together. The clouds had broken and I could see a couple of stars penetrate the smog and ambient city lights. We said good-bye, and Nolan and I drove off with the windows down, enjoying the not-quite-cool night air. "Where am I taking you?"

"I'm staying at Ernie and Miranda's."

We were silent for the next few blocks, both watching the city night slide past. At a stoplight Nolan turned to me and said, "Narcissistic personality disorder."

"Huh?"

"The mark tonight. Shagan. At that fancy fish place on McKinney," she said. "He has NPD. I'll bet Coleman Dupree does too."

"Who are you? Dr. Phil's assistant?"

She ignored my question. "NPDs have a sense of entitlement and are exploitive. Rules don't apply."

The light turned green. "What's your point?"

"Narcissistic personality, operating completely outside the law." She slouched against the door and crossed her legs. "That's a dangerous combination."

I nodded. "Kinda figured that already."

"Be careful."

"He's not the first dangerous guy I've dealt with."

Nolan shrugged but didn't reply.

After a few more blocks she said, "I'm gonna be using Ernie's office for a while."

"I figured as such."

"That okay with you?"

"Do I have a choice?"

"Trying not to step on any toes," she said. "But since he's not going to need it for the immediate future . . ."

"Fine by me. Use it however long you need it." I left unspoken the fact that barring a miracle, Uncle Ernie would never need his office again. "How do you like Dallas?"

"It's been good to me so far. You like living here?"

"It's home." I nodded.

"You ever think about leaving here, starting something fresh?" She looked out the side window, watching the lights blur past.

A strange question. I paused for a moment before answering. Then: "Only on months that end in *r*."

She chuckled but didn't say anything.

I made the right for Ernie's street. A hundred feet later I turned into the Ruibal driveway. "Where'd you learn what you did tonight, the action you put together at the restaurant? That was smooth."

"I worked undercover for a while. Picked up a trick or two." She opened the door and put one foot on the ground, turning back to look at me. "Thanks for the ride." A smile crossed her face briefly. I was conscious of her eyes and how smoky blue they appeared in the moonlight. We looked at each other for a moment, that slightly unsettling jittery gaze people have when they are considering, if only briefly, the possibility of hooking up, the what-would-it-be-like thoughts that pass through the heads of all normal people at one time or the other. The moment passed. This was Ernie's niece.

"See you around," I said.

She waved without turning as she made her way up the sidewalk.

I watched her enter the house of my dying partner and then drove home.

Three fingers of Dewar's filled one of my good, leaded crystal highball glasses to the middle. Two ice cubes raised the level more, but made it look less like a shot of whiskey and more like a nightcap. I made my evening tour of the house, sipping scotch and thinking about Coleman Dupree, Jack the Crack Washington, and Charlie Wesson. Every window and door checked out, locked and bolted. I armed the security system, a series of commercial-grade stuff and a couple of homemade devices. Never hurts to be too careful.

Glenda piled up on her corner of the bed. I turned the air conditioner to arctic, placed my pistol beneath one of the pillows, and slid under the covers, eager for sleep.

CHAPTER SEVEN

My alarm buzzed at seven. I rolled over and looked at the address on the piece of paper sitting on the bedside table. It would have been too easy if Charlie Wesson's apartment had been in the neighborhood. Instead, he lived as far away from me as possible while still being in the city limits.

I groaned and rolled out of bed. A hot shower drove the rest of the scotch out of my system. I fried three eggs in olive oil in one skillet, a thick slab of Virginia ham from the freezer in another. Coffee percolated while I buttered two pieces of toast. I threw all of it on a plate, doused the eggs with Tabasco, and ate the breakfast of the successful private investigator. At 8:03 I started the truck and pulled out of the driveway with my third cup of coffee in an insulated, spill-proof tumbler between my legs.

Charlie lived off Luna Road, on the far west side of the city. With traffic it took an hour and five minutes to get there. The location was a strange place to put an apartment, in the middle of a run-down industrial district. The Trinity River ran north to south through this section of the city, and much of the land lay in the floodplain. Charlie's apartment, Meadowland Estates, would have looked better if it had been under water. It was two stories, about forty units, and sat at the bottom of a hollow. Boards covered the doors and windows of three downstairs units. The middle of the second-floor walkway sagged like a sway-backed mule.

A concrete plant and a warehouse sat on either side. Grimy lettering on the front door of the warehouse proclaimed it to be the world head-quarters of Max's Extruded Plastics. A double-wide trailer with a faded sign that said "April's Massage" sat directly across the street. Trees and overgrown vegetation threatened to return April to the wild. It was the only structure on that side of the road for miles.

I parked facing toward the street and got out. It was hot already, probably in the low nineties, and the air smelled funny, like chemicals, either the concrete or the plastics, I wasn't sure. Charlie rented the apartment on the top right, number 309. The stairs looked solid so I went up, two at a time. No answer when I rapped. No deadbolt, just a locked thumb latch. I looked in both directions and got out my lock picks. Nothing moved anywhere. Not a person, not a dog or cat, not even a bird chirped. I felt like I was in one of those bad 1950s movies where everybody disappears except for the brain-eating zombies.

Years of use had worn the tumblers on the lock. That made picking it more difficult. After almost two minutes I pushed open the door and entered. The AC hadn't been used in a while and hot, musty air bil-lowed out, wrapping around me. I immediately started to sweat.

Charlie dwelled in a spartan world, a clean but simple apartment on the dirt end of town.

The place was tiny; a minuscule kitchen opened onto a combination living/dining area with a bedroom and bath off to the right. I'd owned stereo speakers bigger than that kitchen. In the center of the room a milk-crate coffee table sat in front of a threadbare sofa in the center of the room. Two high-back dining room chairs were on the other side. A thirteen-inch black-and-white TV rested in the corner, on the floor. On one wall, an eight-by-ten picture of Charlie and Vera and what ap-peared to be their mother hung cockeyed. I straightened it. It was an old photograph; Vera had wings for hair and purple eye shadow. That was it for the living area.

The rest of the place wasn't as fancy. A twin bed, freshly made with hospital crispness, dominated the bedroom. On the opposite wall, a cheap, particleboard dresser sat under a cracked mirror. Someone had taped several inspirational poems and sappy friendship cards on the mirror. The cards were signed "Jenny." A gooseneck reading lamp sat on the battered metal folding chair that served as a nightstand. There were two books resting on the makeshift table—a Bible and an Alcoholics Anonymous handbook.

Cue the sad music, please.

I didn't know what I was looking for so I looked at everything. The bathroom was closest and I started there. Charlie preferred discount-brand toiletries. He even used the single-blade, disposable razors. My face hurt just looking at them. There were no drugs of any sort, not even aspirin or cold medicine. Two towels, so worn that light shown through, hung over the shower rod. Everything was clean.

Bedroom next. The door on the closet stuck so I banged on it until it moved. I was groping the pockets in the third of Charlie's fourth pair of khakis when I heard the front door open.

I drew my pistol and disappeared into the closet, leaving the door open slightly so the entrance to the bedroom was visible. I heard the front door shut. Then silence.

One one thousand.

Two one thousand.

I moved my head slightly, straining for a better angle to catch a sound. Sweat drenched my body now. The compressor on the refrigerator kicked in. At the count of thirty, I heard a footfall on the linoleum in the kitchen. Then movement at the bedroom door. I got the faintest whiff of stale cigarette smoke. I drew a bead at the entrance, chest high, pistol clasped in both hands.

The door rested ajar, at a forty-five-degree angle to the wall. It opened inward, toward the closet where I hid. The bathroom was on the opposite side of the room. The door started a slow arc toward me, moving at the speed of dripping honey. Something long and black poked into the room. The barrel of a shotgun, pointed at the bathroom. The intruder had a fifty-fifty shot of where someone would hide—closet or bathroom. Lucky for me, he chose the bathroom first.

More of the weapon slid into view, including the wooden forearm and the hand holding it. Call me old-fashioned, but my personal code of ethics did not allow me to shoot an unknown someone through a door. Even if he was holding a weapon. I jumped out of the closet as quietly as possible and kicked the door, putting everything I had into it. The door splintered into the arm, the gun dropped, and a woman's voice screamed.

I booted the shotgun toward the bed and slung open the door, pistol at the ready. A woman stood there, in the middle of the living area, breathing heavily. She looked to be somewhere between twenty-five and forty, with the hollowed-eyed appearance of one who'd seen too much too soon too often. She was wearing a dirty pair of hip-hugger blue jeans and a worn gray T-shirt. Five foot four, she weighed in at maybe one hundred pounds, and then only after eating Thanksgiving dinner. Everything about her was stringy: her hair, limbs, torso, even her voice.

"Who are you?" Her words came out half shriek, half whisper, a wreck from booze, cigarettes, or just plain bad living. She held her left arm pressed to her body and started to cry.

"My name's Hank. Who are you?"

"Where's Charlie?" She rubbed her nose with her good hand.

"I don't know. I'm looking for him too." I holstered my pistol and picked up the shotgun from the bedroom. It was an old Remington, rusty. And empty. I tossed it on the sofa. "Are you Jenny?"

She nodded and sniffled again. "Where's Charlie?" Half shriek, half wail this time.

I decided to try a different tack. "Is your arm okay?"

She pressed her injured limb tighter into her bony chest and frowned at me, eyes wary. "It hurts." Her voice was a whisper.

"Want me to look at it?" I took a step toward her, a smile on my face. You can trust me, even though I just kicked the shit out of you.

"NO." Back to shrieking again. She took a step backward, toward the front door.

"Look, Jenny. I'm trying to find Charlie too. I don't want to hurt him, or you. Charlie's sister hired me. She's very worried about him." I held my hands out to her, palms upward, in a gesture of openness and honesty.

"Vera hired you?"

"Yeah. Vera hired me." I dug a handkerchief out of my pocket and wiped sweat out of my eyes. "Do you know her?"

She sniffled and wiped her nose on her bare arm. "No. But Charlie talked about her. She was the only family he had. Do you have a cigarette?"

"No. Sorry."

"I want a cigarette."

"There's a store not too far. Want to go with me and we'll buy you a pack?"

She looked at me like I had mush for brains. "I've got my own. They're at my apartment. Next door. I want one now."

Stupid me. "Let's go to your place so you can get a smoke, and then tell me about Charlie. Maybe together we can figure out where he is."

She said okay and trotted out. I followed her, leaving Charlie's place unlocked. I could smell the cigarettes and the garbage can that needed to be emptied when she opened the door. I could also feel the thin trickle of cool air coming from the small air conditioner jammed in the window. The place was still hot but after Charlie's it felt like the North Pole.

Her apartment was identical to his, only dirty and more decorated. Not better decorated, just more. Colored beads dangled in the doorway of the kitchen. Two futons designated the living area. She had an actual coffee table between them. A stack of *People* magazines and an overflowing ashtray littered the top. Several framed posters of animals, cats and dogs doing cute stuff, had been hung haphazardly on one wall. She owned a color television, also a thirteen-inch model. It was tuned to a cartoon show with the sound muted.

"You want something to drink?" Jenny, the hostess with the mostest, was in the kitchen. She lit a cigarette and started rummaging in the refrigerator. "I got some Big Red, and iced tea."

"No thanks, I'm fine." I debated whether to sit down but decided not too. "So how do you know Charlie?"

"We met at an NA meeting. We're both in recovery."

"You and Charlie dating?"

She popped the top on a can of Big Red and took a swig. "Yeah. We were gonna get married too. Only now he's disappeared." Her voice was sad but resigned, as if important people disappeared from her life often. She sat down on one of the futons and looked off into space. "Charlie'd been straight for a long time, lots longer than me. We were gonna make something of ourselves. How'd you get into his apartment?" Something on her ass itched because she shifted her weight and scratched it.

"When was the last time you saw Charlie?"

Five seconds turned into ten as she looked at me and tried to process my question. You could almost hear the synapses firing. "Monday. Monday morning. He asked me if the tie he was wearing looked okay. He had a meeting that afternoon and wanted to look good."

"Who was his meeting with? Did he say?"

"The tie was red with a green little doohickey on it. It looked kinda Christmasy—" She quit talking as a coughing fit racked her body. It rattled deep, sounding of chest congestion and bronchitis. When it subsided, she took a drink of Big Red and fired up another breather.

"Jenny . . . the meeting? Did he say who it was with? What it was about?"

"It was about a lease. He'd just passed his test, you know. So he could do that stuff."

"Right," I said. "He'd just gotten his real estate license and started working at Callahan Real Estate."

She frowned, suspicious. "How did you know where he worked?"

I tried to control my impatience. "Charlie's sister, Vera, told me. Now this is real important, if we want to find Charlie." I sat down beside her. "Tell me what you remember about his appointment. Did he say where it was? Who it was with? Anything?"

Jenny bounced up from her seat like someone had shocked her with a cattle prod. "Ooooh, I know where he went." She did a little two-step jig, hopping from one foot to the other, then ran into the kitchen. She grabbed something off the refrigerator and came back. Proudly, she handed me a piece of glossy paper. "This is where his meeting was."

It was a sales flyer from the Callahan Real Estate Company. Their name, address, and various phone numbers ran across the top. A color picture of a cinder-block building covered most of the remainder of the page. Across the bottom of the picture, it said the address of the property, and "Exclusive Listing—Available Immediately." Below that, in smaller type, was "For Information Contact the Listing Agent—Charlie Wesson." There was a floor plan and technical details about the place on the back.

"Do you remember who it was with? Or what time?"

Jenny kept nodding, but closed her eyes. "The guy. The guy who . . ." She scrunched her face up and curled into a tight little ball on the sofa. "It was at four-thirty. I remember because that's in the middle of *Oprah*."

The time fit. Vera said he left his office at four.

Jenny jumped up again. "The guy next door. It was the guy next door."

"That's who he was meeting with?" I said. "The guy next door? Next door to what?"

She grabbed the flyer out of my hand and waved it at me. "Next door to this. He was meeting with the guy next door. He wanted to move into this place. From next door."

I took the piece of paper from her, folded it, and put it in the pocket of my jeans. I handed her one of my cards. "You've been a big help, Jenny. If you think of something else, call me."

She smiled, as eager to please as a puppy. I asked her if she needed anything, food, smokes, soft drinks, anything at all. She said no, she was set. I stood up and she pulled a telephone off the floor and put it on the coffee table.

"You should probably leave. It's almost time for my shift."

I moved toward the door. "Your shift?"

"Yeah. Phone sex." She said it as a matter of fact, with a blank face, neither ashamed nor proud.

I said good-bye and left her there, lighting another cigarette and drinking Big Red. As I got into my truck I wondered what would become of Jenny, if there was anyone else who could look after her if Charlie didn't come back.

CHAPTER EIGHT

I was halfway down Luna Road, almost to the highway, before I realized I'd left Charlie's front door unlocked and the remainder of his place unsearched. I figured that getting robbed was the least of his worries at the moment. Jenny would probably check on it anyway. As for not completing the search, the real estate sales flyer resting in the passenger's seat was the best clue to be found. I could always go back.

Charlie's listing, the building that was his last known appointment, was on Gano Street, number 919. It must be a good part of town, because I hang out in all the bad areas and that name didn't sound familiar. I pulled into the parking lot of a discount liquor store with one cracked window, and got out the map. I was wrong. Gano Street lay south of the center of town, but north of the Trinity, a no-man's-land between North and South Dallas.

I headed down to Interstate 30, the southern boundary of downtown. City hall and the convention center lay to my left, and I turned right, looking for Charlie Wesson's building. The area was old, like where I lived and worked but less renovated and less populated. There were few houses, just block after block of old brick structures, threadbare and faded like a pair of well-washed blue jeans. Some housed taverns, places with names like South Side Johnnie's and Cleo's Bar and

Social Club; others were occupied by barbecue joints and home-cooking places. But most were used by small businesses: mechanics, appliance repair shops, electrical and plumbing supply houses. Not many cars or people moved about. I drove by four package stores in a single block and wondered who shopped there. Dallas was a patchwork of liquor laws, resembling something designed by an alcoholic Mormon with a split personality. Whiskey was legal to sell by the drink on one side of a given street, yet beer and wine forbidden to be stocked in a supermarket on the other.

I found Gano and followed it until I hit number 919, right before the street ended abruptly at a railroad embankment. It contained only three buildings: Charlie's, the one next door, occupied by Pete's Printing Service, and another vacant property across the street. It looked like the picture: cinder block, peeling paint with a faded awning, and a Callahan Real Estate Company sign. I parked in front and got out, reluctant to leave the cool air of the truck for the midmorning heat.

I'd managed five steps toward the front door when an olive-skinned man in a pair of blue work pants and a matching shirt accosted me. He wore a name tag on his chest that said "Pete." His black hair was shot through with gray that spilled out from underneath a Greek fisherman's cap. He was as wide as he was tall, with a barrel chest and wrists as thick as wine bottles.

"That my building. What you want?" He spoke fractured English with an accent, and blocked my way, hands resting on his hips.

"You must be Pete. From next door." I pointed to the adjacent building.

"That right. My name Pete and this my building. What you want?"

"Trust me, Pete. I don't want your building. I'm looking for Charlie Wesson."

Pete appeared to relax. "You know where Charlie I find?"

I translated that to mean he didn't know his whereabouts either.

"No, not yet. I was hoping you could tell me about the last time you saw him."

"Monday. He come with lease for building. Leave it with me. Say he go outside for minute. Go to see the man at the other building." Pete took off his cap and waved it at the place across the street.

"Who was the man at the other building?" I looked at the third place on the block. It was redbrick, older, and set back from the street. Chipped paint on a window indicated that at one point there had been a restaurant there. It looked like someplace Bonnie and Clyde might have robbed. The ubiquitous green and white sign of one of the larger real estate companies in the area proclaimed that it was for sale or lease.

Pete shrugged his shoulders. "Don't know. Charlie very excited, say he see the big man, he go meet him. Then he never come back." Pete's pocket rang, and he pulled out a cordless phone, babbling in a language I couldn't understand. After a few moments, he covered the mouthpiece with one hand. "You go find Charlie. I sign lease. Need building." He handed me a business card. His last named started with an *S*, and had seven syllables that ended in *olopoulus*.

I walked across the street, to the redbrick building. On the back of Charlie Wesson's sales flyer, I jotted down the number on the sign, and the company name, Strathmore Real Estate. After peering into one of the front windows and not seeing anything, I walked around to the back. A few dozen empty beer cans, faded by the sun, littered the asphalt and gravel. The door was locked. My fingers were warmed up after the earlier break-in and I managed to tweak the tumblers in thirty seconds.

The back half was as hot as Charlie's apartment and divided into a series of offices, four in a row opening onto a hallway that ran along the rear of the building. They were all empty except for the last one, the farthest from the street. There were no windows there, but the overhead fluorescent lights worked. The room was clean, free of the dust and debris cluttering the others, as well as bigger, maybe twenty by thirty. It contained a desk, a half dozen chairs, a dirty sofa, and a late-model Sony portable stereo. The wastebasket held an assortment of empty fast food containers and cigarette butts. And one spent nine-millimeter cartridge. I left everything where it was. Nothing in the desk except a crumpled pack of cigarettes and a disposable lighter.

I had my hand on the doorknob, ready to leave, when it opened on its own and I found myself face-to-face with Mr. Gold Filling, the goateed man from yesterday afternoon. Someone had bandaged his head where I'd kicked him at our last meeting.

He snarled and lunged forward, getting a fast punch in toward my stomach with one hand and wrapping his other around my torso. I twisted and took it as a glancing blow, hitting him in the side of the head with the heel of my hand as he went by.

We went down in a heap, each throwing short jabs and clawing for leverage. He gave as good as he got, not afraid to use knees, fingernails, and teeth. His head butt was a mistake, though, less than twenty-four hours after a concussion. He connected, his temple to my cheekbone. My flesh bruised, the skin split, and I felt a trickle of blood. Mr. Goatee passed out. I rolled away and stood up, wobbly but okay. With a handkerchief, I dabbed at the blood on my cheek and mopped sweat off my face. The ribs on my left side felt sore, and there was a tingly spot on one thigh where his knee had just missed my groin.

Using his belt, I tied his hands behind him and rolled him over. There was a Glock nine-millimeter tucked in his front pocket that I stuck in my waistband. The only other weapon he had was a cheap stiletto hidden in one sock. That went into one of my pockets. The Texas driver's license in the wallet behind his right hip identified him as Carl Albach, age thirty-four, address in northeast Dallas. There were two hundreds, three twenties, and a handful of fives and ones in the wallet. No credit cards. I copied down his name, address, and driver's license number on the back of Charlie Wesson's flyer and returned it all to the same pocket. The only other item on his person was a key to a BMW, housed in its own protective case.

He and Jack the Crack rode in a Mercedes yesterday. Did the BMW belong to Carl, and the Mercedes to Jack? Was Carl alone today or did they always travel in tandem? Was Jack Washington standing in the hallway, waiting to see who came out the door? Too many questions and not enough answers.

I found a piece of twine on the floor and tied up Carl's feet. With my gun out, I crouched by the entrance to the room. Using my free hand, I punched the door open and hit the hallway, running low and fast. Each office lay empty, nothing but dirt and rat droppings. I burst through the back door, ignoring the pain in my thigh and the blood dribbling down my cheek.

A dark green BMW sat by the door, locked and empty. He had pulled around so it wasn't visible from the street. I peered around the front of the building. No other cars or people were evident except for my truck, still parked in front of Charlie Wesson's listing. The sky was cloudless, the air hot, and I felt a fresh sweat bead on my forehead. I walked to the front of the redbrick building. The door was locked so I kicked it in, and explored that section of the place. It was empty. With a chunk of cardboard, I wedged the entrance shut as best I could and went back around the building.

The car was next.

Automobiles can be tricky if you're not careful; there are a lot of nooks and crevices things can hide in. I found a roach clip and half a joint in a plastic Baggie in the ashtray, under a pile of cigarette butts. A cell phone lay on the console. No numbers programmed into memory. I left it where it was. Nothing else in the front except an owner's manual for the BMW and an insurance card, made out for Carl Albach, at the same address as his license. On the floorboard in the back, a dirty denim jacket covered a twelve-pack of Schlitz, a half-off delivery coupon for a Domino's pizza, and a pornographic DVD entitled *Anal Alice and the Alley Cats—Part III*. Carl had some social life.

The trunk got interesting. A package lay in the middle, the only thing there, and measured about eighteen inches square, four or five inches deep. It was wrapped tightly with black plastic trash bags and sealed with duct tape. It felt heavy, twenty or thirty pounds at least. I bet it wasn't Carl's dirty laundry. The smart thing to do would be to leave the package and get out.

Sometimes I'm not the ripest tomato in the basket. I got my truck and pulled around back. The package fit nicely behind the seat. I checked on the unconscious Carl. Still out cold, but breathing. I untied his bonds and left him there, key returned to his pocket where it came from. It was time to leave Gano Street, so I drove back to my part of town, toward the office. There was one stop to make first, at my personal self-storage unit.

A few years ago a friend of mine went to Mexico on business. He never came back, for reasons best left unsaid. He lived not far from Ernie, in an old brick house in the middle of the block, an unkempt two-bedroom cottage on a street that fell somewhere between eclectic and dangerous. He had no family and precious few friends. Before leaving, he asked me to retrieve his mail, water when needed, and get the lawn mowed. Five years later he's taking the eternal siesta in an unmarked grave on the outskirts of Piedras Negras, and I'm still house-sitting. There's no corpse to be found so there's no death certificate. That means there's no probate so technically my dead friend is still the owner and no one is the wiser. I maintain the place, splitting the cost with Delmar and Olson. We call it the unit, and use the place for storage of things we'd rather not keep in a traceable location. Like twenty or so pounds of unidentified stuff found in the back of a small-time hood's BMW.

I made the turn down the alley that ran behind the unit and pulled into the garage. The trees lining the gravel surface formed a canopy on the sides and overhead, keeping out prying eyes. As time passed, there had been some modifications to the house: we'd bricked the windows from the inside, installed steel doors with a complicated locking system, and reinforced the roof.

The unit was relatively empty at the moment. In the dining room I kept an exercise machine I no longer cared for but didn't want to sell. It sat next to a box of china that Delmar's grandmother had given him. The dishes rested on a two-column stack of magazines, a twenty-year collection of *Guns & Ammo*. They belonged to Olson or Delmar, I couldn't remember which. In the bedrooms, the three of us maintained a small stock of ammunition in various calibers and configurations. Bullets are like dollars; you can never have too many.

There was a new addition in the living room, a wooden crate about the size of a desk. Cyrillic lettering stretched across the top. I suspected something fully automatic and highly illegal, property of Olson, the honest and reputable merchant of death. I put the plastic-wrapped package and the Glock in the corner of the living room, and proceeded to check the place, making sure everything was secure. No invaders had breached the fortifications so I left, carefully locking the door behind me.

It was time to go to that place I called an office, to see if my suite mates had scared off Nolan O'Connor. I'd gotten two blocks when my cell phone rang. It was Porter Baxter, an old client of mine who had made and lost several fortunes in the oil fields of East Texas and the divorce courts of Dallas County. His voice was frantic, pleading with me to meet him at an Italian restaurant on Northwest Highway that had last been popular when Martin and Lewis were still a team. Her name was Sue something, he said, and she was a really sweet girl but was being unreasonable. Why do women always think you *love* them when you say you love them? It was just the Viagra talking anyway, dammit.

I didn't get home until three the next morning.

CHAPTER NINE

The talking head who did the weather on the local morning show, the one with the shellacked hair and a fondness for neon-colored bow ties and black dress shirts, predicted an afternoon high of 101. I drank another glass of tepid tap water, positioned the pistol digging into my kidney in a more comfortable place, and left the house, cussing the endless Dallas summer.

Four blocks away from the office, I pulled to the curb and got out a pair of Zeiss binoculars from the glove compartment. I spent several minutes studying the cars parked near the office, as well as the sparse traffic. Satisfied the Camaro was not around, I put the optics back where they belonged. That was when I noticed the banged-up beige Chevy idling behind me. It sat lower than my pickup and obviously had pulled in behind me while I was scoping the office. This was the kind of mistake that could get a body disbarred from the Private Investigators Association. Or killed.

Reiger Street was free of traffic for the moment so I jumped out, pulled the Browning, and flattened myself against the side of my vehicle for cover. I snuck a peek over the bed of the truck. The driver was barely visible, his kinky-curly hair hidden under a San Antonio Spurs ball cap. His lips twisted into a jagged worm when he saw me as his right hand appeared from underneath the dash, holding what looked like a Beretta .25 semiauto. From behind the front windshield of the Camaro, he pointed the tiny gun at me.

I tried not to laugh out loud. Aimed dead-on there was only a fifty-fifty shot that a .25-caliber bullet would even break through a modern windscreen. He held the pistol at a forty-five-degree angle to the glass, virtually guaranteeing a ricochet into the instrument cluster sitting above the driver's knees. This had disgruntled ex-boyfriend written all over it, but I hadn't had that many dates lately. Somebody from a long time ago, maybe. I raised my head another couple of inches and smiled at him.

He frowned and pressed the muzzle of the .25 against the glass. I lowered my gun and stood up straight. The driver's face went blank, his eyes as big as quarters. I took a step toward him, and he dropped the gun on the dash, hand scrambling for the gearshift.

I made another move forward and he burned a layer of rubber off the tires in reverse, squealing into the street and narrowly missing a Yellow Cab parked across the street. He jammed the car into drive and sped off, eyes looking straight ahead. I waved at him as he went by, mildly ticked that a layer of mud obscured his license plate.

I got back into my truck and drove the eighth of a mile to the office. There was a different car parked in the back, a canary yellow Eldorado, made sometime during the Carter administration. One quarter panel was Bondo colored. I guessed it to be Nolan's car since neither of my office mates had clients visit very often.

I entered by way of the front door. There were fresh flowers in a vase on the coffee table, a new addition. My finely tuned detective skills told me that Nolan put them there. The room smelled fresher too, less mildewy. The receptionist station lay empty and bare, the computer and typewriter turned off and covered. Amber must be sick. Again. Ferguson, the lawyer who occupied the office in front of mine, stopped me in the hallway.

"W-w-who is that? In fucking Ernie's office?" Spittle flecked his lips and I could smell last night's whiskey or this morning's eye-opener on his breath. "Yesterday, she put fucking flowers in our fucking office. Then she vacuumed. Today," he paused and looked around to see if anybody was listening, like he had a big secret. "Today, she moved a chair, and then lit some smell-good shit. Place smells like a fucking fruit factory."

I was unclear on what exactly a fruit factory was, except that it was a bad thing in Ferguson's world. I took a few steps down the hall and glanced into Ernie's room. Nolan O'Connor sat behind his desk, talking on the phone. None of the things in Ernie's work space had been disturbed, though there were some flowers on his credenza. Sandalwood incense burned on a small saucer on the desk. She waved at me and continued her conversation. I waved back and went into my office, Ferguson trotting behind me like a besotted Shetland pony. "That's Nolan O'Connor," I said. "Ernie's niece."

"I know who the fuck she is. What the fuck is she doing here?"

The liquor I smelled was definitely from this morning. Booze made Ferguson cuss more, like a drunken sailor with Tourette's syndrome. I suspected that if he weren't able to swear, he wouldn't have the vocabulary to order breakfast. "She's a private investigator, like Ernie. Just moved here; she's using his office, temporarily. Didn't she tell you that?"

"Fuck yeah, she tried to lay some bullshit on me, said it was just for a while." He threw up his hands. "Like I fucking care about what goes on in this crazy fucking place."

"Go take a nap."

Ferguson held his finger up like he was going to make an important point. But the words wouldn't come. Finally he hung his shoulders and wandered away. I stepped into my office.

Ten seconds later Nolan knocked on the door frame and stuck her head in. "He doesn't like me much, does he?"

"Ferguson doesn't like anybody except Johnnie Walker." I clicked and typed and doodled with the computer.

"You guys ever clean this place?"

"Not if we can help it." I checked e-mail. Nothing but spam.

"I found a Hoover in the closet." She pointed down the hall. "He told me to quit using it, too much noise too early."

"Did you?"

"Nah," she said. "Told him to fuck off instead."

I nodded. "You'll fit in fine here."

"The flowers." She nodded her head toward the front of the office. "Miranda had them, and I thought they'd look good here." She gazed at a spot on the far wall, ignoring me. "And, well . . . I did move some things around. There were a couple of chairs that needed . . . replacement. In the front."

I didn't respond to what she said. Instead, I squinted at the hardwoods in front of my desk and said, "Why is there an orange bath mat on my floor?"

She shrugged and rubbed her face. "I was getting to that. About the chairs I moved, I was going to tell you why. See, this place has a good layout, structurally, but it needs the final touches to channel the energy correctly."

I raised an eyebrow. "Channel the whozit?"

"Look. I know you and I probably aren't going to see eye to eye about this—"

I interrupted her. "About what? Orange bath mats, or channeling energy?"

She sighed. "I moved some of the chairs in order to get a better *chi*. That's the life force that flows through everything and everybody. It's part of an ancient Oriental method of improving harmony with nature, called feng shui."

"Fung shway? Did you say fung shway? That Chinese karma stuff?"

Olson had a brief run with the feng shui a few months back. It ended about the third time Delmar tripped over a chair trying to go to the bathroom in the middle of the night.

"Karma. Exactly." Nolan smiled. "Karma's just another word for *chi*."

"So what's that got to do with the orange rug?" I pointed to the terry-cloth fabric on my floor.

Nolan walked to the other side of the bath mat. "A piece of appropriately colored floor covering converts the love *chi* through the power center of the structure, promoting overall harmony throughout."

I rocked back in my chair. "So you're saying my office is the love center of this place?"

"Don't get smug. It's the house. Not you."

I thought back to the night before. Maybe Ms. O'Connor was on to something.

She sat down uninvited. "So how'd it go at Charlie Wesson's place yesterday?"

"He had a girlfriend his sister didn't know about. Named Jenny." I related the rest of the events of the day, only leaving out the location of the unit.

"So that's how you got the shiner." She pointed to my face.

I'd almost forgotten about that. "Yeah, hurt him worse, though."

"What's your next move?"

I sensed that Nolan did not have a particularly full caseload at the moment. "I need to figure out who the 'big man' is. Also, why the head drug honcho of all of Dallas has one of his goons there at that particular place."

"Why don't you start with who owns the building?"

"Yeah. That might be a good idea." I hoped I kept the sarcasm out of my voice. My computer was already on so I typed in the web address for the Dallas Central Appraisal District, the local government agency that keeps track of who owns what. When the page appeared, I clicked the appropriate button and typed in the address of the building on Gano Street.

Nolan stood behind me. She smelled like wood smoke and flowers, not an unpleasant combination. The server finished processing the request and the answer popped up. According to the county, Gano Street Joint Venture owned the building. The deed last transferred in July of 1996. The building contained 8,500 square feet and was built in 1910. The mailing address for the Gano Street Joint Venture was obviously a residence, in North Dallas.

Nolan leaned over my shoulder and looked at the screen. "That doesn't tell you much. I mean a joint venture could be anybody, and there's no way to check."

"You're right." I had a thought and clicked another button.

She tapped her finger on the screen. "Why don't you see who owns the house?"

"That's what I'm doing," I said, clicking things until the search page appeared again. I entered the address and waited.

The place was huge, seven thousand square feet and change, on the books for two million two. Ownership data was the last to materialize as the bits and bytes flew across the Internet. The name of the owner finally appeared on the screen: the Children's Residential Trust Number Four. That's the equivalent of John Smith or Jane Doe. The address for the owner of the trust was yet another trust, someplace on McKinney Avenue. Before Nolan could point out the next thing to do, I entered that address. The name of the owner of that property came with no wait this time. Strathmore Real Estate.

I pulled out Charlie Wesson's flyer and looked at my notes. The sign in front of the building across the street belonged to Strathmore. Nolan started to say something but I waved her off and dialed the number I'd jotted from the sign.

A woman's voice answered. "Thank you for calling Strathmore Real Estate, how may I direct your call?"

"Could I get your delivery address, ma'am?"

"You sure can." Her voice dripped honey as she rattled off the same address as on my computer screen. I thanked her and hung up.

"It goes back to Strathmore Real Estate." I shut down the Web browser.

Nolan sat down. "That's the people with the signs all over town, right?"

"Yeah, that's the company." I made a list of the information in order to keep it all straight. "Strathmore Real Estate owns the building that is listed as the owner's address for the children's trust, which owns the house that is listed as the owner's address for the Gano Street Joint Venture, the owner of the building which is the last place anybody saw Charlie Wesson."

Someone knocked on the door frame and we both looked up.

Davis, my other officemate, stood there, holding the sports page. "The Stars play-off game's tonight. You take the points?"

A long time ago I worked for a bookie named Taco Mulrooney. Taco and I stayed friendly, doing the odd favor for each other on occasion. Davis, in addition to his other compulsions, had started on the long, slow slide into bankruptcy that is the mark of the degenerate gambler. He liked to think that my past association with a professional sports bookie made me some sort of seer, able to divine the outcome of a sporting event by osmosis. He might have stayed even or at least not too far behind if he didn't make stupid wagers.

"Don't bet against the spread." I leaned back in my chair. "What do you know about Strathmore Real Estate?"

"Take the points, huh?" Davis scratched at something in his crotch and studied the paper.

"Yeah. What about Strathmore?"

"They're one of the largest firms in the southwest. Development, brokerage, you name it, they do it."

I kept a small, dorm room–size refrigerator in the corner of my office. It's good to keep the information source lubricated so I got out three cans of Budweiser and came back to the desk. "It's noon somewhere, how about a beer?"

Davis didn't hesitate. He plopped down in the only other available chair. "Sure. What the hell, I stayed home last night."

I handed him a can, placing one on the corner of the desk for Nolan. We opened them and said a toast to midday. The first gulp tasted good. Nolan took a sip of hers and replaced it on my desk. She said, "So what kind of real estate does the Strathmore Company do?"

Davis swirled a mouthful of beer over his tongue, like it was the '82 Rothschild. He swallowed and smiled. "They do all kinds, mostly apartments, retail, and office. Some industrial properties here and there."

"Would they be doing anything south of downtown, say on Gano Street?" I said.

"Nah, nothing down there. Nobody does anything there." Davis took another swig. "Lessee . . . before he retired, I think the Big Man did some apartments in DeSoto, or maybe Duncanville, but that's so far down it's beyond south."

Nolan's eyes lit up but she didn't say anything. I kept my voice casual. "The Big Man?"

Davis drained the last of his beer and helped himself to another. "Yep. The Big Man. That's what they call him. Fagen Strathmore."

"Who calls him that?"

"Everybody in the business. Kinda like Elvis was the King, and Sinatra was the Chairman of the Board."

"Why's he called the Big Man?"

Davis chuckled and cocked an eyebrow. "Because he's big. Like six and a half feet tall big. And he's big as in a big deal businesswise."

"You said he was retired." I took a small sip of beer. "What's he do with himself?"

Davis made a noise, somewhere between and belch and a hiccup. "I think he's working on wife number four or five. She's in the society pages all the time. He's been out for ten years, maybe fifteen. His son, Roger, runs things now. He's still involved, though, just not in the day-to-day stuff. Guy like that never gets all the way out. They're hooked on the deal-making. It's in their blood." A phone rang from the front of the office. Davis stood up. "That's me. Better get it, might be a customer."

After he left, Nolan threw away the beer cans and said, "Type A social drinker or full-blown lush?"

"Just a simple drunk without a title." I moved to the windows and looked outside. "Probably because he doesn't have the love center in his office." The wisps of clouds from earlier in the day had disappeared, leaving only the hot blue sky. I thought out loud. "So the last person we can place Charlie with is the Big Man, Fagen Strathmore, at the Gano Street building Monday afternoon. What happened between them?"

"Also, what's the connection between Strathmore and Dupree?" Nolan said.

"Maybe if we knew that, it would explain how Jack Washington knew I was at Callahan's office."

She nodded and was quiet for a few moments. Then she said, "I think maybe we need to get a little more information on Fagen Strathmore."

"Yeah, you're right." I picked up my address book and thumbed through it. I found the page I was looking for and reached for the telephone. "You ready to take a little drive?"

Nolan smiled and nodded. I made a phone call and a quick conversation ensued. When I hung up, we headed for the suburbs, after a quick stop for Vietnamese food at a little place I knew.

CHAPTER TEN

Traffic ran light and we made good progress. Nolan passed the time by pestering me about the man we were going to see, wanting to know if he knew Strathmore, and if he did, how well. And what he would be able to tell us. I rolled my eyes and dodged her questions until we were about halfway there. Finally I said, "Enough already. Let me do the talking, okay? The Diceman is probably going to know something because he was *connected,* in a big way. If Strathmore is dirty, he'll know. It was his business to keep track of people like that."

"Connected?" she said.

"Yeah. As in mobbed up. You know, a bunch of guys wearing shiny suits, with names like Fat Tony and Earless Mario. Catch my drift?"

"Oh." She paused for a moment and looked out the window as we passed another shopping center with a Strathmore Realty sign on it. "So what do you mean he keeps track of people like that?"

I turned up the AC. "The mob gets a bad rap these days; people tend to underestimate them. They've got an intelligence-gathering apparatus that rivals the CIA. Especially with anybody who's wealthy, they maintain files on them, what they do, where they live, family, friends, vices, their life story, really. Always looking for the weaknesses. Anything that was exploitable."

Nolan nodded. "Antisocial."

"No. Actually, they're pretty fun to hang around with." I slowed as the traffic thickened. "Great parties. I remember one time, the Harrah's in New Orleans had just opened—"

"That's not what I meant." She sighed theatrically. "Antisocial as in a personality type. A lack of regard for moral or legal standards of society."

"Oh. That antisocial. Yeah, that describes most of them perfectly."

"They don't get along with others, or rules. The pain they cause is rationalized away, or not even addressed emotionally." Nolan adjusted her seat belt and then spoke again in a quieter tone. "Sometimes they're called psychopaths."

"Save it for somebody who cares, okay?"

She obliged, the faint smile on her face irritating me more than the psychobabble.

We hit the freeway, and I turned on the cruise control. We had another half hour to travel before we could maybe start to find some answers. If anybody could tell me whether Fagen Strathmore was dirty, the Diceman could.

Victor "the Diceman" Lemieux started life as a seven-and-a-half-pound fuck trophy, in a third-floor walk-up brothel off Canal Street in New Orleans. The product of a forced union between a seventeen-year-old prostitute and an aging vice cop, Victor was busting heads for a local shylock about the age most kids were learning to drive. When he retired forty years later, courtesy of a .38 slug to the abdomen from a cranked-up Jamaican coke dealer, he was in charge of real estate investments for a certain union's pension fund controlled by the Marcello crime family.

We were friends, the Diceman and I, after a nasty street brawl one sultry summer evening in an alley off Conti Street in the French Quarter. For reasons that are best left unsaid, I ended up saving his life that evening. Victor had two blades stuck in him, thigh and ribs. I had a fractured wrist and a two-inch gash in my temple, but still managed to pull him down a narrow alley, just as the police arrived. He directed me to a friendly doctor who patched us up. Despite the fact that he had about as much Sicilian blood in him as did Jerry Falwell, Victor was old school, *omertà* and honor and all that other *Godfather* crap. He maintained that he owed his life to me and never forgot it. After the thing with the Jamaican, the Diceman retired and moved to the Dallas area to be near his only daughter.

He lived in a suburb near the airport now, part of the vast Texas prairie converted haphazardly into a sliver of the American dream, in a three-bedroom slap-up job the developer quaintly called the "Jubilee Floor Plan."

I drove down the main north-south thoroughfare, trying to remember the correct turn. The streets all had western-tinged names like Ponderosa Place and Meandering Canyon. They possessed a dreary sameness, block after block of treeless yards and poorly built brick edifices with miniature turrets and ridiculous-looking two-story arched entryways. I wondered how an old wiseguy called the Diceman fared in this land of minivans, Pottery Barn furniture, and five-digit credit card debt.

His house was in the middle of the block, a dead ringer for all the others except for the LSU pennant hanging over a bay window. We were halfway up the sidewalk when he opened the door, leaning heavily on a cane, his bulk resting against the edge of the entranceway.

"Hot damn. If'n it ain't Mr. Oswald. Done come all the way out here." Victor loved to play up the Cajun accent.

"What's happening, Victor?" I stepped into the foyer and embraced him.

He slapped me on the shoulder and said, "Little of this, little of that. And who might this purty gal be?"

"This is Nolan O'Connor. She's helping me on this thing."

Nolan said hello as he shook her hand. He refused to let go, instead leaning on her as if she were another cane. "Let's go to da den. You can tell me what so important it brings you out thisaway."

Together the three of us made our way into the cavernous family room overlooking the minuscule backyard. Victor still wouldn't let go of Nolan, insisting that she sit next to him on the leather sectional sofa running along one wall. He propped a leg up on the coffee table and turned to me. "Lee Henry, we need us some beer. There's a pile of Dixie in the icebox. Grab some, wouldya?"

I got three cold bottles and passed them around. The Diceman smiled and patted Nolan's knee. "Ask what you need to ask, Lee Henry."

"You know a man named Fagen Strathmore? A real estate guy?"

Victor removed his hand from Nolan's leg and scratched his head. "Whatchoo mixed up with him for? He trying to sell you some swampland?"

"It's a case," Nolan said. "Guy goes to meet Strathmore and is never seen again."

Victor took a long pull of his drink. "That wouldn't be the first person to disappear."

"So you know him?" I said.

"Yeah, we was friends once." He rubbed his eyes, and leaned back. "Lemme tink a minute. Been a long time since I recollected about ole Fagen Strathmore."

After a few moments he told us the story of the boy who would eventually be a multimillionaire, the person they would call the Big Man, about how he grew up poor, in a trailer park in Port Arthur, Texas, where the sulfur stink of the coastal refineries permeated the humid air like smoke in a barroom. Dad died young, a blowout on an oil rig. Mom took care of the tiny family as best she could, slinging hash in a grease trap in Bridge City, and living mostly on Schlitz, Lucky Strikes, and broken dreams. Sometimes she liked to bring home shrimpers, hard, sun-leathered men who smelled of the sea, sweat, and whiskey. Fagen was big for his age, and a challenge to more than one of his mother's boyfriends. For his thirteenth birthday, a doctor at the free clinic downtown set and plastered his broken right arm, and then taped his ribs and nose, the fractures courtesy of a Portuguese fisherman who held no truck with mouthy young men objecting when Mama got slapped around a little.

When he was fourteen he got a paper route, delivering for one of the Houston dailies. At fifteen he was named Paperboy of the Year, and presented with a plaque and a genuine Davy Crockett coonskin cap. At seventeen, he quit high school and bought his first rental house.

The next year proved to be seminal in the life of the young entrepreneur. On his eighteenth birthday, he evicted his first delinquent tenant, skipping the legal niceties and using a baseball bat instead. The next day he bought his fifth lease property, and tracked down the Portuguese man who had put him in the hospital five years before.

The fisherman was never seen again.

At twenty he sold all fifteen of his rental houses, gave half the money to his mother, and took a job with a real estate development company out of Atlanta that wasn't particular about things like a lack of formal training. They bounced him up and down the eastern seaboard, Connecticut, Philly, New York, even a year in Boston. When he had learned all he could, he quit and came home to Texas, settling in Dallas, the concrete mesa on the banks of the Trinity, where it was said a hungry young man could make a name for himself. Strathmore's first project had been an office and shopping center, in what at the time had been little more than a cow pasture. The local banks balked at loaning so much money, unsure of this brash young man. The owner of a strip bar on Commerce, a dingy place called the Carousel Club, put him in touch with a fellow in Shreveport who had sent him to see some dark men in the back room of a social club in New Orleans.

One of the people in that back room had been a much younger Victor Lemieux. The person who put them together, the owner of the bar, was named Jack Ruby.

"Fagen always paid back promptly, every time, never gave us the chance to get our hooks in him for real," Victor said, draining his second beer.

"He kept borrowing mob money?" I said.

"Yeah. It helped us too, sometimes." Victor shrugged. "Clean funds, you know."

Nolan stood up and stretched. "So he was doing you guys favors?"

"Uh-huh." Victor nodded. "Hell, one time he gave us some money so that we could loan it to a certain person for him. Guy's name was Peabody somethingerother. Went through a savings and loan we had at the time, in Tyler. Peabody was small time, trying to buy property and build some offices. Unfortunately, he had stuff that Fagen wanted. Guy owned the last teeny chunk in a strip of dirt that Strathmore already owned. Bad thing to be Peabody."

"What happened?" Nolan pulled a pack of Marlboro Lights from her pocket and stuck one in her mouth. She made no move to light it.

Victor looked at her smoke and licked his lips, breathing heavily. Finally he snapped out of it and said, "Huh? Oh yeah, well, Fagen says let me buy it. Peabody says no. Fagen ups his offer. Peabody says no again. See, he's got plans, needs that building to use as collateral because he wants to borrow some money. So he borrows the money, using this certain savings and loan I done mentioned already. Then guess what happened? Had 'em a little case of Jewish lightning. Damn shame too; his family had an antique store in the place, been there for years." Victor paused and looked at a spot on the wall. "Peabody's mother was there that day. She didn't make it out."

"Jewish lightning?" Nolan said.

Victor grabbed her pack of cigarettes and stuck it under his nose, inhaling the scent of the tobacco deeply. "Whoowee, that smells damn good. Guddam doctors say no more smokes, no more sausage, no booze 'cept for a Dixie or two a day." He took another whiff of the demon weed and put the pack down. "Where was we, oh yeah, Jewish lightning. That's a fire. Usually you do it to collect the insurance money. Only this time, there weren't no insurance because the S&L's supposed to take care of it. But that bank didn't and Peabody lost his ma and his property. To good ole Fagen Strathmore."

"Whatever happened to Peabody?" I said.

"Humph." Victor waved a hand and shrugged. He pulled a cigarette out of Nolan's pack and stuck it in his mouth, leaving it unlit. "Peabody threatened to sue. Started calling the papers, shit like that. He had a car wreck a little bit after. Died."

I turned to Nolan. "I hope you're not going to say Strathmore's got narcissism whatever."

She shook her head. "His basic personality type sounds like self-confident with narcissistic disorder overlays. Most definitely a Type A."

I sighed. "Are you making this stuff up as you go?"

"I have a degree in psychology."

"That makes her smarter than you and me put together, Hank." The old man laughed and removed the smoke from his mouth, running it lengthwise under his nose like it was a Monte Cristo No. 1.

"When I was on the job, I specialized in profiling." Nolan looked at me. "You got a problem with understanding the way the mind works?"

I didn't reply. She held a Zippo out to the Diceman. He shook his head, and sucked the dry, unlit tobacco.

"I'm trying to quit too." Nolan slid the lighter back into her jeans. "Sometimes it feels good to just hold one in your mouth."

"Orally fixated, are we?" A brief smirk crossed my face as Victor chuckled. Nolan rolled her eyes.

I decided to get back on track. "What's Strathmore been up to lately? Any ideas?"

The Diceman shook his head. "I'm out of the game. No idea. Ain't talked to that crooked son of a bitch in ten years, I'll bet."

We made small talk for another half hour. As we were leaving, my cell phone rang. A muffled voice was on the other end, crying. I waved good-bye to Victor and we walked outside, listening to Vera Drinkwater's voice in my ear. "Hank. They've found Charlie." More tears now; her voice became ragged. "He's dead. They found him dead."

"Tell me what happened, Vera." My tone was sharp, trying to snap her out of hysteria. Nolan and I got in the truck. She raised her eyebrows at me. I shrugged and mouthed, *Charlie's sister.*

"They said he shot himself." More crying, then the sounds of deep breathing. She was trying to get control of herself. "They said he committed suicide. They found him in a crack house. With drugs."

"When?"

"When what?"

"When did they find him?"

"I don't know, they just called me, just now." She started sobbing again. "He had one of those emergency contact cards in his wallet. He had my name on it. I remember when he filled it out—" She started to cry harder. I let her sob for a few moments. The crying subsided and she spoke again. "He didn't kill himself, Hank. There's no way, not after what he'd been through. He was on the upside. People don't kill themselves when they are on the upside, do they, Hank?"

"I don't know." My voice was low and calm.

She quit crying and her tone became cold. "I want you to find whoever did this. I want you to find who murdered my baby brother. Will you do that for me, Hank?"

I sighed and stared at a greasy spot on the floor mats, feeling older than I should have. I grabbed a pencil out of the console. "Tell me where they found him."

She told me the address and we hung up, after I promised her I'd be in touch later in the day with what I found.

CHAPTER ELEVEN

Charlie Wesson died on a toilet, like Elvis.

The similarities ended there. The King croaked in the bathroom of his mansion in Memphis, amid a sea of flocked wallpaper, shag carpet, and fried banana sandwiches. Charlie died in West Dallas, in a condemned crack house with a needle in his arm and cockroach shit on the dirty linoleum floor. The blackened spoon and lighter used to cook a dose of heroin lay nearby. The gun he used to shoot out the back of his head rested in his lap, right hand still clenched on the grip. It was a Glock. Charlie had been there for a couple of days if I had to guess, based on the condition of the body. I brushed a fly away from in front of my face and wiped a trickle of sweat off my temple, trying to breathe through my mouth because of the stench.

"That your guy?" The police officer named Cloyd was a burly man in his mid-fifties, with a whiskey-tanned face and stubby fingers. We'd been acquaintances since his partner had become involved with a slick-talking hooker a few years back. I'd helped end the relationship on terms amicable to almost everybody. He didn't let me in the bathroom, just peer through the door. Nolan was outside.

"Yeah. That's him. Charlie Wesson." Even given the trauma of death and the beginning of the decomposition process, the face still bore a remarkable resemblance to the decade-old picture I'd found on the wall of his apartment.

"Huh. That's what his ID said too. Charles Wesson."

I didn't bother to point out that I would not have been there if they hadn't called his sister, which meant they already knew his name. I left the house and stood in the front yard. Where the lawn should have been was a mass of weeds, beer cans, and other trash. The humid air buzzed with mosquitos that had bred in the pools of stagnant water in two worn tires by the front porch. A cloud passed in front of the sun, providing a momentary relief from the heat.

The house itself was a small wood-frame structure, unattractive when new, now just plain ugly, with boarded-up windows and an orange sign from the city denoting its status as condemned. All the houses on the block bore the same sticker. A sign on the corner said that this was the future home of the New Canaan Baptist Church and Apartments of Hope. I hoped that the people of New Canaan fared better than did Charlie Wesson.

Nolan got out of the truck and joined me. "Was it him?"

"Yep."

"Dead?"

"Uh-huh, stuck a gun in his mouth."

"Suicide?"

I kicked an empty beer can. "That's what they're going to say. An ex-junkie, with a needle in his arm. It doesn't work, though. Why would you shoot up, get the buzz working, and then go and blow your brains out?"

Nolan slapped at a mosquito. "You kill yourself on the way down, when you're depressed about using again."

"Maybe it's the house," I said. "Got some bad feng shui." I didn't even laugh at my own joke.

"Maybe Charlie was just supposed to die now." Nolan patted my arm. "Doesn't make it right, just makes it what it is."

Her touch was strangely comforting. A few more clouds appeared, dotting the sky like fat dirty cotton balls. A hot wind whipped around us, blowing dirt and garbage into the street. The house sat on a side street, off Westmoreland and Fishtrap Road, in an area still waiting for the promised urban renewal. The places that weren't condemned were colored a cross between the clouds in the sky and the dirt below my feet. An ambulance pulled into the graveled rut that passed for a drive-way, no sirens or light. A white Crown Victoria, bristling with antennas, followed.

"How'd they know about the body?" Nolan said.

"Two kids saw the door was open, wandered in."

The ambulance attendants stayed in their ride, waiting further in-struction. The Crown Vic pulled up until it was a couple of feet from my legs. Two men got out. One was black, late forties or thereabouts, in shape, and wearing a tailored dark suit, white shirt, and muted tie. He could have been a stockbroker or a well-dressed insurance salesman. The other guy was the same age but white. Twenty years of chicken-fried steaks and pitchers of Lone Star at the local Elks lodge had left a gut that spilled over the top of his maroon polyester slacks. The yellow and purple tie he wore stopped about midway down the front of his brown dress shirt. An orange and navy herringbone sports coat fin-ished out the ensemble. The jacket looked like someone had skinned the seat covers off a 1973 Pinto. He was a cop, no question.

The black man took off his suit coat and his badge became visible, clipped to the leather belt. He positioned himself between me and the car. "My name is Sergeant Jessup. Homicide." He smelled like Ralph Lauren aftershave. "What are you planning to tell me that explains why you are standing in front of this house with a dead body inside?"

I didn't move and my eyes never wavered. "My name is Oswald. The deceased's name is Charlie Wesson. Until an hour ago, a missing person. His sister hired me to find him."

At the word *hired* Jessup held up his hand, palm outward. He placed one finger on his lips. "That means you're a . . . private detective." He made the two words sound like *child molester*.

"Yeah, I'm a private investigator." I pulled out my ID and held it up. "In my free time I train telemarketers in new and better ways to be intrusive."

Sergeant Jessup smirked, a smile with no humor. A dangerous face. He read from my license. "Lee H. Oswald. You any relation to the other Lee Oswald?"

"Nope."

"What's the *H* stand for?"

"Henry. Hank for short."

Jessup examined my PI license again. "Says here you were born after Lee Harvey whacked Kennedy. That mean your parents went ahead and named you Lee H. Oswald? That's pretty fucking weird, don't you think, Lee Henry?"

I stuffed the license back in my pocket. "My name's not important. I'm here about the dead body you've got in there."

"How long had he been missing?"

"Four days."

"This guy have a history of disappearing?"

I didn't answer because I knew it was just a short distance to discussing Charlie's drug use.

Jessup didn't press it. He said, "Well then, the stiff is no longer missing. There's no need for you to be here, is there?"

"I don't suppose you want to know any of the particulars of this case, do you?"

"We need your help, we'll let you know." If he was trying to keep the sarcasm out of his voice, he failed. Again a smile that had no apparent gladness behind it creased his face, and he moved toward the front door.

His partner followed. They ignored Nolan. Cloyd came out and stood on the sagging front porch. He and Jessup huddled, heads together. Jessup's partner listened in but kept an eye on me. I hadn't moved from in front of the Crown Victoria.

Jessup nodded and then shrugged his shoulders. All three police officers turned and looked at me. Jessup spoke. "A fucking junkie? Somebody actually hired you to find a junkie? You could've just waited at the morgue, he would've shown up there sooner rather than later."

I walked toward the truck. "Take a look at the body. Why would he shoot up, then commit suicide?"

"Whaddya expect?"

"I expected to make some calls, check some things out, and find Charlie Wesson strung out somewhere. I didn't expect to get tangled up with Coleman Dupree."

Jessup had his hand on the torn screen door, ready to enter. Instead, he sauntered down the rickety stairs of the crack house, hands held behind his back, a leisurely stroll. At the bottom of the stairs, he paused to examine a small patch of paint remaining on the railing. He picked at it with a fingernail and then continued his walk over to me. When we were face-to-face he stopped and pulled out a piece of gum from his pocket. His face was oily with sweat, a thin sheen coating his mahogany skin. The heat was like a third person standing between us. He fiddled with the wrapper while talking to me. "Who exactly are you talking about, Lee Oswald?"

"Coleman Dupree." I felt a trickle of sweat meander down my back as a thin cloud moved past the sun, exposing us both to the full brunt of the afternoon heat. "And his buddy Jack Washington. They're tied up in this somehow."

Jessup didn't say anything. He just fixed me with that thousand-yard stare perfected by cops the world over, displaying nothing but utter and total blankness.

I kept on. "Dupree's goons warned me off asking any more questions about Charlie Wesson. Then less than forty-eight hours later, Charlie turns up dead in this shit hole."

Jessup looked off into the distance, toward a liquor store on the corner. Three old men in overalls sat in front, leaning back in lawn chairs. Without taking his eyes off them, he spoke to me, his voice so quiet I had to strain to hear. "You think you're some hot shit PI from North Dallas, don'tcha, Lee Harvey?" When I didn't respond he continued. "Well, lemme tell you something, you *Spenser: For Hire* motherfucker. You are nothing down here. They eat people like you in this part of town. Just because some white guy scores a load of the good stuff and then offs himself, don't go blaming the latest colored boogeyman." Jessup stuck the piece of gum in his mouth. He turned to me and said, "So go home."

When he said the last part I caught a whiff of the mint gum he was chewing. It triggered some weird mnemonic signal in my head and I remembered the last time I had seen Charlie Wesson, so many years ago. Right after a baseball game, with my graduation only a few weeks past, I'd stumbled into the locker room immediately after Charlie had dropped an easy pop fly. His father had been there, alone with him. I smelled the mint of the gum that Ketch Wesson always seemed to chew, saw the sinews in his jaws working. He'd had ahold of Charlie's arm and the only thing I heard before he noticed me was something about "the best part of the Wesson genes musta spilled out of your mama, you dumb piece of shit." Charlie had looked at me with mournful eyes, way beyond fear and embarrassment, more of a despondent acceptance of what was to come. Ketch saw me and said to get the hell out. I did, retreating quickly down the hallway to the sound of a fist hitting flesh.

That had been the last time I'd seen Charlie Wesson alive.

Jessup was still talking, rattling on about how I needed to get my ass home. Then because I smelled his gum and I remembered Charlie's eyes, right before his father hit him, I did a stupid thing. I pushed Sergeant Jessup out of my way, and headed for my car.

The next thing I knew I was facedown on the hood of the Crown Victoria. I resisted the urge to fight back, as that would make a small mistake much bigger. I heard the door of my truck slam shut, and then two or three sets of feet running toward me; one of them obviously had to be Nolan.

"Lee Henry Oswald." Jessup's voice was harsh in my ear. "You're one dumb son of a bitch. You are under arrest for assaulting an officer." The cold metal of the handcuffs bit into my wrist. The hood of the car was hot like a branding iron against my cheek. Rough hands patted me down and found the Browning on my hip, clanking it on the top of the car. "Hope you got a license for that. What else you carrying?"

My voice was muffled. "I'm legal for the piece. There's a thirty-two on my right ankle."

Jessup found the backup pistol and pitched it next to the Browning, dragging me toward the back of the unit. He stopped when he saw Nolan O'Connor standing there, holding a San Antonio PD shield. The fat cop with the bad clothes stood behind her with his hands raised in a questioning gesture. "Says she's on the job, Sarge. Homicide, Bexar County."

Jessup hesitated, hanging on to me by one elbow.

"You know, Sergeant, there's nothing that would give me more pleasure than seeing his butt thrown in jail," Nolan said. "But there's a lot of people counting on this loser, and I need him on the street."

"You're a long way from the Alamo, aren't you, honey?" Jessup tightened his grip on my arm.

Something sparked in Nolan's eye, but she kept her cool. "Sarge? I'm reaching out to you here. A favor. I'm sure he's sorry. Aren't you sorry, Hank?"

"Yeah, I'm sorry. Really sorry. Don't know what came over me." I tried to sound like I meant it.

"Let it go, Sarge," Fat Cop Bad Clothes said. "We got a full plate today."

Nobody said anything for a few moments. Finally Jessup sighed and said, "Fuck it." He unlocked the cuffs. I stepped away from him and moved to retrieve my weapons, rubbing my wrists as I went.

Jessup put his bracelets back on his belt and turned to me. "That's a professional courtesy. For the little lady. Next time you won't be so lucky. Stay the hell out of this part of town."

I ignored him and headed for my truck, Nolan walking by my side. We'd gotten halfway there when Jessup called out to me. "Man named Carl Albach turned up in the hospital yesterday. Brain trauma, they say. In a coma, and the doctors don't think he'll wake up. For some reason his . . . associates are damn upset about the whole thing. You wouldn't know anything about that, wouldya, Mr. Private Eye?"

I didn't say anything, just shook my head. He stared at me for what seemed like a long time, then turned and walked into the house.

Nolan and I returned to my truck and stood there in the heat and mosquitoes, watching the slow procession of cars and uniformed personnel peculiar to a young man passing on under violent circumstances. Medical examiner, crime scene investigators, photographers; all came and went, each a part of the equation needed to determine that Charlie Wesson had gotten so euphoric from a load of heroin that he decided to blow his brains out. I should have left and gone to track down Fagen Strathmore, but for some reason I remained. Maybe I wanted to bring Charlie home in some way. Maybe I wanted to honor his passing, however ignominious it may have been. After a while, Nolan got in the truck and turned it on. I could see her fiddling with the air-conditioning. I stayed where I was, heedless of the sun and the sweat oozing down my body.

An hour passed and they brought the body out, a black plastic capsule of Charlie Wesson's earthly remains. As the medical examiner's people wheeled him over the uneven terrain of the front yard, a blue Lexus pulled up. It was eight or nine years old, but spotless, wheels and chrome gleaming, even in the overcast light. A black man in gray pinstripe suit pants and a cream-colored dress shirt unfolded himself and emerged from the car. His skin was the color of one of those four-dollar coffee drinks that's half milk, half java. He was NBA tall, athletic but thin, with short hair and a cell phone stuck to one ear. He didn't so much walk as he stalked, his movements conveying frantic energy barely contained. The day did not have enough hours for this man.

He hung up the phone and approached one of the uniformed officers. They talked until the cop waved him off. He then tried to enter the small house but was rebuffed by another officer. He and the uniform engaged in a conversation, with a lot of hand-waving and pointing. The officer shrugged his shoulders. The tall man didn't say anything more, just huffed off.

At that point, he seemed to notice me and walked toward the truck. On the way he paused for two phone calls. The first one stopped him in the middle of the dirty front yard, talking animatedly into the tiny speaker, gesturing at the other party. The second one forced him to retrieve some papers from his car. He spread a file on the roof and talked, occasionally consulting something on a page.

After five or six minutes he ended that call and headed toward me. "Hey. You got any idea what the hell's going on here?" He jerked a thumb toward the police congregated at the front door. His voice was friendly, with an us-against-them tone.

"Man died." My voice was not so friendly.

"I figured that. You know who it is?"

"Yeah." I turned from the scene and faced the man as the attendants slammed shut the ambulance. "Why do you care?"

The man held out his hand. "My name's Aaron Young. I own the property." His voice changed; curious morphed into smooth and forceful. Velvety yet powerful at the same time. I turned and met his gaze. His entire attention was focused on me, as if every word I might utter would be the most important thing spoken on the planet on this day. The eyes sparkled with intelligence and something else: determination, grit, or just regular stubbornness. I'd seen the look before, in faces of powerful people: politicians, master salesmen, generals, entrepreneurs. I shook his hand but didn't say anything. The fingers that engulfed mine were thin, long, and too skinny in proportion to the rest of him. I told him my first name.

"What's your function in all this, Hank? Why are you here?" Sincerity smothered his voice. The scene in front of us, the dead body in a condemned crack house, was a million miles away.

I debated what to tell him, finally settling on a variation of the truth. "I'm a repairman."

Aaron said mmm and stroked his chin. "That's interesting, Hank. I am always in need of repair work. What is it that you fix?" Rapport Building 101. Use the person's name a lot and talk about his interests. Even as I recognized the technique, I realized how good he was, how smooth.

I watched as Cloyd the Cop came out onto the porch, cleared his throat, and spit into the dirt. "People mostly. I fix people and their problems."

Aaron laughed. "I need that kind of repair work from time to time. But I was referring to a handyman sort of fix-it guy." His tone became serious. "So who's the guy in the house?" He turned back to watch the actions at the ramshackle dwelling. We stood shoulder to shoulder.

"The man who died on your property was named Charlie Wesson. That mean anything to you?"

"No. Should it?"

"Not really, not unless you're in the drug business."

The anger in Aaron Young's voice stopped birds from flying overhead and killed what little grass remained below our feet. "Since I don't know you, Hank, I'll pretend I didn't hear that, or that you didn't really mean it. Drugs are not something I take lightly. I have seen the damage they have done in this community, even in my own family."

It was an Oscar-winning performance, or he really didn't like dope. "When'd you buy it?" I said.

"We closed on the last two houses in the block a month ago." His voice returned to normal.

The ambulance pulled away, no sirens. The mosquitoes were worse now but the heat had begun to dissipate a little. A knot of police officers huddled around the unmarked Crown Victoria, listening to Sergeant Jessup. "And you bought all those houses because you don't like drugs? What about the New Caanan church and apartments?" I pointed to the sign.

Aaron tugged open his tie, a thin film of sweat now visible on his forehead. "The houses are to be demolished in the next week or two. After that we break ground on the apartments, then the church."

"Why the apartments first?"

"We got funding for them, based on the rent we'll receive. There's a tremendous need for quality, affordable homes in this area. The rent will also help fund the church."

I watched the police start to disperse, heading to investigate other crimes and misdemeanors. "And what's your function in all of this?"

"I put the deal together, negotiated financing, hired the contractor, arranged for the church's participation. That sort of thing."

I turned and looked at him. "And you did all this because you don't like drugs?"

He smiled, the quickest of grins that was replaced with a dead-pan expression. "Well, there's a little profit in the deal for me too." He handed me a card. "I have to be at a meeting, gotta run. Time kills deals, you know." He waved and walked back to his Lexus.

I twirled the business card in my fingers like it was a tarot with all the answers. Jessup and his partner walked by. They ignored me and got in their unmarked car to leave. The last police unit idled in front of the house, two officers fiddling with paperwork. Except for the autopsy, that was it; the last sad chapter of Charlie Wesson's dismal life. Dead, sitting on a toilet, in a filthy house about to fall down.

I got in the truck and soaked up the air-conditioning.

Nolan leaned against the door, staring out the front window. "It's a good thing that cop didn't look too closely at my badge." She held it up for me to see. Blue letters, stamped at an angle across her picture, read, "NOT IN SERVICE."

"Thanks for doing that." I found a paper towel in the glove compartment and mopped sweat off my face. "That saved a lot of hassle."

"Not to mention an assault charge." She paused for a moment and then said, "What the hell got to you; it's just another case, isn't it?"

I pulled out into the late afternoon traffic, heading for the office. "Forget about it. You wouldn't understand; I'm not sure that I do."

"That's classic. The macho PI bullshit; keep it bottled up until you explode." She adjusted the AC vents on her side. "Got a psychotic, alcoholic ex-husband who had that problem. Except for when he was drunk, it was like talking to a lump of coal. Then it was dodging fists and praying you could keep your cool so you don't smoke him with your service piece. The night before I filed for divorce, he's passed out on the bed, buck naked. I'd had enough so I got a tube of that miracle glue shit and proceeded to glue *both* his hands to his dick."

In spite of myself, I was laughing. "So what happened?"

"The dumb sonuvabitch had the nerve to send me the bill from the urologist."

I was still chuckling when I dropped her off at the office, twenty minutes later. I stayed in the truck. Nolan got out and leaned back through the door, placing one hand on my forearm. Her touch was smooth and cool.

"You sure you don't want me to go with you?"

I shook my head.

"You couldn't have prevented it. Guy was a walking morgue ticket, looking for a place to happen."

I didn't reply.

"Don't beat yourself up over it."

I nodded and grunted, an affirmative that didn't sound very believable.

"Call if you need anything." Nolan patted my arm, a single lock of hair free from her ponytail, partially obscuring one of her blue eyes. The shadows from the trees over the driveway dappled the sunlight on her skin, giving her face the depth and complexity of an Impressionist painting. I felt a tickle in the pit of my stomach, the first feeble outriders of desire beginning their march toward my libido. But she was Ernie's niece and I squashed anything approaching lust or feeling with the knowledge of what I had to do next.

I put the truck in drive. Nolan said good-bye again and shut the door. I made a quick stop at the hospital and then on to the visit I dreaded—Charlie's sister.

CHAPTER TWELVE

Vera Drinkwater lived on a street in northwest Dallas named after a Disney character, not too far from where we'd both grown up. When my family moved there from central Texas, the area had had a certain suburban seventies-style quaintness to it, sort of Norman Rockwell meets the Brady Bunch.

But the intervening years had bleached the charm from the squat two- and three-bedroom ranch-style homes lining the streets. The peeling paint, gap-toothed shutters, and weed-infested lawns combined with the cars on blocks and omnipresent sirens to drain any nostalgic enchantment I might have felt. The 7-Eleven where I used to ride my bike and buy Slurpees was now an adult video store. The next right was the turn for Vera's.

Her house was two blocks down, on a corner. Half a dozen cars were parked in front. In the yard of the house next door, a group of Indians milled about, chatting quietly, the women a riot of color in their richly pigmented saris. I parked across the street, got out, and smelled something exotic and spicy simmering on a stovetop nearby.

The front door to Vera's lay open and I walked in. Five or six blue-haired, polyester-clad women sat on a purple, crushed-velvet sectional sofa, sipping coffee and eating pound cake. Hook rugs and needle-pointed pictures of dogs and cats covered the wood-paneled walls in the living room. The whole place smelled like pine disinfectant and cinnamon potpourri. I stifled the urge to sneeze.

A pudgy woman wearing a lime green pantsuit and white pumps, evidently the head blue hair, stood when I entered. "Duane and his . . . friend are in the garage. Just go through the kitchen." She jerked a thumb to the back and sneered, leaving no doubt her opinion of Duane and his acquaintances.

"Who's Duane?"

"Vera's husband." The woman frowned and looked at her people sitting on the couch, then back at me. "Who are you?"

"A friend of Vera's." I smiled and tried to look nonthreatening. "Where is she?"

Heads came together followed by a clucking of tongues and clanking of coffee cups. Blue hair number one replied for the group: "Vera's in her bedroom, on the phone."

"Do you think you could tell her I'm here?"

The woman smiled for half a second. "I-I-I'll get her." She disappeared down a hallway.

The sister of the deceased emerged a few moments later, looking like six miles of bad country roads. Her face was red and puffy, and the faded blue jeans and threadbare Dallas Mavericks sweatshirt she wore looked a couple of sizes too big.

"Hi, Hank. Thanks for coming." She sniffled once. "Let's go in the back and talk."

We disappeared through a doorway, away from the whispering of elderly women.

The kitchen was mercifully empty. Casserole dishes covered every square inch of the avocado green Formica countertops. Vera went to the sink and filled a glass with tap water. She drank it in one gulp and then apparently remembered me. "I'm sorry, Hank. You want anything to drink?" I said no.

She downed another glass of water. "The women out there. One's my great-aunt. She's about the only family I got left. The others are from the church." She sighed. "They've been a big help."

"I didn't know you were married."

Vera opened a cabinet and got out a carton of cigarettes. She removed a pack and pounded the top of it against her palm. "Oh, Duane. Yeah, we've been together about three years now." Her tone was on the edge of condescending, between despair and hostility, at the mention of her spouse.

I nodded. "What's Duane's function in life?"

"He's a personal trainer." She lit a cigarette. "At Rudy's Gym over on Hall Street."

"Where is he now?"

"In the garage, with a lifting buddy." She blew a plume of smoke into the air. "It's one of the nights they work out. They've got all the weights set up here so they decided to go ahead. What the hell, it wasn't his brother that died." The tone of her voice didn't bode well for Duane's continued marital bliss.

I got a check out of my wallet and filled it out. "This is repayment of your retainer, minus a small amount for expenses." I handed it to her. "I didn't do a very good job of finding your brother. I'm sorry about Charlie, Vera."

She took the check and held it in her hand without looking at it. "Do you remember that night we got so drunk, back in high school?"

"You and I?"

Vera nodded and turned to the sink. She held a lighter under my check until it flamed, then dropped it. "Yeah. Prom night, junior year. Our dates flaked out on us both for some reason. We ended up at that park on Forest Lane, drinking and talking. I thanked you for looking after Charlie."

"He told you about all that?"

"Uh-huh." She nodded. "Charlie needed taking care of."

A vague recollection crept out of some dark corner of my mind. Prom night. I mentally shuddered. Ruffled dress shirts and baby blue tuxedos should be outlawed. Had that been Vera I'd gotten drunk with that night? "You shouldn't have torched the check," I said. "You don't owe me anything."

"Yeah, I do." She reached into her jeans pocket and pulled out a wad of hundred-dollar bills and placed it on the end of the kitchen table, next to a plate of something greenish covered in plastic wrap. "Do you think my brother killed himself?"

I looked at the money, hesitating for a few moments, and then said what I really thought. "Not in my opinion."

"Do the police think he was murdered?"

I looked at a worn spot on the floor. "No."

"They think he committed suicide, don't they?"

I nodded.

"But you don't and neither do I. So I want to pay you to find out who killed him."

"Vera, I'm not a cop. I've got some friends on the force who I can call. Maybe get them to look at this thing harder."

"You're a private investigator, Hank. Fucking investigate it yourself." I looked up and saw that she was crying, soundlessly, just the steady drip of tears running down her face. "For chrissakes, Hank, he was the only family I've got. 'Cept for a prune of an aunt out there and fucking Schwarzenegger in the garage."

I picked up the money but didn't do anything with it.

Vera walked over to my side of the room and leaned against the counter next to me. "Please, Hank." She put a hand on my arm.

I put the money in my pocket. "There's a couple of people I can talk to. They may know something that—"

The slamming of the door leading into the garage cut me off.

"What's going on in here? Am I interrupting anything?" The voice was pinched and nasally, not too far from a whine, and belonged to a five-foot-two-inch-tall, greased-up fireplug standing in the entranceway to the kitchen. The man was flushed and pumped from lifting, his scalp shining pink through the stringy comb-over that had been carefully arranged on the top of his head.

Vera rubbed her eyes. "You're not interrupting anything, Terry. What do you want?"

"Protein shake." The squat little man kept his eyes on me as he waddled toward the refrigerator. His muscles bulged so much he had to walk almost spread-eagled. "This sure seems like something." Sexual innuendo dripped from his voice. I hated him instantly.

"Nope," I said. "I just stopped by to offer my condolences to Vera on the untimely death of her brother."

Incredibly, the man appeared not to have known about Charlie's passing. He looked shocked, then confused, and mumbled something vaguely sympathetic as he got a plastic container out of the fridge. Still with a bewildered face, he started to speak again but clamped his mouth shut instead and disappeared back into the garage.

"I'd better get out of here, Vera. Tomorrow I'll start nosing around. I'm not making any promises, though."

"Thank you, Hank. You have no idea how much I appreciate it." She leaned forward and gave me a hug at the exact moment the kinky-haired man from the beige Camaro stormed into the room.

"W-w-what the hell's going on in here?" the man said, spluttering protein shake everywhere.

"See, Duane. See, I told you. Something's going on. This dude's in here hugging on your old lady. See. Just like I told you." Terry stood behind the larger man, hopping from one foot to the other, the tone of his voice whinier and more subservient than I thought possible.

"Hey, Duane." I took a step away from the counter I'd been leaning on. "What was the estimate on getting the Camaro fixed?"

Vera pointed a cigarette at her husband. "You told me Carlos from work trashed your car."

Duane looked at his wife and said, "Shut the hell up, willya?" To me: "Suppose you tell me 'xactly who the fuck you are?"

Something about the tone of his voice and the way his corded muscles bunched in his shoulders made me think of Ketch Wesson, Vera's abusive stepfather. I felt sad and tired suddenly and wondered about the dark things fluttering around in the back of Vera Drinkwater's mind. "Your wife has hired me to investigate the death of her brother."

He balled his fists. "Bullshit. Y-you're in here, coming on to my wife, a-and—"

I held my palm out in a conciliatory gesture. "Duane. Ease off. In case you haven't noticed, your brother-in-law died. Your wife's upset. Let's think of her right now, okay?"

I'm guessing here, but I think somewhere deep down a tiny spark of humanity came alive. He hesitated a moment, then took a step back and let out his breath. "Yeah, you're right. Damn shame about that little fucker. Wasn't a bad dude when he was sober." He paused and took several deep breaths, a troubled look on his face. Finally, he turned to his wife. "S-s-sorry, Vera."

Vera rolled her eyes as she shook her head, but didn't reply. She pulled a cigarette out of the fresh pack and busied herself getting another glass of water.

Terry hopped around his alpha male. "Whaddya talking about, Duane, this shithead's fucking around with your wife and you're just gonna let him walk? I say let's pound him."

Duane didn't say anything but I could see his face darken and his eyes frown. It wouldn't do to look like a wuss in front of your people, however smarmy they may be. He bowed up again and said, "I think you better get your ass out of here 'fore me and Terry decide to have a little fun."

Vera piped up from over by the sink. "Oh, shut the hell up. Can't you lose the macho weight lifter bullshit for three seconds?"

Duane turned to his betrothed. "Listen here, woman, I've had enough of you already today. Don't make me shut you up."

"You ain't got the balls to handle a real woman." Vera waved her cigarette at the man she promised to love, honor, and cherish. The conversation degenerated from there, a verbal slugfest reminiscent of some reality cop TV show. They were following a well-worn groove in the record of their marriage, each playing a part he or she knew intimately. I wondered if Duane had ever struck Vera. Probably not. Yet.

I put two fingers in my mouth and whistled, getting everybody's attention. "Vera. Shut the hell up."

She looked startled but complied.

I turned to her husband. "Duane, don't ever, ever, I mean ever, threaten her again. Don't even think about it. You threaten her again or lay a finger on her, I'll come back and break your legs so bad you'll never walk again without crutches. Forget about the Mr. Universe competition."

Duane laughed and clenched his fists. "You sonuvabitch, I'll—"

I held up a finger and wagged it. "Quiet now. Listen closely, Duane, and everything will be all right."

He flexed his pecs. "Don't you tell me what to do. You come in my fucking house, acting like you're a tough ass, and—"

I shrugged. "Duane, buddy. Work with me here, okay? I'm trying to help you out."

"Help me out of what?" He frowned.

"Keep you from getting hurt, okay?"

He laughed. "Whaddya talking about? You know how much I can dead-lift?"

I scratched behind my ear. "You pump iron for a living. I take down people who do that. Every day. It's my job."

He furrowed his brow in concentration, and I could imagine the wheels turning in his mind. After a few moments he nodded. I figured he finally realized his ability to bench-press a Toyota did not necessarily mean he had the skills to win in a dirty street brawl.

Terry, the muscle-bound midget, hadn't seen the light yet. Out of the corner of my eye I saw him charge, head down, arms out. I tried to step out of the way but the food-laden table and the kitchen counters conspired against me, and I took Terry's combed-over head in the solar plexus. We crashed to the floor, me gasping for air. He might have done some damage if his short, stubby, overdeveloped arms could've gotten some room to swing. As it was he got in two short stabs, both hitting my ribs painfully, before he rolled away and got to his feet. A pair of nunchucks—two sticks held together by six inches of chain—appeared in his hand out of nowhere.

I didn't waste the time it would take to get up, opting instead for one quick kick at Terry's knee. My steel-toed work boot connected with the target, producing a crunching sound. Terry shrieked and fell face forward onto the table, scattering covered dishes and utensils everywhere.

I jumped up. Vera and Duane had not moved; both stood still watching the screaming man as he rolled around on the kitchen floor, covered in tomato aspic and green bean casserole.

"W-w-what the hell'd you do to him?" Duane said.

"I kicked his kneecap because he was trying to tear my head off. You gotta problem with that?" It had been a long day and my patience was growing thin. My ribs hurt, as did my cheek where I had hit Carl Albach's head the day before.

"You broke his leg." Duane couldn't decide what to do, help his little buddy or take a swing at me.

"Yeah . . . maybe. That's for a doctor to decide. You wanna get some of that, Duane? Maybe take a header into the macaroni salad?" I made a move toward him but he stepped away, hands out.

"No. No. Back off, dude. It's cool. We're cool here." Duane moved away from me and knelt by his moaning friend. "Everything's cool. I'm just gonna take care of Terry, and everything'll be fine."

"Cool," I said.

"Yeah, that's it. Cool." He began wiping green beans off the top of his partner's head.

Vera ran water over the glowing end of her smoke. She pitched it in the trash can and turned to me. "I'll walk you out." She ignored the two men kneeling in the pile of food in her kitchen. I followed her through the door leading into the living room, scattering the cluster of eavesdropping old women like dandelions in a tornado. She ignored them, ushering me to the front door. Once there, she kissed me on the cheek and said, "Thanks for everything, Hank." Her eyes filled with tears again. "A-a-after I bury Charlie, I want you to tell me the name of a good divorce lawyer. It's not supposed to be this way. Even I know that."

I left her there, crying softly in the doorway of a home filled with bitter old women, an egotistical, abusive husband, and one musclehead with a Napoléon complex, currently cleaning tomato aspic out of his ears. I went home to my little house and mean dog in East Dallas, grateful for the small things in life.

The next morning I hit the office early, meeting Nolan there. We started the search for Fagen Strathmore, the man I regarded as our best lead to date. One full hour of telephoning and networking yielded a lot of promises to call back but no solid information. Strathmore maintained an office at his namesake company on McKinney Avenue but the owner of the janitorial service who cleaned the place, who owed me several favors, said that the man was rarely there, and that his secretary had indicated he was on vacation all week anyway.

We were stuck until someone called back.

That left the only other option, a weak one at best, Aaron Johnson, the owner of the house where Charlie Wesson had been found. I dug his card out of my wallet, and Nolan and I piled into my truck.

CHAPTER THIRTEEN

Due east from downtown, almost on the exact opposite side of the city from where Charlie Wesson took a bullet, lay the nightclub district clustered along Elm Street, better known as Deep Ellum. In the latter part of the nineteenth century the area had been home to the city's brothels, gambling houses, and opium dens as well as a series of narrow clubs and taverns, long-since-forgotten places where the black men of the day had come to hear their music, the blues, played with smoky authenticity by people like Blind Lemon Jefferson, Robert Johnson, and Leadbelly Ledbetter. Elm Street ended a few blocks from the entrance to Fair Park, the 277-acre, art deco wonderland that hosted the Texas State Fair every year and was home to the Cotton Bowl.

Aaron Young kept his office on Second Avenue, on the south end of the fairgrounds. We skirted the edges of downtown, made our way down Elm Street, passed the neon of the bars darkened by daylight, and approached from the west, on MLK Boulevard, following the edge of the fair. The monstrous Ferris wheel that dominated the midway cast a long shadow across the road. I took a short cut through a residential section, the houses small and wood-sided. The only faces I saw on the street were black.

At Second, I turned south into Aaron's neighborhood. The buildings on either side were old and brick, worn but maintained, and most were painted or decorated in some flamboyant fashion. Someone had made a lot of money selling neon-colored pennants this year. Every third storefront promised to have the best barbecue in Dallas. The rest housed dusty bars and narrow shops selling secondhand appliances or used tires. Old men sat in lawn chairs, leaning against the sides of buildings, smoking and visiting as children dashed down the crowded sidewalks, threading between the adults who made a slow promenade in the June sunshine.

I drove below the speed limit so as not to miss Aaron Young's office. It also helped to avoid potholes and the children on bikes careening down the avenue. Nolan spotted it first. "There. On the left." The place was the newest on the street, a one-story, shiny redbrick strip of a building, half a block long. Young Enterprises occupied the south end. A daycare center and a beauty shop rented the northern spaces. I eased the truck into the parking area and turned off the motor, leaving the keys in the ignition.

"What do you want me to do?" Nolan said.

"Stay out here. I don't want to overwhelm this guy." Truthfully it would have been better to have two sets of eyes and ears during the interview. In reality, I was used to working on my own, even though Ernie and I were partners. The other part of the equation was that the interview was a long shot, but until I found the whereabouts of Fagen Strathmore, it was the best I could do. Plus, I didn't want to hear that Young had narcissistic sexual hydrophobia or whatever the psychosis of the week was.

"Keep an eye out for Coleman Dupree." I said the last in jest. Even if we were in Dupree's part of the world, it was a sunny morning with people on the street. His kind favored the anonymity of the night. Besides, we didn't know what he looked like, and only I had seen his chief enforcer, Jack the Crack.

The front door to Aaron Young's office was metal, painted to look like wood. I pushed it open and entered the reception area, enjoying the blast of cold air that hit me in the face. Parquet flooring and beige walls dominated the small but well-appointed room. A navy sofa and two wing-back chairs formed a small sitting area to the left. To the right was a receptionist desk. A conservatively dressed woman in her fifties sat behind the desk. She was sorting a stack of papers when I walked in, and did a half-second double take when she saw a white man in an untucked denim shirt with a bruised cheek enter the office.

"May I help you?" Her tone was courteous but clipped.

I tried to smile, but it hurt my face so it probably ended up as a grimace. "I'd like to speak to Mr. Young. My name is Hank Oswald." Definitely a grimace because she peered at me, eyes narrowed into a frown. Finally she arched one brow. "I'll see if he's available."

I nodded and she punched some numbers into the phone beside her. As she spoke into the receiver the door opened behind me and a young woman with a group of children entered. There was a blizzard of activity—talking, teensy arms and school bags flurrying about. The swarm stopped when they saw me standing there. I nodded hello and tried to smile. The woman smiled back and corralled the children over to the sitting area, shushing them. She was in her late twenties and pretty.

The door behind the receptionist desk burst open and Aaron Young swept into the room. He breezed by me, touching my elbow for a moment before embracing the woman on the other side of the room. "Coleeta, my dear, how are you? It's been too long."

"I'm fine, Aaron." She pulled away and gestured toward the children. "I wanted to show you what some of my pupils have done. Children, this is Mr. Young."

A chorus of small voices said, "Hello, Mr. Young."

Aaron Young beamed. "Hello, children. Sit down and tell me what you've done." He plopped down on the sofa and gathered the youngsters around. At Coleeta's prompting, they took turns reciting their accomplishments, a piano recital well played, a good grade in a hard subject, a difficulty overcome. Aaron listened and nodded appropriately to each child. When everyone had their say, he produced a wad of five-dollar bills from a pocket. Amid the squealing he doled out one bill per child.

Coleeta kept her attention focused on me, her expression somewhere between curiosity and hostility. After the noise from the children died down to a low hum, Young and Coleeta herded the group toward the door. She kept looking back to me as the children shuffled out the door.

Calmness returned to the office as the door closed. Aaron turned his attention to me, the thousand-watt smile never diminishing, just changing hue from juvenile to adult. "Well then, Mr. Oswald. I'm not surprised to see you here. You have the look of someone who doesn't give up easily."

"That's me, Mr. Stubborn. I had a few more questions."

"And I may or may not have answers; we'll see." He gestured to the door. "Why don't we talk about this in my office." Before I could respond, he strode out of the reception area, leaving me to follow. The receptionist frowned as I walked by. I winked at her and shut the door behind me.

We were in a long hallway, and Aaron was already at the end, motioning me to hurry up. There were six or eight offices off the hallway, each with an occupant or occupants on the phone or banging away on a computer. Several looked at me as I passed, faces impassive.

Aaron sat behind his desk when I finally entered his office. It was surprisingly small, not much larger than my converted bedroom on Reiger Street. Just nicer, newer with better furnishings. Windows overlooking Second Avenue covered one wall. A map of the southern sector of Dallas, up to downtown, covered the opposite side. Stick pins of various colors and sizes dotted the surface. A bookcase dominated the wall behind the desk. It was half books and half plaques and awards, various recognitions for civic activities. It contained a great deal of community recognition for a man who appeared to be barely forty.

A complicated stainless-steel apparatus sat on a counter against one wall. Aaron hopped up, talking to me as he moved. "Espresso, Mr. Oswald? Maybe some cappuccino?"

"Coffee'd be good. Nothing in it."

"Black coffee it is." He twisted and turned and tweaked things, and a few moments later brought me a steaming mug emblazoned with the Young Realty logo, a *Y* and an *R* intertwined. "That's a special roast, from northern Sumatra."

"Oh." I blew on it and took a small sip. It had a unique taste, a cross between something left on the burner too long at Waffle House and shoe polish. I tried not to frown and said, "Good coffee."

Aaron took a long pull of his and then leaned back in his chair. "That's quite a bruise you got there; looks like it's better than yesterday. Got anything to do with the guy that died?"

"Indirectly." I took another small swig of the Sumatran blend and placed it on the edge of his desk, on a Texas-shaped coaster superimposed with a silhouette of Martin Luther King. "So what's that with the kids out there?"

Aaron chuckled. "It's a thing I do with several of the schools in the area. A private reward system I developed. They need a pattern of reinforcement for making good choices. Also, it's important to provide the kids in this section of Dallas with positive role models." He took another sip of coffee. "I don't want to bore you with the statistics but over half the families fall below the poverty line. Two-thirds of the children in this neighborhood come from a single-parent household. That means no daddy at home. If they see me, somebody who came from their same background and made something of themselves, then maybe, just maybe, the allure of the street life, the gangs and the drug dealers, won't be as strong."

I didn't want to get into a discussion of the socioeconomic factors in the North Texas area, so I said, "You from Dallas?"

"Born in New York City, raised here, though, grew up near Redbird Airport."

I picked up my coffee but didn't take a drink. "New York City? That's quite a change."

"Yeah, I guess it is." Aaron smiled. "My mother had dreams of dancing on Broadway, really making it big up there . . . until I came along. My father took off, and she moved back here to be near family."

I nodded politely but shifted gears. "Tell me about the house where Charlie Wesson died. Who had access to it?"

Aaron pursed his lips. "No one, really. It was boarded over. Plywood on the windows and doors. But as I mentioned, it's an old place, scheduled to be demolished, so it's not like we keep it guarded or anything."

"So nobody could get in or out?"

Aaron pursed his lips. "Well . . . there's my head of maintenance."

"Who's that?"

"Guy named Marvin Jones. Been with me for years. Good man."

I nodded and tried to look thoughtful, while filing the name away. It was those good ones you had to be careful about, kind of like an unloaded gun. "Would you mind if I talked to Mr. Jones?"

Aaron Young sighed. "I don't mind, really." He paused a moment. "Besides, I've talked to the police and it's their understanding that Charlie Wesson committed suicide."

"That may very well be so," I said. "But the family has hired me to determine the particular details of this case."

Aaron didn't say anything for a long period, just stared at me without blinking. I made no move to fill the void. Finally he said, "And would you be this conscientious if I'd owned the house that Charlie Wesson had died in and it was in North Dallas? And Marvin Jones was a white man?" His voice was soft but firm.

I met his gaze. "Until you mentioned it, I had no clue as to Marvin Jones's race. But I assure you that since I have taken this case, I'm going to give it my best shot, no matter what part of town it may take me to."

He had a point. Things happened differently in the southern part of

Dallas, where most of the black population lived. Crime was higher, police response slower. Disease ravaged more people, but fewer doctors practiced there. Unemployment was higher but there were fewer jobs available and less money to buy cars to get to the work centers in other areas. Which would have been okay if there were decent public transportation. Then there was the school system, an antiquated district full of overworked teachers, too-full classrooms, and test scores falling somewhere between ditch digger and assistant ditch digger.

"Do you have any other leads at the moment?" Aaron said. "Other than me and my house?"

"I've got a couple of things to follow up." The bruise on my cheek started to itch. I resisted the urge to scratch it. "The place had been a drug house before you bought it. Any idea who used it?"

"At the risk of sounding trite, I believe drug users were the ones using it for drug purposes."

"What I mean is, who was the supplier, the dealer?" I tried another sip of the rank coffee.

Slap. Aaron Young's palms hit the desktop as he leaned forward. A vein in his temple throbbed. "What are you trying to say, Mr. Oswald? Just because I'm black, you think I know all the crack dealers in Dallas? Does your last name mean you know a lot of presidential assassins?" His café-au-lait complexion purpled with rage.

I kept my voice calm and even. "No offense meant, Mr. Young. I'm just looking for information."

As quickly as it erupted, the storm passed. Aaron sank back in his chair and said, "I am sorry if I seem to have overreacted. I value my position in the community very much." He rubbed the bridge of his nose and leaned back in his chair. "I also have . . . I am—" He seemed unable to find the right words and stopped for a moment. "I have a number of projects under development at the moment. All of which require my personal attention."

"Don't worry about it. I appreciate the time you've given me." I stood up and put my coffee cup back on his desk. "Could I get a contact number for Marvin Jones?"

Anger flashed across his face for an instant. Then he smiled and scribbled something on a piece of paper. "Sure. This is his cell phone. Tell him I said it's okay to talk to you."

I took the piece of paper. "Thanks. I appreciate it." I gestured toward the hallway. "How many people do you have in your operation?"

He jumped out of his chair, energized by my question. "We've got sixteen here, and another thirty people on site at various properties. Most of them are managers and maintenance people at our apartment projects." He turned to the map across the room. "The majority of the apartments are west of here, in Oak Cliff." He pointed to a series of red pins, south of downtown and the river, and west of Interstate 35.

I walked over to the map. It started in DeSoto and Lancaster, at the extreme southern portion of Dallas County, and ran to the Oak Lawn and uptown areas north of downtown. In the process it covered the entire wall. I spotted the location of my house and office, about eye level on the right side. There were several different-colored pins a few blocks south of me. "What are the green pins?"

Aaron beamed, that deep, broad smile he'd shown the children. "That's for retail properties, shopping centers, things like that. We have ten of them now, over six hundred thousand square feet of retail property, new shopping in the southern sector. We've put grocery stores back in neighborhoods that had been without a place to buy food for years. The red pins, as I mentioned, are for apartments. We've got more than sixty complexes, almost eighteen hundred units, of clean, decent, affordable homes."

"And the blue pins?" There were eight or ten, scattered about in no particular concentration.

"Those are offices or miscellaneous properties we own or manage. I have a couple I am particularly proud of here on Jefferson." He pointed to the map. "These were two older buildings, long since written off by most investors. I took them and cleaned them up; now they're ninety-five percent full and cash flowing."

"That's impressive," I said. Jefferson Avenue was the main thoroughfare of Oak Cliff, the largest section of the southern half of Dallas. The street was a vibrant but run-down little nugget of the city, all but unknown to the people north of the river. "What's the gold pin?"

Aaron laughed. "That's headquarters, where we are right now."

I nodded and turned to leave. Something on the map caught my eye. It was an outline, not a pin, and it was in the Trinity River bottom, between North and South Dallas. "What's that?"

Aaron's voice took on the same intensity as when he'd chastised me about drugs, only without the anger. "That parcel there, Mr. Oswald? That's going to be my crowning glory. That's the Trinity Vista, something that will finally link North and South Dallas."

"What do you mean?" I moved closer to the map.

"White Dallas has done its best to keep us separate." He traced the Trinity River channel with one thin finger. "But not equal."

I didn't reply.

"But this will be the bridge." The phone on his desk rang. He moved toward it. "You do understand what I'm saying, don't you?"

I nodded as he answered the phone and slipped out, smiling as best I could at the woman at the front. She managed not to frown at me as I left.

CHAPTER FOURTEEN

The thin cloud cover present since early morning had burned off, leaving a heated layer of smoggy air blanketing the street. Something else was different too. I felt my skin tighten and knew it wasn't from the change in temperature after Young's cold office. I've always had that ability, even as a child, to spot trouble long before it becomes visible. One of my earliest memories involved a man robbing a liquor store, near the small central-Texas town where I was born. Our home at the time was a four-room shack on the ass-end of some property my father's people owned in western McLennan County. That branch of my family was a dour lot, creased and dusty from the sun, the earth, and the fatalistic attitude that whatever waters they tried to fish, someone had long since been there and caught everything worth keeping. Still, that was where they threw their line.

One August afternoon, when the sun made the air shimmer and each breath felt like an oven blast in your lungs, Daddy and I stopped at a bottle shop after putting out a new salt lick for the cattle in the south field. I was probably three or four years old, and remember holding a pack of those candy cigarettes they had back then, waving them at my father in hopes that he would buy me a treat. He ignored my pleadings and stood there at the counter, talking to the owner of the store.

As I waited in front of the candy display, the cowbell hanging over the front door jangled and a young man entered. He was ordinary for the time and place, dirty jeans and a denim shirt with a greasy baseball cap. To this day I remember the way the bill of that cap had been creased and the name of the seeds advertised on the front. I'd like to say that the eyes gave him away but those too were unremarkable. I knew, though, as soon as his boots squeaked across the hardwood floor, he was there for trouble. My insides felt still and nervous at the same time, as butterflies fluttered across my stomach. The man walked to the rear of the store and grabbed a six-pack of beer. As he returned to the front I tottered my way to the other side of the candy rack, some portion of my cerebellum already wired to seek cover.

By the time he reached the counter, he had a firearm drawn, an old Colt .45, a John Wayne gun. After that, things moved slowly, like they were underwater. There were shouts and yelling and hard, strange movements from the adults. My father stepped back, looking for me but keeping his eye on the robber. The owner held his hands up as the man grabbed money from the register. Daddy dragged me to the rear of the store, away from the danger at the front. It became very quiet; the only sound I was aware of was our feet scuffling on the floor as we made our way down the aisle. I had a clear view of the man with the gun. The hammer cocking back sounded like a piece of dry kindling breaking on a cold morning. The sound of the gun firing was loud and soft at the same time, kind of like the feeling I had in my stomach when the man entered the store. There was no mistaking the thumb-size hole that appeared in the owner's chest and the way he fell backward into the rack of cigarettes. After that, I don't remember much.

My skin was clammy and those same butterflies skittered in my diaphragm when I walked out of Aaron Young's office. The street felt different than when I had entered, only twenty minutes before. There were fewer people milling about. Those that were out weren't smiling anymore. They kept their eyes down and hurried along. Before I could reach the parking lot, Nolan pulled my truck up to the curb. She rolled down the passenger's window. "Get in."

I complied and she drove away. "Two Cadillacs been making the circuit for the last few minutes. Four people in each one. All the windows rolled down." She had a revolver resting in her lap. "They've been checking out this truck."

"When's the last time they went by?" I pulled my Browning from its holster.

"About thirty seconds ago." She stopped for a light. "There. In the next block. There's one of them." A ten-year-old Seville, dented and colored half gray and half rust, idled in front of a liquor store fifty yards ahead. The tires were new, bigger than normal for a car that size. Nolan put one hand on her gun and said, "How do want to do this?"

"I want to get the hell out of here is how I want to do this."

"Okay then." The light changed and she punched the accelerator. "Hang on." We blew past the Cadillac at forty miles per hour. At fifty we hit a pothole and our heads banged the roof of the truck. The Seville followed on our tail, no more than two car lengths behind. The driver avoided the potholes that we seemed to hit. Nolan swerved to miss a battered Pontiac and almost collided with two small children crossing the street. "You want me to hit a side street, see if I can lose them?" She held on to the wheel with both hands. We were going sixty, as fast as we could on a narrow, cluttered roadway.

I looked back at the pursuing car. "This is their turf, we'd be goners on the back streets." So far the occupants of the Seville hadn't flashed any artillery, just given chase. We entered a stretch of Second Avenue where there was nothing, just vacant land pockmarked every few hundred yards with the occasional abandoned building. "Keep doing what you're doing. Maybe they're just trying to run us out of their neighborhood." I didn't believe that even as I said it.

"I think we're gonna need a new option." Nolan's voice made me turn back around, just in time to see the front windshield star-burst from a bullet. The second Cadillac, an early eighties Coupe deVille, blocked the road ahead. I could just make out a figure in the backseat, poking a handgun out the window. I saw a flash and heard a pop but the bullet went wild.

"Hold tight," Nolan said, her teeth clenched. Before I could respond or grab anything, she stood on the brakes and jerked the wheel around. Pickups aren't Porsches and balk at moves like that. Mine was no exception. We went up on two wheels before plopping back down. The force of the impact knocked me into Nolan so that my head was in her lap. I figured that was what saved my life because the next shot from the Coupe hit the rear windshield, right where my skull would have been.

"Hope you don't mind if I stay down for a while. It's a little dicey up top."

A horn sounded and Nolan wrenched the steering wheel. Her elbow hit me in the ear. "How about you get up here and do something constructive, like shoot back."

"How am I supposed to aim, with you driving like this?" I sat up and punched out the rest of the rear window. Wind whipped through the cab of the truck as the two Caddies raced behind us. We were about to be out of the deserted section of Second Avenue and back where we started. The Seville led and a hand holding a pistol snaked out of the passenger-side window. Two flashes but both shots missed. I steadied my right arm as best possible and let loose four rounds in quick succession, aiming for the radiator. Good luck shined upon us because a cloud of steam billowed from the front of the car. The engine seized and they pulled to the side. "That's one down."

With a screech of the tires, we were on two wheels again, turning left onto a side street. I slammed into the passenger's door, where my bruised cheek connected with the glass.

"Traffic up ahead. Didn't have a choice," Nolan said. The street was narrower than Second Avenue, lined now with small houses. Cars and trees speckled both sides of the road. Nolan slowed down to about fifty, still way too fast. It was a matter of time before we wrecked. The Cadillac followed but not as closely. We blew past a sky blue house on a corner, the trim a fresh white. A thirty-year-old Chevy sat in the driveway with an old man behind the wheel, adjusting his seat belt before driving off. As we passed, he eased the antique into the street. The Seville hit the gas and tried to make it, but got clipped by the Chevy. It wobbled, side-swiping the cars on either side of the street. We gained ground, rounded a curve, and were out of sight of the car.

"Make a turn," I said. "Let's lose 'em."

Nolan hung a right, then immediately another right. I was looking out the rear window so I didn't understand why she had stopped. "Why are you—" I turned around and saw the dead end.

We were on a half street, only five homes long. The road ended in a tangled mass of trees and bamboo. The houses appeared to be vacant. We sat silent for a few seconds until we heard the squealing tires.

I opened the door and said, "Out of the car." I grabbed my cell phone and we ran to the second house from the end, on the left. It was the most overgrown. Ten years' worth of unkempt hedges hid the front of the house. We melted into the vegetation and rotted wood at one end of the porch, trying to be still. We waited. It didn't take long.

I'd barely pushed the safety off my Browning when the Seville eased around the corner. It stopped at the end of the street and a lone figure hopped out. He slipped behind a tree and pointed a rifle at the truck. Another figure exited from the other side of the car and took up a position on the opposite side of the street, rifle in hand. They signaled each other and opened fire on the truck. I recognized the distinctive chatter of the AK-47. The shooters were well trained, and concentrated on the cab of the truck, a careful and controlled barrage of bullets that destroyed where we'd been sitting moments before.

The shots ceased and they approached the remains of the truck. The man on the left was the first to reach it. He whistled and waved his hand when he saw the empty cab. Two more figures got out of the car and the four of them spread out. They were preparing to search the surrounding houses.

"Ready or not, here they come." I gripped the pistol tighter.

CHAPTER FIFTEEN

An old gunny sergeant I used to know said that one of the stupidest things you could do was to bring a knife to a gunfight. Our situation wasn't quite that bad, but close. I had a Browning Hi-Power with one extra thirteen-round magazine. Nolan had a six-shot revolver. The four stalking us, getting closer by the second, each carried an AK-47 with a long, curved banana clip. Twenty or thirty rounds per weapon. They'd outlawed those high-capacity magazines years ago, but these guys obviously hadn't heard about that.

The other problem we had was that I can't shoot a pistol worth a damn. The army even sent me to study with a special group of folks, sort of a graduate course in all the latest techniques of murder and mayhem.

They called themselves the Rangers and were exceptionally good at what they did. They taught me to kill with all sorts of things: grenades, rifles, shotguns, even the odd household instruments lying around, like a butter knife or piano wire. And of course: handguns.

I flunked pistol killing.

Our best bet was to sneak away, if that turned out to be an option, which I doubted. I assumed the two on our side were mimicking what their counterparts were doing across the street: slowly making their way down the block, one checking out the abandoned houses, the other standing guard on the sidewalk.

They were progressing at the same speed because when the two opposite us reached the house directly across, I heard a rustling in the bushes of our hiding place. Nolan looked at me, eyebrows raised. I held the Browning in my right hand and waited, blinking the sweat out of my eyes. More rustling and the wooden porch creaked.

He looked like he was barely out of high school, a skinny kid wearing low-slung jeans and a dirty Lakers jersey. He knew how to carry a rifle, though, shoulder mounted with both eyes open. He stepped on the rickety porch from the opposite end as us, cautiously pushing his way through the tangle of wisteria and holly. If we were lucky he wouldn't see us, crouched behind a wreck of a Barcalounger. It would help if he were blind too.

An instant after he saw us he fired two rounds our way. He was scared or a bad shot or both, because they went high, into the corner of the house. I aimed for his chest and fired twice. The bullets hit the thin wooden column supporting the porch, about two feet to his right. Stupid pistol.

A shower of wood rained on him and he put one hand to his eyes and fired another round that went into the floor. Nolan and I bolted, scrambling off the porch. We'd just landed in the dirt of the side yard when the shrubbery and the front of the house disintegrated in a shower of bullets.

We whipped around the side of the house, where I tapped out three quick shots toward the source of the fire. He or they returned the favor but we were already gone, racing through the backyard and breaking through the foliage to hop the fence and land in a gravel alley, overgrown and empty. We headed left, toward the street from where we'd turned. After passing two houses, I pulled Nolan into the backyard of the third. We hid in the brush line, Nolan looking toward the street while I kept watch the other way.

I heard tree limbs crackle and break as our pursuer brushed through the vegetation and entered the alley. I couldn't see him, and after the initial noise, couldn't hear him either.

I strained to sense something, a sight, a sound, anything. I held my pistol at ready and counted Mississippis. At ten, a rat zipped across the alley, a few feet in front of us. An old tomcat bounded after it, stopping for a moment in the middle before continuing the pursuit. He was dirty orange, fat with one crooked ear, and I almost shot at him.

Something rustled a tree limb, startling both me and the cat. The tom darted away from the noise as the trunk of a tree about ten yards past us exploded in a cloud of wood chips. A bullet plowed into the fence line on the opposite side. Then another one on our side, a few feet closer to us from the tree. The shooter was working his way down the alley, firing in a pattern of sorts to see what he could stir up.

"Let's go." I grabbed at Nolan and then felt someone mash a lit cigar on the inside of my thigh, midway between my crotch and knee. I was vaguely aware of the sound of a gunshot associated with the pain. I steered Nolan into the yard of the deserted house and squeezed the trigger three times as fast as I could, aiming in the direction of the sound. Another shot zinged against the front half of a rusted El Camino sitting in the yard. Without aiming, I fired again toward the sound of the shot and was rewarded with a yelp.

"Head toward the street." An obstacle course of crap lay in the yard, abandoned appliances and unidentifiable rusted things. Nolan led the way, threading through the maze. I could feel blood, warm and sticky, coating my leg, mixing with sweat. We reached the side of the house and paused.

"What's the plan now?" she said, wiping the perspiration off the palm of her gun hand and onto her jeans. "Wait for nightfall and try to make it back to camp?"

"Like to be out of here before then." I examined the wound in my thigh as best I could. It was only a graze but there was a streak of red running down the inside of my blue jeans. "We've got to get off this block."

She huffed trying to get her breath back. "No kidding. You went to private eye school to figure that out?"

Sirens rang in the distance. Usually that sound didn't make me happy, but this time I hoped they were headed toward us and if so, they got here in time. Nolan started to say something when I heard movement ahead. The stand of bamboo hiding us from the front shivered and crackled as someone pushed through. A finger of flame licked out of the cane poles and a bullet slammed into the rusted refrigerator Nolan was leaning against. If I were older, I thought, I'd be having a Vietnam flashback. Instead I fired twice at the dense brush, hopefully near the muzzle blast. Nolan squeezed off one round.

One more shot erupted from the bamboo, then nothing. We ran around to the opposite side of the house, where the brush wasn't as thick. A old pecan tree grew flush with the rotting wood of the home, seeming to sprout from the foundation. I crept up behind it, not eager to break into the open front yard.

My caution was rewarded when I saw the sea of red lights swarming in the street. The heat had arrived. Clusters of uniforms stood around the empty Coupe deVille and my pickup, peering inside and talking on radios. Three officers bearing shotguns stood in front of the house where we were hiding. This was as dicey as escaping the guys chasing us. As a rule, police officers do not like to be startled. And there wasn't much more startling than two grimy, sweaty, gun-toting private investigators popping out of the bushes at the scene of a twelve-alarm firefight. I pulled out my cell phone and hit the speed dial for my lawyer's voice mail. As fast and quiet as possible, I spit out the basic facts of the situation, including the location.

I turned to Nolan, who was slouched beside me. "You still got your San Antonio PD badge?"

She patted her pockets. "Dammit. No. In the truck."

"Holster your piece and raise your arms over your head." She did just that and I followed suit. "No sudden movements and let me do the talking." I started to ease through the vegetation.

"Keep your palms facing out and fingers wide," she said.

I held my hands in the suggested manner and we broke free into the front yard. I whistled once, a sharp, piercing, come-hither tone.

Hither they came and we found ourselves facedown in the dirt, spread-eagled and devoid of all our hardware and ID. Handcuffs clinked on our wrists as heavy footfalls shuffled in the muck around us. Radios squawked. Cops talked to one another. Finally they pulled us up and somebody noticed my bleeding leg. Fifteen minutes later I was sitting in an ambulance as a paramedic cut away my jeans. She was pretty, petite with red hair and a long, thin nose. I was about to start with my charm and say something about a nice girl in a place like this, when she dumped some alcohol on the wound. I swore instead.

A skinny cop, fiftyish, with bloodshot eyes and a handlebar mustache, ambled over and leaned against the ambulance door, one hand scratching at something on his belly while the other rested on the butt of his revolver. He was sweating and wore his gun belt slung low, like a TV-western gunfighter, and looked like how I imagined Doc Holliday would appear, only without the tuberculosis. As the paramedic worked, he started in on me about shooting and killing and how unlucky the Dallas jail was for guys named Lee Oswald and I better damn well tell him what the hell was going on down here.

I nodded politely and kept a blank face. After a couple of minutes the emergency tech taped a bandage over the wound and pronounced me fit.

Doc Holliday leaned over so eye contact couldn't be avoided. "Isn't that great, Lee Harvey? You don't have to go to the hospital. We can take a trip straight to Lew Sterret."

He was talking about the county jail. Originally designed to hold only a few hundred inmates it usually housed enough lawbreakers to populate a midsize city and seemed to be perpetually under some federal judge's scrutiny. Not a good place. I started to say something but was interrupted.

"Perhaps you could tell me what my client is charged with?" The newscaster-smooth voice came from behind the officer. Doc Holliday turned around and there stood Bertrand Delarosso, my attorney. He had a movie star face framed by thick waves of brown hair. Even in the steamy heat in a two-thousand-dollar suit, he didn't appear out of place. He was in his element, manipulating the criminal justice system.

He slid the jacket off and draped it over one arm, making a great show out of looking at his watch, a digital Timex. Bertrand didn't like to be pretentious.

Doc Holliday made a face like he'd bitten into a pile of weasel shit. He ignored Bertrand and spoke to me. "Is this man your lawyer?"

I nodded. The paramedic had given me a safety pin and I was trying to close up the rip in my jeans. "He also represents Nolan O'Connor, the woman you're holding in the car over there." I pointed to Nolan's silhouette, in the squad car across the street. I wanted Bertrand to know about all his clients as soon as possible.

He never missed a beat. "Yes, Officer, I represent Ms. O'Connor and Mr. Oswald. Now then, could you tell me what the charges are?"

The officer shook his head and sighed. "We're in the preliminary stages of investigating a shooting. Your clients were involved. I am not sure what the charges will be." He emphasized *will be.*

Bertrand pursed his lips as if in deep thought. "Hmm, yes, I see. A shooting. How many victims are there?"

"Victims?" the cop said.

"Victims," Bertrand said back.

The officer scratched the back of his neck and looked off into the distance. "Like I said, this is the preliminary stage of the investigation. We haven't found all the victims yet."

"Oh, I see." Bertrand's pocket chirped and he pulled out a cell phone. He turned it off in midring. "So how many victims have you found as of this point?"

"Well, actually, none."

"None?" Bertrand said.

"None," the officer said back. "But there's a lot of empty casings in several spots, and a couple of places we've found blood."

Bertrand nodded and then pointed to my leg. "My client has been wounded, perhaps that was his blood?"

The officer pulled out a rumpled pack of Marlboros and lit one. He blew a plume of smoke into Bertrand's face. "Perhaps. Maybe if I could ask your client some questions, we could determine that."

Bertrand didn't so much as blink as the cloud of tobacco smoke enveloped his head. "By all means. Ask my client anything you want. I am sure that we can do that here or at my office rather than the county jail, don't you think so, Officer?"

I sensed that Doc Holliday would rather take me to the lockup but he said yeah, he supposed so, then turned to me and began the interrogation. Forty minutes later, he'd run out of things to ask. I had answered everything truthfully, if not completely. Bertrand had not interrupted once. They left me sitting in the ambulance while they went to talk to Nolan. I watched the police wrecker hitch up what was left of my pickup truck and haul it away. Another thirty minutes passed and we were in Bertrand's BMW, headed north. The conversation stayed light, nothing concerning the afternoon's events. Bertrand's a big believer in plausible deniability. Instead, we talked about his matrimonial status with wife number three, Sandra Jo, Miss June of 1991 and also an ex–Cowboys cheerleader. She'd maxed out her American Express Gold Card, something that was theoretically impossible, when she charged a new Ford pickup on it last week. The truck was for her little brother who had started a pool business. Bertrand was quick to clarify it was pool as in billiards, not swimming.

I'd met Sandra Jo a couple of times. I'd let her max out anything of mine.

Bertrand wheeled onto the freeway. "Where do you want me to drop you? Home or office?"

"Hold on a second." I dialed Olson. He answered on the second ring and we had a quick conversation. I hung up. "The Texaco, Stemmons and Inwood. Olson's picking us up there."

Bertrand nodded and headed that way. He knew better than to ask why, and I knew better than to explain that since the police had confiscated our guns for the duration of the investigation of the shooting, I needed a firearm on my hip before I went anywhere.

It was full-on rush hour when we pulled into the Texaco. Olson was there as promised. We hopped out of the BMW. Bertrand said he'd send me the bill.

We got into Olson's truck. Before he pulled out into the traffic, he took a long look at us and raised his eyebrows. "You stink. What the hell have you kids been up to today, besides getting shot and dirty?"

Nolan looked out the window while I detailed the events of the last few hours.

"Two cars full of hoods, huh." Olson whistled. "That means six or eight heavily armed guys. All of them looking for you. What's up with that?"

"I don't know, but I'm getting tired of it."

"Maybe you shouldn't have taken that package."

"Yeah. I'm thinking that wasn't the smartest move. Still, at least I've got it for a little leverage. If I can just figure out how to use it without getting killed."

"Where do you guys want to go now?" We were driving down Lemmon Avenue, a mile-long strip of car dealers, bars, and greasy burger joints.

"I need to rent a car. It's tough to be a private eye in Dallas without wheels."

"I've got wheels," Nolan said.

"Would that be the Eldorado?"

"Yeah. What's wrong with that?" Her tone was wary.

"I need something that's not too obvious," I said. "Especially if we're gonna find Aaron Young's maintenance guy."

Olson swerved to miss an old man shuffling across the street. "What're you still doing on the deal? I thought it'd be over since Wesson turned up stiff."

"Charlie's sister doesn't think he'd kill himself. Neither do I."

Nolan leaned into the space between the two front seats. "Addicts rarely kill themselves intentionally."

"Nolan has a degree in psychology," I said.

Olson nodded and looked at her in the rearview mirror. "It all has to do with sex. And Mom. Right?"

Nolan nodded and winked. "Exactly."

I ran my hand lightly over the bandage on my thigh. "Take me home so I can start looking for a replacement ride."

"Ten-four." Olson made a turn. "Then what's your plan?"

I dug a piece of dirt out of my left ear. "I've got two leads. The maintenance man who had access to the place where Charlie died, and a guy I can't seem to track down named Fagen Strathmore."

Olson chuckled. "That's an easy one."

"What is?"

"Fagen Strathmore."

"What the hell do you mean?" My tone was sharp; I wasn't in the mood for Olson's circuitous logic.

He sighed, as if explaining something to a particularly slow-witted child. "Seeing that guy. It'll be easy."

"Why?"

"Because Delmar is meeting with him tomorrow, to sell him a gun."

"Fagen Strathmore?"

"Yep."

"You sure it's the same guy?"

"How many cats in this city named Fagen Strathmore? Rich guys willing to buy one of Delmar's overpriced shotguns?" He had a point.

I scratched at the wound on my thigh and tried to make sense of it all. "Strathmore buys guns, huh?"

"Oh yeah, he's a big collector. And a shooter too. 'Fact, that's where Delmar's meeting him tomorrow,"

"Where?" Nolan said.

"At a shoot. A tournament."

I felt the bandage on my leg to make sure it was secure. "What kind of shoot?"

Olson laughed, as if he'd just thought of a joke. "It's kind of hush-hush. It's a pigeon shoot, at a place south of town."

I'd heard of them before, a shotgun tournament where the targets were living birds instead of clay targets. They were supposed to be big along the border. Not popular at all among your animal rights types.

"Well, that should make for a fun and interesting day tomorrow."

Olson slowed down as a Maxima switched lanes abruptly. "Unless you're a pigeon."

He dropped us off at Reiger Street, at the office. The windows lay dark, my suite mates long since departed for the tavern of the month. The only car there was Nolan's Eldorado. The yellow didn't appear nearly as neon in the early twilight. Olson flipped the Suburban's lights off, and waited while we slipped in the back door. I carried one of his spare pieces, a .44 Magnum with a three-inch barrel. I prayed I wouldn't have to use it during the time it took me to get to my other weapons. The muzzle blast and recoil of the thing would kill me as well as whatever I was shooting at. I wasn't expecting trouble, but after the events of the day, I considered myself in a state of war. No threats in the office, so I called Olson on his cell phone and told him he could leave. My fridge was empty but Nolan rummaged around in the kitchen and came back with two Pabst Blue Ribbons. They belonged to Davis. I didn't think he'd notice, nor did I care. We popped them open and drank. Then I called Delmar and told him what I wanted. He pondered it for a moment and said he would call back. Next I turned to my closet and opened the safe I keep there. It's small and fits neatly into the narrow space.

"You got an extra gun?" I said.

"Not handy."

"You want to stick with a thirty-eight?"

Nolan hiccupped. "Huh?"

"Your gun? You want to go with the same kind? Or something bigger?"

"That's fine." She frowned and tried to peer around my shoulder into the closet. "What's with the extra firepower?"

"I hang out with Delmar and Olson; they give out guns with their Christmas cards." Weapons were almost a birthright in the state of Texas; rich or poor, urban or rural, people like their guns. They were a rite of passage for many young men, a symbol of maturity, when they received their first .22 rifle, usually sometime in the second or third grade. But don't try to take them away. Never can tell when you might have to shoot a rabid armadillo or somebody climbing through the window of your seventeenth-story apartment in Houston.

I pulled out a stainless Smith and a Browning, similar to the ones the police had confiscated. "Here you go. There's some hollow-points on the shelf over there." I pointed to the built-in bookcases across the room. While Nolan loaded her new weapon, and I worked the action on the Browning, the phone rang. It was Delmar. "Nine o'clock tomorrow. Your office. I scrounged you up an invitation. You owe me on this one."

"Thanks." I shoved a loaded clip into the Browning and stuck it into the holster on my hip. "Put it on my account. Say, if I'm going to do this thing, I'll need a shotgun. My riot gun with the extended magazine probably won't fit in too well."

Delmar sighed dramatically. "I'll see if I have anything lying around you can use."

I drained the last of my beer. "Oh, and I'll need a car. Unless you want us to ride with you. My truck is fried and . . . well, I could use Nolan's Caddy, but a well-to-do pigeon killer wouldn't be caught dead in a canary yellow—"

"You're pushing it, Hank."

"See you at nine." I hung up. It was a game he played, see how grouchy he could be. But Olson considered himself in my debt, and by extension so did Delmar.

"You want me to take you home?" Nolan said.

"Nope. To the hospital, gotta see Ernie." My wounded leg throbbed and I made no move to stand.

"Yeah, me too." She tugged at her ponytail and sighed, suddenly looking as tired as I felt. "What's gonna happen when he dies?"

"I'll be . . . sad?" I tried to keep my tone from being sarcastic.

"No shit." She sounded exasperated. "We all will. I meant about Miranda, will she be okay? I don't really know her that well."

"She's a survivor. She'll do fine." I wanted to say more but couldn't think of anything. Miranda was a survivor; so was Ernie. Until the cancer. I felt a lump in my throat. We were both silent. I looked over and saw Nolan rub the corner of one eye. I said, "Were you and Ernie close?"

She nodded. "My old man was not exactly father-of-the-year material. Uncle Ernie was there when I needed him. H-h-he was so good to me. . . ." Her voice trailed off. Neither of us spoke for a while.

After a few minutes I stood up and said, "Let's go to the hospital."

CHAPTER SIXTEEN

The Mercedes rode hard, the suspension stiffer than I was used to in my recently deceased pickup. Navy blue and four years old, it was the top of the line, loaded with all the options. It smelled like an ashtray at a VFW Hall. The wheelless can't be picky about their wheels, though. The German auto belonged to Raul, a friend of Delmar and Olson's. The car was his second or third, and he didn't have need of it for the foreseeable future. It was better not to ask too many questions.

Nolan and I were following Delmar down a two-lane blacktop in rural Navarro County, south and east of Dallas. I was tired and grumpy. Sleep proved elusive the night before, with Charlie Wesson and Ernie wrestling for control of my subconscious. Charlie, with the back of his head blown out, made me lurch awake and remember Ernie lying in the hospital bed, looking ten pounds thinner than he had on my last visit. He hadn't said much during our time there, halfhearted stabs at conversations punctuated by gravel-sounding wheezes as his lungs struggled to make it through one more day of pain. We sat, Nolan on one side of the bed and me on the other, and made small talk. He seemed to hear us but not be listening.

When it had been time to leave, Miranda kissed us both with tears in her eyes. I declined Nolan's offer of a ride home and walked instead,

preferring the company of the street. It was midevening when I sauntered down Gaston. The concrete and asphalt held the heat of the day
like boulders in the desert and soon the sweat dripped down my back. I
walked past the bars and the *vatos* loitering about, past the dilapidated
apartments with the soft-spoken families of Vietnamese refugees sitting
outside in the humid evening, past the occasional hooker plying her
trade, past everything that makes up my neighborhood, my home that
is the colorful little slice of East Dallas. The air smelled of charcoal fires,
car exhaust, and the faint traces of alcohol coming from the small knots
of people passing the evening hours with a twelve-pack of discount-
brand beer. The precise angles of the illuminated skyline, pristine and
cold against the blankness of the night sky, provided a stark contrast to
the warmth and humanity along the street.

Along the way I stopped at a taqueria and ate two carne asada tacos,
washing them down with more Tecates than I cared to admit. I left the
last one half empty, and stumbled the rest of the way home, daring anybody to get in my way. The pedestrian traffic gave me wide berth, leery
of the mumbling, drunken Anglo. Somehow I managed to feed the dog,
and make it to bed, sleeping fully clothed on top of the covers, pistol
next to me.

I jolted myself out of last night and into this morning as I almost
slammed into Delmar when he slowed for a curve. As it was, I managed
to spill the last quarter inch of tepid coffee from the cup between my
legs onto my lap. It left a nice, brown stain in the crotch of my starched
khakis. Now I was going to be a well-dressed but soiled pigeon shooter
in my lizard-skin boots, khakis, and black T-shirt. The footwear was already starting to pinch. I hate cowboy boots and only wear them for occasions such as this. I'm not a cowboy, why pretend? I shifted in the
leather seat and that made the bandaged flesh wound on my thigh itch.
To take my mind off it, I dabbed at the tears in my eye from the pancake
makeup Nolan provided to cover my bruise. Look out world, here I
come—pissed off and crying.

Nolan fidgeted in the passenger seat. "How much longer?"

I threw the empty coffee cup in the backseat. "This is my first trip. I'll let you know when we get there." I looked at the crude map Delmar had scribbled earlier, in case we got separated on the way down. We shouldn't be more than a few minutes away from the CenTex Paloma Club, the site of the tournament. *Paloma* means "pigeon" in Spanish.

We passed a bunch of cows standing in the shade of a mesquite grove, then an old farmhouse. Decades of exposure to the raw elements had reduced the structure to little more than a wooden skeleton, grayed to the color of old concrete, roofless and held together by a layer of dirt. Farther on lay the remains of a similar house, the wood structure long since gone, leaving only a crumbling brick chimney pointing heavenward, a mute testimony to whoever had lived, loved, and dreamed there. The land was partially wooded; post oaks and scrub trees dotted the open pastures. More abandoned buildings swept by, interspersed with the occasional occupied structure denoted by the presence of a pickup or two.

"I hate the country," I said.

Nolan had turned on the radio and was fiddling with the buttons. "Huh?"

"The country, I hate it. Too much wide-open space. Not enough places to eat or get a drink. Too many cows."

"Uh-huh." She found a station playing something twangy, about a guy named Earl and his cheating wife. "Whatever you say." Her feet tapped in time to the music.

We rounded another curve and saw Delmar pull across a cattle guard, onto a caliche road. Two men in hats and jeans guarded the entrance gate. He handed them something and they waved him through. At our turn, I gave the man a slip of green paper that Delmar had given me that morning, an invitation with today's date printed on it.

The man smiled and let us in. I followed Delmar's cloud of dust down the road. The white gravel surface was long and winding, and we passed cows, live oak trees, mesquite trees, more cows, some horses, and a creek before we turned past a stand of cedars and hit a parking area. I parked between a Lexus sport-utility vehicle and a Range Rover that still bore the dealer tags. Delmar parked on the other side of the lot, next to a black, three-quarter-ton Suburban with a group of people clustered around the back end, all of them fussing with shotguns.

I opened the door of the Mercedes and stepped out, into a fresh pile of cow manure. Nolan came around to see what I was cussing about.

She pointed to my foot. "You stepped in cow shit."

I paused for a moment and calmed my breathing. "Yeah. I see that." I grabbed a small branch and started scraping off the offensive material. "Why don't you get the shotgun out of the trunk." She muttered something under her breath and went to the back of the car. By the time she returned I had cleaned off most of the manure.

In addition to the car and the invitation, Delmar had provided a shotgun for me to carry around. It was a Beretta double gun, luxury grade, and I was afraid to ask how much it cost. It had gold inlays on the receiver and two polished blue twelve-gauge barrels that were as long as a broom handle. They were thirty-two-inchers, Delmar had explained, the preferred length for pigeons as well as sporting clays. I figured if you didn't want to shoot them, you could always uses the barrels as a swatter. I cracked open the shotgun and slung it over my shoulder, mimicking the other men who wandered about. Delmar was nowhere to be seen. Per our arrangement, we were on our own.

The first two shotgun blasts startled us, making us both reach for our pistols at the same time. The sound came from the other side of the clubhouse. A few seconds later a gray-speckled pigeon flew overhead, circling before coming to roost in the larger of the two live oaks shading the parking lot.

"Score one for the birds," I said. "Let's go inside, see if we can find the Big Man."

The clubhouse was built from wood and stone, and had originally been a home. It had since been added onto, long, low wings coming off either side, sheltered by the overhanging trees. We entered into a small reception area, which opened up to a glass-walled room that ran the length of the building. Oriental rugs covered the hardwood floors, and the walls that weren't glass were wood-paneled and tastefully decorated with what appeared to be original oil paintings. Dead animals were the predominant artistic theme. Clusters of leather easy chairs dotted the room, all of them looking out onto two circular grassy areas, each delineated by an eighteen-inch-high wrought iron fence.

The fenced area was manicured to a lush, verdant sheen, and except for the concrete walkway jutting into the middle, resembled nothing so much as a putting green. It didn't take long to figure out that the walkway, striped with yardage markers, served as a handicap system. The better shooters stood farther back. The object of their attention was the lowly *pigeonus commonus,* which popped out unannounced from one of a half dozen boxes embedded in the ground at the far end of the ring. After a few more minutes we deciphered the rules of the game—kill the pigeon before it leaves the ring. The sport was brutal and left a sour taste in the back of my throat.

I set the Beretta down in one of the wooden gun racks provided. Nobody had said anything to us, no challenges to our presence, and I felt stupid toting around the long-barreled weapon. The bar that sat against one of the back walls was doing a big business, considering the early hour. Nolan and I sidled to the far end where an urn of coffee simmered. We helped ourselves to a cup and then wandered the rest of the clubhouse.

The place was full and I couldn't begin to guess how many people were there, fifty or sixty or more. Excluding the handful of women present, all of them were white, middle-aged men. Lots of gold watches and soft bellies. The accents indicated wide geographic representation. Except for the incessant sound of guns firing from outside, we might as well have been in the card room at the country club.

"What's the predominant personality type here?" I took a sip of coffee.

"Sadistic, maybe." A shotgun fired twice so fast it sounded fully automatic. Another bird went down.

"This is like a dogfight but the people are better dressed."

"You go to those often?" Nolan said.

"All the time." I kept my voice deadpan.

"There's a theory about the spectators at aggressive games. The mob psychology at work legitimizes the individual's—"

"And if I want to hear it, I'll let you know." I put the coffee cup down at the same time as Fagen Strathmore moved where we could see him. As the tallest person there he was hard to miss. He was standing at the far end of the second wing, talking to Delmar. Evidently they had just concluded their deal because they laughed and shook hands. Strathmore held a shotgun over one shoulder. He slapped Delmar on the back and then turned, pointing to another table.

I caught a glimpse of the Big Man's face. Even from across the room, his presence was palpable; the power in his eyes felt like a beam of raw energy, sweeping the entire place. He was in his midsixties, tall and still rail thin except for a tiny paunch that his navy double-breasted sport coat hid well. He wore a golf shirt underneath that and a pair of gabardine slacks that broke just so over the tops of his exotic skin boots. I couldn't tell what they were made from, probably bald eagle, maybe albino tiger. The person Strathmore had pointed to at the next table, a short, pudgy dumpling of a man with a ten-inch cigar growing out of one side of his mouth, waddled over and handed Delmar an envelope. The man's cowboy hat was as big around as a wagon wheel and he looked like Boss Hogg from *The Dukes of Hazzard*. Delmar examined the contents and smiled. He shook the man's hand and walked out, ignoring us.

Fagen and the pudgy man sat down and began to examine the shotgun. There were two empty seats at their table. I slid into one and Nolan took the other. Nolan looked good: pretty and fresh in tight black Wrangler jeans and a western-styled beige silk blouse that showed just enough cleavage. I looked like the out-of-place burnout I was: a fifty-cent ham sandwich in a world of twenty-dollar steaks, an angry and cynical private eye who was old enough to know better but young enough to still enjoy pissing off people. In boots that pinched.

Not surprisingly, Fagen Strathmore chose to ignore me and talk to Nolan. "How're you doing, little lady?" He appeared confused as to why we had sat down at his table, but not alarmed. His voice was deep and masculine; the twang of the Texas Gulf Coast combined something from the south, all of which was filtered through what sounded like a mouthful of gravel. The accent did not match the clothes.

"I'm fine," Nolan said, her voice warm and inviting. "Nice fire stick you got there." She pointed to the new gun resting on his lap.

Boss Hogg frowned at her and then spoke before Strathmore could respond. "This here's that ole boy from Orlando I was telling you about." He waved his cigar toward the window where a man in a leather shooting vest stood midway down the concrete walkway, preparing to shoot. The boy from Orlando was about fifty and wore enough gold jewelry to start a rap band.

Fagen said something I couldn't catch. He pulled a hundred-dollar bill out of his pocket and slapped it down on the table. Boss Hogg said you're on and put down a matching note.

The boy from Orlando squared off and loaded his gun, facing the line of boxes at the other side of the ring. He shouldered the weapon and pointed it toward the middle of the line. We couldn't hear because we were inside, but he must have called for the release of the target because a pigeon popped out of the box second from the right. Even a novice like myself recognized that he'd gotten an easy target: a fat, gray-black bird, hovering about ten feet above the ground, undecided as to where to fly. One quick blast put the target down in a cloud of feathers, a couple of feet from where it had started.

The man reloaded while a Hispanic-looking kid dashed across the field and scooped up the carcass of the dead bird. He snatched it on the run and threw it into a garbage can outside the ring. Kind of like a ball boy at a tennis match. Only much different.

Boss Hogg moved to pick up the money but Fagen put down two more bills and said, "Double or nothing?"

"You're on." The chubby man pulled out his money.

The recently deceased bird must have radioed back to his compatriots about the danger that lay ahead because the next bird screamed out of the box like it had a Roman candle up its ass. It flew straight at the Orlando shooter and surprised him, throwing his aim off. He hit the bird but not enough to kill it. There was a short, quick spray of feathers and the target flew out of the ring, counting as a loss. It wobbled, wings not functioning properly, and flew straight into the window in front of where we sat. The pigeon hit the glass with a thud and slid down, leaving a smear of blood.

Strathmore pocketed the money then held the gun up for us to see, balancing the butt on his thigh. "So you like shotguns, huh?"

"I like things that go bang." Nolan smiled and smoothed a nonexistent wrinkle down the side of her blouse, drawing everyone's attention to her chest.

Strathmore was silent for a few moments, then: "Uh . . . yeah. This is a pretty one, just bought it, as a matter of fact." He rubbed his hand on the forearm, the grain of the wood swirling into a creamy chocolate pattern that had been polished to a high gloss. "I particularly like the engraving on the receiver." He put the gun on the table so we could get a better view.

The metal on the side of the firearm was burnished to a high luster and inlayed with gold. A rendition of a reclining nude woman stretched along the length of the receiver. The image was a frontal shot, with her head tossed back, hiding her face. The likeness was very detailed. Very.

"That's as pretty as a picture, ain't it?" Boss Hogg decided to get in on the fun. "I don't believe I've had the privilege." He pulled off his

Stetson and held out a handful of stubby, sweating fingers. "Name's James Ethridge Snodgrass. Mah friends call me Jimmy."

Nolan introduced herself and shook hands. I did the same.

Jimmy turned to the Big Man sitting next to him. "And this is my friend and bidness associate, Mr. Fagen Strathmore."

Strathmore greeted us each by name and shook hands. His fingers were as long and thin as Jimmy's had been short and fat. He gripped my hand and bobbed it twice, cool and firm. He lingered over Nolan's touch, smiling at her and making eye contact. His eyes were trouble—deep, blue, and penetrating; they sucked at the marrow of your being, drew you in like a tractor beam.

"Nolan O'Connor," Strathmore said. "That's an interesting name, but you don't look Irish. Tell me about it." Jimmy Snodgrass and I weren't even at the table anymore, it was just the two of them.

"Not much to tell. It's just a name." Nolan's voice took on a sultry quality, and she fluttered her eyelashes a lot. I wondered where this was going. On the ride down she'd wanted a plan, for each of us to play a role and to work some sort of an information con. I favored a more direct route: just ask the man some questions and see what developed.

I decided to get us back on track. "Tell me about your gun."

"You like guns too, son?" The word *son* had the barest beginning of condescension in it.

"Yeah. I like guns."

He stroked the wooden stock. "This is a Perazzi. That's an Italian make. Same as that Beretta you carried in a little bit ago." Score one for Fagen Strathmore and his eyes that didn't miss even the tiniest detail.

"Wanna sell it?" Score zero for me with a weak comeback.

Jimmy Snodgrass snorted. "Shit, boy, he just bought it. Not ten minutes ago."

"So it's not for sale?" I said.

Strathmore had been about to say something else to Nolan, but instead turned to address me. He fixed his full attention my way, a penetrating gaze that gave me just a taste of why he was an extremely wealthy and powerful individual. "Oh, it's for sale. It just depends on what the deal is." His voice was calm and deadly serious, and had lost all traces of cornpone.

"How much do you want for it?" I said.

"I asked you first, what deal do you have in mind?"

I shrugged. "I don't know what kind of deal you want. I just want to know how much money for the gun."

He smiled at me but it wasn't friendly. "I don't care about the money, son. Money's just for keeping score. The deal's what I'm interested in." His voice remained quiet.

"I don't have any deal, just money."

"Then I'm not interested. I got enough of that."

A Mexican guy in a tuxedo walked by carrying a tray of drinks. Fagen Strathmore signaled to him and ordered four Bloody Marys. I didn't know if they were all for him or if we each got one. He hadn't asked.

"So, sugar, tell me what brings you to our little club way out here in the middle of nowhere."

Nolan got out a cigarette and tapped it on the tabletop, while looking around the room. She sighed. "Boredom, I guess. There's only so much to do in the city. It's the same people and the same places. I'm sure you know how it is." She put the cigarette in her mouth and waited.

Strathmore pulled out a Dunhill lighter that could double as a cutting torch and lit her smoke. "It never gets boring around here. Especially with someone like yourself in attendance."

Nolan fluttered her eyelids and started to reply when she was interrupted by a presence looming over the table.

It was blond and female, and held a half-empty martini glass. "What. The fuck. Is going on here?"

She stood behind Strathmore, hands on her hip, wearing a short, black skirt and a sleeveless denim top. I gathered from her stance and his reaction that they were together. Tall and lingerie-model pretty, she looked to be in her mid-thirties. Her breasts were obvious upgrades, D-cups that appeared as moveable and pliant as Mount Kilimanjaro. Diamonds and gold and other shiny things bobbled off her like candy canes on a Christmas tree. The legs belonged to a professional athlete or dancer, not an ounce of anything extra and curved in all the right places. The expression on her face belonged to a dental hygienist I used to date right about the time she found me in a compromising position with her second cousin, a Miss Waco runner-up.

"Hello, Corrine." Strathmore kept his composure. "Where you been?"

"Don't you 'hello, Corrine' me, you bastard," the woman said. "I've been talking to your fucking worthless son, Roger, trying to get some fucking opera tickets out of him so I can take the girls from bunco to see that goddamn Spanish faggot everybody's raving about." The movement was subtle but I noticed that the three of them—Jimmy, Strathmore, and Corrine—collectively rolled their eyes at the mention of Roger.

Strathmore fiddled with the lighter, spinning it around in his hand. "Let me handle Roger. I pay for all that damn artsy shit anyway. I'll get your tickets."

"Damn right you'll handle Roger." Corrine took a swallow of her drink and turned her attention to us, specifically Nolan. "And who are you, darling? I don't believe we've met." She placed a hand on her taut bosom and gasped. "And however do I love your top. I've heard such wonderful things about the couture section at Wal-Mart. Or did you get that at Target?"

Nolan kept cool. "Well, hello to you too. We were having just the most delightful time visiting with your father here." She pointed her cigarette at Strathmore, who looked like he had all the paternal instincts of a foreign exchange student moonlighting as a sperm donor.

Some signal passed between Strathmore and Jimmy because the latter popped to his feet and began murmuring to Corrine, a soft tone, sooth-ing. Before I knew it, he had her by the hand and was leading her out. As she walked away she scratched at something on the back of her neck, us-ing her middle finger. Classy.

"That was my wife. She's feeling poorly, you'll have to excuse her." The Bloody Marys arrived and we each got one. Fagen took a drink and smiled. "Now where were we?"

I drained half of mine. "You were just about to tell me about the building on Gano Street you're trying to lease and why it was the last place that a guy name Charlie Wesson was seen before he ended up dead in a crack house." I took another sip. "Thanks for the drink, by the way."

Strathmore didn't scare easily. He ignored me and spoke to my part-ner. "Darling, who is this guy?"

Nolan blew a plume of smoke across the table. "Tell us about Char-lie Wesson. Tell us why someone would want to kill him."

Strathmore finished his drink and stood up. "I'm going to leave now." The smile never left his face. "Say, you two never said who your host was for today. Or are you members here?"

I leaned back in my chair and did my best to look relaxed. "We're here as guests of Mr. Coleman Dupree."

That was the money shot. Strathmore sat back down and took a sip of his empty drink, ice clinking against ice. The smile never left his lips, but his eyes told a different story. "What is it you want?"

"I want to know who killed Charlie Wesson."

"I don't know any Charlie Wesson."

"Charlie Wesson knew who you were. He came over to see you, the Big Man, at the building on Gano Street on Monday afternoon. He wanted to meet you."

"I wasn't at any building on Gano Street. I haven't been down there in years."

Nolan leaned forward and put her cigarette out. "That's funny then. If you weren't at the building, then how come there's a picture of you there?" I smiled. I was about to say the same thing but she beat me to it. It was a bluff, of course, but he didn't know that.

Real poker players don't blink. They often get a thin trickle of sweat down the side of the hairline, but they don't blink. A pinprick of moisture meandered its way down Strathmore's temple, but his eyes held steady.

"I don't know this Wesson fellow or Coleman Dupree."

"Dupree's an entrepreneur, like you. Sure you don't know him?" I smiled and took another slug of my drink.

"No. I don't know who he is. And the only time anybody took my picture recently was at city hall, last week. I was with the mayor and the city council. And the chief of police." He enunciated the last very carefully, making sure I caught the implied threat in every syllable. "Some award, the council was giving me. Lots of folks from South Dallas there; maybe this Dupree fellow was one of them."

I smiled. "How do you know Coleman Dupree is from South Dallas?"

"Well, I—" He started to say something but stopped, aware of his gaffe. The eyes, the gaze that launched a thousand office buildings, clouded, just for a moment. Even the Big Man made mistakes.

"Hmm." I scratched the side of my head. "Wonder what the mayor and chief of police would think about that?" I quit talking when I saw Strathmore start to grin. Something cold and metallic poked in my ear and I heard the hammer cock back on a revolver.

"Now then, I think it's a good idea if you two left," Strathmore said. People moved about in front of us, walking, talking, and watching shooters blast pigeons outside. I guessed that somebody with a gun stuck in his ear wasn't that big of a deal at the CenTex Paloma Club.

Strathmore started talking again. "It would probably be best if you two forgot about me and this Coleman Dupree fellow and that other guy . . . you know, the dead one." He stood up and threw the shotgun over his shoulder. His sport coat shifted and I could see the pistol he carried on his right hip. "And one more thing. If somebody has done something stupid like some techno-computer bullshit and made me look like I'm in a picture with some fucking crack dealer, it would probably be best if that picture and all the negatives were to disappear."

I started to say something about how if it were a computer picture there wouldn't be any negatives, but I thought better of it. The gun barrel left my ear and Jimmy Snodgrass came into view, a shooting vest draped over his right forearm keeping the pistol out of sight. "Get out. Now."

Nolan and I stood up and left.

CHAPTER SEVENTEEN

No one accosted us on the way out, no more guns stuck into ears or up our asses or anywhere else, no shots fired or anything. Fortunately, I remembered to grab Delmar's shotgun off the rack. I'd rather face Coleman Dupree, Jimmy Snodgrass, and the hired guns from yesterday than Delmar had I forgotten his Beretta. I stowed the weapon in the trunk of the Mercedes and navigated my way through growing throngs of cars now crowding the parking area. Nolan tapped me on the elbow and pointed out a black Cadillac sport-utility vehicle parked to one side of the clubhouse. The license plate read STRATH1.

She said, "Bet that's Fagen's car, whaddya think?"

"Uh-huh. Wonder what sweet little Corrine drives?"

Nolan looked back at the clubhouse. "Probably a broom. With leather seats and a CD changer."

I squinted at the bumper stickers plastered on the back of the Caddy. You can learn a lot about somebody by what they put on their car. Back when I had a car, before it got shot up, I didn't have any stickers. I don't want anybody knowing anything about me.

Fagen Strathmore struck me as a play-the-cards-close-to-the-vest kind of guy so I was surprised when I saw the half dozen on the rear of his truck. In addition to ones for the local country radio station and a pro-business congressional candidate, there was one that read "The Trinity Vista—the time for tomorrow is today." It sat next to a Texas Hunting Association sticker.

Trinity Vista . . . there was that name again.

Nolan poked me in the ribs. "Uh, I think we'd better get going."

I looked up. Jimmy Snodgrass stood on the back steps, shading his eyes from the sun with one hand, pointing at us with the other. Two men stood on either side of him. Very large and mean-looking men. They started toward us with an ass-kicking look on their faces.

I threw the car into drive, punched the accelerator, and fishtailed it out of the parking lot, throwing a cloud of gravel all over them and Fagen Strathmore's shiny truck. We burned down the caliche road and blew past the men at the front gate. I pointed the star of Daimler Benz toward the interstate and drove.

After a few miles we came to a section of land with no trees, just endless acres of milo and alfalfa as green as Ireland, growing tall under a cloudless sky. The massive irrigation sprinklers used to supplement Mother Nature's output looked like aluminum toothpicks caught between the endless blue horizon and the emerald earth. I punched the accelerator on the Benz, and the car lunged forward. The carpet of vegetation became a blur. A few more miles whizzed by before a flashing stoplight in the distance caused me to slow down.

We stopped at the intersection of two no-name farm-to-market roads. There was nothing there, except for a couple of trees and dirt and an ancient aluminum travel trailer. A blackened smoker stood nearby, next to a couple of faded picnic tables underneath the shade of a live oak tree. A hand-painted sign on the trailer said "Bobby's Bobby-Que— the Best in Navarro County."

Nolan started shaking her head even before I pulled into the dirt parking area. "Nope, no, uh-uh. Don't even think about. I am not eating there. Bet they've never even heard of a health inspector."

I tried for humor. "Maybe they have squab on the menu today."

"I've seen enough dead pigeons."

I hopped out of the car. "It's a perfect day for a little rural al fresco dining experience."

Nolan reluctantly followed. The aroma of slow-cooked meat wafted over us, tangy and smoky. I ordered two blue plate specials—brisket and ribs, pinto beans and coleslaw on the side—and two Dr Peppers. The meat was so tender you could cut it with a harsh word. Nolan finished before I did.

We didn't talk much on the way back. I thought about Coleman Dupree and Fagen Strathmore and what the next move should be. I thought about Vera Drinkwater getting ready to bury her little brother. I thought about a lot of things, and came to conclusions on none of them.

At the Dallas County line, some idiot had rammed a Trans Am into an Isuzu. Both cars had flipped, taking out two of the four lanes and backing up traffic for miles. While we puttered along Nolan told me the story of her elderly Cadillac Eldorado and how that came to be her sole means of transportation. The tale began with a former Houston call girl named Penelope, Nolan's ex-husband, and a South Texas gun runner for one of the El Paso drug cartels. It ended with Nolan fleeing north one night in her second cousin's Caddy. Her usually immaculate Toyota Camry was full of blood and brain matter from the El Paso shooter and the hooker. The bullets used to kill them came from the nine-millimeter she'd bought from the SAPD when she'd quit. Her weapon and the ex-husband who had begged to borrow the car allegedly for a job interview were nowhere to be found. Old friends on the force suggested she might want to head out of town for a while since the cartels had started to operate with impunity far north of the border and the dead gunman was a grand-nephew to the head of the El Paso branch. Just to be safe. Hence the quick trip to Dallas. Things would cool down once they ran the ex to ground, they assured her.

I nodded at the appropriate times but made no comment, impressed with her coolness over the whole affair and more than a little miffed that my partner had not thought to tell me any of the details. I tried to blame that on the pain medication for his cancer.

When we arrived back at the office it was late afternoon. I wanted to ask Davis about the Trinity Vista but he was gone. I shuffled into my office and sat down, pondering the next move. Nolan disappeared into the kitchen and returned with a sixteen-ounce Miller High Life Genuine Draft and two avocado green water glasses. She split the beer and handed me one of the tumblers.

"It's Saturday night," she said. "You got big plans?"

"See Ernie for a while. Then a pizza and HBO probably. What about you?"

"The same." She took a sip of beer. "I need to look for a place to rent."

"You here permanently, even if they catch your ex-husband?"

She shrugged but didn't reply.

"Why?"

"What do you mean?"

"San Antonio's your home." I drank half my eight ounces of beer in one swallow. It was cold and warming at the same time and felt great. "You leaving town because of him?"

"I'm just leaving. Okay?" She drained her glass, set it down, and stared out the window. After a few moments she started talking: "The hostage negotiator for the SAPD is a fat lush name Vinnie Decambra. Vinnie could talk the pope into turning tricks on the west side if he wanted to. He was that good."

I nodded but didn't say anything.

"So one day a few months ago the SWAT team gets a roll-out,

hostage situation. Only problem is Vinnie is getting drunk with a beautician he sees on the side, at a bar across town. Since it's on the sly he's turned off his cell phone and beeper. Of course the backup guys are at Quantico doing some new training thing."

I said, "And that left you?"

She nodded. "I'd had some luck with a sociopath who was killing hookers. Pegged his next location. To the brass that makes me a negotiator."

"They're completely different things." I shook my head.

"No shit." Nolan covered her eyes with one hand, her voice so low it was hard to understand. "A speedfreak was holed up in his apartment with his common-law wife and their three-year-old little boy. Guy's convinced he's got ants coming out of his skin. All he's got is an old thirty-two and a pocketknife."

"What happened?" I leaned forward in my seat.

She shook her head, still covering her eyes. "I did everything I could, which wasn't fucking much. Had him on the phone saying what you're supposed to say when he decided the ants were in his son. So he slits his little boy down the middle, looking for the bugs. We hear the screaming and everybody rushes in."

"The child? Did he . . . ?"

She looked across the desk at me but her eyes were somewhere else. "I got to him first. His intestines are laying on the floor, on this filthy carpet, and he's crying for his daddy, why were they arresting his daddy. He died with his guts in my hand, me trying to shove 'em back in and praying the EMTs get there in time."

"You did what you could, under the circumstances," I said.

"Shut up, Hank."

I fiddled with a stapler lying on the desktop. "Just trying to help."

"You can't."

"I got that message now."

"It's all bullshit, you know."

"What is?"

"Everything." She stood up and crossed the room to the window on the far wall. She didn't say anything for a while. When she turned back around it was like the previous conversation hadn't occurred. We talked for a few more minutes about the course of action: Coleman Dupree or the maintenance man for Aaron Young. But not tonight, I said. We should go to the hospital. Nolan agreed. We decided to take separate cars to visit Ernie. Tomorrow was soon enough to find Coleman Dupree, not today. Little did I know that he would find me.

CHAPTER EIGHTEEN

Back before the first Persian Gulf War, I'd lived in Waco for a while, working for a guy named Frankie Rebozo. Frankie owned a little joint right outside the city limits called Spanky's. The bar was not what you'd call a family place, if you catch my drift. Smoky and dirty, an air of depravity littered the place like cigarette butts at an AA meeting.

Spanky's didn't even have a liquor license, so the girls could dance naked, rather than just topless. For this, you paid a cover charge and a setup fee, and brought in your own alcohol so you could sit at a cramped, wobbly table and watch a strung-out nineteen-year-old with three kids shake her ass to Metallica. The bar was also where I met my ex-wife, Amber, but not in the capacity most imagine.

Frankie hired me as a bouncer. It didn't take much skill or energy, mostly slapping around the Baylor fraternity dipshits who acted like they owned the place, or mixing it up with the drunken day-shift guys from the chicken-processing plant down the road when they got cross-ways and thought that one of the girls really did love them. After a couple of weeks I received an on-the-spot promotion when the manager got stabbed by a redneck kid hopped up on angel dust.

Mother was so proud.

The guy Frankie hired to replace me was a bullet-headed sociopath named Clairol Johnson. Clairol hailed from one of the swampier parts of East Texas, where the double-wides sat hidden beneath the pines and anybody who graduated from high school was called Professor.

I hadn't seen Clairol in over a decade so I was surprised when I bounded out of my house Sunday morning and saw him leaning against the borrowed Mercedes in my driveway. He hadn't changed much; the reddish hair had thinned, the pale face that always looked sunburned or flushed had a few more lines. His hands were the size of grapefruits, and still looked capable of smashing through a car window and pulling a person out. I should know, I'd seen him do it.

"Heya, Hank," he said.

"Hi, Clairol." I transferred my tumbler of coffee to my left hand, keeping my right hand free to grab my piece. I didn't think he was there for a social call.

"What's up?" He hadn't moved, just remained leaning against the car, arms crossed.

"Not much, this and that. How about you?"

He shrugged. "Same shit, different day. I got this new thing going, working up here now. I work for this guy . . . and well . . . he wants to see you."

"Would his name be Coleman Dupree?" I took a stab in the dark.

"Uh-huh."

"And you're here to take me to him?"

"Uh-huh."

"See, Clairol, here's the deal. I'd really like to visit with Coleman, but on my own terms."

Clairol's beady little eyes frowned and I could see the wheels turning. He'd always been a few clowns short of a circus but I was surprised that he hadn't thought it through. Like I was just going to hop in the car with him.

The gravel crunched behind the Mercedes. I had my fingers on the butt of the pistol when a burning sensation like a sliver of the sun hit my leg. My last impression before I hit the ground was of a younger, fatter Clairol standing behind the car, holding a Taser in his hand.

When I was with myself again I was in the backseat of a Lincoln, speeding down Gaston. My arms and legs had duct tape around them. Clairol was driving and his mirror image sat next to him, working the action on my Browning. I rubbed my ankles together and felt the backup .32-caliber still there. With one hand Clairol reached across the seat and bopped his partner's ear. "Put that fucking thing down before you shoot somebody."

The younger, fatter Clairol made a noise that sounded like a donkey trying to pass a kidney stone but put the pistol on the floorboards. He muttered something I couldn't understand, gibberish, and began playing with the switchblade I usually carried tucked in my waistband.

"Don't cut yourself either, dumbass," Clairol said.

Younger, fatter Clairol gurgled to himself and kept flicking the blade.

Clairol looked in the mirror and noticed I was awake. "Sorry about the laser thingie, Hank. Poon gets carried away sometimes."

"Poon?" I said. "What the hell is a Poon?" My left leg felt like a twelfth-degree sunburn.

"He's my kid brother." Clairol pointed to his sibling.

"Your brother is named Poon?" I asked this of the man whose parents had given him the moniker of Clairol after seeing an advertisement for how silky it made your hair.

"Yeah," Clairol said matter-of-factly. "Poon Otis Johnson."

"I see." We drove in silence for a few blocks, the flicking of the switchblade the only sound in the car.

"Where're we going? This isn't any way to greet an old friend, is it?"

"Dupree."

"How about untying me and giving me back my gun first?"

Clairol shook his head. "It don't work that way, Hank, you kno—"

His words were cut off when Poon started to howl. He'd cut himself. Clairol jerked his arm away from the spurting blood and the car swerved. An eighteen-wheeler blasted its horn, as Clairol cussed at Poon and pulled us back into the correct lane. He started digging around in the front seat looking for something. An Oldsmobile loomed ahead, its rear end about to connect with us.

I shouted Clairol's name. He looked up with nanoseconds to spare and tugged the wheel. Tires squealed and horns honked but we missed the Olds.

"Fucking shit," he said. "Quit fucking blubbering, you mush-headed piece of shit." To me he said, "Hank, you got a paper napkin or a towel or something? Poon, he's a bleeding motherfucker, I'll tell you what."

"Got a handkerchief, but I can't really get to it now." I'd been trying to wiggle out of the duct tape but to no avail. If my life wasn't on the line, this would all be real funny.

"Oh yeah," Clairol said. He kept one hand on the wheel and jammed the other one under the seat. He came up with a greasy rag and handed it to his brother. Poon wrapped the dirty cloth around his wound and then turned to look at me. The okra patch of his mind had not gotten the proper amount of water during its formative years. His eyes looked buggy and twitchy. And angry. He gurgled something and his good hand shot to my throat and squeezed. Colored lights began to flash in my head as oxygen drained from my brain.

From a long way away, I heard a series of whopping sounds as some-one said "Dammit, you fuckstain" repeatedly, and the pressure on my throat was released. I wheezed my way back to a semblance of con-sciousness and saw Poon huddled in the far corner of the front seat, whimpering.

"How much farther we got to go, Clairol?" My voice was a croak.

"I don't think you should be in a hurry."

A dozen minutes later I'd hyperventilated myself back to a state nearing normalcy, and we turned onto Harry Hines Boulevard. Poon muttered to himself while Clairol drove the speed limit and sang along with the Eddie Arnold tape he'd popped in a few minutes before.

Harry Hines split the western sector of North Dallas, running north and south, six lanes of vice and commerce catering to the blue collar/immigrant crowd: adult entertainment venues, working-class saloons, and windowless, steel-doored liquor stores peddling Schlitz and Thunderbird. The bottom was a bunch of sleazy motor court motels, hookers, and the hospital district, all enjoying some sort of symbiotic relationship I never quite grasped, at least the hospital part. Next came the Mexican shopping area, a couple of miles of *supermercados*, gigantic flea markets and pawnshops, all advertising *en español*. After that, the Koreans took over with a stretch of cheesy import-export houses, hawking cheap electronics, gold and silver and perfume. Every third place was going out of business.

We wheeled into the parking lot of a dingy strip center located somewhere between Little Monterrey and Koreatown. The building ran lengthwise, perpendicular to the street and back. A tavern called Sue's Easy Times II sat at the front while the back was a topless bar named Roxy's. Clairol pulled to the rear of Roxy's and stopped the car. He tapped the horn and the door opened. Two large black men, both wearing gold chains and running suits, came out and stood guard while Clairol cut the tape off my ankles and wrists. I held my breath as his hands came near my backup piece. He missed it again. When he was finished, they each grabbed an arm and dragged me inside.

If there's anything more depressing than the back entrance to a sleazy topless bar on Sunday morning, let me know. Harsh fluorescent lights, only used during the off hours, lit the joint with an unnatural glow, exacerbating the natural tackiness of a bar that prided itself on being the Home of the Five Dollar Table Dance. The shag carpet on the walls was worn and soiled with things I didn't care to know about. The whole place smelled like a whore's drawers: stale booze and smoke with the faintest aroma of disinfectant. They pulled me through the bar out into the main sitting area. One lone, red open-toed pump with a six-inch heel sat forlornly on the empty stage, a silent witness to the revelries of the previous evening.

The two men plopped me down in a seat midway between the bar and the stage, and retreated to the next table. I was vaguely aware of Clairol and Poon somewhere in the background.

A door, leading to the dancers' dressing rooms, I guessed, opened and out walked Jack "the Crack" Washington. He looked GQ in a three-button dark gray suit with an open-collar navy shirt. A skinny white guy in dirty chinos and a greasy ponytail followed him. From somewhere out of the shadows to the left of the stage a huge mass of flesh waddled out. He got in the lights and I could see he was Asian, Korean probably, wearing a Roxy's sweatshirt. The gathering was a veritable Rainbow Coalition of hoods.

Jack Washington slid into the seat opposite me, drew back his arm, and backhanded me with all he had. My head whipped to one side and I fell over. By the time I had righted myself and gotten back into the chair, Jack had a cigarette lit, resting in one of the ashtrays. Gingerly, I felt my swollen lip where a trickle of blood ran down my chin.

Jack took a drag and laughed. "Boy, you hurt one of my cousins. His mama is pissed off, and so am I."

The Korean and the white guy sat at the next table, opposite where the two guys in running suits were. Everybody but me was smoking. I'd rather have had a cocktail but I didn't want to impose. Instead, I said, "So where's this Coleman Dupree fellow? I've got things to do." I made a great show of looking at my watch.

Jack laughed until he choked. "Shit, boy. Only thing you got to do is cough up what you know and then die."

I had an idea that me dying was part of the plan since nobody had covered his face or hid where we were. My mind goes cold in situations such as these, which allows me to start running through escape possibilities and filtering the current situation through my subconscious.

I began to ease my leg up to get to the .32-caliber backup gun strapped on my ankle, calculating the distance across the table to Washington. Concentrating on slowly moving my leg like that, it took me a few moments to register the sound of a cell phone ringing. One of the running suits, the maroon one, pulled a Motorola out of his pocket and answered. He grunted a couple of times, hung up, and nodded to his partner in the beige running suit. They stood up and began to move tables out of the way, clearing a path to the front door.

The Korean walked to the entrance and opened it with a key on a chain attached to his belt. Sunlight streamed in. Jack Washington's attention faltered for a moment and I pulled the tiny pistol out and palmed it in my right hand. Everybody extinguished their cigarettes.

A short, squat figure appeared in the doorway, hazy and backlit by the midmorning sun. Another person materialized behind the first, much taller and thinner. Together they entered the bar and the door closed.

The woman was tall and pretty, her hair a henna red, wearing a pair of low-slung jeans and a tight black T-shirt, a couple of inches of midriff showing. She pushed the wheelchair carrying Coleman Dupree into the bar, navigating through the path left where the tables had been. They maneuvered to where we were. It was hard to tell much about Dupree, sitting like that. He wore a plain white shirt with an open collar and a baseball hat from the Gap. His skin was the color of watered-down coffee and looked unhealthy, pasty, and drawn. Jack Washington stood up and embraced him, leaning down to place his arms around the man. The white guy with the ponytail came over and shook his hand, as did the two running suits and the Korean thug. It was all so Don Corleone.

Jack Washington moved aside and let the wheelchaired man ease up to the table. Nobody said anything. Coleman waved his hand and the girl sprang to his side. She handed him some sort of inhaler and he took a puff. He held the dispenser in his hands, toying with it, as he took several deep breaths. Finally he turned his attention to me. "So this is the great Lee Oswald. We've only crossed paths here in the last few days but already it seems like an eternity."

I didn't respond, crunching the numbers instead. The Seecamp .32 held seven rounds. Coleman, Jack Washington, the two running suits, and Clairol and Poon. That was six. Then there was the white guy and the Korean. That was eight. Nine counting Dupree's friend, Miss Rent-a-Babe in the skintight clothes. Two would be left standing, assuming I didn't miss. And that the pip-squeak .32 put each one down for the count.

Coleman spun the inhaler around on the lacquered wood of the table. "There's lots of things I'd like to know about you, but over the course of my career, I've learned to prioritize. So we'll start with the most important item first. One of my employees was to store a shipment of merchandise for me at a certain location. He turns up at this location, comatose, with the merchandise and his firearm missing. I believe that you know where that bit of product is."

"I don't know what you're talking about."

Coleman smiled. "After you tell the location to my vice president of security here—I believe you've met Mr. Washington—I'd really like to know what you are up to. Why don't you leave it all alone?" He began to push himself back from the table.

I started to say something to buy some more time when a screech from the end of the bar interrupted me. Everybody turned to see Poon Johnson blubbering and banging his good hand against the Formica countertop. His brother had been trying to clean the wound on his other hand with a bottle of rubbing alcohol.

Dupree spun his wheelchair around. "What the hell's wrong with that fucking cracker?"

Maroon running suit spoke. "Cut himself. With this boy's knife." He pointed to me.

Poon bawled again. Clairol tried to shush him.

Coleman turned to Washington. "Who the hell is that, anyway?"

Jack the Crack shrugged. "Two guys from Waco. He used to work with Oswald. 'Fact, we used him for the snatch this morning."

Coleman wheeled closer to the two men at the end of the bar. "And the younger one?"

"Package deal, I guess," Jack said. "I'll ask their supervisor." He turned to the guy in the beige running suit. "Hey, Supervisor, these crackers a package deal or what?"

"Yeah," the man said, chuckling. "We got the older one, and the younger came along for free."

Coleman had wheeled closer, until he was only a few feet away from the Johnson brothers. "Somebody better tell me this ain't no retard working in my operation."

Beige Running Suit and Jack Washington made a big deal out of not looking at anything in particular. Finally Running Suit spoke. "Jack told me to hire 'em, said we need some more muscle, 'specially with the—"

"Mr. Dupree." Clairol cut off the other man. "It'll be all right. I'll get Poon all cleaned up and we'll be out of your hair in no time." He looked nervously from his boss to his brother, standing at the bar with a towel pressed against his wounded hand.

Jack slapped the table, ignoring Clairol and speaking to his underling. "Shit, niggah, please. You smoking crack again? I never said nothing like that."

Running Suit rolled his eyes and put his hands on his hips. "The hell you talking about, Jack? You told me—"

Coleman Dupree interrupted, his voice rising above that of his squabbling lieutenants. "I don't give a flying fuck who hired what. Get rid of that drooling motherfucker." He smiled and then wheeled back to where I was sitting. "Matter of fact, why don't you clip him. Now. In front of Oswald here. Maybe that'll soften him up a little before you go to work, Jack."

Jack shrugged and made a face that carried all the concern of someone who'd just been told, "Okay, we'll have turkey sandwiches instead of roast beef."

Coleman's woman wheeled him away. When they reached the door, he spun around and faced me again. "You've caused me a great deal of discomfort lately. I'm going to return the favor."

Before I could say anything, Jack "the Crack" Washington stood up and pointed to Poon Johnson. He spoke to Beige Running Suit. "Ice Forrest Gump for me, will ya? I'm saving my strength for Oswald here."

CHAPTER NINETEEN

I decided three of the seven bullets in my mouse gun would go to Jack the Crack. The rest would be doled out on a first-come, first-serve basis.

Beige Running Suit made a move for Poon Johnson, a thin strip of wire dangling from one hand, two wooden dowels at either end. A garotte. Poon's brother had other ideas. Beige Running Suit had taken maybe three steps when a pistol appeared in Clairol's hand. He fired twice into the center of the man's chest. The guy was dead before he hit the floor.

After that, things moved fast but seemed in slow motion. I brought my .32 up to bear on Jack Washington and slapped the trigger twice, as fast as I could. At the same instant, he shoved the table into my diaphragm, throwing my aim off, and drew a Glock, squeezing off two quick rounds at the Johnson brothers.

My first shot went wild, hitting a fire extinguisher across the room, which began to spew white foamy stuff everywhere.

My second shot hit the Korean in the crotch.

Jack fired three or four shots as he ran for cover, including one my way. I felt it whiz by my ear. The ponytail guy grabbed something out of his windbreaker that looked dangerously like a MAC-10, a nasty, street-sweeping pisser of a submachine gun. He swung it toward me and pulled the trigger. Nothing happened. He swore, and began to yank on knobs and levers.

I turned my attention to the bar. Jack Washington and Maroon Running Suit were at one end, the Johnson brothers at the other. Both parties were firing at each other, but to little effect. I ignored the squealing Korean and the swearing machine gun man, and steadied my arm on the upturned table. I aimed at the center of Washington's torso, took a deep breath and carefully squeezed the trigger. My efforts were rewarded by a dead-solid, perfect graze on the shoulder of Maroon Running Suit. He swatted at his shoulder like it was a mosquito bite and stepped away from the cover of the bar for a moment. Someone from the Johnson end nailed him in the chest.

Jack Washington leapt over the bar at the same time as the guy with the machine gun got his piece working.

An angry hornet's nest of nine-millimeters exploded as I ducked. Bullets flew everywhere as it became apparent that Machine Gun Man did not know much about that particular firearm. He sprayed the entire room, floor to ceiling. Glass and lights and breakable shit rained down, blanketing the whole place. Gloom descended as the fluorescents overhead broke, and the only illumination came from the exit lamps over the two doorways.

The gun jammed or the clip emptied and silence rang in the air. I thought about peeking from behind the upturned table where I was hiding. Someone moaned. From across the room I heard Jack Washington calling me. "Hey, Oswald."

I didn't reply.

"Hope you like fire. Because hell's getting ready for your ass."

I had the sensation of something flying over my head, and then there was a breaking sound. Flames spread out along the wall.

Molotov cocktails.

Washington was using the liquor behind the bar to make the bombs.

He was nothing if not resourceful. Another bottle followed the first and I could feel the heat now. Still kneeling, I slid a chair toward the front door, pushing it hard enough to knock over several others. Washington fired two rounds at the movement and threw another whiskey grenade. I kept my head low and slithered the opposite way, toward the back entrance. Flames engulfed half the bar now. The plastic and carpeting started to melt, emitting a harsh, chemical smell.

The machine gun began working again, better controlled this time. It raked the upturned table where I'd been. A wasp stung the calf of my left leg. I peered through the forest of table and chair legs and saw I was even with the Johnson end of the bar. They were nowhere to be seen but still around because there were another half dozen shots fired from each end of the room.

I stuck my head up for a quick peek and was rewarded with a glimpse of thick smoke and dancing flames, punctuated by the occasional muzzle flash. The Korean was screaming again. I ducked as another bottle jetted over the bar toward the main stage. It broke at the back of the runway and spread flames into the area backstage.

I had just started to crawl toward the exit when Lucifer himself upchucked in the form of a blast from the dancers' dressing area. The walls shook like there had been an earthquake. Sunlight streamed in as the roof on the front half of the club collapsed in a mass of flames. A gust of muggy air stoked the fires as the smoke threatened to overcome my lungs. With my last bit of energy I dashed for the back door.

I hit it on the run, with my shoulder, and mercifully it opened without a protest, dumping me in a heap on the dirty asphalt. I saw blue sky and took a breath of sweet, beautiful, clean air.

Then I passed out.

When I opened my eyes again, I was back where I had started the day, the rear seat of Clairol Johnson's Lincoln. This time there wasn't any duct tape around my arms and legs and only Clairol sat in the front seat. We were in the alley behind the inferno that used to be the strip center housing Roxy's. My hand still clutched the tiny .32.

Fire engines blocked our access to Harry Hines. Cars and people from the Mexican flea market down the street stopped our alley escape. We sat and watched the firefighters battle the blaze. That nasty house fire smell lingered over everything.

My calf itched and I scratched it. Blood covered my hand. I started to ask Clairol for a rag but thought better of it. Instead I rolled up my jeans leg and examined the wound. The bullet had passed through the muscle part of the calf cleanly, more than a graze but not much more. No major damage. I pulled a handkerchief out of my pocket and bandaged the wound as best I could. I was getting sick of dodging bullets.

I'd been back in the world of consciousness for a couple of minutes now and Clairol still hadn't said a word. I leaned forward and spoke to him. "Where's Poon?"

He pointed to the blazing building. "In there. He took one in the throat, right at the end." Other than a slight tremor, his voice was blank, no emotion whatsoever at the death of his brother.

"Sorry." What else was there to say. Poor Poon.

Clairol grunted and then was quiet. After a few moments he said, "We need to get out of here." Another fire truck pulled up, followed by a police unit.

I agreed wholeheartedly and said, "Let's head down the alley, see if we can ease around all the people."

Clairol didn't say anything. He stuck the key in the ignition and cranked it. And cranked it again. And one more time. He slumped his shoulders. "The car won't start."

"Yeah." I nodded my head slowly. "I can see that. Gonna be a problem."

"Uh-huh." He removed the key and twirled the chain around one finger.

I sighed and tightened the makeshift bandage on my leg. "I guess we're gonna have to walk."

"Yep. You want your gun back?"

I said yeah and he handed me back my Browning. We both got out of the car. He went to the trunk and got another pistol out. "Lost my piece in there." He stuck a .45 in his waistband. Together we headed down the alley, toward the flea market. I tried not to limp.

Hacking up God-knows-what out of my lungs, bleeding from the calf and lip, I entered the back of the *mercado*, Clairol following close behind. The place was a riot to the senses, a whirlwind of sights and smells and sounds: piñatas and brightly colored clothing hanging from the ceiling, chiles roasting, tamales cooking, people bargaining with one another in Spanish.

My head ached and I began to grow dizzy. From somewhere up ahead came the smell of baking bread. We turned a corner and found a *panaderia*, a Mexican bakery. I stumbled in and ordered a cup of coffee and a *pan de huevo*. The coffee was thick and syrupy, almost espresso. The sweet bread was sugared and chewy from the egg-based dough. The sugar and caffeine amped me up and my head started to feel something approaching normal.

Clairol finished his second sopaipilla and took another slug of Coca-Cola. He burped and said, "How the hell are we gonna get out of this mess?"

I choked on the last sip of coffee. "We? What's this *we* shit? You gotta mouse in your pocket?"

"Well, I just figured that we're sort of in this together and—"

"And nothing. If you hadn't kidnapped me this morning, then none of this would have happened." I stood up to leave.

"Sorry, Hank." Clairol got up also, hovering around where I was trying to walk. "I didn't know it was gonna be like that. I thought you'd tell 'em what they needed to know and everything would be cool."

"Try not to think anymore."

Clairol chewed on his lip for a moment. "B-b-but now they're gonna be after me. I mean they're coming after both of us now, after what just went down."

"Welcome to my world." I walked back out into the teaming mass of humanity. Clairol followed and together we threaded our way through the shoppers. I headed for the front door, without much of a plan. I wanted to get away from the flea market, get somewhere safe and regroup. I figured to call Nolan once I got outside. I'd see what kind of police presence there was, and get her to pick me up.

Two men wheeled a refrigerator out of a stall up ahead so we stopped. We were in front of a place selling roosters, the proprietor an old man with long, gray hair. He was petting his critters and making them squawk so I didn't hear what Clairol said at first.

He tapped me on the shoulder. "Don't you want to know, Hank? Huh?"

"Know what?" Foghorn Leghorn cock-a-doodle-doo'ed in my ear.

"Don't you want to know what I know about Coleman Dupree?"

The thought had already crossed my mind that Clairol might have some useful information. Probably not, since he was at the bottom of the food chain, in more ways than one, but maybe. "Okay. Tell me what you know about Coleman Dupree. Where's he stay? Where's headquarters?"

Clairol's beady eyes frowned and he looked from side to side. "Well, uh, I don't know that but—"

"Okay, let's try this one. What about Jack Washington? Where does he work out of?"

"I don't know that either. See, the first time I've ever laid eyes on him was this morning. Don't matter, he's dead."

"He's dead when I can see his body. Otherwise, don't count your bales of hay until they're in the barn."

The blockage in the aisle cleared and we continued on our way. "Well, I know where Marvin worked," Clairol said.

"Who's Marvin?"

"He's the guy that hired me."

Marvin was also the name of the maintenance man for Aaron Young's company, though I didn't mention that to Clairol. I don't like coincidences. We paused our conversation again as we made our way past the electronics stall. Boom boxes blared a wall of *conjunto* music, the accordions that I normally liked grating on my nerves now. When the noise died down, I spoke again. "So Marvin would be the guy that you shot first back there?"

"Uh, yeah."

"Where'd he hang out?"

"This Denny's on . . . the expressway?"

"That's narrowing it down. What expressway?"

Clairol stuck a stubby index finger in his ear and twisted, either scratching something or tweaking the linear amp in his brain. "The north expressway in . . . Richardson." He smiled, evidently proud of himself for remembering.

I figured it out, and it made sense. North Central Expressway in Richardson, which lay on the northwest side, was a gateway into the white-flight suburbs of Plano, Allen, and McKinney. They were separate municipalities, with the small-town values and the schools everybody liked. That's code talking for not a lot of people of color living nearby. That's also a lot of kids with affluent parents. New market share.

I decided to get back to the coincidence. "Ever hear of a guy named Aaron Young?"

Clairol stopped to let a herd of small children sweep by, two tired-looking parents following, loaded down with shopping bags. He spoke out of the side of his mouth. "The real estate guy."

I nodded. The last of the people moved from the aisle and I started walking again.

"We weren't supposed to sell on blocks where he had property."

"Why was that?"

Clairol stepped around a dropped pile of cotton candy. He told me. I tried to process the information but my head hurt and another pile of coal-miner phlegm sputtered out of my mouth.

We'd made it to the front door. The outside was a bigger party than the inside; mariachi bands, more food vendors, and carnival rides dotted the parking lot. A black cloud plumed from the remains of the strip center to our left. Fire engines and police units had blocked Harry Hines completely, making a quick exit difficult if not impossible, even if we had a working car.

We slinked along the outside wall of the place, skirting the edges of the parking lot. Clairol was talking again. "See, Hank, we could go hang out at the Denny's and when one of Coleman's guys comes in, we could snatch him. Then we could make him tell us where the headquarters is. Then we could go and hit the pla—"

"That's not a good idea, Clairol."

"Huh. Why not?"

I stopped walking and felt the swollen part of my lip again. "First of all, they're going to have people watching for us. They know what we look like. Second, I've got something they want. The smart thing to do is to give it to them."

A police cruiser made its way through the crowd, windows down and the two uniforms scanning the herd of people. We turned our backs and examined a stall of Mexican statuary. I hoped they were just looking, not for us in particular.

"Well, we could wait to hear when they're going to do this park thing," Clairol said. "Washington's supposed to be taking care of that himself."

"What park thing?"

"I dunno, I heard Marvin talking about it a couple of days ago. Jack was going to take care of this thing in this park."

"What 'thing'? He supposed to kill somebody?"

"Uh-uh," Clairol said. "Wasn't a clip job. He didn't say. It was this problem he was gonna have to do in the park. Marvin saw me and Poon standing there so he shut up."

"Where?"

Clairol did the thing with his finger in the ear again. He switched to the other side but to no avail. "I dunno. Some park. The problem in the park."

"Keep thinking, maybe it'll come to you." We watched another fire truck race up Harry Hines. I tried Nolan's cell phone. No answer. "While you're studying on that, Clairol, be working on a way for us to get out of here."

"No problem." He smiled like the slow kid at a spelling bee whose first word was *dog* and disappeared into the crowd. I started to stop him but didn't. I guess I was hoping he wouldn't come back. I thought I would make my way to Harry Hines and head south, try to reach Nolan again, or Delmar and Olson.

Clairol came back.

In an early 1980s Chevy pickup, with a Mexican flag hanging in the back. He rolled down the window and said, "Hop in."

"Not a chance." I rubbed my eyes and shook my head, tired to the core all of a sudden. From somewhere deep down, a cough leapt out of my lungs and I spit up something black and carcinogenic-looking. My calf started to ache where the bullet had passed through. "What the hell." I jumped in the passenger seat. The inside of the truck was immaculate, spotless serape seat covers and a carpeted dashboard. A plastic Virgin Mary overlooked everything.

Clairol headed south through the parking lot, jumped the curb at the end, and got to the street from the parking lot of a nightclub called El Conquistador. We managed to miss the owner of the truck, as well as any law enforcement. At my request, he stopped two streets from my house. I opened the door and put one foot on the pavement.

"How'd you know where to find me?" The question was valid. My number was unlisted. The house was registered to a corporation and all the bills came to a post office box.

"Marvin, he had me doing some collection work a couple of blocks over. Saw you turning down this street."

"Anybody else in Dupree's organization know where I live?"

Clairol shook his head.

I got out and stretched. That was a mistake. I felt something give way in my side and my calf started to hurt again.

"Heya, Hank. How do I get in touch with you? You know, in case I hear anything else."

"Preferably not with a Taser." I flipped him a card with my cell phone number on it.

"I'm sorry it got ugly back there." Clairol squinted at the card before stuffing it in his shirt pocket. "What I told you, that'll help, right?"

I shut the door of the old pickup and walked away.

CHAPTER TWENTY

I limped the rest of the way home, dodging cracks in the sidewalk and Mr. Martinez's grandkids playing soccer next door. He sat in a lawn chair in front of the house, in the shade of a willow tree, watching his progeny scurry after the ball. The sun was high in the sky and it was hot. I could feel sweat hit my various abrasions and sting. Mr. Martinez raised his can of Coors to me but made no move to visit. He was a smart man and knew not to ask questions. He'd been to the river and back, walking up to the fringes of this world, the gray area between normal workaday life and the other side, the place where outlaws dwell, the thieves, the hookers, the gamblers, the bad folks like Coleman Dupree. I knew he saw the marks on my face and the limp and decided to keep to his own business. Sometimes I wish I were that smart.

I walked to the front of my home and picked up the Sunday paper, leaning down carefully. When I came back up, Edwin, my neighbor on the other side, stood there. He held an uprooted flower in one hand, the other hand perched on his hip.

He thrust the plant in my face and said, "Look at this." His tone was that of an exasperated parent with a disobedient child.

"Yeah." I tried to keep the anger out of my voice.

"What do you have to say about it?"

I didn't have anything to say since I didn't know what he was talking about.

Edwin smirked. "This is the result of your visitors this morning. Those two men in the Lincoln. They parked on my flowers."

That would be Poon and Clairol, right before they blasted me with nine thousand volts and hauled my ass to the bar on Harry Hines, which subsequently exploded with me in it. I shrugged but didn't say anything.

"Just because you don't plant any color doesn't mean the rest of us shouldn't. Now look at them. Ruined." He pointed to a flower bed in his yard, flush with the curb. It had a tire track in the middle. About half the people on the block had some flowers planted. Everybody but Edwin planted them adjacent to the house, not up against the street, where they might get run over.

I smiled as much as my split lip allowed.

His smirk deepened. He made a tsking sound. "You know the trouble with you is that you have no appreciation for anything aesthetic." He stuck the damaged plant closer to my face and a tiny piece of dirt landed on my chest. "Just look at this, can't you—"

Edwin's harangue stopped with a wheezing sound as my fist wrapped around his throat. He clawed at my fingers.

I pulled him closer. "Edwin. I want you to blink if you can hear me."

Edwin blinked. Lots and lots of blinks, coming as fast as a hummingbird's wings.

"Good," I said. "Now then, here's the deal. Don't ever touch me again. With your finger, with a speck of dirt, with anything at all. Don't even let your breath get on me. Do you understand me, Edwin? Blink if you do."

A blizzard of blinks.

"That's good." I released him with a shove toward his house. "Go sculpt something. It'll make you feel better." He looked at me and started to reply. Instead, he took several deep breaths and stalked back to his front door.

I went around back, let myself in, and checked every door and window in the place, making sure everything was secure. The dog seemed halfway excited to see me so I gave her a Milkbone. I popped open the top of a people Milkbone, an ice-cold Coors Light. The first gulp was so good I decided to share, and poured a half inch into the dog's bowl. Together we finished the beer. I opened another one, took a sip, and left it on the kitchen counter.

Still limping, I went to the basement and opened the safe I kept there. I grabbed another blade, a Benchmade auto this time, and stuck it in my waistband. Next I pulled out a shotgun. It was a Remington pump and kicked like a pissed-off hippo but never failed to fire when I pulled the trigger. Olson had added a magazine extension tube that ran along the bottom of the eighteen-and-a-half-inch barrel so that it could hold eight rounds. I stuffed Winchester double-aught buckshot into its feeding hole until no more would fit. The sling doubled as a bandolero and held another ten shells. I filled it, too. On my workbench, I disassembled the .32 and cleaned it. When I was finished I reloaded it and stuck it back in the ankle holster. I repeated the process with my Browning, even though it was already clean.

My work in the basement was finished. I went upstairs and reexamined all the bolts and locks and other safety measures. I kept the shotgun hung over one shoulder. Jack Washington didn't know where I lived. Yet.

Back in the kitchen I grabbed a strip steak from the freezer and set it on the counter to thaw. Ten ounces of marbled red meat sounded good for lunch. Beer in hand, I went into the office I'd set up in one of the bedrooms. The room was bare except for an old pine table with a Dell desktop and a printer on it. I pulled the drapes and turned on the computer.

While the machine did its thing I drank beer. After a few moments I punched and clicked the right buttons at the right times. Pretty soon the Yahoo! screen appeared. I typed in "Trinity Vista Dallas" and waited. The answer came back in the form of a couple of dozen hits, ranked by relevance.

Everybody and everything has a Web page. Pro–Trinity Vista and anti–Trinity Vista. Pro-Trinity, but anti-Vista. Anti-Trinity, anti-Vista, pro–Area 51.

I clicked and surfed and hyperlinked and the picture became a little clearer. Part of it I knew already, other bits were new. The Trinity River, little more than a slow, trickling puddle most of the time, ran down the middle of a two-mile-wide floodway, between two dirt embankments. The area around the river was flat and grassy. It was also as dry as a Baptist picnic for 95 percent of the year. But get a few days of continuous storms and it soon resembled the Amazon during rainy season. The waterway also split the city of Dallas in two. North and south. For whatever reason, that had turned into the haves and have-nots.

But then a funny thing happened.

Dallas ran out of dirt.

Except for suburbs two counties away, and the occasional vacant tract, the city was full, nowhere else to build. Too bad you couldn't build on all that great river bottom land. Too bad it was floodplain and the structures would wash away.

The person with the original idea was unclear but someone, either a city hall booster or a planner with the U.S. Army Corps of Engineers, had wondered aloud about recovering part of the floodplain of the Trinity. A couple of million dollars in feasability studies later, the answer emerged.

It could be done.

A series of levees and other reclamation projects would net close to a thousand acres of usable land. One thousand acres of prime terra firma, adjacent to downtown and the convention and tourist district, straddling north and south. The developers went apeshit at the suggestion, salivating at the thought of that much land ready to be covered with income-generating structures. Their spinmeisters pushed the notion that except for the large buildings everywhere, it would be an urban greenbelt of sorts, an oasis in the middle of a major metropolitan area.

Then the guys with funny-sounding names and strange accents showed up. The people from the Olympics Committee. The city was still smarting over getting cut from the shortlist for 2012. When the U.S. Olympics officials put out feelers for host cities for the 2020 games at about the same time the Trinity Vista began to appear in the public consciousness, the powers that be realized this was Dallas's one big shot at international respectability.

Place the Olympic Village smack dab in the middle of the Trinity River.

On the official Trinity Vista home page, I found a master plan of the proposed area. The oasis mentioned on the other page was tough to see, what with all the apartments, offices, and retail projects surrounding the Olympic Village. And of course the 100,000-seat stadium dead-center of the project.

I drank the last of the beer and crushed the can. What had Aaron Young called it, a bridge between North and South Dallas? It didn't take much of a real estate whiz to understand that it would be a very valuable bridge.

Which led directly to my next question: Who gets to be in charge of the goose that's going to lay that big, pretty golden egg?

I was fairly sure of the answer but I needed confirmation. The computer hung on a recalcitrant Web page, so I went to the kitchen for another beer while the routers routed and the servers served.

The steak was almost thawed. I got out a bag of salad and another Coors Light. By the time I returned the Internet was again cooperating and the Web page appeared. And I was wrong.

The answer was not Strathmore Realty.

The project was to be under the auspices of a consortium of developers, assuring that everyone got a piece of the pie. There were a couple of different companies for each type of development—office, apartments, and retail. A committee pulled from these groups would implement the Olympic Village. The head of the entire project, the lead developer, had yet to be decided. That position was between two companies.

Click, click.

Strathmore Real Estate.

And the Aaron Young Company.

The lead organization would be in charge and have a hand in every decision and piece of development. There would of course be compensation, by way of a percentage of the rents. More important, though, there would be power and prestige.

And it had come down to Young and Strathmore. More specifically, Aaron Young and Roger Strathmore, Fagen's son. On the Strathmore company's home page, I found a picture of the family scion. He looked like his father but seemed lesser somehow, at least by way of my computer screen. Where Fagen had a prominent jaw, Roger had a slight overbite and a weak chin. His eyes were narrower than his father's, but the nose was the same. I read the accompanying statement regarding the firm's participation in the Trinity Vista project. The document was a panorama of power verbs, words like *thrust* and *triumph* and *dominate*. The term *phalanx of empowerment* appeared four times. According to the text, the fate of Dallas itself hung on the Trinity Vista; the city's status as an economic powerhouse and cosmopolitan center of the arts would wither and fade away if the Vista wasn't developed properly.

I laughed out loud at that one. Cosmopolitan in Dallas was a vodka and cranberry cocktail, not a state of mind. It was something you bought.

Before shutting off the computer, I clicked to the appraisal district Web site and did a search for Roger Strathmore, looking for where his home might be. He lived the good life, a six-thousand-foot estate in

Highland Park, the wealthy island of a town sitting in the middle of Dallas. I wrote down the address. Next I ran Aaron Young's name. Nothing came up. That didn't prove anything, just that he didn't own a house in Dallas County under his own name.

Power off to the computer and I went to the kitchen. Growling sounds came from my stomach and my head felt funny again. Nothing quite like getting shot, Tasered, and almost burned up on Sunday morning to make a body shaky.

I debated the wisdom of another beer but decided that maybe a wee tot of the Scottish Highlands would ease the nerves. I poured two fingers of Cutty Sark into a highball glass, sipping it as I heated up a heavy iron frying pan, dry. When it was hot, I sprinkled the thawed piece of meat with salt and pepper and placed it in the pan.

Smoke and steam shot to the ceiling as the fat in the steak melted into the skillet. Four minutes on each side yielded a perfectly cooked strip steak, pink all the way through. I dumped some olive oil and balsamic vinegar on the lettuce and sat down to eat, another half a finger of scotch in my glass.

Roger Strathmore lived on Miramar Avenue in Highland Park. It would take me about ten minutes to get there. I hoped he didn't have big plans for the afternoon. I wanted to have a visit with him, see what he could tell me about the whereabouts of his father, and maybe a little info on the Trinity Vista. I ate steak and drank scotch. The plate had just gone into the dishwasher when my cell phone trilled. The number was unfamiliar.

"Hello."

Clinking glasses. Laughter. Music in the background. Vera Drinkwater's voice muffled and tipsy sounding: "H-Hank."

"Vera." I sat on the kitchen counter and massaged a previously unidentified ache in my left thigh.

"I'm at the Blue Goose, on Greenville Avenue." The scratch of a lighter paused her voice for a moment. "Woman I work with called. Said to meet her and her boyfriend. He's got a new Hog."

"That's nice, Vera." The Blue Goose was a Mexican restaurant sitting in the middle of a string of bars and eateries. Facing the street was a large patio with built-in misters and fans to keep the heat at bay. Sunday afternoons the place became the semi-official hangout of the biker wannabes, the fifty-something dentists and CPAs wearing leather vests and riding gleaming Harley-Davidsons. They parked their machines in front and sat on the patio, drinking beer, eating nachos, and talking bikes. Vera sounded like she'd skipped the food part and concentrated mainly on the beer.

"Everybody's having a good time," she said. "But my brother's still dead."

I didn't reply.

"Can I come over?" The noise faded and I could tell she was moving. "You're the only person who knew Charlie too."

"Got some stuff to do this afternoon." I slid off the counter. "It's about your brother."

"He was all I had." A car door slammed and the ambient noise stopped. "Where are you now?"

"I'm at home."

"What's the address?"

Don't tell her. "Sycamore Street." I recited the number.

"Where's that?" Automobile ignition noise in the background now. *Don't give her directions.* "Head south on Abrams Road. You'll find it."

She hung up without saying anything else. I washed down two aspirin with the last half inch of scotch, brushed my teeth, and sat down in the living room to wait. Nine minutes later the doorbell rang and Glenda went bonkers. I grabbed the dog and shoved her in the backyard. I returned to the living room and opened the front door.

A wave of heat and humidity rushed in, enveloping the wobbly figure of Vera Drinkwater leaning against the door frame, sunglasses perched on her blond head. She wore a denim skirt that stopped midthigh and a pink sleeveless top with red ruffles on the sides. The front was unbuttoned to her sternum, exposing the tops of her breasts encased in a black push-up bra. Perspiration dappled her chest and upper lip.

"It's hot as shit out here." She fanned herself with one hand. "Aren't you going to let me in?"

I stood aside and closed the door as soon as she walked into the living room.

"What happened to your face?" She squinted at the cut on my lip.

"It's been an interesting day so far."

She nodded and then seemed to become aware of her surroundings. "Nice place. You always were a classy guy." She did a quick turn around and took in the front third of my house. "Got any beer?"

"Sure." I led her into the kitchen and got two Coronas from the refrigerator. "Where's Duane?"

"Probably taking it up the butt from that pisswad Terry." She drank a quarter of the beer in one gulp and rolled the bottle across her forehead. "Duane's not exactly a stallion when it comes to the bedroom. Too many steroids. Too much looking at himself in the mirror."

I took a sip of beer but didn't say anything.

"But what am I gonna do?" Her tone was resigned. "There's no looking back. Can't start over now."

"Why be unhappy, Vera?"

She placed her bottle on the counter and moved to where I was, standing by the fridge. "Help me, Hank. My brother's dead and nobody gives a shit but you and me." Her voice choked with emotion.

"Vera, let's concentrate on finding who did this to your brother, okay?"

"Please, Hank." She stepped closer.

I hesitated a moment and then took her in my arms. That would have been okay except she tilted her head up and kissed me on the cheek. I tried to push her away but she held on tight, moving her lips to mine. After a few seconds I kissed back. She pressed her body into me and what sounded like a whimper or a moan came from deep inside her. I felt her pain as a tangible force, wondering where her suffering ended and mine started. Pretty soon we stumbled out of the kitchen and left a trail of clothes in the hallway leading to the bedroom. We fell on the bed in a tangle of arms and legs. Her breasts were chalky white compared with the tanned skin of her shoulders and torso. She filled my senses, a heady mix of perfume, sweat, alcohol, and cigarette smoke. When we finished, she cried a little, over what had just occurred or her brother or something else, I couldn't tell. She drifted off to sleep as I struggled to control my sinking eyelids.

From a long way off I heard a buzzing sound. I opened my eyes and swatted at the noise by my ear. Long shadows dappled the far wall. I looked at the alarm clock and saw that it was three hours later than it should be. The buzzing was my cell phone. I looked at the number on the caller ID. Miranda and Ernie's house. *Please don't let Ernie have died.*

"Hello." Sleep colored my voice. Vera stirred beside me.

"Hank?" It was Nolan.

"Yeah. What is it?" I shook my head, trying to push out the fog.

"Were you asleep?"

I burped and tasted scotch and steak. "Maybe."

Vera sat upright in the bed and groaned as if she'd been having a bad dream.

"Are you alone?"

"Uhhh . . . yes. I mean no." I rolled off the bed and rummaged around on the floor for my boxer shorts. My wounded calf started to hurt. "Lemme call you back." I disconnected.

Vera stood up beside the bed. "W-w-what happened?"

I stepped into my shorts. "What do you think happened?"

She looked at the bed and then back to me. "I've got to get out of here."

"Me too." I found my jeans in the doorway and slipped them on.

"This isn't the way I am." Vera put on her underwear. "I'm sorry, Hank."

"There's nothing to apologize for."

She found the rest of her clothes in the hallway. "Don't forget Charlie."

"I won't, Vera. That's what I was working on when you came over."

She looked at me for a few moments, both of us standing in the dim light of the hall. Without a word she turned and left. I called Nolan.

She said, "Did I interrupt anything?"

"No." I went to the kitchen and pulled the coffeemaker out. "Vera came by."

"You screwed the client?" Her tone was incredulous.

"Why do you psych types always assume there's sex involved?" I turned the tap on and filled Mr. Coffee with Mr. Water.

Nolan must have heard the activity. "What are you doing now?"

"Getting ready to go see Roger Strathmore, Fagen's son. Wanna go?"

"Yeah." Her voice dropped lower. "I need to get out of the house. Ernie's not doing well. Miranda just cries. I try to say something, to do something, but it doesn't help. She just cries."

"How is Ernie?" The coffee filter drawer lay empty, so I fashioned a substitute out of a paper towel. Taste wasn't important at this point, wattage mattered.

"Coma. They don't know if he'll come out of it or not."

I stopped shoveling coffee out of the can for a moment to let that sink in. I'd screwed and slept through my visit to Ernie.

"Hank? Hank, you still there?"

"Yeah. Meet me at the office in half an hour." We hung up.

CHAPTER TWENTY-ONE

Women are a pain in the ass sometimes.

One little gunshot wound (okay, so it's the *second* one in twenty-four hours) and they think you should go see a doctor. I said I was fine. Nolan said no, you should go see a doctor. I said no, really, it's nothing to worry about. This went on for some minutes at the office, after I told her about the events of the morning. She looked suitably horrified at first, but then started in on me about going to the emergency room and how men in general are reluctant to see their primary care physician for anything. After asking her what a primary care physician was, I said that if I went to a hospital with a GSW then I'd have to fill out reports and explain what happened, which she could see from the puffy-haired anchorwoman here on Channel 8 was this really sleazy bar that burned down with a bunch of people in it.

She quieted down a little, and together we watched the early news. The current version of the story went that it was a drug buy gone bad. Two bodies found so far. Tentative IDs put one of them as Kim Pak Yung, owner of the bar Roxy's. Kim was a model citizen, if you didn't mind the arrests for public lewdness, solicitation of prostitution, possession of a controlled substance with intent to sell, and a child pornography charge pending. The rap sheet made me feel better about shooting him in the crotch. Police speculated there was a) a gas leak; or b) he was operating a methamphetamine lab in the back of his club. Hence the explosion.

A wallet on the second body identified the stiff as one Harvey McMillian, a former accountant now reputed to be a bookkeeper for the Russian mob. Three other bodies were found, no identities as of yet.

Eventually, I assuaged Nolan's concerns and we left for our unscheduled interview with the Strathmore son, Roger.

I turned past the Dallas Country Club onto Beverly Drive, the main east-west thoroughfare in the small enclave of Highland Park.

It was late Sunday afternoon, and the summer sun seemed to kiss the immaculate grounds of the town in a special way. The grass was greener, the flowers more vibrant than in the rest of Dallas. The people we saw were tanned and healthy-looking, in cars that cost more than I paid for my cottage in East Dallas next to Mr. Martinez and his chickens in the backyard.

We passed a crew of Mexican yardmen tending a lawn that looked like the fairway at Augusta. One man drove a riding mower in a diagonal pattern across the immaculate turf, shaving off another half inch. The other worked a monofilament weed cutter on the edge of the grass as if it were an extension of his body, a third arm. They possessed an economy of movement and a synchronicity I found amazing, like the owner of the mansion paid them extra to look good while they worked.

I was glad we were in the borrowed Mercedes; it fit in better. Nolan played swivel head, gaping at one large house after the other.

"Nice cribs, aren't they?" I said.

She didn't say anything for a moment. Then, "What? Oh yeah. Nice. Real nice. What do these people do? I mean, where do they get this kind of money?"

"You got your oil guys, your real estate guys, your stocks and bonds guys, and a whole plethora of your captains-of-industry types. Lots of lawyers too, I would imagine. Some computer and software folks. And don't forget the members of the lucky sperm club."

Nolan frowned. "Captains of what? The lucky who?"

"The lucky—Never mind. Lots of trust funds out there too." I made a turn past a lake. A group of ducks paddled serenely while two young lovers exchanged a kiss underneath a towering oak tree. One more left and we were on Roger Strathmore's street. The lots were big, with the houses set back from the street. Roger's house was on a corner, a two-story brick home with a circular driveway and a deep bed running along the front, stuffed with thousands of flowering plants, reds and yellows and blues, a French landscape painting on speed. The lawn was so green it looked like it had been applied with spray paint. I pulled into the driveway and shut off the car.

"Just gonna walk up and knock on the door?" Nolan said.

"Yep."

"And you're going to ask Roger Strathmore if he knows where his father is and maybe could he tell you about the warehouse on Gano Street and what he knows about a hood named Coleman Dupree?"

I opened the car door and the afternoon heat spilled in. "Yeah, that pretty much sums it up."

Nolan clicked her tongue. "Maybe we could be a little more subtle." She got out of the car too.

"Nope." We stood for a moment by the Mercedes and looked at the house. The air smelled of bougainvillea and magnolia blossoms.

"How about you let me at least get a read on this guy's body language?" She tugged at the bottom of her blouse.

I waved my hand at her in a dismissive gesture and touched the butt of the Browning underneath my denim shirt with my elbow, making sure it was in place.

"You have the cell phone with your lawyer's number in it?"

I wiggled the tiny Nokia at her and started up the walk. When we got to the front steps the door opened. A woman stood there, one hand holding the door and the other grasping a tumbler full of something milky and bubbling. She was attractive, a nip-and-tucked forty-five, tanned, wearing a tennis outfit and a gold Rolex.

"You the guys from *Designer Week*?" *Designer* came out as *s-ssigner* and I could smell the alcohol from eight feet away.

Before I could say anything, Nolan took the lead. "Yes, we are. Are you Mrs. . . . ?"

The woman hiccupped. "Strathmore. Mrs. Roger Strathmore. Carla." She took a big slug of whatever it was she was drinking and smacked her lips. "Y'all want to come in?"

We said we did and followed her into the house. The entry was cavernous, a black and white marbled floor leading to a circular stairway. Two oil paintings of some fuzzy-haired lap dogs dominated the far wall. Each dog wore a pink bow and gazed idiotically at the other.

"Roger's in the study. Been looking forward to meeting you two." She finished her drink and set the empty glass down on an antique sideboard resting against the wall. A middle-aged black man wearing a white jacket and dark tie materialized.

"Missus Carla, you want another of Henry's potions?"

The woman stifled a burp. "I sure as shit do, Henry. That was a frickin' damn good batch last time." She turned to us. "You guys want to try one of Henry's potions? Damn fine, I'm here to tell you. Makes 'em with lemonade and gin and some other good stuff. Mmm, mmm, tasty."

Carla smacked her lips, Henry looked at us and winked, and Roger Strathmore swept into the room from our right.

I'm not sure what I was expecting, but it wasn't what I got. Roger Strathmore was younger than his wife, by at least a couple of presidential administrations. He wore a pair of beige linen trousers and a lavender silk shirt. The weak chin was more pronounced in person. Receding hairline. He was shorter than his dad, maybe only six feet. The eyes, partially hidden behind a pair of narrow, horn-rimmed glasses, didn't have the intensity of the father's. He held a cordless phone in one hand and chewed on the end of the antenna absentmindedly.

He sighed and said, "Carla, the last thing you need is another drink. Go lie down, for heaven's sake. We've got the museum steering committee meeting tonight."

Carla rattled the ice in her empty drink and glanced at Henry. "Oh yeah, the steering committee. How could I forget? I'll be upstairs then." The black man nodded at her and left the room.

Roger Strathmore turned to us and clasped his hands to his breast. "Do my ears deceive me or did I hear you're from *Designer Week*?"

"Your ears are marvelous, simply marvelous. As is this lovely house." Nolan's voice beamed, and she swept her arm around, indicating all the objets d'art.

"You must be Phyllis and Terry." He approached us with his hand outstretched. Either I was Phyllis or he shook my hand first because I was closest. "Roger Strathmore. So nice to meet you." Firm handshake with the left hand grasping the elbow. Mr. Sincerity. He repeated the operation with Nolan. "Let's go back to my study and we can get started."

Nolan and I shrugged at each other and followed him into the interior of the house. We passed through several rooms, each with a different theme. The solarium was light and airy, done in yellows and other soothing pastels. It overlooked a garden with a fountain, and a half dozen Greco–Roman-style statues. Most were of nude or partially nude men. Next came a library, a large room with dark paneling and walls of bookshelves stuffed with leather-bound volumes that appeared to match the coffee-colored leather furniture. A large birdcage containing a white cockatoo sat in one corner.

The last room was undefinable, a cowboy/western motif with rugged sofas covered in Indian blankets and deer mounts on the walls. And everything done in some shade of pink.

Finally, we entered Roger Strathmore's study. The room was only slightly smaller than my entire house. Crucifixes and other religious icons dotted the white plaster walls. The whole place was taken up with various arrangements of chairs and tables, each set up just so. Lots of china and porcelain stuff everywhere else, the kind of crap my ex-girlfriend from a couple of years ago, the interior designer, would have called decorative accessories.

In the middle of the room sat a Queen Anne–style desk, really a table with a couple of drawers. A young man with short, gel-spiked hair, a stretchy T-shirt, and khakis sat on one side of the desk, scribbling something on a yellow pad. He looked Queen Anne style too.

Roger breezed into the room and sat behind the desk. "Phyllis, Terry, this is my assistant, Dirk."

Dirk stayed sitting, and in lieu of shaking, held his right hand out, palm down, and allowed us to grasp it. "Charmed, I'm sure," he said.

Roger smiled at us, clasped his hands together, and scrunched his shoulders up. "This is so exciting. *Designer Week,* interviewing me."

"We're excited too." Nolan sat on one of the spindly chairs in front of the desk.

"I'm all tingly," was probably not the right thing for me to say judging by the looks I got from Nolan and Dirk.

Roger ignored me and concentrated on Nolan. "So tell me where you want to start."

She pursed her lips. "Let's get some background first. What you do when you're not . . . well, you know—"

Roger interrupted her with a chuckle. "When I'm not designing award-winning apartment interiors that bring such fun people as you two to my front door, is that what you mean?"

Nolan and I both nodded enthusiastically.

"Well, my day job is as executive vice president of Strathmore Realty. That's one of the ways that I got involved in apartments since we build quite a few of them."

"Tell us a little bit about your company," I said.

Roger quit smiling and put on his serious face. "Strathmore Realty is a full-service real estate firm. We offer development, brokerage, leasing, and management for all aspects of commercial real estate. Strathmore currently has eighty million square feet of office space in twelve metropolitan areas. In terms of multifamily development we have seven thousand units in—"

"Hold on just a sec." I pulled a pen that didn't work very well from my back pocket along with last week's grocery list. "That's seven thousand units, right?"

Roger nodded. He looked relieved to have quit reading from the corporate brochure.

I scribbled some more. "So what do you have going on here in Dallas?"

Roger and Dirk frowned, looking puzzled. Wrong question.

"This is just for background," Nolan said matter-of-factly, trying to get us back on track.

Roger scratched his forehead. "Well, the biggest thing we've got going on is the Trinity Vista."

"Of course," I said. "The Trinity Vista. As I understand, that's a group of developers."

"Well, yes. That's right," he said. "But we're supposed to be the lead entity."

Nolan cut me off before I could ask another question. "I think we've got enough background info. Let's get to the fun stuff."

Roger brightened at the same time as a phone rang. Dirk picked up a receiver from the desk and spoke into it. The expression on his face went from puzzled to hostile. He hung up.

"That was Henry. The people from *Designer Week* are here." He looked at us. "At the front door."

After a couple of heartbeats' worth of silence, Roger Strathmore said, "Who are you two?"

I thought about bracing him with the Trinity Vista and why was a hood named Coleman Dupree interested in his building on Gano Street. I passed on all that. I said, "What's up with Corrine? Is that your stepmother?"

Dirk clicked his tongue and snorted, rolling his eyes skyward. "That woman."

Roger Strathmore lost all traces of his smile. For an instant, his eyes took on the intensity of his father's, a penetrating gaze that laid you bare. He smiled without humor and said, "Dear, sweet Corrine. Is that what this is about? She using me to try and do some end run around the prenup?"

I didn't reply.

Roger filled the silence. "That woman is a piece of work. Dad always had a thing for the leggy types, the dancers. 'Course, the only place that slut ever danced was on the main stage at the Men's Club." I nodded. Dirk stood up and flexed his pectorals through the thin material of his T-shirt. "I think you two should leave now." He'd butched his voice up.

Nolan scratched the corner of one eye and said, "Shut the hell up, Dirk. We'll leave in a minute."

"We're not here about Corrine," I said to Roger, before Dirk could strike another pose. "Tell me about the Trinity Vista."

Roger snorted. "Oh, it's not about Corrine. Hmm, let me guess, you two are reporters and looking to get the inside story on Strathmore's participation in the Vista project. That right? Well, there is no inside story."

"Tell us about Aaron Young," I said, aware that our window of opportunity was fading away.

"I'm calling the police now." He picked up the phone but didn't dial. "For the record, Strathmore Realty will be the leader of the Trinity Vista project. Aaron Young does not have the expertise or capital to undergo such a venture." He sounded like he was reading from a teleprompter. The next part didn't come from a script, it came from the heart, judging by the intensity in his voice. "I will get the Vista project, if for no other reason than the Big Man thinks I can't."

"What's Coleman Dupree have to do with it?"

"Who?" Both Dirk and Roger at the same time. Genuine puzzlement at the name.

I started to say something else but Dirk interrupted me. "This has gone on long enough, you need—"

I raised my voice, drowning out Dirk. "Somebody died, Roger. I'm trying to find out how and why."

"I think we're finished here." Dirk's voice had gotten deeper still. I turned to him and noticed he held something silvery and tiny in his right hand.

"That's not a gun, is it, Dirk?" I said.

"I know how to use it." He waved it at us and scowled, trying to look menacing.

Roger gasped. "Dirk, put that thing away."

Nolan and I stood up slowly. She said, "You know, Dirk, some psychiatrists consider a pistol to be a phallic extension. What are you trying to tell us?"

Dirk smirked, and then rolled his eyes. In midroll, I grabbed his right hand and twisted. He yelped and I came away with the gun. It was a .22 derringer, about as big as a book of matches.

"We're leaving," I said. "I'll drop this with Henry at the front."

"I think that's a good idea." Roger Strathmore's voice sounded weary and resigned.

I flipped a card onto the desk. "If you ever need to get in touch with me . . ." He didn't respond.

We turned and made our way to the door on the far side of the room. Before I left I turned around and said, "Hey, Roger. If you want to get the Big Man going, ask him about Coleman Dupree."

"Just leave." Roger sat back down behind the desk and crossed his arms.

I held the door open for Nolan and she walked through. As I closed the door behind me, I said, "Ask him, Roger."

In the hallway, Nolan whistled. "Well, Mr. Phyllis, you've got the Strathmore clan all stirred up."

"Uh-huh. It's been a busy Sunday."

We threaded our way back toward the front. I found what I thought was the door to the foyer and pushed it open. There was a flash of light and I almost went for my gun. What I figured were the real Phyllis and Terry, and a photographer, stood in the foyer, admiring the dog paintings. Henry was talking. ". . . and these were commissioned by the Strathmores. Portraits of their dogs, Mildred and Lady."

We nodded at the three newcomers. Henry winked at us and smiled. I bet not much got by him. I went over to the mahogany sideboard and dropped the tiny .22 into a silver dish of candy. "Thanks for everything, Henry. It's been swell."

He said it had been grand and we should drop on by again, anytime. I couldn't tell, but it seemed like he was trying not to laugh. We stepped outside. The smell of cigarette smoke drifted across the front porch. Carla Strathmore leaned against one of the columns, puffing on a breather. She wore a white terry-cloth robe that came to midthigh. Her hair was wet.

"My husband doesn't let me smoke inside. Says it's bad for the paintings."

I put my hands in the pockets of my jeans. "Roger's got too many rules. That's no good for someone like you, is it, Carla?"

She flicked the butt into the flower bed, pushed off the column, and sauntered over to me. When she stopped our faces were only a few inches apart. The robe slid open a couple of notches, exposing most of her breasts. She didn't seem to care. She flipped her wet hair in Nolan's direction. "You two got something going on?"

I didn't say anything.

"You know, you're a pretty good-looking guy."

The robe came apart another inch. I could smell her: cigarettes and booze, perfume and fresh shampoo. And something else I couldn't put my finger on. It came to me suddenly, in the form of a *Jeopardy,* question. *Alex, I'll take middle-aged women who've made deals they now regret, for five hundred.*

"We'd have a good time, you and me," she said, moving closer. "I promise."

What is the smell of desperation?

"Good evening, Mrs. Strathmore." I walked around her. Nolan and I got in the Mercedes and drove off.

CHAPTER TWENTY-TWO

It was the time between late afternoon and early evening when the wind died and the heat of the day rested over everything like invisible smoke from a forest fire, suffocating and deadly. I turned the AC to high and drove away from the home of Roger and Carla Strathmore.

Going just under the speed limit, I nodded once at the uniformed man behind the wheel of the SUV. The town of Highland Park is only about two square miles and has more police officers per capita than anywhere else in the world, except maybe the Vatican or Monaco. They were well trained, well paid, and well equipped, and spent most of their time patrolling. Their response time was measured in seconds, not minutes. They rode in late-model Chevy Tahoes, one unit cruising the perimeter of the town while the others prowled the interior streets, all in an effort to keep the all but nonexistent crime rate from racheting up even a fraction. Once again I was glad to be in the Mercedes instead of my recently deceased pickup.

We headed down Beverly Drive, toward Preston. Neither of us said anything. The sun had begun to sink, and it was the quiet time of the weekend in Highland Park, people eating dinner together, planning the week. I supposed they worried about the same kind of things as the rest of us—is Junior burning through his trust fund too fast, which stock options to cash in, how much are the servants stealing, and so on.

That kind of stuff.

Nolan pantomimed eating and drinking while I dialed the number to Ernie's room at the hospital. Miranda answered and we talked quietly. Yes, Ernie was still in a coma. No, don't come and see him like this. She'd taken a tranquilizer and felt better. Her sister was on the way. Thanks for calling.

I headed toward Love Field and a bar I knew.

"Food," Nolan said.

"Cocktails," I said back. "And maybe a little information."

The Time Out Tavern sits on the west side of the Park Cities, near Love Field. It's one of a handful of neighborhood bars in a city with few real neighborhoods. Consequently, people drive from all over town to hang out there. It was Sunday evening and the sports crowd were winding down when we wheeled into an empty spot in front of the bar. A baseball bat hung on the steel door, serving as a handle, and a faded awning striped to look like a referee's shirt covered the blacked-out windows.

The denizens of the tavern do not care for natural light.

I pushed open the door and we entered. A month or so had passed since I'd last been there and not much had changed. The place was still long and thin, dark with a low ceiling and a bar running down one side, a shuffleboard on the opposite wall. The smoke hung thick over the solitary pool table, lit up like a fluorescent, carcinogenic fog by the neon beer signs on the walls. The glowing advertisements punctuated the space between sports pennants and pictures of patrons. A big-screen television set sat at the far end, ESPN talking heads babbling silently about something.

Two women in their late thirties, wearing Mavericks sweatshirts and a couple of kilos of eyeshadow apiece, sat at a table by the front. They waved their cigarettes at each other while they cussed somebody named Daryl.

A half dozen people sat at the bar. At one end was a gray-haired couple leaning against each other, palsied hands holding smokes while they sipped drinks. When they spoke it sounded like gravel in a blender. Next to them were two men in navy slacks talking loudly about the new configuration on the Boeing 767s and how screwed up it was. Each had a half-full beer mug and an empty shot glass sitting on the bar. Everybody needs to unwind, even pilots.

And at the far end sat Davis Marcy Howell, my office mate. Reading glasses perched on the end of his nose as he sipped a draft beer and read the personal ads in the *Dallas Observer*.

By the time we reached the bar, an icy longneck of Coors Light awaited me on a coaster. The bartender nodded at me and Nolan. "And for the lady?"

The lady rolled her eyes and said, "Scotch, on the rocks."

We took seats on opposite sides of Davis. He finally looked up. "Heya, Hank. N-n-nolan." His eyes rattled in their sockets like marbles in an ashtray as he wobbled atop his bar stool. "What's up?"

"Not much, Davis," I said. "Just grabbing a couple of drinks before calling it a weekend. What's up with you?"

He folded his glasses and put them in his pocket. "Yeah, me too. A couple or three drinks. Not much else. Nothing good anyway." The newspaper slid over and I could see a cocktail napkin covered with scribblings, the names of teams and dollar figures.

I pointed to the markings. "You had a good day?"

"Nah. Not really. S-s-s-no big deal." He tilted the glass of beer to his mouth and took a swallow. A thin stream dribbled down his chin, but he made no move to wipe it up. Nolan reached over and dabbed at it with a paper towel, a tender gesture out of place with the surroundings.

Tears welled in his eyes. "Thanks."

I pulled the napkin over so I could read it. "How bad?"

"Not good." He took another swig of beer, managing not to spill any this time.

"How much?"

"Twelve hundred."

"That's bad but not a killer."

He sighed and fumbled with a cigarette and lighter. "That's for today. I was trying to get even from yesterday."

"What's the total for the weekend?"

He blew a cloud of smoke skyward and then hung his head. "Seven." It came out as a whisper.

"Seven thousand?" I tried not to sound shocked. "Is that American dollars?"

He nodded at the same time as his cell phone chimed. He squinted at the screen, pursed his lips several times, and turned it off. About ten seconds later, the phone behind the bar rang. The bartender answered and said, "Lemme look around." He covered the mouthpiece with one hand. "You here or not, Davis?"

Davis shook his head, mouthing a frantic no.

"Nope, he's gone already . . . Uh-huh . . . Yeah. Yeah, I'll tell him." He hung up. "Some guy named James. He said he'd be in touch. Soon."

I whistled soundlessly and took a sip of beer. James was a bookie who worked for some people from deep in East Texas, who in turn worked for a couple of very rough fellows from Shreveport. Who were bad people to owe money to. "How much does James need right now, to keep you in one piece?"

"I dunno. Doesn't matter. I don't have it."

"I do, and I'll pay him for you," I said. Davis looked confused. I continued. "Here's the deal, though. You quit betting. On anything. You can keep drinking yourself comatose but lay off the wagering. Man like you doesn't need that many vices. Now how much do you think you need to buy some time?" Sometimes I wondered how stupid I could actually be, offering to help pay for this guy's markers while conducting a mini-intervention. Still, I needed info, and fast.

"Probably a grand."

I pulled out my wallet and counted out five one-hundred-dollar bills. Cash is like a gun or a knife in my line of work, another tool of the trade. I rolled them around in my hand for a moment and then put them back. I would only make the problem worse by giving him the money now. "I'll arrange a payment plan with James; we've got mutual acquaintances and he'll work with me. Now I need some information."

Davis pumped my hand, tears in his eyes again. "Thanks, Hank. Anything you need. Anything at all."

I ordered us another round of drinks. "Tell me about Roger Strathmore."

"Roger the homo?"

"You tell me."

Davis stubbed out his cigarette. "He's married but she's way older. No kids either. Whatever he is, he's supposed to be running the show over there."

"Over where?" I said.

"The Strathmore Company. Strathmore Real Estate."

"And?"

"And, Roger's running things but not like the old man. I mean Fagen squeezed every last dollar from every project. Roger, he doesn't have the killer instinct." Davis spoke the last sentence with a trace of condescension in his voice, seemingly unaware of the irony of sitting drunk in a bar on a Sunday night, seven grand in the hole to a mobster named James.

"What about the Trinity Vista?"

Davis took a drink of beer and it dribbled again. Nolan made no move to wipe it up this time. "The fucking holy grail of Dallas real estate?"

"Roger's in charge, right?"

Davis laughed. "Roger may think he's in charge. But I'm here to tell you the word out there is that Fagen Strathmore is not gonna let Roger handle that one solo. It's Fagen's deal all the way. His biggest single deal ever. So he's not gonna let that pansy fuck it up."

Nolan rattled the ice in her drink. "How come Fagen doesn't just can Roger, if he doesn't have the *cojones* to get the job done?"

"Roger gets the job done, sort of. Plus, he can't fire him since Roger and his mom and sister own too much stock in some holding company." Davis hiccupped. "But one thing is for sure: Fagen Strathmore's not gonna lose control of the Trinity Vista."

"So how big a deal is the project?"

A man came in wearing what looked like a pilot's uniform and joined the other two. We were quiet as he ordered a Michelob and a shot of Jim Beam.

Davis scratched his chin. "Ultimately? Hell, I dunno."

I drank the last of my beer and signaled for the tab. "You're a real estate appraiser. Take an educated guess."

"How much does it need to be worth?" He cackled at his own statement, evidently some form of appraiser humor. Nolan and I looked at each other with raised eyebrows.

"Just give me a ballpark figure," I said.

Davis quit laughing. "Ultimately, that deal is probably gonna be worth . . . oh . . . one point two, maybe one and a half."

"One and a half what?"

"Billion. Dollars."

Nolan put out her cigarette and whistled. "Hot damn. Is that American money?"

I poured Davis into a cab and then hopped in the Mercedes with Nolan. Her eyes looked unfocused and she made a vague, rambling threat to my manhood if I didn't feed her soon. Dunston's Steakhouse was only a few blocks down Lovers so I took her there. Dunston's had been grilling red meat over an indoor, mesquite-fired grill since sometime right after the Bronze Age, and the decor hadn't changed much, nor had many of the patrons. If you can find a better piece of dead cow in the state for under ten bucks, I want to know about it. We sat between two plumbers wearing "Proud to Be Union" ball caps and a table full of gin-swilling, cigarette-smoking blue hairs blabbing about how awful the country club's food had become since they'd fired Juan for stealing.

Nolan got a ten-ounce New York strip shot through with marbling. I ordered pork chops. We drank a bottle of screw-top Merlot aged six months to perfection, ate, and talked about what to do next. Rather I talked and Nolan chewed, offering the occasional grunt. With five ounces of her steak left, my cell phone rang. Olson was calling.

"You know a guy named Dirk?"

I washed down the last bite of pork with a mouthful of wine. "Personal assistant to Roger Strathmore?"

"Yeah. That Dirk. He's over here now, in a bad way."

"He's over where? At your place?" I paid the tab and leaned back in my chair. "Well, that's too damn bad for Dirk. I didn't try to hurt him. Did he happen to mention pulling his pistol on me?"

"No, he didn't. This doesn't have anything to do with you. He showed up here a few minutes ago. Hysterical."

I leaned forward in my chair, attentive now. "About what?"

"Something to do with his boss, about Roger Strathmore. Something happened to him."

Things weren't computing. What could have happened to Roger in the couple of hours since we left him? "What's he saying happened?"

I heard babbling in the background and then Olson's voice with the phone away from his mouth. "Delmar, shut him up, will you?" To me, "I dunno what the hell he's whining about. Something about a guy and woman scamming their way into the house then he chased them off. They were in a blue Mercedes. Then something happens to Roger and he gets all hysterical. I put two and two together with the Mercedes and called you."

The little rodents in my brain were running on their treadmills just as fast as they could but no answers were coming out. I said, "We'll be there in a few minutes. Try to figure out what happened."

"Hurry up, will you, I think he's gonna wet himself or something and I just got the rugs cleaned." He hung up.

Nolan downed the last of her wine and said, "Lemme guess. We're not through for the night?"

I nodded and stood up to leave. If only I'd known how prophetic her words were to be, I would have stayed there and ordered another bottle.

Olson and Delmar lived in a converted duplex on Herschel Avenue, between the Oak Lawn district of town and Highland Park. Their place sat between a hair salon and the local office of the Gay and Lesbian Alliance Against Defamation. I don't know whom they thought they were fooling but I knew better than to mention it.

Nine minutes after leaving Dunston's, I turned into their driveway and tapped the horn. A closed-circuit TV camera mounted on the side of the house swiveled toward the Mercedes. A few seconds later the iron gate swung inward, allowing us to enter. I parked by the back door, next to a lime green VW bug, and hopped out. Olson stuck his head out and waved us in.

We entered into the den, a stucco and brick add-on with surround sound for the twin plasma televisions over the fireplace and a zebra-skin rug in the center. A dartboard with a picture of the gun control advocate Sarah Brady hung on one wall. Two stacks, six cases each, of shotgun shells stood in the middle of the rug, a dolly sitting next to them. On top of the cases of shells were eight or ten Smith & Wesson pistol boxes. Just another Sunday at home.

Olson greeted us and then walked back over to the leather sofa and picked up what looked like a broom handle with a muffler on one end. He began polishing it with a cloth. "Delmar took him in the back room and gave him a Zantac. They'll be out in a minute."

The kitchen and media room were one big conglomeration so I went to the refrigerator and got out two beers. I gave one to Nolan and plopped down on the sofa next to Olson.

"What the hell is that?" I pointed to the thing in his hand. The object was metallic and three or four feet long.

"It's the barrel to my new fifty-caliber," he said, with more than a little exasperation in his voice, like I was supposed to know that it didn't go with the old .50-caliber.

"Oh." I drank some beer and decided not to ask any more questions. A .50-caliber bullet was about the size of a banana and originally designed to shoot down an airplane. Better not to pry.

There was movement from the kitchen, and Delmar entered the room, followed by Dirk. He didn't look as cocksure as he had earlier in the day. His face was pale and his eyes were red-rimmed. He jumped and started to whimper when he saw Nolan and me sitting there. Delmar shushed him, then got a beer and sat down in the easy chair by the fireplace.

"All right, Dirk. Tell Hank what you told me."

The young man crossed his arms and kept his eyes on me. "It was about t-t-thirty minutes after you left." He nodded his head toward me. "Thirty minutes. They came."

I leaned forward and put my beer down on the coffee table, using the latest issue of *The NRA Today* as a coaster. "Who are you talking about, Dirk?"

"Two men. I thought it was you two again. But it wasn't." He shuddered.

"Where were the people for *Designer Week*?"

"They'd already left. Roger had to go to the committee meeting so they couldn't stay long." He paused for a moment. "They just walked in the front door."

"Tell me what happened exactly."

"These two men came in. Henry was in the kitchen and Carla was upstairs, passed out. Roger and I were in the foyer since I was getting ready to leave for the day. They just opened the door like it was their house. One of them said, 'Hi, Roger,' and Roger said, 'Who the hell are you?' and then they said, 'We need to talk to you.'" Dirk paused for a breath. "It was t-t-terrible." Delmar rolled his eyes.

I said, "Let's get to the terrible part, huh?"

Dirk whimpered but managed to continue. "Roger went over to them and talked alone, where I couldn't hear. After a couple of minutes he turned to me and said he was going to go with them and that it would be okay. Then he winked at me." Dirk started to cry. "But he didn't smile. He always smiles at me when he winks. Always." More sobbing.

I looked at Delmar again. "You want to fill in the blanks for me? So far all I've got is Roger leaving with a couple of strangers, and Kato here doesn't know who they are."

Delmar drained his beer and crushed the can. "Doesn't sound like a big deal to me either. He said the guys were average-looking white dudes, bad suits. The only thing off is that the one talking had a funny accent."

Dirk let out a caterwaul. "Roger just didn't do that kind of thing. He would never have gone away with someone he didn't know."

I sighed. "Isn't it possible that he might have known them?"

"No. I would have known who they were. Besides, he had the committee meeting." Dirk fluttered his eyelids and waved one hand to make the point. "Roger never misses a committee meeting."

Nolan said, "What's Carla have to say about it?"

Dirk quit sobbing long enough to sneer. "Carla? I couldn't wake her up. One too many of Henry's potions."

I felt the bandage on my calf, making sure it was in place. The wound was beginning to itch. "How exactly did you end up here?"

Delmar answered for him. "His mother's neighbor's brother is an old friend of mine from college. He and I keep in touch. When Dirk moved here from Baton Rouge, he asked me to look after hi—"

Olson piped in. "And this is what happens. He ends up hysterical on our doorstep once every couple of months. Remember last time, Delmar? He got in a fight with that hairdresser and runs here, with that idiot following him. The fucker drove across our lawn right after we sodded, then—"

I whistled and held up my hands. "Uh, fellows? Little more info than I need." I turned to Dirk. "Tell me about the accent."

"I dunno. They just didn't talk American." If Dirk were a dog, he'd be a cocker spaniel: dumb with fluffy hair.

I scratched at my chin and tried to look serious. "Let's see if we can pin down what kind of accent it was, huh? Was it Mexican?"

Dirk shook his head. "Uh-uh. They weren't Mexicans. They were white guys. Real pale, with funny accents."

"Scandinavian mobsters," I said. "Who would have figured?"

Olson shot me the finger.

"What do you mean funny accents?" Delmar scratched his head. "German?"

Dirk hesitated a minute then shook his head. "They had . . . bad teeth. You know, lots of fillings."

Olson and I said it at the same time: "Russians." Delmar slapped his head. "Of course, that makes perfect sense." Dirk jumped like we were going to hit him.

"Russians?" Dirk said.

"Russians," I said back.

"What does that mean?" He sniffled and rubbed at his nose with the palm of his hand.

I drank the rest of my beer and stood up. "I have no idea."

CHAPTER TWENTY-THREE

Delmar gave Dirk a handful of Xanax and a bottle of Chardonnay. He warned him not to take all of the pills with the whole bottle of wine, and to call if he heard anything from Roger. When Delmar left the room for a moment Olson told Dirk to go ahead and take all the pills with the wine, and here are a couple of dozen Valium, go ahead and pop those too and you'll sleep real well. Nolan shot Olson a look that could peel the paint off the walls, grabbed the Valium, and told Dirk to just drink the wine. I told him to do what Olson had said.

"What exactly did Olson say?" Delmar had snuck back in the room.

"Oh nothing," I said. Olson got very interested in his gun barrel.

Delmar handed the young man a wad of cash. "Why don't you stay at a hotel tonight. Just to be careful."

Dirk started to whimper and asked if it would be all right if he stayed there. Olson pointed the .50-caliber barrel at him and began to make gunfire noises. Dirk scampered out, money and wine in hand. Delmar scowled at Olson. Nolan and I laughed.

Then, because they asked, and because Delmar went and got two more beers, I told them about the events of the morning. Delmar looked attentive and Olson quit fiddling with his gun barrel while I related how Clairol Johnson had kidnapped me and we had ended up at the bar on Harry Hines. I finished up with our conversations with Roger Strathmore and Davis Howell.

Delmar leaned back in an easy chair. "So what's your next move?"

"Fagen Strathmore, Coleman Dupree, and Aaron Young all tie in together somehow." I pondered my next words. "And the guy who snatched me this morning says Coleman and Aaron Young are brothers. Maybe that's why Aaron hates drugs. Which brings up the problem of that package I took off the guy on Gano Street."

"Gotta have a game plan," Olson said. "And stick with it."

"Thanks, Coach Landry. I'll get right on that." I turned to Delmar. "The best thing to do is to leave the stuff somewhere and tell Coleman's people to pick it up." I finished the beer and put the can down. " 'Course, I'll also let a couple of cops know about it too."

Everybody chuckled. Delmar said, "You'll lose your leverage."

"Better than losing your life," Nolan said. "Being dead won't bring back Charlie Wesson."

I nodded slowly but didn't say anything. She was right.

"When do you want to do the drop?" Delmar said.

I looked at my watch. "It's almost ten. I'll set it up for tomorrow. You guys got any ideas about how to get in touch with Coleman Dupree?"

"Let me make a call," Delmar said.

He left the room, and Olson flipped on the news. The fire and subsequent deaths at the bar on Harry Hines was not the lead story. I was surprised. The first segment was live at the scene of a triple homicide at a vacant warehouse. On Gano Street.

The police spokesman theorized it was a drug deal gone bad.

Delmar came back into the room right as they wound up the report. "That's another thing you're responsible for." He was speaking to me.

"What are you talking about?" I said.

He waved at the television before handing me a piece of paper. "That shit there. The 'drug deal gone bad.' That wasn't any deal. There aren't any drugs to sell on account of the supply's dried up. Seems a real big shipment has gone missing, stuff that's promised to a lot of different people."

"Way to go, Hank," Olson said. "That's not very nice of you, making people miss their deliveries." He talked without looking up, intent on reassembling his rifle from the dozens of pieces he now had scattered on the coffee table.

"How do you know that's my fault?"

"From the same guy that gave me that phone number. Mr. DEA." Delmar plopped back down in his easy chair. "Two guys got whacked in Richardson too. Didn't make the news yet. They were supposed to make a delivery to a retail guy in Plano."

"I think I'd stay away from the house and office until you get that stuff back to them." Olson spoke through clenched teeth, holding a screwdriver in his mouth while he whacked a metallic piece into the rifle.

I looked at the slip of paper. One phone number. "What's this?"

"That's the cell number of Coleman Dupree's personal bodyguard," Delmar said. "Don't ask any more questions about it. Tomorrow, find someplace safe but public and drop that shit off. Call me and I'll call my guy. Then ring that number."

I stood up to leave, and Nolan followed suit. Olson banged one more time at something with a soft rubber mallet and held out his toy for us to see.

I sat back down. "What the hell is that?"

"It's my new rifle," he said proudly. "I call her Miss Clarita."

I blinked a couple of times to see if my eyes were okay. Miss Clarita was an oversize, bolt-action .50-caliber rifle, and about four feet long. The muffler-looking thing on the end of the barrel was a muzzle break, designed to mitigate the recoil. There was a scope mounted on top that looked like two wine bottles cemented neck to neck. But the really strange part of the firearm was the stock, the nonmetal part where the barrel and action fit in. It was painted neon pink and splattered with white. Something sparkly had been embedded in the finish.

Miss Clarita looked like a deer rifle on steroids. With sexual orientation issues.

"You name your guns?" Nolan said.

"Just this one." Olson wiped down the barrel with a cloth. "I got Miss Clarita back today from the gunsmith." He stroked the twinkly pink fiberglass lovingly. "I designed the stock myself. Got it lacquered over at a body shop on Ross Avenue. Neat, huh?"

I leaned over to examine the paintwork. It was pink and glittery up close too. "That's real cool. You gonna get some curb feelers next? Maybe a pair of fuzzy dice to hang off the barrel?"

Delmar and Nolan tried not to laugh. Olson made a growling sound. Nolan got ahold of herself and said, "I know I'm probably going to regret asking this, but where did the name come from? *Miss Clarita?*"

I looked over at Delmar. He was sitting in the easy chair, eyes closed, shaking his head.

Olson stood up and shouldered the rifle. It must have been heavy because his arms trembled with effort as he held the weapon. After a few moments he put it back down on the coffee table. "I named it after my third-grade teacher, Miss Clarita Sue Dawson. She encouraged my artistic side." He said the last part with a certain smugness on his face.

I'd had enough of artistic third-grade teachers and pink sniper rifles, so I stood up for the second time. "I bet she'd be proud to know that you named a gun after her. We need to be going, it's getting late and tomorrow is looking busy." Nolan and I walked to the door.

Delmar said good night while Olson let us out. We walked to the car and he said, "Good luck tomorrow. Call if you need any help. I'll be around."

I cut through Highland Park on the way back home, feeling good that at least I could get the bad guys off my back for a little bit, until there was a chance to regroup. I didn't really pay attention to the BMW until it was too late. The driver and his two passengers were white, and Coleman Dupree and his thugs were black, so the Beemer didn't raise any alarms until they started shooting. That's what racial profiling will get you, I guess.

We were on Preston Road, headed north, when Nolan screamed at the same time as a shotgun blast took out the passenger-side front tire. I jammed on the brakes and slid into the oncoming traffic. The back side of the Mercedes connected with a Cadillac. We spun around again and the front window disappeared in a cloud of glass fragments, the boom of a shotgun sounding strangely distant.

The front tires connected with a curb and something exploded in the interior of the car. Nothing like a couple of gun blasts directed your way followed by an air bag to the face to disorient a body.

Sirens.

Two more shots.

Screeching tires, more gunfire.

Nolan screamed, sounding far away.

I got the knife out of my waistband to cut away the bag, but it deflated on its own. A hose gave way under the hood and the odor of a hot radiator wafted through the passenger compartment.

I rolled out of the car onto the pavement, dropped the knife and pulled my gun. Kneeling by the ruined Mercedes, I held the pistol pointed out, not sure what I was going to shoot since I couldn't see anything.

I felt hot rain on my face and tongue and smelled something coppery and metallic. Warm, sticky. Tangy. I wiped blood out of my eyes and could see. A shape appeared at the back side of the Mercedes. White guy, wearing a pair of sweatpants and a dark shirt.

A pistol materialized in his hand. He pointed at me and pulled the trigger. A millisecond later someone hit my stomach with a two-by-four. My knees wouldn't support my body anymore and I fell, squeezing the trigger of the Browning one time as I went over.

Darkness.

CHAPTER TWENTY-FOUR

I became aware of lights and movements and sounds, somewhere far off, like the world was covered in a layer of gauze. My stomach hurt.

I debated with myself the possibility of opening my eyes. A voice that sounded like Charlie Wesson's told me to go back to sleep, everything would be okay.

When my lids parted a few seconds, minutes, or hours later I could not have been more surprised. What a lovely sight; a pair of perfectly formed breasts dangled a few inches above my head. Larger than most, and all natural judging by their . . . fluidity; they were tightly encased in a sheer silk cloth, beige and cut low. The tanned flesh contrasted nicely with the smooth material.

They wobbled and began to speak. "I think he's awake." The arms attached to the breasts finished fussing with the pillow under my head and moved back. It was Sandra Jo Delarosso, wife of my attorney, Bertrand Delarosso. She moved another few inches and stood beside her husband. They were on one side of my hospital bed. I shifted my eyes the other way and saw Olson. Delmar was at the extreme edge of my vision, leaning against the far wall, murmuring into a cell phone.

"How are you feeling, sugar?" Sandra Jo said.

In my mind I wanted to say something witty and urbane and end it with "—and I'm feeling better now that you're here." With my mouth I said, "Urrgh."

Sandra Jo stroked my arm. "There, there, Hank. It's okay. How about a drink of water?"

I managed to nod.

She held out a plastic tumbler and guided the straw to my lips. I drank, suddenly aware of a deep thirst. When I was finished, she put the cup down and resumed her place next to Bertrand.

"Where am I?" My voice was a croak.

"Parkland Hospital," Olson said. "You were hit, right after leaving our house. Two BMWs. Don't know how they tracked you down yet."

I was aware of something on my face so I moved one hand that way. Bandages on my forehead. "How bad?"

"The doctor'll be back around in a minute and give it to you in Latin terms." Olson rubbed his eyes and looked tired. "You took a nine-millimeter to the side. Passed through the fleshy part, grazed the large intestine but no penetration. Exited out the back. Full metal jacket so there wasn't any expansion. You were extremely lucky."

"I feel lucky. Or something." I touched the bandages on my face.

"That's from glass fragments and where you banged your head on the curb," Olson said. "They hit you with shotguns, front wheels and engine compartment. They were trying for another snatch."

A thought blasted in my mind. "What about Nolan?"

After an eighth of a second too long of a pause, Olson continued. "They were out-of-town guys, Russians, just off the boat. Didn't know that doing a job in Highland Park is close to suicide. Two patrol units going opposite directions saw the whole thing go down. They said—"

"Where's Nolan?" I put what little strength I had into my voice. It was loud in the small hospital room.

Delmar appeared by the bed, snapping shut his cell phone. "Nolan is . . . missing."

"WHAT?" I tried to sit up but a wave of nausea hit me. "Whaddya mean? Is she all right?"

Delmar pulled up a chair and sat by the bed, at my level. His voice was low and firm. "We don't know. They snatched her." He and I locked eyeballs.

He continued. "She got two rounds into the first car, the one that shot out your tires. They wrecked too. Coming from the other way was the second BMW. They stopped and grabbed her. She didn't appear to be wounded."

"How do you know?"

"We've seen the police video," he said. "They were there almost immediately but didn't realize there were two cars involved."

I started to ask how he could have seen the tape but realized it must have been through his DEA connection. The fog began to lift from my head and I realized where this was headed. The drugs for Nolan. A trade. "Have you heard anything from them?" I kept my voice low.

Delmar understood and looked up at Bertrand. "Counselor, would you mind stepping out of the room for a moment?"

Bertrand didn't so much as twitch a facial muscle. "Of course. Sandra Jo, let's get some coffee, shall we?" When the door opened as they left the room I was aware of a commotion outside, in the hallway.

I could see that Delmar heard the activity also. "We don't have much time," he said. "LEO is wanting to talk to you in the worst way."

"Yeah, I would imagine." LEO is an acronym Delmar and Olson often use for a law enforcement officer. "But why's Bertrand here? I didn't do anything except get shot."

"That and nail one of the bad guys in the chest."

"What?"

"Yeah, you, Mr. Pistolero, you popped one of the bad guys. Dead center."

I remembered the crash and the air bag. Then the gun was in my hand. The act of pulling the trigger danced around the edges of my memory, like fireflies in the yard on a warm summer's evening.

The door opened a few inches and then slammed shut. We heard raised voices.

Delmar spoke again. "Listen. We don't have much time. You killed a guy. No ID, no nothing. Fingerprints don't show up anywhere. The only thing is that he had stainless steel fillings, which means he's Russian. They have gotta go through the investigation on this. It's the second time in as many days that you've used your piece. Even if it's a legit shoot, they still don't like it." There was hesitation in his voice. "And—"

"And what?" I said. "What else is there?"

"There's the stuff at the unit." He lowered his voice even more. "The drugs. Evidently there's been a lot of missed deliveries. Four more people have been killed since last night. None of them have exactly been pillars of the community but it's getting to be a war zone out there."

Olson came around to the other side of the bed and leaned in. "Say the word and we'll set up the delivery. Get rid of that stuff." There was a lack of enthusiasm in his voice that I recognized.

"That's not gonna bring back Nolan." My mind ran through possibilities. "We get her back. You don't leave your people behind."

Olson nodded and smiled faintly. He understood, as did Delmar.

"Where's my cell phone?" I said.

Delmar pointed to the nightstand. "We got it at the scene. Nobody's called. The number we got last night doesn't work today. Disconnected."

I tried hard to put the emotional aspects of Nolan's dilemma out of my mind. The situation required cool, level-headed thinking. Then a rather obvious question dawned on me. "What time is it?"

"Noon, Monday," Olson said.

I swore to myself. Please let her be in one piece.

"You got hit a little less than fourteen hours ago. We're doing what we can for Nolan." Olson seemed to read my mind. "We've reached out to some of your contacts who might know anything. So far nothing. The police know to look for her. So does our guy at the DEA. But it's a delicate situation. He's aware there's a missing shipment. And we're pretty sure he knows we know something about it. And, well . . ." His voice trailed off and I understood. You couldn't exactly tell your cop buddy that you were sitting on thirty pounds of cocaine.

Over half a day, poof, and gone.

Nolan kidnapped.

I felt the bandage on my side and started to say something but the door opened before I could. Bertrand and a skinny guy wearing scrubs and a white lab coat, stethoscope dangling from around his neck, entered. No Sandra Jo.

Bertrand spoke first. "The police are outside. They're going to want to ask some questions. But first of all, Dr. Morgan here needs to check you out again."

Dr. Morgan looked like he should still be an undergrad somewhere, copping a feel off a Delta Gamma while the pledges tapped another keg of Schlitz. He harrumphed at Delmar and Olson. "I thought I specified this patient required complete rest."

Bertrand spoke up before anyone else could. "These men are my, uh . . . paralegals. They're assisting me with Mr. Oswald's case."

The paralegals glared at the doctor, then turned and said good-bye to me. Olson shook my hand and pressed something metallic into my palm. "We'll be around."

I clasped my fingers around what felt like a small semiautomatic pistol and slid it under the pillow. Dr. Morgan examined my side and pronounced it free from infection. He then told me he had taken the liberty of rebandaging the flesh wound in my calf.

"It certainly seems like you've had an interesting few days," he said.

"Yeah. Guess you could say that." I scratched at my bandaged forehead. "When do you think I can get out of here?"

"Out of the hospital?" The doctor appeared horrified. "It'll be at least a couple days. Even though no major blood vessels or organs were damaged, you've still sustained a serious wound."

I nodded solemnly and tried to look contrite for even asking. The doctor's cell phone chirped and he answered, turning his back to me for a moment. Bertrand leaned over and whispered that he'd sent Sandra Jo to get me some clean clothes. It's nice to have a full-service attorney.

Dr. Morgan hung up his phone and made some notes on my chart while clucking his tongue. "I've prescribed some Tylenol Threes for any discomfort you may have."

"I'm in a lot of pain, Doc. How about some Percodan?"

He frowned and left without replying.

He'd been gone for about a second and a half when the door opened again and a passel of LEOs barged in. There were two Highland Park plainclothes, since the attack happened in their jurisdiction, a Dallas narcotics investigator, somebody from the district attorney's office, and a DEA agent. I didn't know if he was Delmar and Olson's guy or not. They asked a bunch of questions and I answered all of them, some even truthfully. The DEA guy kept looking at me whenever the inquiries got around to why these guys were after me. For a moment I debated telling them about the debacle at Roxy's and Coleman Dupree. Only for a moment.

It didn't take a crystal ball to see that I had signed the death sentence for Nolan O'Connor, my dying partner's niece, who had been kidnapped because I was a dumbass and took something that wasn't mine, trying to bust open a case.

After thirty minutes, a nurse's aid came in with a tray of an unidentifiable protein and carbohydrate mixture, cleverly designed to resemble food. Bertrand looked at his watch and said I needed to eat and rest, what with the gunshot and the trauma and all. There was a lot of posturing and zingers about grand jury investigations and threats to not leave the county. Bertrand nodded a bunch and said hmm while he looked thoughtful and stroked his chin.

Finally everybody left. I devoured the tasteless food like I had just been released from a Soviet gulag. When I was finished I washed down a couple of the codeine Tylenols.

"You know, Hank, I don't usually pry into my clients', uh . . . activities."

"Then don't start now." I looked at my cell phone to make sure it was still juiced up and switched on.

He ignored me and continued. "But you seemed to have reached a new plateau vis-à-vis your involvement with certain criminal elements—"

The door to my room opened and Sandra Jo came in, cutting short her husband's sermonizing. She carried an oversize shopping bag that said "Prada" on the side and was breathless. "Got back as fast as I could. Not many decent shops around here."

Bertrand and I both watched her as she plopped the bag on the foot of my bed. He closed his eyes and shook his head. "You went to *Prada* to get Hank some clothes?" The first traces of anger started to show up in his otherwise unruffled voice.

"What exactly is a Prada?" I asked, afraid of how much it was going to cost me.

Sandra Jo ignored me and talked to her husband. "Don't be silly, sugar. I got Hank some stuff at the Gap. While I was out, I just happened to stop at the Prada store, and there was this most adorable leather jacket. It'll be perfect for the bar association meeting next month." She pulled out khaki pants, some socks, a denim shirt, and a set of underwear, including two pairs of maroon boxer shorts, and handed them to me.

"Hmm. Yes. I see. The bar association meeting." Bertrand took several deep breaths and pursed his lips. "Hank, do you feel able to leave the hospital?"

I pulled the clothes toward me. "Yeah, I'll be fine." Gingerly I swung my legs off the bed. Not a smart thing to do so fast. I got an eight-beer, dizzy head. I closed my eyes for a moment. I opened them again when I heard a fizzing noise.

It wasn't a beer, but a Fresca. Sandra Jo sat next to the bed, leafing through a fashion magazine and sipping on the soft drink. I blinked my eyes.

"What time is it?" My voice had returned to a croak.

Sandra Jo looked at her Rolex. "Little after three." She put the magazine down. "You fell asleep, right after trying to stand up. Bertrand left."

I eased myself up to a sitting position. "I've got to get dressed. Get out of here."

Sandra Jo took a sip of Fresca. "Are you sure, Hank? You've been shot."

"Yeah, I'm sure." I grabbed the soft drink from her without asking and drank half of it in one gulp. "Where're the clothes you brought?"

She handed them to me. "This is about that girl, isn't it? The one called Nolan."

"Yep. How'd you know about her?"

"I heard them talking. Your two friends, the blond one and the other guy." She stood up and went over to the window. The sun accentuated her profile, the strong jawline. She brushed her hair behind an ear and turned around. "You're very loyal, Hank. I've always known that about you. Remember that time at our Christmas open house a couple of years ago? You left early because your friend was in trouble. I admired you for that."

I vaguely remembered the party in question. I seemed to recall leaving early with one of the caterers after I told her I was in the CIA. I may or may not have come up with some excuse for Sandra Jo about helping a friend in need. It had been a while ago.

She turned back from the glass, leaned against the windowsill, and looked at me, arms crossed underneath her breasts. "Yeah, Hank. You're very loyal. I like that. Bertrand, he's not loyal to anything except money, and a piece of ass. You know he's got somebody new, don't you? Met her at a conference. She's a second-year law student. Twenty-five years old."

I stood up beside the bed on wobbly legs, new clothes clutched to my chest. "I'm sorry. I didn't know." I rummaged around and found my wallet, keys, money clip, and pocketknife. I left them on the nightstand but grabbed the pistol from under the pillow, and my cell phone. "I'm going to go in the bathroom and clean up. Then get dressed." I wobbled a little more but managed to stay standing.

Sandra Jo reached out and took hold of one arm, her fingers caressing rather than holding. "Are you sure you're okay, Hank? I could help you." She took a step closer. "If you wanted me to." She tugged at the bottom of her blouse, a quick gesture that accentuated the slimness of her belly and made her breasts bobble. We were both quiet, staring at each other. I picked up the pile of clothes and clutched them to my chest as my breath became shallow.

She was only a few inches away now, the guest star of more than a couple of my fantasies, dancing close to the edge of offering herself to me because her husband, my attorney, had tired of her, as was his pattern. One of her lovely, exquisite breasts pressed against my arm. I could smell her, some herbal shampoo and a trace of expensive perfume. Visions of her—naked—skittered around in my mind until the ugly picture of an abducted Nolan O'Connor forced them away.

"S-S-Sandra Jo." My voice faltered and I cleared my throat. "I don't think—" She moved closer until our thighs touched. I cleared my throat again and willed my body not to react. "Thanks. I think I'll be okay. I'll holler if I need help." I pulled away from her and turned to the bathroom, holding the wad of new clothes in front of the thin hospital gown.

"Really, I'll be okay." I shut the door. Once inside I leaned against the cold tile wall and took several deep breaths. Today of all days. Gut shot and a kidnapped partner. I set the clothes down and left the gun and cell phone within easy reach.

There was some plastic of the type used to cover dry cleaning and a roll of adhesive tape in a drawer. I made a waterproof cover for my latest gunshot wound and hopped into the tiny, hospital-size shower. Soap and warm water did wonders for my outlook, washing away the remainder of the dirt and dried blood from the attack as well as a small layer of fatigue. I brushed my teeth and slipped into the new clothes. Sandra Jo was better at picking sizes than husbands. Everything fit fine.

When I left the bathroom she was still there, sitting quietly in the chair, magazine laying open on her lap. "The nurse came in. I told her you were in the john."

"Thanks." I put the keys and stuff in my pockets. My shoes were in the closet and I retrieved them. Bending was not fun but hurt less than I thought, sort of like someone had replaced my liver with a nail-studded brick.

She stood and grabbed her purse. "What do you want me to do? Bertrand told me to do anything you asked. *Anything.*"

I ignored the breathiness in her voice and the implied offer. "Sandra Jo, here's the deal. You and I are gonna walk out of here like nothing's going on. It's important for me to not check out, so that the bad guys think I'm here for a while longer. Then I need you to get me to a car, because I'm having the worst luck with automobiles the last few days."

She pulled a compact out of her purse and fluffed her hair. "I can handle that. How about I take you home and you use one of the Cadillacs? Or you can drive the Range Rover." She pursed her lips in a kissy face to the mirror, checking her makeup.

"Uh, no thanks. I've got a better idea." With that, I eased open the door to my room and slid out, Sandra Jo following in my wake. It was another typical day at the county medical facility, sick people and doctors and nurses, blaring intercoms and clanging bells. Nobody paid us any mind, and we slipped out.

CHAPTER TWENTY-FIVE

I don't think I've ever actually been on this stretch of Ross Avenue," Sandra Jo said. A pothole loomed ahead. She jerked the wheel of the Porsche, narrowly missing the cleft in the asphalt, instead almost side-swiping a stooped Hispanic man pushing an ice cream cart. I held on to the dash in a death grip, willing away the potholes and sudden turns. They were hell on a fresh bullet wound.

"It's just like any other part of Dallas," I said. "Maybe a little rougher. People are the same everywhere. Just trying to get by in this big, bad world."

Before she could respond, something red and tomatoey splattered on the front windshield. We turned to see a large man with flowing auburn hair and matching beard standing on the sidewalk, cackling. He wore a pink and teal sundress and a straw cowboy hat, and leaned on a grocery cart full of crushed aluminum cans. He pushed the cart into the street and disappeared into a bar called Treading Water as a group of Vietnamese teenagers strutted down the street, their hair slicked back as if they were extras from the movie *Grease*. I made them for one of the new Asian Triads, a vicious group of newcomers intent on conquering turf belonging to the traditional Hispanic and black gangs.

"Just trying to get by, huh?" Sandra Jo turned on the windshield wipers, smearing the red stuff everywhere.

I didn't say anything.

She laughed and then flipped on the auto washer, and the sprayers streamed water on the soiled glass.

When we passed the Croatian Food Mart, Sandra Jo broke the silence. "How much farther?"

"The next block, on the right." She slowed down until we pulled abreast of Calamity Jane's House of Used Cars. I said, "Stop. This is it."

She pulled to the curb and I eased out, moving gingerly. The asphalt street was hot, absorbing the relentless heat from the sun high overhead in the empty sky. A trickle of sweat dribbled down my back. Sandra Jo leaned across the console and said good-bye. I said see you around and to find a good lawyer and start rat-holing money if she was gonna dump Bertrand because she'd need it. She pondered that for a moment and then drove off without saying anything more.

I turned my attention to the used car lot in front of me and shuffled my way into the Quonset hut that served as a sales office. Jane, of Calamity Jane's, was my former mother-in-law, *mater* to the demon child Amber, whom I met in the aforementioned bar in Waco when she was conducting research for her doctoral thesis on the similarities between the male orangutang during mating season and American men. My contribution had been the title, *Of Monkeys and Men,* and the tome had eventually been published by some company in San Francisco.

I always had more in common with Jane than I did with her penis-hating daughter, and she was glad to see me. She hadn't changed much, hair still dyed the color of the sun, skin still fake-'n'-baked the hue of mahogany, same uniform of a denim prairie skirt and a pearl, snap-button western blouse. Lizard-skin boots and enough turquoise to feed a family of Navahos for a year completed the look. I did some quick math. She must have been past retirement age but still had the figure of someone half her years.

She'd been in the used car business for a long time, as well as several other lucrative but not-entirely-legal enterprises, and took no note of my condition or request. I've got just the thing for you, she said, when I asked her for a clean rig, nondescript but in good shape. And no title problems. She called in one of the fender lizards she employed as a salesman and threw a key at him.

Ten minutes later I heard a horn honk. Jane and I went outside. The salesman sat behind the wheel of a five-year-old Ford Taurus, idling smoothly next to a row of cars for sale. The body was the color of emptiness, a pale gray like fresh concrete. It had new tires, a police suspension, and a rebuilt engine. Gassed up and a clean title, what else did I need?

I asked Jane another question, one I knew she wouldn't like but would answer anyway. She swore and pointed across the street to an emaciated Hispanic guy loitering near the front door of a Mexican supermarket, next to a shopworn quartet of mariachi players. The man watched me hobble across the street as the mariachis strummed their guitars and sang into the oily air of Ross Avenue. He nodded once and uttered a few words and the transaction was complete. I passed him some folded bills and he handed me a cellophane package of small white tablets. The finest meth money could buy, he assured me, enough speed to keep me rocking for as long as I wanted. The way things were shaping up, I would need it.

The time had come to visit Aaron Young, but on my terms and after a quick stop. I said good-bye to Jane, eased myself into the Taurus, and headed south to Interstate 30. I got on the freeway and stayed in the right-hand lane. Traffic was light.

Cars zoomed by as I held to a steady fifty miles an hour. One mile passed. Another quarter of a mile and I pulled even with the Dolphin Road off-ramp. At the last possible instant, I exited, yanking the wheel hard to the right and running across the part where you're not supposed to drive. I missed the concrete embankment by a couple of feet but saw that no one followed me. Back under the highway, I turned left on Samuell Boulevard and headed back toward town. The neighborhood was rough, even for this section of East Dallas, a row of dark taverns and smoky nightclubs where the sound of dice tumbling in the back rooms often competed with the rattle of gunfire when the sun went down.

After a half dozen more blocks of double-backs and speeding through yellow lights, I was convinced that no one was trailing me. Three minutes later I idled down the alley behind the unit. A needle of pain shot through my side when I got out of the Ford. I bit a Tylenol in two and swallowed half, dry, while I punched codes and unlocked deadbolts. Once inside, I Fort-Knoxed the door behind me and wandered into the gun room.

My supply of Browning Hi-Powers was running low. One in the safe at home, then the ones here. I took the next to the last one and wiped it down. I cracked open a case of nine-millimeters and loaded up five magazines. I jammed one in the pistol and went looking for a holster. I found another inside-the-waistband rig lying on a shelf, so I stuck the gun in that and threaded it onto my belt. The weight pulled on my wounded side, but felt comforting nonetheless.

The tiny Smith & Wesson that Olson had given me in the hospital went to his corner of the room. I dug around and found another Seecamp .32, complete with an ankle holster. I frowned and tried to remember what happened to my shotgun. A vague recollection skittered through my head about sticking it in the backseat of the Mercedes before I went to see Roger Strathmore. That meant the police had it.

Damn. It had been a hard few days on equipment, of all sorts.

I found a black-stocked Remington in the hall closet. After pilfering fifty or so rounds of double-aught buckshot from Olson's section, I went over to my corner and sat down, pulling the brown-wrapped package between my legs. I plunged my pocketknife in the top and eased it out. White powder clung to the blade, the consistency of baking soda. I touched my gum line with the tip of the blade, and then pressed my finger on the spot.

Numbness. Enough to do surgery.

No wonder they were pissed off. There had to be almost thirty or so pounds here, pure stuff. I didn't know that much about the drug business, despite that thing in Houston the one time, but I figure that they could cut this three or four ways and come up with almost two hundred pounds of retail-level cocaine.

I shuddered involuntarily and realized I was hyperventilating. Where the hell was Nolan? What had I done to her by taking this stuff out of the warehouse? How dumb was I to think it would get me closer to finding Charlie Wesson? I started to shake and my side hurt. I was on the verge of losing it, the enormity of the situation dawning on me. I no longer cared who killed Charlie Wesson or why Roger Strathmore had gone missing or any of that other stuff. I wanted Nolan back. This wasn't her battle, it belonged to me. Why hadn't there been any contact from them?

I stuck the parcel back in the corner and pushed myself up, using the shotgun as a cane. The time had come to go see Aaron Young. The half brother of Coleman Dupree.

Monday evening lay quiet on Second Avenue, the stores and daytime businesses closed since dusk. The only activity came from the occasional bar that dotted the thoroughfare. A solitary light burned in the window of Aaron Young's office. I peered into the parking lot as I passed. A dark-colored Lexus, similar to the one he'd been driving the other day, sat under a floodlight, nestled against the building.

By the time I'd turned around, the Lexus had pulled out of its parking spot and up to the street, waiting for a break in traffic. By the light of a passing eighteen-wheeler, I caught a glimpse of Aaron Young's profile as he motored onto Second Avenue, three cars ahead of me. I maintained the distance and followed him up Second to Hatcher Street. He signaled and took a left, with me and the ugly Taurus a hundred yards behind.

Hatchet Street, as it's called by some of your more hard-nosed law enforcement types, runs across the bottom half of southeast Dallas and has seen more than its fair share of violence. Block after block of apartments and tiny, shotgun-style homes peeled past my window. Some were well maintained. Some were not. All of them looked like they were built during the Coolidge administration. Hubcap-size satellite dishes sprouted from most of them, like toadstools after the spring rains. The weather was warm so there were people out, cooking on grills resting on bare dirt lawns, drinking beer, milling about in the sultry evening.

Aaron Young drove on, past the man and woman arguing in the thin light from the open door of their Pontiac, while a toddler sat on the sidewalk crying. He drove past the group of young men standing on a corner, wearing Raiders T-shirts and jeans with two inches of boxer shorts visible at the top. They glared at Aaron in the Lexus, then at the tinted-window Ford, angry at us or the world, or maybe the grittiness of life on Hatcher Street.

I kept going, following the dark Lexus as it swung onto South Central and headed south toward the interstate and Houston. Before the cutoff for H-town, he exited at Illinois and headed west, toward Oak Cliff. The traffic had thinned and I struggled to keep a car between us yet not get too far behind.

He crossed Interstate 35 and we were in the Cliff, the road unfolding in front of us in a series of hills and valleys unique to the usually bland terrain of north Texas. The houses were different here too, quaint, 1920s-era Tudors that hadn't been scraped away to make room for the latest in overbuilt tackiness, as had been done to great chunks of land in the northern half of the city. At Colorado Boulevard, Aaron turned left and then a quick left again.

We were in Winnetka Heights, twenty or so square blocks of prairie-style houses on steep lots, home to the middle tier of Dallas civic and business leaders a century ago. Aaron Young pulled into the driveway of a sand-colored stucco place in the middle of the block. I stopped two houses away, lights off. As he got out of the Lexus, I pulled out the dome light of the Taurus and slipped out the door, easing it shut. The evening air was humid and I felt perspiration bead on my forehead.

No movement whatsoever on this particular block. It was early evening and the street lay dark except for the porch lights on several of the houses, including the one where Aaron Young had parked. While he rummaged around in the backseat, I moved down the sidewalk as quietly as possible. I was halfway across the front lawn when he stood up, holding a wad of papers and a briefcase. He saw me at the same time as I cleared the Browning from its holster.

"What the hell?"

"Remember me, Aaron?" I stepped in close and knocked the briefcase to the ground and spun him around, all in one motion. "Put your hands on the car and don't say a word."

"Who are—?"

"That's a word." I whopped him in a kidney with the barrel of the Browning. He groaned but didn't say anything. "Now let's do this the easy way, what do you say? You and I are gonna take a little drive and you're gonna tell me what I need to know. Then I'll drop you off here and everything will be back to normal."

I grabbed the back of his suit coat and pulled him off the car. "Put your hands behind you."

He hesitated a beat and then complied. I grasped the cuffs of his coat in one hand, making an informal pair of handcuffs, and stuck the gun in his back. "Now we're gonna walk to my car, down the street, and you're going to get in the backseat and lay on the floorboards." I prodded him with the Browning and we moved across the lawn toward my auto.

I heard the stretch and springing sound of a screen door open and close, followed by footsteps on creaking wood. "Aaron? Aaron, honey, is that you?"

I dug the muzzle harder into his ribs, turned, and looked at the porch. A slim woman stood there, leaning against one of the wooden columns along the front. The light on the door frame silhouetted her, making it difficult to see her features.

"It's okay, Mother. I'll be there in just a minute." Aaron yanked his arms out of my grip and stepped around to face me. I cursed my codeine- and fatigue-numbed reflexes, and the bullet wound in my side, that made his escape possible. I held the gun close to my hip, out of sight of the woman on the porch. Nobody said anything, the three of us staring at one another in some bizarre triangle.

"So what are you going to do? Gun me down in the yard, in front of my mother?" Aaron kept his voice low.

"I want some answers and I'll do what it takes."

"Who the hell are you?"

I moved a few inches closer to the light on the porch. "It's been a rough few days, but you sure you don't recognize me?"

He squinted and then nodded. "The private investigator. Yeah, that's you, from the other day. Man, you look like shit."

"If I don't get some answers from you, you're going to feel the same."

"I'll be glad to answer anything you want to talk about. I don't understand the need for violence. Ask me what you want, and I'll answer. I assume this is about that fellow you were trying to find, the one that turned up dead at my place."

"It started with Charlie Wesson, but it's gone beyond that." I cranked up the volume in my voice. "Let's talk about your brother, Coleman Dupree."

Stone-cold silence.

Finally the woman spoke. "Who is that out there with you, Aaron? Walk into the light where I can see you."

Aaron had his eyes closed and his shoulders sagged. "Put the gun away, Oswald. Let's go inside and talk."

I holstered the Browning and followed him to the porch and inside.

His mother held the door open for me and expressed no dismay at my condition. I saw her now, clearly, with the light. Tall enough to almost look me in the eye, she grasped my hand and said, "Lydia Bryson. And you are?"

"Oswald. Hank Oswald."

She must have been in her sixties but could have passed for a hard forty-five. Her skin was flawless, all but unlined and the color of chocolate ice cream. The tailored linen suit she wore accented her long legs. She possessed a certain regalness and poise I found engaging.

"Why don't we sit in the living room?" She gestured to the spacious room to the left of the hallway. Muted lighting illuminated the leather sofa and easy chairs, casually arranged on the polished hardwood floors and Oriental throw rugs. "Is that all right with you, Aaron?"

Aaron eyed me warily, rubbing his back where I had punched him. "Yeah, Mom. That'll be fine, we'll sit in the living room."

I let the two of them go in first. Lydia sat down in a wing-back. Aaron sprawled on the sofa. I stayed standing, suddenly weary and afraid that sitting down would be a bad move. Nobody said anything for a moment. Aaron looked at a spot on the floor. His mother stared at me, expressionless.

"I need to know where to locate your brother, Coleman. He's got something of mine and I need it back."

"Coleman Dupree is my half brother," Aaron said, evidently anxious to get the degree of sibling connection established. "Not my full brother."

"Okay then. Half brother. I need to find him. It's real important." I debated taking the speed. Not yet.

"I don't know how to get in touch with him."

"Why don't you take an educated guess." I reached in my pocket and pulled out the cellophane package with the white pills.

"I know some people who might know some other people who— Well, you get the idea." Aaron rubbed his eyes and leaned his head back. "My brother and I have chosen different paths for our lives. We don't keep in contact. If you've had any dealings with him, if you know anything about him, I'm sure you'll understand why."

I kneaded the package of diet pills. "Not exactly Wally and the Beaver, huh? How come you turned out the way you did and he's—"

"A criminal? A drug dealer?" Aaron made a noise that was a laugh but wasn't funny. "Who knows why anything is the way it is. We're both entrepreneurs, you know, just in different fields."

Lydia had not uttered a word. I decided it was time to switch it up. "So . . . uh, Mom. You got any ideas where to find Coleman?"

I wasn't even sure she had borne the two men. Something told me that she was the common denominator, though. She sat stiffly in the chair, hands held in her lap and her legs crossed at the ankles. Without moving anything but her lips, she said, "I did not raise my child to be what he is. He was a good boy. Both my kids were good. Raised them to be Christians. But Coleman, he turned out differently. I don't know why."

She blinked her eyes. Twice.

Then she started talking again. "Maybe he fell in with a bad crowd. Maybe his father was a thing with him, maybe not. He wasn't a bad man, his father. He liked to drink and gamble, but Lordy, so did Aaron's father. I tried to do the right thing."

"All I need to know is where to find him."

"You're going to hurt him, aren't you?"

"No. I'm not going to harm your boy." Nobody said anything for a few moments. I broke the silence. "I'm trying to help him."

The woman snorted. "A white man helping Coleman out?"

"Lives are at stake."

She blinked her eyes two more times, then took a deep breath. "What does he have of yours that's so important?"

I debated with myself over what to tell her. "It's not a what. It's a who. A woman. He's taken a woman. And I'm going to get her back."

"My boy is not a kidnapper."

"No," I said. "He's just a drug dealer and a murderer. Not a kidnapper."

Aaron laughed once, a sharp burst, before smothering it. His mother glared at him, then turned to me. "A mother's love is unconditional. The mind knows things that the heart refuses to see. My Coleman is a good boy underneath all that stuff they say. Surely you can understand that, can't you?" There were tears in her eyes.

I nodded. "Uh-huh. But this woman he's taken, her family wants her back too."

Her chocolate complexion darkened and her voice became angry. "You're the *man* and you lying. Gonna get what you want and kill my son."

"I can't change how you feel, but I will tell you one thing." The wound on my side ached, reminding me again of the stakes. Fatigue smothered me now, to the core, a weariness that no amphetamine would fix.

"The next time they come looking for Coleman, whether it's to get this girl back or something else, they're not gonna be as pleasant as I am, sitting around in the nice living room you got here." I pushed myself off the wall.

Lydia Bryson blinked her eyes, but this time she didn't open them immediately. A tear trickled out of one, running down her cheek. "You promise you won't hurt him?"

I nodded.

"I have a phone number," she said. "It's to his nurse. That's how I get in touch with him. You won't hurt him, will you?" She pulled a piece of paper out of the pocket of her jacket.

I walked over and took it from her. "Ma'am, all I want is my friend back. I'm done hurting people or being hurt."

"Do you know why my son is in a wheelchair?"

"Mother." Aaron Young's voice was an angry hiss. "Why he is in a wheelchair has nothing to do with what he is."

"He is my son, and they put him in that damn chair."

"He is my brother and he's a murderer." Aaron's voice had cracked.

I felt for them, sensed their pain as a palpable thing in the conservatively decorated living room. It hung over everything like a layer of smog over a dirty city. You knew it was there, suffocating life, but you couldn't see it.

"My son was stopped by the police," the woman said, pausing for a moment to regain her composure. "He was stopped in some little cracker town in East Texas, near the Louisiana border. Stopped for nothing, nothing at all. Driving while black. They hauled him out and laid him over the hood of his car. It was nighttime. His car was on the shoulder but they'd pulled off the road onto the grassy area. It was their county and they knew. They knew, dammit."

"Knew what?" I said.

"They knew to pull off the road at that stretch of highway. It was at a bend, everybody in the county knew it was a blind spot and you shouldn't stop your car there. They went back to the squad car to see what they was gonna charge my boy with. Left him spread out on the hood of his car. They left there and damn straight if one of their cracker friends didn't come around the bend, drunk, and hit my boy."

She paused and wiped fresh tears away. Her voice got husky. "Then they left him there, torn up and bleeding, while they searched his car. Finally, they decided they better call an ambulance or they might have 'em a dead niggah on their hands."

I didn't say anything. Aaron sat on the sofa, leaning over, elbows on his knees. He stared at a spot on the wall. He said, "Tell him the rest of it, Mother. Tell him about what they found in his car."

The woman didn't want to tell. She got up and stalked out of the room.

He turned to me. "I'm sorry about that. It's a difficult part of our life. You got what you needed. I think it's best if you leave."

I pushed myself off the wall and walked to the hall, turning around in the doorway. "One more thing, Aaron. How's the bid going?"

If he was surprised, it didn't show. He managed to swallow all the family trauma and turn on the charisma. "Ah yes, the Trinity Vista. The board meets tomorrow. That's when we know."

"We?"

"Yeah, me and the other people up for the contract."

"And who would the other people be?"

He looked a little confused, but not reluctant. "Well, there's me and then the Strathmore team, and a couple of others. They really don't count. The competition is between me and Strathmore." He wasn't smug, just stating a fact in his mind.

"You and Roger Strathmore?"

He chuckled. "Yeah, I guess you could say it's between me and Roger Strathmore."

I headed to the front door. "So you think you're gonna get it, huh?"

The charisma left his face and voice. The eyes were hard and cold. The voice flat. "Oh, I'll get it Mr. Oswald. I like to win, I always have."

He shut the door behind me, and I stepped off the front porch into the evening. The time to go hunting had arrived.

CHAPTER TWENTY-SIX

Before I could do much of anything, my phone rang. I was stopped at a light on Colorado Avenue, headed I didn't know where.

"Yeah."

"Don't go home." Delmar's voice sounded tinny.

"Why?"

"They found where you live."

"Details." The light changed and I headed toward downtown.

"Olson had somebody watching your place. The bad guys showed up about half an hour ago. Four of them. They kicked in the door; that fancy alarm you got went ballistic for about ten seconds until they got to it." Static noises obscured the next few words. ". . . had the cell number of the patrol unit for your precinct and called it in, but the heat didn't get there in time. They were in and out in ninety seconds. Trashed the place, but didn't get in the safe."

"What about the dog?" I hated that mutt, but didn't want anything bad to happen to her.

"Rover hightailed it to the neighbor's, that old Mexican guy next door." More cell phone noises. ". . . police got there right after they drove away. Our guy had the license and they found the car a few blocks away. It'd been stolen."

A low-riding Oldsmobile pulled even with me. It had been new back when Reagan still was in the White House. Now it was rusted and ratty-looking, except for the tinted windows and new tires. I sped up and it matched me. Same thing when I slowed down.

"So why can't I go home? Bet they don't come back for a while." I whipped down a side street. The Olds didn't follow.

"You shouldn't go to your house unless you want to get bogged down in a crime scene."

I pulled to the side of the narrow street and flipped the lights off. "What are you talking about?"

Delmar said, "They left a dead body in the living room."

A ripple of emotion caught in my throat. "Nolan?"

"No. Wasn't her. A guy. White male. Dead and way messed up. They'd Joe Theismanned him big-time. I do believe it was meant to be a message."

Somebody turned on a porch light across the street. I pulled away from the curb and went in search of a main thoroughfare and a way out.

"The dead guy, what'd he look like?"

"Hang on."

I heard shuffling sounds and then he was talking to someone else on another phone. Voices and mumbling, too indistinct to understand.

He came back on the line. "The stiff's about five-five, chunky, red hair. It's hard to tell much more about him. They've been working on him for a while. Ended it with GSW between the eyes."

"That's Clairol."

"He the guy that snatched you the other morning?"

I got on Hampton, headed north. "Yeah. He's the only one who knew where I lived. Something must have tipped them off. Then they got the info out of him." There was silence while both of us tried really hard not to think about Nolan. Delmar asked where I was. I related the events of the evening.

"Did you tell Aaron Young that Roger Strathmore's turned up missing?"

"I left that out."

"What are you gonna do next?"

"Call the nurse's number. It's time to get this deal done."

Delmar grunted in agreement and ended the call.

I pulled into a boarded-up Taco Bell, near Singleton Boulevard, only a few blocks from where Charlie Wesson had swallowed a lead sleeping pill. The dome light rattled around in the ashtray. I fished it out and stuck it back in the socket. With the door cracked and the lamp flickering overhead, I squinted at the piece of paper Aaron Young's mother had given me. Something new and unfamiliar filtered through my mind.

Reluctance, fear, maybe.

I was scared to call the number. Not of what might happen to me, but of what might have occurred to Nolan O'Connor because of my actions. A vision of Clairol Johnson, bloody and broken, swam in my head.

I punched "send" and waited while the phone rang.

A woman's voice, sleepy or disoriented, answered. "H-h-hello."

"Put Coleman on the phone." I kept my tone deadpan.

"W-w-what? Who is this?"

"I'm not talking to you. I'm talking to Coleman. Put him on."

"Where'd you get this number?" Her tone was incredulous.

"Off a bathroom wall, and it said your name was Sally Syphilis. Is your last name *really* Syphilis?"

"Who the hell are you?" A tinge of anger crept into her voice.

"Put Coleman on the phone." A gun fired not too many blocks away. I put the car in gear and headed north again.

"He . . . uh, he can't come to the phone right now. Tell me wha—"

"This is the guy who's got about thirty pounds of what he needs." I hit the bridge over the Trinity, the river and accompanying floodplain an inky black ribbon in comparison to the lights on either side. "Tell him I'm gonna dump it in the Trinity and whack out a couple thousand alligator gars and turtles."

Even with the cell noises and sounds of the car, I heard movement and voices in the background. Finally she said, "He can't be talking to you right now. No shit, okay. He really can't. He'll call you back at this number."

"Fifteen minutes. That's how long he's got to call back. Then I start feeding the fish."

"Look, buddy, you're making a big mistake, gonna get your ass whipped—"

I interrupted her. "Fifteen minutes, starting now." I hung up.

The darkness of the river gave way to the spotty lights of Industrial Boulevard. Low-end topless bars, massage parlors, and bail bond offices lined the street. I headed south to a little place I knew called Harper's Bar and Grill. I parked in front, between an Asian modeling studio and a burglar-barred 7-Eleven.

The grill part had burned about ten years back, along with Harper and a seventeen-year-old hooker named Sarsparilla. They never bothered to replace the sign or Harper. His widow, Selma, ran it now, perched on a stool by the cash register with a never-empty glass of beer sitting next to a pack of Winstons. When she wasn't smoking, she'd light matches and watch them burn. It gave me the creeps, what with the extra-crispy husband, but we were sort of friends after some stuff a couple of years ago.

She had a beer waiting for me when I got to the bar. I waved it away and asked for coffee. She raised her eyebrows but poured a cup. I took it to a booth in the back, away from the two greasy bikers talking Harleys, and a skinny guy in a dirty Jiffy Lube shirt, twitching and mumbling to himself.

In the dim light of the corner, I pulled up my shirt and checked the wound. It didn't appear to be bleeding but I could feel the Tylenol wearing off. I washed down another half a pill with coffee and placed the cell phone on the table.

Fourteen and a half minutes after I hung up with the nurse, they called back.

I answered after two rings. "Yeah."

Nolan's voice came on the line; she talked fast, eager to get the words out. "Don't give it to them, Hank—"

As quickly as her voice started, it stopped, replaced by the sounds of a struggle. I could just make out another woman's voice talking, a funny accent, words too indistinct to understand. Finally there was a slapping sound and then Jack Washington's monotone. "I wouldn't listen to her."

"Don't hurt her, Washington." I kept my voice low. "That would be bad. For you."

"You're not driving the bus right now." He chuckled into the phone. "The stuff for the girl, or we start messing with her."

I made a circular motion on the tabletop with my coffee cup. "One hour from now. The warehouse on Gano Street. You bring the girl and I'll—"

"Shut the fuck up and listen. Ain't no way we're going there again. You want the ho back, you follow what I say, real close."

"How bad do you want the drugs?" I was anxious to get control of the conversation again. Once you start reacting instead of acting, your position is considerably weakened.

Washington made no reply. Instead I heard what sounded like an open-palm slap followed by a moan.

"Tomorrow morning, at dawn." He came back on the line, voice low. "We're gonna meet out in the open, away from any buildings where anybody can be hiding. You know where the Continental Street Viaduct is?"

I said I did, and my mind started to race. The viaduct was one of the bridges crossing the river, connecting north to south. Out in the open, he had said, and it appeared he meant it. On the floodplains of the Trinity River.

"Good, there's an old campground just south. Wetbacks run cockfights there on the weekends. You be there, alone, tomorrow at sunrise, with the shit."

"Put Nolan on the phone, I need to—"

"She ain't talking to you right now. Y'all can be visiting all you want tomorrow. You get her for the shit. And one more thing: stay the fuck away from Aaron Young and the Strathmores. You dig?" He ended the call before I could answer.

I leaned back into the booth and sipped coffee, trying to formulate a plan. I tried to keep calm but my heart pounded and I felt the blood pulsate in my temples.

The bikers left the bar. The guy in the Jiffy Lube shirt shuffled over to my table and asked if I had any pot to sell. I stuck the muzzle of the Browning under his nose and told him to get the hell away from me or there'd be an immediate opening on the lube rack tomorrow. He scurried off, toward the jukebox on the other side of the room. Selma grinned at me and shook her head. I threw a couple of dollars on the bar and left as she lit another match and watched it burn.

In the car, I called Olson and told him about the conversation with Jack Washington. We talked about it for a few minutes and then made plans to meet at the unit. There was much to do before sunrise.

Once there, we worked and planned until about two in the morning. Delmar made a few calls and arranged for another man to join our team, an ex–marine recon named Cyrus. In spite of the dishonorable discharge for striking an officer, he came highly recommended, someone who would keep his mouth shut. He arrived at midnight and helped with the final preparations. After that we slept, or tried to. At about four, we woke up, ate something, and left.

The river bottom runs through downtown, a mile-or-more-wide strip of soggy dirt sandwiched between two levees, with the Trinity threading its way down the middle of the track. The river itself is nothing remarkable, a thin trickle of muddy water slowly oozing its way toward the coast. Shallow and narrow, in most other places it would be called a creek. The area between the levees belongs to the U.S. Army Corps of Engineers, who forbid trespassing with signs and locked gates and all sorts of deterrents.

All the barricades accomplish is to keep out law-abiding citizens, doing nothing to stop the scofflaws who use the land as their in-town recreation area. For years it had been the playground of illegal hunters looking for the out-of-season dove, teenagers looking to party and score, and Mexicans looking to escape the daily grind and violence of life in a foreign land with the things they remember from home.

Like cockfights.

It was into one of these illegal sporting areas that we were headed in the cool stillness just before dawn. It was about 4:30 A.M. Olson stopped at a spot along Canada Drive, the potholed street running along the south levee. He left us between a burned-out house and a white-washed church called the Full Gospel Tabernacle of Christ, the Reverend Delaware Monroe presiding. The Reverend Monroe was nowhere to be seen, so we used the back of his church to shield our activities from the nonexistent traffic. The plan was simple. The other three would cover me while I went and made the deal. My specialty had been CQB, close quarters combat. Room-to-room fighting. This was going to be different, an open fighting arena. Fortunately, all four of us had spent some time in the sandboxes and hot zones of the Middle East, working similar ops. We were better trained and better equipped than a couple of strung-out dope peddlers and their goon squad. The only variable was how many of the bad guys would appear. Lack of intel makes me nervous but you have to play with what you've got.

While Olson headed to a location farther up from the rendezvous point, Delmar, Cyrus, and I huddled behind the church and checked our equipment. We wore black combat fatigues. Cyrus carried a thirty-pound pack on his back, full of you-know-what. Delmar carried extra ammo and some other fun things. I traveled light, due to my wound, only carrying my Browning, and a Heckler & Koch MP-5 submachine gun.

The subgun had a silencer and two thirty-round mags, taped opposite each other for a quick reload. It was the Cadillac of machine guns. Never skimp on hardware, that was my motto.

We checked our comm units, minuscule little things with tiny earpieces and throat-mounted mikes. Everything worked properly, reaching all the way to Olson, who was stationed upriver in an abandoned minivan sitting on top of the south levee. He carried a couple of sidearms and an M-16, along with about eight zillion bullets.

And Miss Clarita, the .50-caliber sniper rifle from hell.

After making sure everything worked and was secure, we began the hump over the levee. Cyrus and Delmar went first, spread out about twenty yards apart, with me forming the bottom point of the triangle. The night-vision goggles gave everything a greenish tint. The air was humid and smelled of rain. I started to sweat.

Once on the bottoms, Delmar took the point, pushing through the knee-high grass with Cyrus and the delivery twenty or thirty yards behind. I rode as tailgunner. My side began to hurt, but I ignored it. After a few hundred yards I took another half a Tylenol.

The cockfighting place was in a stand of cottonwoods, next to the river. The trees loomed ahead, darker than the night sky. We'd determined the exact location with a couple of calls to some hombres who knew of such matters.

One lone, sickly mesquite tree stood between us and the meeting point. I spoke a few words, and Cyrus dropped the pack ten paces away from the tree, toward the river. Delmar and I waited for him to finish his tasks. After a few minutes he clicked twice on the comm unit and the three of us continued through the grass to the grove.

We flanked out and entered the stand of trees from three different directions. It was empty, as I had thought. The meeting time was not for two hours. I suspected they would have people guarding the barricaded entry points to the bottoms, not actually in place at the clearing in the trees.

Someone had left four or five old lawn chairs scattered around a campfire pit. I pulled one underneath a tree while Delmar got the inflatable dummy out of his pack. He huffed and puffed until the thing began to resemble a human. We dressed it in black fatigues and a matching cap, and sat it in the chair, pulling the whole setup deep into the shadows. To one side, we put a package of wadded-up newspaper, wrapped to look like the missing drug shipment.

This was the fallback position.

Delmar and Cyrus melted into the shadows, their mission to hide in the grass surrounding the stand of trees and wait for the bad guys. My position was behind the trunk of a dead or dying elm, near the tree line closest to the Continental Viaduct, presumably the direction from where they would arrive.

I took another Tylenol, along with one of the white meth tablets, and waited.

CHAPTER TWENTY-SEVEN

The sky had lightened to a pale gray when the first man appeared. Olson, with the fancy rifle scope, saw him first. He radioed the rest of us.

"Car stopped on the viaduct. One man, getting out. And . . ." There was a long pause. Even with all the optics, I guessed it was hard to make out details. Finally he clicked back on. ". . . and he's carrying a rifle. Hold on. Another one, I think. Come on, dude. Get out of the car. Oh yeah. Got two now. Second one's packing a rifle also. And a backpack."

Then he was silent. I slipped to the edge of the trees and peered out. It was still too dark to see anything.

Olson spoke again. "Okay, you've got these two moving. Down the levee." Long pause. "They're on the ground. Your level. They're flanking out and heading toward the trees. I'm gonna lose sight of them."

I was on the levee side of the trees, farthest from the river. The morning was in that between time, where the night goggles helped as much as they hindered. I took them off, squinted, and finally saw movement, maybe a football field away. "I got the one on the levee side. Designate him Levee Boy, and call it a hundred and fifty meters out."

I got back a chorus of acknowledgments.

Levee Boy walked a few more feet, then evidently hunkered down near a bush because there wasn't any more movement. Cyrus radioed that he thought he'd sighted the one on the river side, holding steady. We designated him River Boy, except for Delmar, who wanted to call him Soon-to-Be-Dead Guy.

Nervous laughter. Somebody made gunfire noises. More chuckles at the gallows humor.

Then, silence. Five minutes stretched to ten, then to thirty, as the sky lightened. Olson came back on. "Different car's at the same place. Three, no, four guys getting out. All of 'em carrying AKs. They're moving down the levee."

I pulled out a pair of small field glasses and could just make out the activity.

"Oops, that had to hurt," Olson said. "These must be city boys. One of 'em just lost his footing and busted his ass."

"Any of them look like Nolan?" I said.

Olson came back, subdued. "Negative."

Nobody said anything for a few moments until the cellular vibrated against my leg.

"Got a call," I radioed to the others. From the thigh pocket of my fatigues, I pulled out the phone. "Yeah."

"You got my shit?" Jack Washington's voice sounded clear and crisp, as if in the next room.

"Yeah, I have it. Where's the girl?"

"We'll worry about the bitch later, after I get my product."

"No, we'll worry about her now."

Washington ignored me. "Where're you at?"

"I'm by the trees. Where's Nolan?"

"Step out where I can see you. On the river side."

I started that way, talking as I moved. "Put Nolan on the phone."

"Shit, motherfucker, ain't you got it yet? We doing this my way, not yours."

Before I could say anything, I heard Cyrus's voice in my other ear. "I got the four. They're on the river side. They're flanked out. Wait. Hold it. One's dropped behind a bush. You've got three visible. One hiding, plus the other three."

I covered the mouthpiece on the cell phone with my thumb and acknowledged his information. A thin, watery dawn filtered through the trees as I threaded my way to the other side. Cigarette butts, beer cans, and other garbage, now visible, littered the ground. I stepped around a pile of old tires and scared two rats the size of poodles. At the edge of the tree line someone had left two ancient television sets stacked one on top of the each other. I used them as cover and eased myself around to look out.

Three figures stood about seventy-five yards away, toward the Continental Street Viaduct. I brought the phone back up and said, "I only see three men. Where's Nolan?"

The group moved toward my hiding place. No communication.

At thirty yards away, Jack Washington came back on the line. "Out. Where I can see you."

"First you tell me where the girl is."

Jack chuckled and hung up the phone. Before I could ponder what that meant, I heard movement behind me. All the amphetamines in the world couldn't help. I reacted in time, but the suppressor hung on a tree branch. I turned to see the muzzle of a bolt-action rifle pointed about five feet from my head.

"Please. Gun down. Hands up." The accent was Slavic and matched the pale face that peered at me from underneath a hooded cape of burlap. A forest of artfully arranged plastic foliage covered the cloth. The outfit was called a ghillie suit by those who knew of such things, and was used mostly by snipers. It perfectly matched the surrounding terrain. The man's belly was covered in mud, indicating a long crawl. I figured him to be ex–Soviet military, probably special forces.

"Valk. Out." He waved his weapon.

"Yeah, I'll *valk*," I said, speaking for the benefit of my crew. "Quit pointing that rifle at me. Where the hell did you come from?" The throat mike was hidden by the collar of my shirt. The earpiece was clear and on the opposite side and would hopefully remain unnoticed.

"Gun on the ground." He pointed the muzzle of the rifle downward. I complied. He indicated the pistol on my belt and I dropped that too.

"Valk." He scooped up the MP-5 with one hand, leaving the sidearm on the ground.

I "valked" out of the trees and into Jack Washington and his posse of thugs. He stood between the two others, no gun visible. His companions had AKs pointed my way. The Russian slung his sniper rifle over his shoulder and waited.

"You don't look like you're carrying my shit," Washington said. "Where is it?"

"It's within reach, but hidden. Where's Nolan?"

"She's not exactly where you can help her." He laughed.

"She better be in one piece, Washington."

He smiled and said something, but it was difficult to process two conversations at once. I couldn't understand his reply because of the noise in my ear. "Cyrus says he's got a shot at River Boy." Washington took a step toward me, talking; Delmar said something else. Olson's voice was louder than everyone: "Go on my signal. I've got the Levee Guy. GO DOWN NOW, HANK."

Pay no mind when someone talks about the glory of battle and the thrill of combat. It's a dirty, nasty business that no sane man would search out. It's a series of disjointed sights, sounds, and smells, magnified a thousand times by adrenaline. Your skin alternates between clammy and sweaty. Your head spins and your stomach flutters with anticipation of the next shot. Everything jumbles in your brain and comes out surreal. It makes no sense. It's horrible.

I headed down as directed by Olson, right as River Boy squealed and dropped. At the same time, a reddish mist sprayed off to my right as the torso of the Russian sniper disappeared. A half second later there was a sonic boom in the distance followed by the faint sound of a car alarm. A pile of something red and livery landed a few feet in front of me.

Miss Clarita had spoken.

I crawled toward the remains of the Russian, through the mess that had been his chest cavity, and grabbed the MP-5. Small arms chattered all around me. The stench of blood and the contents of the Russian's bowels filled my nose. I could feel my own life force dripping from the wound in my side, reinjured during the movement.

Shouting.

Swearing.

More gunfire.

A cloud of dirt erupted from the ground, ten feet in front of me, followed by the sound of the .50-caliber. Noises in my ear, my team talking to one another. Olson broke through the fog. "Hank, sweep it at twelve o'clock."

I pushed the safety off and sprayed an ankle-high swath of bullets in front of me, the working of the bolt the only noise until a scream pierced the air.

Olson's voice again. "Hank, you need to get out of there. They've got reinforcements coming. Make for the tree line."

Mama Oswald's boy doesn't need to be told twice. I jumped up and ran for cover, ignoring the pain in my side. Another Slavic-looking guy emerged out of the grass, thirty yards in front of me, shooting my way with a semiautomatic pistol held sideways, gangster-style. I dumped half a mag at him, as did someone behind me. The figure convulsed and fell, spasmodically firing into the ground on the way down.

I entered the grove at the same place I'd left and managed to scoop up my Browning on the way. I paused for a moment and wiped sweat out of my eyes. Even early in the day, the heat was suffocating in the trees, compounded by the lack of breeze and the heavy fatigues I wore.

More gunfire erupted, a lot more, coming from the direction of the Continental Viaduct. A couple of stray bullets slammed into trees nearby. From a long way off I heard sirens.

I made my way back toward my team, running as quietly as possible, one hand holding the wound on my side, the other leading with the subgun. I pressed through a group of saplings toward where we'd placed the dummy. There was a gunshot close by and then Jack Washington's voice swearing.

I stopped cold, willing myself to be as quiet as possible.

He howled, a banshee screaming in the light of dawn. He'd found the fake stash. I peered through the brush and could see a blur of movement as he ran through the woods. I lost sight of him, but then his voice exploded again in the stillness of the grove. "Hey, Oswald. You out there? Well, guess what? Your bitch is dead and so are you."

The trees deflected and twisted his words. I quashed any feelings I had and tried to get a bead on his location but couldn't. There was another boom from the .50-caliber followed by a prolonged rattle of fully automatic fire.

"You hear me, Oswald? You are one dead motherfucker." The words came from one direction, then another. "I will hunt you down if it's the last thing I do."

My foot brushed against a rock. I picked it up and threw it as far as I could manage in the undergrowth, heading in the opposite direction before it landed.

Washington fired at the sound and ran toward the clearing. I caught a glimpse of him moving and let loose with the silenced machine gun. The nine-millimeter chewed a path through the brush, toward the target. Then he was gone.

I heard crashing off to my left. Then, "She screamed a lot. Didn't break easy." He fired at something and the bullet hit a tree ten yards behind me. I moved to the right as quietly as possible, and resisted the urge to let him bait me and draw fire before I was ready. He continued to shoot randomly. Olson started talking in my ear. I switched the comm unit off and wiped sweat from my palms, breathing shallowly through my mouth.

Then Jack "the Crack" Washington made a mistake.

Another barrage of small-arms fire crackled in the distance. He took the noise as an opportunity to dart across the edge of the clearing where I had a clean view. I dumped half a clip at him and he went down, landing hard in the dirt. Shaking, I jammed a fresh magazine in the gun and approached the still figure carefully. Blood mixed with earth as it trickled out of his wounds. I kept the muzzle trained on him. When I was about six feet away, he opened his eyes and coughed. Blood flecked his lips.

"F-f-fuck you." His voice was weak.

"Eloquent."

He spat at me, a mixture of blood and saliva that barely made it past his chin.

"Where's Nolan?" I said.

"Too late."

I felt nothing but coldness and amphetamine-induced jitteriness. "Where's Coleman Dupree?"

Washington's eyes rolled upward in his head, then came back down. He coughed again, a gurgling noise like someone blowing bubbles in a soft drink. "He'll find you when he's ready." He made a sound like a laugh, and smiled. Then he died. Something deep inside him rattled and a bloody bubble blew out of his mouth. It was time for me to move. Sporadic gunfire competed with sirens in the distance.

I switched on the tiny radio unit.

"—come in. Hank, come in, please." Delmar's voice.

"Yeah, I'm back with you."

"You gotta problem with maintaining radio communication like we agreed on?"

I headed away from the shooting and sirens, toward where Olson had dropped us off. "Sorry. Been a little busy. Fill me in."

"Smokey the Bear has inun-fucking-dated the viaduct."

"What's the plan?"

"Head back the way we came. Cyrus and I are in a stand of willows at the edge of the river, right under the Sylvan Street Bridge. There're no cops at this end. Yet. You better belly-crawl it anyway."

"Yeah." I stood at the edge of the trees and got my bearings. "I'm gonna pass on the belly crawl."

Daggers shot through my side and I felt blood dribble. I ran low and headed for the willows by the underpass. I gave wide clearance to the tree where Cyrus had left the package. After what seemed like an eternity, I slogged my way into the meager shelter of brush on the river's edge. My two compatriots huddled there. Cyrus kept guard, scanning for trouble. Delmar had the backpack we'd left in the truck, now lying open on the ground.

He held a drill bit in his teeth, while he worked the chuck on a cordless Makita. "Olson dropped this off for cleanup." He stuck the bit where it belonged and tightened down. "He's at the base of the bridge. We're gonna dump the guns and then head that way." He handed me the drill. "It's set up for a nine-millimeter."

I nodded and pushed the magazine release button on the MP-5, then cleared the chamber of the live round. After checking to make sure the hardened drill bit was secure, I jammed it into the muzzle of the subgun. Four or five passes with the extra-hard cutting tool obliterated the rifled grooves of the barrel. No ballistic test would ever be able to match a specific bullet to this gun. Expensive, yes, it was, but better than getting caught with a gun linked to a bunch of dead people.

Cyrus and Delmar repeated the operation with their firearms. Not counting my Browning, which had not been fired, we were down to one now, a short-barreled M-16 that had been stuck in the backpack and was clean. Delmar radioed Olson that we were almost ready. I gathered up the weapons and tossed them into the muddy water one at a time.

I dropped the last one and turned to my companions. "Welcome to Gun River."

Delmar chuckled without humor. "Let's get the hell out of here."

Ten minutes later, we were in Olson's Suburban, sweaty and dirty but in one piece. I mopped up blood from my side as best I could and put a fresh field dressing on the wound. Olson handed me a pint of Dewar's and I washed down a codeine. Upon short reflection I decided to have another.

I gave Cyrus twenty one-hundred-dollar bills. He told us the address of a girl in Carrollton where he wanted to be dropped off. Olson pulled the truck off Canada Drive, looping around to get on the Sylvan Street Bridge.

The traffic on the overpass was slow as everybody tried to make out the scene at the Continental Viaduct. When we reached the middle, the traffic stopped again. From a long way off came a thudding sound. Somebody had hit the perimeter trip wire Cyrus had set up in a circle thirty yards in all directions of the package. I rolled down the window and could just make out a white cloud drifting with the wind through the rain.

Delmar said, "Two ounces was just right." I nodded but didn't reply. We'd put on quite a show for the assembled police and spectators.

Two ounces for thirty pounds. Gone in a cloud of smoke.

CHAPTER TWENTY-EIGHT

The day after the battle at the river, I attended a memorial service for Charles Michael Wesson. The intermittent thunderstorms promised by the TV weatherman in the purple shirt never materialized, replaced instead by an extra-thick band of humid air layering the city like marijuana smoke at a Grateful Dead concert as the low pressure trough held its place over the Gulf. A record broke for that day when the temperature hit 102 about the time the funeral started. I wanted to wear shorts and a T-shirt but instead put on a lightweight suit.

The event took place at a Baptist church on Marsh Lane, not far from where Vera Drinkwater lived with her husband, Duane. The church was small, befitting the number of mourners. A couple more people and we could have fielded a football team.

Afterward, I told Vera what I could, which wasn't much. I promised I would learn more and fill her in later. She started to cry and talk at the same time, but I couldn't understand her through the sobbing. Duane stalked up at that moment, resplendent in a light green double-breasted suit and white loafers. The jacket had been cut to accentuate his shoulders. A guy stood behind him who looked like a hairless gorilla in sweatpants and a wife-beater T-shirt. The gorilla had on so much cologne he left a puddle when he stood still.

Duane said something derogatory about my mother and then suggested that I do an anatomical impossibility. A surge of anger spiked through me. The next thing I knew, a black guy in a suit had ahold of me, and was shoving me into an unmarked police car. They said later that Duane's collarbone did *not* break, but the Paco Rabanne–wearing simian would be walking funny for the next few weeks.

When I snapped back to the land of sanity and reasonableness, we were pulling into the parking lot of a Denny's on Forest Lane. The black guy in question was Sergeant Jessup, the investigating officer in Charlie Wesson's death. His partner, Sonny Conroy, rode in the passenger seat.

We took a booth in the back and ordered coffee. Jessup pulled a pack of Merit Ultra Lights out of his pocket and sparked one up, defying the No Smoking signs. He spoke through a cloud of nicotine. "Next time you assault somebody, make sure the police aren't standing around watching."

"I'll make a note of that."

Conroy grunted and dumped a couple of pounds of sugar in his coffee.

Jessup spoke again. "You read the papers, Oswald? Follow your local current events much?"

"Yeah, sort of." I shrugged my shoulders.

"You read the newspaper this morning?"

"Uh-huh. You mean about the new Cowboy running back and that prostitute?"

Jessup chuckled and rolled the cigarette in his mouth. "No. I'm talking about the firefight at the Continental Viaduct."

"Oh, *that* story." I drank some coffee. "What about it?"

Jessup stubbed out his smoke. "Seven people killed. Two police officers wounded. One critically."

I nodded but didn't say anything, figuring that he didn't want me to point out the obvious, how six of the seven people killed had forty-three arrests, seven convictions, and nine outstanding warrants among them.

Jessup pulled out another cigarette but didn't light it. "Then of course there was the explosion. A shitload of white stuff blown every which way."

"Does this conversation have a point?"

He didn't say anything, just fiddled with his lighter. Sonny Conroy grunted again, and shifted his weight to scratch his left buttock. The waitress came around and poured everybody another cup of coffee. She was young and pretty, not coarsened by the years of bad food, bad booze, and bad love that were yet to come. As she left I watched her move down the aisle, back toward the cash register. Nice legs. Why was I thinking about legs now?

When she sat down at the counter, Jessup said, "The point is, maybe you could help us clarify the who and the what of the activities on the river."

"You've got the wrong guy, Officer Jessup. I'm afraid I can't tell you anything."

Conroy spoke for the first time. "We were late getting the choppers up but one of our people on the ground thought he saw some men, dressed in black, towards the Sylvan Street Bridge. So yesterday, we got a crime scene team to the site. Somebody had been there. Found a bunch of nine-millimeter casings and fresh footprints. The officer in charge got the bright idea of dragging the river, seeing what comes up."

He paused for a drink of coffee. "They pulled out a pile of guns. Military-type stuff with serial numbers that go nowhere. And here's the funny part: the barrels, they've all been blown out, the rifling gone. That's not a gangbanger trick. That's a professional move."

"Really." I drained the last of my coffee, wishing I could get another cup and Irish it up. "Think that has anything to do with the dead bodies that keep showing up all over town?"

Jessup sighed and leaned back in the booth. "That kept us hopping for a while. That's over for the time being. The longhairs in narcotics tell us there's been a shift in the power structure of the dope trade." His tone was casual and he affected a relaxed demeanor.

Neither man spoke for a moment. Sonny Conroy fiddled with the salt and pepper shakers, moving them around on the tabletop like some peculiar chess game only he understood. Finally Jessup spoke. "Coleman Dupree has disappeared. After the shit storm at the river, he had a small manpower shortage. Packed up and gone. It's too bad, we'd like to have a talk with him."

"Have you asked his brother where he is?" Score one for my side. By the looks on their faces they didn't know what I was talking about.

"His brother," Jessup said. "Who's that?"

"You don't know?" I enjoyed drawing out the moment. "Actually, it's his half brother. Name's Aaron Young."

Jessup leaned forward. "Coleman Dupree's brother is Aaron Young? The same guy that got the contract for the—"

"Yeah, the guy in charge of the Trinity Vista."

They dropped me back at the church. I got in the Taurus and headed toward the tollway and Baylor Hospital. I'd been there already that morning, before the funeral, but wanted to go again. Ernie was still in a coma and I guessed that was a good thing since he wasn't in pain. Also, I didn't have to tell him that there'd been no word from his niece for three days now. I didn't have to tell him that she was probably dead and it would be a miracle if her body was ever found. I'd told all I could to Miranda. She'd nodded and cried and then took a couple of pills.

At Northwest Highway, I exited. It was the wrong place to get off, but I did anyway. I headed west until I got to a topless bar called the Amazon Club. There used to be a dancer who worked there named Connie or Karen or something like that. I'd helped her out with a problem involving a certain local televangelist who had a thing for handcuffs, tall redheads, and crotchless panties, not necessarily in that order or in the way you might think.

Unfortunately, that had been a long time ago and she no longer worked there. I sat at the bar and tried to figure out what I wanted to ask her. Something about dancers. I was midway through my second beer when it came to me. I threw some money down and left.

I burned it down the tollway this time, anxious to get to the office and the phone number I needed. Fifteen minutes later I rolled in the front door, passed my two remarkably sober suite mates, and went into my office. It took a few minutes but I found the card I was looking for, hiding underneath a box of .38 Specials in the bottom drawer. Rick Haggard, private investigator. New York City.

I got him on the first try with the second number. We small-talked for a few minutes, chatting about the thing we'd worked on in L.A. a few years back, and a couple of grifters we knew in common. Finally I told him what I needed. He said it would be no problem and he'd get back to me in a day or so. It was a freebie, a professional courtesy, so I couldn't rush him. It didn't matter. The info wasn't going anywhere.

I left and went to the hospital. Miranda sat outside the room, leafing through a magazine and looking at a blank spot on the far wall. The pills were good and bad at the same time.

"Doctor's in there now. He's a new one." She let the magazine slide off her lap and onto the floor as I walked up. "Dr. Mort, one of the candy stripers told me. He's the one they call when there's nothing left to do."

"How're you doing?" I pulled a chair next to hers and sat down.

"I'm doing for shit, Hank." Her voice was flat, monotone, no emotion whatsoever.

I patted her hand. "Ernie still in a coma?"

"Yeah. Goddamn coma. Nurse said he's got edema. That's a fancy name for swollen feet." She exhaled loudly. "And that means his heart's shutting down. So he's gonna die sooner rather than later, and that's when they call in Dr. Mort." Still no tears or emotion. I guessed there was only so much anguish a body could hold.

I didn't know what to say. "Miranda, I am so sorry—"

She interrupted me. "And you know what, Hank? It's about damn time."

I looked at her but didn't say anything.

"Hope you don't think bad of me. But I don't give a shit." She lowered her voice and leaned closer to me. "I can't see him like this anymore. I can't do it."

The door to Ernie's room opened. A doctor and two nurses came out. The doc wore a set of three-day-old scrubs and a four-day-old beard. His eyes were red-rimmed, his hair was disheveled. I'd seen gutter slut cokeheads who looked better.

"Mrs. Ruibal, I'm Dr. Mort Silverberg." His breath smelled like cigarettes. "Your husband is in the end stages of hepatocellular carcinoma. It's probably metastasized even farther than we'd thought. I'm afraid he won't live out the night." He tried to look like he cared but didn't quiet pull it off. Miranda asked a couple of questions. He answered them. Then he left. We went inside and sat on either side of the bed.

In the end there's nothing to it, really. About ten, the monitors did that flat-line thing, and that was it. Finito. *No más Ernesto Ruibal.* Another spark extinguished in the vast cosmos. I thought I would feel more, but I didn't. Too much had happened in too short a period. Miranda got on the phone and pretty soon the room was filled with extended family and friends. Old women I didn't know, crying and wailing. She was in good hands.

Before they came and wheeled out my padre and my partner, I leaned down and kissed him on the forehead. Then I slipped out, into the night. I walked around for a while, then went home, drank scotch, and stared at a spot on the floor.

CHAPTER TWENTY-NINE

The next morning I woke sweating, the sour taste of Dewar's coating my tongue and the pain deep inside me. The low the night before had been eighty-three, a phenomenon that usually only occurred in the dog days of August. Anything above eighty for the low kept the city from properly cooling at night, which made everyone's air-conditioning less efficient. My body felt greasy with perspiration, and jittery. I ached like a decayed tooth that couldn't be removed.

My various wounds and bruises hurt more than usual, and I stubbed my toe on the way to the bathroom. Once there I showered and scrubbed and brushed and soaped under cool water and repeated all of the above until I felt a little less bad, physically anyway. Dripping, still in my towel, I called Jessup to see if anything had turned up on Nolan.

Nada. Again.

I dressed and went to the Ruibal house to . . . to do whatever it was that people like me do in situations like this. Olson and Delmar came along to help. Olson had brought a chicken casserole. Once we got there, Delmar pulled me aside and told me to act like it tasted good because Olson had stayed up until three making the damn thing. Delmar was the cook in the family but Olson had insisted that he wanted to do something, and his contribution was to fix a chicken casserole. Both men were unusually subdued. Ernie had meant a lot to them also.

The small house was filled with mourners, friends, extended family, even a couple of representatives from the Hispanic Police League of Dallas. A former city councilman was drinking coffee in the living room, talking to a silver-haired man who'd just flown in from El Paso. Ernie had been a friend and adviser to a great many people from all walks of life over the years.

Olson, Delmar, and I stood in the kitchen, sipping coffee and trying to stay out of the way. Somebody dropped that day's issue of the *Dallas Morning News* on the table. We each took a section and skimmed it, as the people and preparations for a traditional Mexican funeral whirled around us.

Olson grunted and handed me the business pages. "Read this. Third page toward the bottom."

I looked where he indicated. It was in the Business Briefs section, the stuff deemed barely worthy of newsprint. I read it aloud. "Mr. Roger Strathmore announced today his retirement from his family's company, Strathmore Realty. In a prepared statement Mr. Strathmore said that he was looking for a lifestyle change and would be moving to Santa Fe, New Mexico, to pursue a career as an artist. There was no mention of his unexplained absence from the U.S. Corps of Engineers meeting where he was to deliver a proposal on his company's desire to manage the Trinity Vista project. Observers say that his unexplained nonattendance was part of the reason, but not the only one, that resulted in the project being awarded to a South Dallas firm headed by Aaron Young, a prominent real estate developer in that area. Minority activists hailed the Aaron Young decision as a milestone in race relations in Dallas. Calls to Strathmore Realty were not returned."

Olson whistled. "So Roger's not a corpus delicti after all. Wonder what that's all about?"

I had a real good idea but didn't say anything.

Miranda breezed into the kitchen, a herd of middle-aged women following in her wake. She shooed them away and then came over to me.

"Hank? *Por favor, un—*" She stopped abruptly and sighed. "Sorry. Haven't spoken this much Spanish in years. Hank, I need to talk to you for a moment."

I followed her into the small utility room off the kitchen.

"Nolan's mother just got here." She paused and looked at me. "I wanted you to know. Since Nolan is missing I thought you could talk to her. It must be difficult losing a brother and not knowing about her child." She paused to clear her throat, and I patted her arm.

She started talking again. "I-I-I thought that . . . I thought that since . . . since Nolan—" Her voice broke. "Oh, Hank, Ernie's dead." She cried then, big wails of agony, tears of what was left of the pain and sadness she thought were all gone after the drawn-out, bitter death of Ernesto Ruibal.

I held on to her and murmured soft things. Several of her posse of mourners poked their heads in, tongues clucking that they were not comforting the widow Ruibal. After a while she quit crying and left. I sat on the dented Kenmore for a while, in the tiny room utility room at the back of the late Ernie Ruibal's house in East Dallas. I didn't want to talk to Nolan O'Connor's mother. What would I say? *Sorry?*

From where I rested, I could see a slice of the kitchen, people coming and going as the activity level increased in the house. Food smells wafted in, corn tortillas, coffee, and cinnamon rolls. I wondered where Nolan was at that exact moment and said a quick prayer for her safe return. I missed her. The psychoanalysis that actually proved to be pretty astute. The skepticism of the street so often apparent in the deep blue eyes. The fact that she had been a partner when I needed one. And I had let her down. Just like I had done with Charlie Wesson and Vera.

After a few minutes a gray-haired man with a bushy mustache sauntered into my field of view. Several of the hens clustered around the stove greeted him, making a fuss. He spoke to Miranda, and the way he positioned his head, and the way she moved her body, told me a tiny story about what the future held, the years to come without Ernie Ruibal walking this earth.

Anger coursed through my body, and I fought the urge to grab my pistol and shoot the man with the bushy mustache. Instead, I answered my cell phone. The voice of my friend in New York sounded crackly in my ear. I heard what he said, though, and asked him to fax the info to me. I hung up. That's when the woman screamed and I knew they'd found Nolan.

I bounded out of the room and into the kitchen. A groundswell of voices came from the dining room, yelling and crying. I pressed through the crowd and saw a middle-aged woman in a dark shawl crying. I didn't recognize her but knew instantly it was Nolan O'Connor's mother by the way she moved her head and the line of her jaw. She cried and grasped a cordless phone in front of her as if it were on fire. Miranda stood on one side of her, holding on and weeping, her face contorted so much it looked like a smile.

All the other women were crying and talking excitedly at the same time. Delmar appeared beside me. "They found her."

I nodded and closed my eyes.

"Hank." He grabbed my arm and squeezed. "She's alive."

Parkland Hospital emergency room. The same doors through which they had wheeled me only days before.

My Browning set off the metal detectors. Olson intervened as the guard tried to frisk me. Delmar held me in a bear hug so I wouldn't hurt anybody or myself. Shouts and threats. More yelling. Another guard appeared and drew his revolver. Then there was silence. Delmar kept his arms wrapped around me and his eye on the gun. Olson had the first guard on the ground, hands behind his back. The second guard, the one with the gun, opened his mouth to speak but the metal detector went off again. We all looked up to see Officer Jessup standing there, holding his shield in one hand. He spoke to the guards: "Let 'em go. They're with me."

The rent-a-cops didn't like it but complied. Olson released the one on the ground and muttered an apology. The four of us left them and found the nurses' station. Once again the badge worked its magic and we soon found ourselves talking to an ER doc wearing bloody scrubs and a bad attitude.

He was older than the one who had treated me, maybe mid-forties. He looked at Olson and Delmar, then at me. Finally he turned to Jessup. "Are any of you family?"

"Do I look like family?" the black man said. "Dallas Police. Homicide. What can you tell me?" He flashed his badge again.

"She's not dead." The doctor pulled a lollipop from a pocket. It looked like a skinny cigarette hanging out of his mouth. "What do you want with her?"

"I need to talk to her." Jessup sighed dramatically. "About a homicide." I took a step forward. "How is she?"

The doctor looked from Jessup to me. He sucked on his lollipop for a few seconds longer than necessary. "Who are you?"

Jessup put a hand on my arm as I took another step toward the man. "He's another party concerned with the health and welfare of a certain Nolan O'Connor, who I believe you are treating at the moment. Which gets back to my original question. What can you tell me about her condition?"

"You should know about the new medical privacy laws." The doctor pointed to Jessup with the lollipop. "Can't tell anybody anything until I see some documentation on a case you are investigating or the patient says it's okay."

Olson growled. Delmar flexed his fists. I got very cold and still.

"Suit yourself." Jessup shrugged. "Here's how I see it. You're pushing fifty and still working the ER. That's a young man's game. You're not the head doc either because nobody treats you that way."

The man didn't say anything.

Jessup continued. "Which means you've either fucked up somewhere along the line, or pissed off somebody. Based on your attitude, I'm guessing the latter."

The doctor opened his mouth but didn't say anything.

"So why don't you tell me how the woman is, before you piss *me* off." Jessup cocked his head to one side and stared at the man.

The ER doc hesitated for a few moments and then talked. An elderly Russian woman, bad to no English, had dropped her off that morning. She'd found her in a vacant apartment, in East Richardson, an area where most Russian immigrants settled. She wasn't in bad shape except for a GSW to the leg, which hadn't been treated and was now infected. A few cuts and bruises. Nothing major. She was unconscious due to surgery to remove the bullet. Jessup questioned him further, about the Russian woman and other details. The doctor led us to a small window where we could see her still figure, hooked up to an array of machines. I stayed there for a moment and watched her chest rise and fall underneath the thin hospital blankets. Jessup continued to ask questions of the ER doctor.

Delmar, Olson, and I slipped out after determining that we wouldn't be allowed to visit with her. In the parking lot, Olson asked what I was planning to do. I ignored him, got in the Ford and headed for the office, with a quick stop at the unit.

CHAPTER THIRTY

For a prominent, socially connected, rich-ass son of bitch, Fagen Strathmore was damn tough to find. How hard is it to hide a six-and-a-half-foot-tall multimillionaire? According to a directory for one of the country clubs, he lived on the twentieth floor of a high-rise on Turtle Creek. I scammed my way past the front-desk security with a set of INS credentials. A middle-aged black woman in a maid's outfit answered the door and said that Mr. Strathmore didn't live there anymore on account of he and Mrs. Corrine were getting a divorce and no, she didn't know where he was staying. The tone of her voice did not indicate a great deal of respect for either employer. I gave her fifty dollars and my cell phone number, and told her to call me if she heard anything.

From there I hit a couple of bars and social clubs, putting out the word on the Mexo-American grapevine of wait staff and cleaning people that I was searching for Señor Hombre Grande, Fagen Strathmore, and that I would pay *mucho dinero* for information on where he might be staying, eating, or drinking. On the third day after we put Ernie Ruibal in the ground, a waiter at the Dallas Country Club called me. He said Señor Strathmore was there now, finishing lunch with two men. I was in the car, close by, so I headed that way.

A block away, the phone rang again. He was leaving, in a black Cadillac SUV, out of the Mockingbird Lane exit. I ran a red light, not the smartest thing to do considering what I was planning, and made Mockingbird just as a black truck turned north on Preston Road. Traffic ran light for noon on a weekday. I punched the gas on the Taurus and passed an Oldsmobile. The light changed and several cars stopped ahead of me. I cut through the parking lot of the gas station on the corner, tires squealing on the asphalt.

The congestion was heavier on Preston, and I could barely see the truck, ten or twelve blocks ahead. With one eye in the mirror and the other looking forward, I darted in and out of the line of cars, trying to go only ten miles over the speed limit. By Northwest Highway, I'd closed the gap to three cars. The Cadillac turned left and I followed, keeping two or three cars between us.

Wherever he was headed, time was not a concern. Strathmore stuck to the middle lane, a steady and sedate thirty-five miles an hour. He passed the topless bars at Bachman Lake, then the megaplex movie theater and restaurants at Stemmons Freeway, and kept going. At Newkirk Lane, he turned north, into a run-down warehouse district built on the old City of Dallas landfill.

A few more streets passed and he turned left, then right into the parking lot of a squat, one-story building. It was made of prefab concrete, weathered to the color of a corpse. Idling at the corner, I could barely read the sign over the metal door that said, "Opal's Printing Service and Modeling Studio." I had no problem making out the long legs and black miniskirt of the girl that dashed out of the place and hopped in the passenger seat of the truck. I bet she wasn't named Opal. The SUV sat there for a few minutes until three more girls scampered out of the building, similarly clad. They got in the backseat.

The truck backed out of the parking lot and headed away from me. There was no traffic so I waited until it made the turn at the far corner before following. We left Dumpville and headed back to town. They were in a hurry now, and I was guessing Miss Legs and her three pals had something to do with that. They crossed Stemmons, weaving in and out of traffic.

We hit Walnut Hill Lane, headed east, into the middle of North Dallas. The Caddy slowed as it passed a squad car at Midway Road, and I did the same, keeping my hands on the wheel in the driver's ed position of ten and two. The police paid us no mind.

The truck turned onto Strait Lane, a strip of asphalt famous for its five-acre lots and garish mansions hidden by elaborate stone fences and massive oak trees. Three houses past the domicile of America's last viable third-party presidential candidate, the Caddy pulled into the driveway of a smallish place for the area, maybe only two acres and a five-bedroom ranch-style home nestled underneath two sweeping magnolia trees. I drove past, counting the number of mansions to the end of the block.

From there I drove down the alley, numbering lots until I got to the back of the home with the magnolias. I parked up against the fence of a house across the way, one down. I pulled on a pair of latex gloves and got two magnetic signs out of the trunk, slapping them on either side of the car. They said, "Owen's Pest Control Service. Don't Be Bugged by Bugs." It was approaching the hottest part of the day, the temperature near or just past 100. A drop of sweat meandered down the side of my face.

The gate was not locked, and I stepped into the rear of a gigantic backyard, in an area shielded from the house by a small hedge planted next to the side of the garage, to hide the pool equipment and garbage cans. I peered through the vegetation. The entire back of the house was glass, opening onto a large deck, pool, and hot tub. Before I could decide the next move, a sliding glass door opened and two of the girls came out, struggling with a loaded cooler between them. They were naked except for matching yellow bikini bottoms. One of them dropped her end and turned around to pick it up. A yellow *thong* bikini bottom.

They continued to the pool and dropped the cooler by the hot tub. The taller of the two, a redhead with breasts the size of cantaloupes, found the switch for the Jacuzzi and turned it on. They grabbed two beers from the cooler and hopped in at the same time as the door to the house opened again and Fagen Strathmore emerged with the other two G-string–clad girls. He walked like he'd been mainlining Viagra, stiffly and with his eyes glued to the chests of his two buddies. When he was almost to the pool I took the opportunity to do a little more reconnaissance. I slipped out the gate and went around the back of the four-car garage. There was a small gap between the side of the structure and the neighbor's fence. I squeezed through and soon found myself in the eighteen inches of no-man's-land between the two fences belonging to Strathmore's house and his neighbors. I stepped on one of the cross timbers and peered over the top. The side of the house was fifty yards away, hidden by more hedges. I figured there must be a walkway on the other side of the vegetation.

The overhead door was open and the Cadillac SUV sat at an angle in the middle of the garage. I looked down the driveway toward the street. No other cars were visible.

I jumped the fence and landed on the concrete, wincing at the pain in my side. As quickly as possible I made my way to where the hedges met the edge of the house. Once there I squeezed through and found myself by the kitchen door, at the end of a sidewalk leading toward the garage. The patio and glass doors leading to the pool were not visible from where I stood, nor was the hot tub. I could faintly hear squeals and giggles coming from that way.

I tried the kitchen door.

It opened without a hitch and I slipped inside, grateful for the cool air. A small entry area led into the kitchen, a vast room with two islands in the center and custom built-in appliances along the walls. One of the island counters housed a commercial gas range big enough for Emeril to sauté an entire pig. The next room was a cavernous family area where the glass door leading to the pool was located. I crawled in and peered over the edge of a large sofa. The activity in the hot tub was barely visible. I counted five heads in the churning water.

Before I did anything else, I wanted to know if the rest of the place was empty. The search took a while, but I was alone. Four bedrooms and a media chamber upstairs, expansive dining and living areas, a wine room, a library, another media room, and a master down. Not much furniture anywhere. What was there looked brand-new, just off the dealer's floor. The master bedroom had a king-size bed and a big-screen TV. There was a bunch of forty-three-inch-inseam khakis in the closet. The nightstand held a box of condoms, a Colt .45, and a bottle of Viagra. My superior detecting skills told me that this was Fagen Strathmore's lair.

A wallet and money clip lay on the dresser. I ignored those and picked up what I'd come inside for. A set of keys. A few minutes later I did what needed to be accomplished and returned them to where they belonged. I slipped out of the house again and went to the garage, surveying the meager set of yard tools lining one wall. A couple of items caught my eye and helped settle the best course of action.

Showtime.

CHAPTER THIRTY-ONE

The hot tub was the size of a Chevy Suburban and shaped like the state of Texas. Strathmore was in the panhandle region, near Amarillo, eyes closed as one of the girls bounced up and down on his lap in the unmistakable rhythm of copulation, her bare breasts swaying in tempo with the movement. She was the redhead, young and pretty, and shouldn't have to be exposed to people like him, no matter what her career choice. I almost felt sorry for her.

The other three noticed me but hadn't said anything. One smiled and waved. Maybe they thought I was the gardener or maybe they were used to Strathmore inviting people in to share their bounties.

For a moment, I thought about letting the man finish the act, but my side hurt and the sun was a furnace overhead. When I was about four feet away, I wiped the sweat off my face, turned on the electric blower that I had found, the orange extension cord snaking behind me to a plug in the garage.

The girls screamed and Strathmore pushed the redhead away. He looked at what I held in my hand and I could tell that he was slowly becoming aware of his predicament.

I shut off the blower. The only sound was the bubbles from the hot tub. One of the girls, a blonde with a small overbite who reminded me of Vera Drinkwater, tried to climb out.

"Don't do it. I'll drop this thing into the water."

She thought better of it, and sat back down, causing a small tidal wave in the confined area. The redhead crossed her arms over her breasts and sank down until only her head was out of the water.

Strathmore was breathing heavily, eyes glaring at me with a look that would cause sterility in lesser private investigators. He groped around in the bubbles until he found his swimming trunks. He yanked them under and fought the wave action of the tub until he could pull them on. After that he tried to regain a modicum of composure, plastering a smile on his face and reaching for his beer can. "Well, if it isn't Mr. Oswald."

"You've had enough beer." As his hand reached for the drink I turned the blower on and whooshed the can across the concrete. "Now's the time for answers."

The redhead started screaming, shaking her hands in front of her face like they were on fire. Fagen reached for a towel lying on the deck. I hit him with a blast of air, grabbed the towel, and found a stainless .38 Smith. Plop. It went into the deep end of the pool.

"I'm not kidding, Fagen. Any more funny shit, I'll drop this thing in there, and you'll fry like a piece of cheap steak. Be the main course, right after an appetizer of hooker soup." I blew a stream of air into the face of the screaming girl and then turned off the blower. "Honey? Hey, you. Naked chick. Shut the hell up." She quieted down to a whimper.

"Let's see you do it then." Fagen's voice was a growl. "You ain't got the balls."

I sat on my haunches and dangled the motor end of the tool over the surface of the water, three small inches from electrocution. "You really want to try me, Strathmore? Do you think I've never killed anybody?"

Fagen looked at me, then at the blower, and then back at my face. "All right, Oswald. What do you want?"

I rocked the electric blower back and forth in my hand like it was a six-shooter and I was Marshal Dillon. "I want to know why you picked one son over the other."

His mouth was already open and I could tell he'd been ready to say something, a snappy one-size-fits-all comeback that would allow him time to think and plan a proper response. My question stopped him cold.

"*What?*"

"You heard me."

Strathmore stared at me. He knew I knew.

I bammed the snout of the electric blower in the water, splashing everybody. "Quit stalling, Strathmore. I'm asking about your son Aaron Young, born to Lydia Mae Bryson on April 2, 1965, at Bellevue Hospital, in New York."

Strathmore's eyes got wide.

"Yeah," I said. "*That* son. How come he got the Trinity Vista?"

Fagen quit with the blustering and leaned back against the side of the tub. "You are a persistent fucker, aren't you?"

"You're a leg man. Aaron Young's mother hoofed it on Broadway for a while. The women I've met associated with you have all been attractive, with a certain look." I shrugged my shoulders.

Strathmore started to say something, jabbing his finger at me to emphasize a point. He thought better of it and remained quiet.

I continued. "Plus, I found Aaron's birth certificate and a copy of the paternity suit, filed in Superior Court, Borough of Manhattan." I pulled a sheaf of papers out of my pocket and tossed them into the bubbling waters.

Fagen's voice was resigned. "What do you want? Or should I say, how much do you want?"

I smiled. "Don't want any money. I want to know why two people had to die."

"I'm as clean as a whistle." The last was said with some pride.

I almost lost control and forgot my plan, said the hell with it and dropped the blower in the water and electrocuted the lot of them. Instead, I counted to five and took a deep breath. "Yeah, how'd you manage it? I mean, that was pretty damn clever of you . . ." I let my voice trail off, hoping that an appeal to his vanity would snag him.

His eyes narrowed but he didn't say anything.

"I figured you had it planned all the time. Somewhere along the line, you found out your illegitimate son had come to Dallas, and was making a name for himself in the real estate business. You probably learned about Aaron Young the same time you figured out that your other son really didn't have what it takes."

Fagen Strathmore nodded slowly and smiled.

I continued. "Then along comes the Trinity Vista: the cream puff, cat daddy of all deals, and you've got to have it. But there's just one problem. You've more or less retired and the company is run by your son, Roger, who unfortunately controls his mom and sister's stock. Which means you can't just kick him out. So he gets a run at the Trinity Vista project and a chance to lose it. I bet you were mighty pissed off when all that became clear."

Fagen laughed and nodded. "Yeah, you could say that."

"So you look around and damned if you don't see that you've got another kid in Dallas, only this one's got the same drive and entrepreneurial spirit as you."

Strathmore snorted but smiled.

"You decided it would be great if Aaron's company gets the contract for the Trinity Vista. That way you could slide in as long-lost Daddy, help him out, and still be in control. For all I know you might have arranged some financing. You might already own part of him or his company."

Strathmore's face clouded, and I realized that I'd hit a nerve.

I continued. "Because of who you are, you can steer the contract away from any firm in North Dallas. Hell, it'll just look like you were positioning your namesake company. Nobody suspected a thing. Only problem in the way, other than your son Roger, is a couple of pesky competitors from the southern sector." I opened the cooler and grabbed a Coors Light.

"Like most people north of the Trinity, you think South Dallas is just a grease spot on the way to Waco. Which means you don't have a lot of connections down there. But you are Fagen Strathmore, the Big Man, and you're one lucky son of a bitch because it just so happens that your bastard son's got him a half brother who is plugged in down there, in all kinds of ways. My guess is that you made a deal with Coleman Dupree, something along the lines of 'You make sure no blacks or Mexicans get in the way of Aaron Young and Young Enterprises, and I'll use my influence at city hall to make the police go easy on you and your operation.'"

Fagen Strathmore's face was stony, no expression whatsoever. "Fuck you."

I stuck the nose of the blower about three inches under the water and turned it on. A stream of water erupted, like King Kong had just passed gas, hitting everybody in the face. One of the girls started to climb out but changed her mind.

I continued. "That left your acknowledged son, Roger, as the only problem. Couldn't exactly tell him so sorry, we're giving the deal to Aaron Young. That wouldn't do at all, would it? So what you did was let Roger think he was going to go through with the presentation, but at the last minute, you had some friends of Jack 'the Crack' Washington's— Russians so that they were white and wouldn't raise suspicion in Highland Park—you had them take your son for a little ride just long enough to miss the Trinity Vista get-together."

"You've got the best bullshit I've heard in a long time." Fagen laughed. "Matter of fact, I could use a guy like you. Pay you good money."

One thing was for sure: he had balls the size of Montana. "Not interested," I said. "I'm fine with my gig." I finished my beer and flipped the can into the pool. "So you've got this real nice deal working, except you screwed up one time. For whatever reason you decided to actually have a meeting with Coleman Dupree or maybe one of his flunkies. Maybe some money needed to change hands. Maybe one or both of you wanted to meet in person to size each other up, maybe . . . who the hell knows. The one thing that matters is you picked a place that you own, in roundabout fashion, out of the way, on a dead end street. A place where nobody would see you or recognize you if they did."

I waited for a reaction. When there was none, I continued. "It was a good idea except that coincidence or fate or whatever you want to call it put Charlie Wesson on the same dead end street at the same time. Charlie, Mr. Clean and Sober, Gung Ho, New Real Estate Guy, instantly recognized the Big Man. But the Big Man didn't want to be recognized, not with the company he was keeping."

Fagen yawned, affecting a bored demeanor. "Guessing is all you got, son. Because the only guy who could have seen me there is dead."

"That sure is convenient," I said.

Fagen frowned and then said, "One thing that's bothered me. What the fuck did you care about the little shit Charlie whasshisname?"

I thought about Charlie Wesson. I thought about his father and that time in the locker room after Charlie had lost the baseball game. I couldn't put it into words. Charlie was one of those people who needed somebody to look out for them, a lost soul in a world that preys on the weak and the sick and the stragglers in life. "Vera Drinkwater hired me to find her brother. When he turned up dead, she hired me to find who did it."

Fagen shrugged his shoulders. "The boy was a whiner, anyway. World's better off without him. Carrying on about how it wasn't fair now that he'd cleaned up, crying and shit. Damn pussy."

"Do you want to get electrocuted?"

"Shut the hell up, dumbass. He's a dead motherfucker and if you're not careful, you'll end up that way too." Fagen stretched and fondled a breast on the girl huddled in the corner of the tub, near the Oklahoma border.

"Better men than you have tried."

Fagen ignored my statement. "Mr. Hot Shit Private Investigator, we about done here? Because from where I sit, you ain't got nothing on me. Nobody does."

I stood up. "Just one more thing. How much does your illegitimate son know about all this?"

"Aaron? Shit. Aaron wants to have it but he doesn't want to get his hands dirty. 'Bout near threw me out of his office when I suggested getting his brother Coleman to help. He's got the drive, but he lets his morals get in the way."

Nobody said anything for a few moments. Then Strathmore stood up. "I'm getting out of here. Feel like a damn stewed prune."

I didn't reply, just lobbed the electric blower up in a slow arc toward the hot tub. Time seemed to hang still, and all five of them gasped. As the blower began its descent I gave the cord a yank and it came unplugged. The yard tool splashed harmlessly in the frothy water.

I turned and walked away.

"Goddammit, boy," Strathmore yelled after me. "You nearly gave me a heart attack. You little fucking pissant. I'm gonna get your ass, run you out of town. No place for anybody named Lee Oswald in Dallas."

His voice became fainter as I opened the gate and stepped into the garage.

"I got friends in city hall, the mayor, the fucking chief of police. You're in a world of shit. . . ."

The sound of his words trailed off as I slipped back into the alley and got in the Taurus. It was about two o'clock, the hottest part of the day. I drove around front and parked a few hundred yards away in the shade.

The shadows lengthened as the afternoon wore on. At three-thirty, the Cadillac backed down the driveway. Fortunately for me there was still no traffic.

They turned my way.

I put a pair of foam earplugs in and pulled a black mask over my head. And stepped out of the car.

CHAPTER THIRTY-TWO

Too many people in too many hospitals lately. Ernie. Me. Now Nolan. I slipped into the antiseptic-smelling room on the fifth floor of Parkland Hospital, carefully shutting the door so as not to make any noise.

Nolan's bed was upright, the white sheets accentuating her dark hair. Except for the bruising on one side, her normally olive face was now pale and drawn. But alive. She opened her eyes when I entered. An IV tube ran from the back of one hand to a plastic container suspended on a stainless steel rack. I moved to the foot of her bed. We stared at each other for a few moments, neither saying a word. I heard a siren scream outside. The only movement was the steady drip of her IV.

When the siren quieted she spoke. "Hey."

"Hi."

"You look like shit." She smiled and fiddled with the plastic tubing connected to her body.

"Everything's relative." I did indeed look bad. The contusion and split flesh on my cheekbone from connecting with Carl Albach's head had started to heal but it was still a nasty shade of yellow and purple. Plus I hadn't slept much lately. But I hadn't been through what she had either.

Silence for a minute or so. Then she said, "I don't blame you."

I didn't reply.

"Tell me what happened."

"You first," I said.

"A round penetrated the door and hit me in the thigh." She brushed her free hand through her hair. "There was a lot of shooting and yelling and somewhere in there I knocked my head. I think I tried to walk and my leg buckled."

"Then what?"

"I woke up in a rat-hole apartment somewhere." She looked out the window. "A woman brought me some water and then left me alone again."

"What did she look like?"

"Older. Mid-sixties. Russian." Nolan turned her head from the window. "She tried to be nice to me. My leg, it got infected."

"When did Washington show up?" I sat in an armchair by her bed.

"When he called you." She rubbed her eyes. "Guy needs his lights turned out. Permanently."

"What did he do to you?" I kept my voice low.

"It wasn't that bad," she said. "He slapped me around a few times after I talked to you. I've had worse."

A nurse came into the room. She ignored me and handed a paper cup containing several pills to Nolan. She tapped on the IV bag a couple of times and asked if the patient needed anything else. Nolan shook her head.

When the door shut I said, "He's dead."

"You do it?"

I nodded.

"Tell me what happened."

I stood up and walked to the window. The sun looked like a faded tennis ball behind the smog and haze. A mass of dark clouds had gathered in the distance; the thunderstorm promised to break the triple-digit temperatures teasing the city once again. I placed one hand on the glass and felt the heat of the day on my palm. Then I turned around and explained what had occurred, starting with the connection between Fagen Strathmore, Aaron Young, and Coleman Dupree. Next, I told her about the activities at the river and the explosion of thirty pounds of white powder. She raised her eyebrows and smiled at the mention of destroying all that cocaine. I smiled back and let her in on the secret: it hadn't been drugs that we blew up, but rather thirty pounds of something else.

Cornstarch.

I talked faster so she wouldn't interrupt, continuing with the story about Fagen and a Cadillac full of hookers easing down the driveway of a mansion on Strait Lane.

From the glove compartment of the car with the pest control signs on the side, I removed a battered Glock nine-millimeter last fired the month before in a liquor store robbery in Fort Worth. Delmar had provided it, and I didn't ask questions. I could have used the pistol I took from Carl Albach at the warehouse on Gano Street but I had planted that one underneath the driver's seat of the Cadillac.

I got out of the car. The truck headed toward me slowly. I could see Strathmore in the driver's seat, one of the girls next to him. The silhouettes of the other three were barely visible in the backseat.

When the SUV was twenty yards out, I dumped five rounds into the radiator, as fast as I could pull the trigger. All hit their mark.

I dropped the pistol on the pavement and hopped in the car, jamming it into gear and heading north, past the Cadillac with Fagen Strathmore staring at me, his eyes wide and his face white as cotton. As I drove I removed the mask and earplugs. After two blocks I pulled into an alley and removed the two magnetic signs on the side of the car.

Sirens sounded in the direction of where I'd left Fagen Strathmore in a shot-up truck with four prostitutes and thirty pounds of uncut cocaine, nestled in the back cargo area next to a set of golf clubs. What with the drugs, and the two dirty pistols, he'd have a challenging time explaining it all to the police. I bet that the chief and the mayor wouldn't be very helpful, given the circumstances.

I drove the speed limit for a couple of miles, to an empty school parking lot on the other side of Preston Road. I pulled off my dark T-shirt and put on a button-down and a tie. The car was clean, no number to trace anywhere but to a recently deceased widower in Tyler. I wiped down every surface for the third time and shut the door. A few blocks away was a small strip center. I wandered into the Starbucks and got a cup of decaf. From the pay phone in the back I called Olson's cell. Delmar had a state legislator who owed him big, as in life-or-death, for reasons I was afraid to ask. The good senator had graciously volunteered to be my alibi if need be. Hopefully, his services would never be required.

O lson picked me up," I said. "We took a drive down Strait Lane. They had Fagen handcuffed and facedown on the hood of the Cadillac. After that he dropped me off here."

Nolan closed her eyes for a few moments, like she was tired. Then she said, "Ernie died."

"Uh-huh." I turned back to the window. The bottom of the sun kissed the horizon. The thunderclouds had increased, moving across the city from the east. A jagged flash of lightning ripped somewhere over the suburbs.

"Coleman Dupree's MIA," she said. "Aaron Young gets the brass ring. And Charlie Wesson is still dead."

"Yeah, that pretty much sums it up."

"Where does that leave us?"

I stared out the window at the clouds moving toward us, the edge of the rainstorm plainly visible now. "Very much alive."

TURN THE PAGE FOR AN EXCERPT FROM HARRY HUNSICKER'S
NEXT LEE HENRY OSWALD MYSTERY

THE NEXT TIME YOU DIE

AVAILABLE IN HARDCOVER FROM ST. MARTIN'S MINOTAUR

My workload came from one of several distinct groups, a pattern I figured was typical for any moderately successful private investigator in a major metropolitan area.

Most PIs thought of the first group as their best clients. The business was steady and they paid well and on time. They were lawyers in all their various shades and flavors. What could be more recession-proof than litigation and the ancillary investigations required?

Next came the people missing something of value. An inheritance. A loved one. A spouses's sexual attention. The company's checkbook. Et cetera. This was a diverse group and paid in a diverse manner. Still, work was work.

Finally, there was the miscellaneous category. These were the people who walked on the dark side of the street. The half-bent cops. The occasional call girl with a dead politician stinking up a hotel room somewhere.

And my personal favorites: the dimwit wise guys who had screwed, stolen or ingested something that didn't exactly belong to them and needed help, off-the-books and pronto. If they didn't try to kill you, this group always paid, no questions asked.

The tires of my Chevy Tahoe crunched on the gravel parking lot as I came to a stop in front of a stone-and-brick building nestled under two old hackberry trees. I slid the gear shift into PARK, turned off the ignition and listened to the motor tick. Two guys who looked like out-of-work musicians or maybe the creative team at a small ad agency sat at a picnic table and watched me as they drank from long-neck bottles of beer. I watched back for a moment and then opened the door of my truck, steeling myself against the wave of heat and humidity typical of mid-September in Texas.

My concern was that the person who had requested this meeting didn't fall into any of the usual categories, or so it seemed based on our initial, cryptic phone conversation. He'd said his name was Lucas Linville and he was: (a) a preacher; (b) of the Baptist persuasion; and (c) wanting to meet in a drinking establishment. If that wasn't enough to give a body pause, I didn't know what was.

I walked across the gravel and dirt yard in front of Lee Harvey's, a bar located a few blocks south of the new Dallas police headquarters in a part of town a friend of mine refers to as the corner of Gun and Knife Streets. I pushed open the front door and welcomed the dim light as a relief from the afternoon sun. The air-conditioning was set somewhere between the Arctic Circle and Iceland. The place smelled like beer and burgers and stale smoke.

Originally a house a century or so back, the bar occupied what had once been the living/dining area. It split the room in two, running parallel to the front wall, and had seating on either side. The bedrooms were to the left and had been converted into one big area which now contained a pool table. The kitchen was to the right.

I picked a stool on the opposite side, facing the front door. Nothing behind me except empty room. No other access points. The guy next to me had a portable oxygen tank slung over his shoulder, a cigarette in one hand and draft beer in the other. He was dressed in a rumpled tuxedo, no tie. He looked to be somewhere between fifty and ninety years old, give or take.

I nodded hello to the bartender, a guy I sort of knew from previous visits, and ordered a Shiner Bock. Across the room the front door opened, and I squinted against the sunlight as the man I took to be Lucas Linville entered.

Five-eight or -nine. Skinny. Late fifties. The pink bow tie was the giveaway, the article of clothing he had mentioned he would be wearing. It was tied tightly around the neck of a beige dress shirt underneath a brown suit. Even from across the room, I could see the outfit was worn at the edges.

He blinked a couple of times against the gloom of the place and then walked to the bar, leaned in and whispered something to the guy who had just served me a beer. The bartender cut a glance my way without breaking his conversation with Linville.

I nodded.

He pointed to me with an ashtray he'd been polishing.

Linville took a moment to examine his surroundings and then walked around the bar past Mr. Emphysema and took the empty stool next to me. He stuck out a hand and introduced himself. His breath smelled like Wrigley Doublemint chewing gum, and I caught the faint aroma of drugstore aftershave on my hand where it had pressed against his palm.

Before I could say much of anything other than my name, Linville ordered a shot of Jim Beam with a Budweiser chaser and said, "Did you have any trouble finding the place?"

I didn't reply for a moment as I watched the bartender serve up my newest favorite concoction: a Baptist Boilermaker. Might have to start going to church.

"I know my way around town pretty well," I said. A few blocks away a bullet had punched a hole through the side of my new Hugo Boss leather jacket a couple of winters ago. I was still pissed about it.

"I have a small ministry not far from here." He downed the glass of whiskey in one gulp, followed it up with a swig of beer. "This is a troubled part of town, wouldn't you say?"

"No offense." I looked at my watch. "But I didn't come here to talk about urban blight."

Linville leaned back and stared at me, a blank expression on his face. "You find stuff for people, right?"

"Sometimes." Category Two. People missing something. I felt a little better. "Depends on what it is."

"A file was stolen from my office yesterday."

I nodded but didn't say anything.

"My ministry helps the people on the fringes." He steepled his fingers underneath his scrawny chin. "Drug addicts. Prostitutes. What society thinks of as the gutter."

He paused for a drink of beer. "Sometimes the people who find themselves on the bottom started out on top."

"Debutantes turned street walkers, next on Jerry Springer." I'd been hired once to find the daughter of a social bigwig. It turned out a busboy at the country club had introduced the flaxen-haired lass to the joys of injectable methamphetamines. The situation turned out poorly for all concerned.

Linville nodded. "Yeah. More or less."

"What was in the file?"

"Records on a former employee of mine, a young man named Reese." Linville tugged on an earlobe as he talked. "Came from a prominent family. Dad was a lawyer. Mother was involved with all those charity balls. He could have done anything, been anything he wanted."

"What was Reese's problem?"

"He had trouble with opiates, and cocaine too. Ended up on the streets in a bad way until I gave him a job." Linville clinked the empty shot glass against his beer bottle and asked the bartender for another Jim Beam. "His family has been more than generous to my ministry."

"When did he quit working for you?"

The older man frowned and ran his index finger around the rim of his beer can. "Four or five months ago."

"It's an employment file," I said. "So that means it has his last name."

"Yes." He lowered his voice and looked around the room. "Reese Cunningham."

The name sounded vaguely familiar. It conjured up an image of yacht clubs and cotillion dances. I said, "And Mumsy and Daddy won't be too eager to fund your operation if it gets out that their precious angel was a homeless addict."

"Certain segments of society care about appearances at all costs." He downed his second shot.

"When did you notice it missing?"

"Yesterday, right after lunch."

"Anything else gone?"

He shook his head.

"Who had access—" I stopped and mentally slapped myself on the forehead. The people he ministered to were not exactly pillars of the community.

"I know what you're thinking." Linville's eyes glowed with alcohol, watery yet intense. "Only one other person had keys to my office."

"What's his name?" I got out a pen and grabbed a cocktail napkin from a pile by the beer taps.

"How do you know it was a he?"

I sighed. "Okay. What was *her* name?"

"Oh, never mind. *He* was my assistant." Linville rubbed the bridge of his nose, his voice now sounding distant. "Carlos. He didn't come to work today."

"Last name?"

"Jimenez."

The old guy on the other side of me erupted into a fit of coughing, his chest cavity sounding like a tin can full of gravel. When his wheezing subsided I said, "How long has he worked for you?"

"Must be six months now." Linville drained his beer. "Started as a court-ordered DWI thing. He's been clean ever since."

I fanned away a cloud of smoke from Mr. Emphysema's fresh cigarette. "Where does Carlos live?"

"A boarding house. In Oak Cliff." Linville grabbed my pen and scribbled something on the cocktail napkin. His hand trembled as he slid the paper in my direction.

I put the information in my pocket but didn't say anything.

"Discretion is—" Linville covered his mouth with one hand and hiccoughed. "Uh . . . imperative. That's why I didn't call the police."

I mentioned my fee. He produced an already-made-out check. The amount was for a week's worth of my time, a sum of money incongruous with the man's shabby appearance. He described Carlos. Overweight, Hispanic. Mid-twenties. A tattoo of the Virgin Mary on his left arm.

A shaft of sunlight penetrated the darkened room as the front door opened and two people entered. Mr. Emphysema coughed a couple of times and spat something on the floor. He ordered an Absolut Martini, one hundred proof, straight up. I debated taking up smoking again.

"One more question for now," I said. "Why haven't you tried to track down Carlos yourself?"

"My work demands a lot of time. And . . ." Linville stood and looked at two men who had just entered. "I believe certain people mean me harm."

I stood also. The two newcomers flanked out, their attention plainly focused on Linville and me. Their hands were balled into fists. Everything about their demeanor screamed attack.

"Oh dear." Linville's face drained of color. "Now I've got you involved."

The larger of the two produced a semi-automatic pistol from a pocket. He started toward us.